Caroline Anderson is a matriarch, writer, armchair gardener, unofficial tearoom researcher and eater of lovely cakes. Not necessarily in that order! *What Caroline loves:* her family. Her friends. Reading. Writing contemporary love stories. Hearing from readers. Walks by the sea with coffee/ice cream/cake thrown in! Torrential rain. Sunshine in spring/autumn. *What Caroline hates:* losing her pets. Fighting with her family. Cold weather. Hot weather. Computers. Clothes shopping. *Caroline's plans:* keep smiling and writing!

Alison Roberts is a New Zealander, currently lucky enough to be living in the South of France. She is also lucky enough to write for the Mills & Boon Medical Romance line. A primary school teacher in a former life, she is now a qualified paramedic. She loves to travel and dance, drink champagne, and spend time with her daughter and her friends.

We hope you've enjoyed

A Single Dad to Heal Her Heart
Caroline Anderson's 100th book

Also by Caroline Anderson

One Night, One Unexpected Miracle

Yoxburgh Park Hospital miniseries

Their Meant-to-Be Baby
The Midwife's Longed-for Baby
Bound by Their Babies
Their Own Little Miracle

Also by Alison Roberts

The Shy Nurse's Rebel Doc
Rescued by Her Mr Right
Their Newborn Baby Gift
Twins on Her Doorstep

Rescued Hearts miniseries

The Doctor's Wife for Keeps
Twin Surprise for the Italian Doc

Discover more at millsandboon.co.uk.

A SINGLE DAD TO HEAL HER HEART

CAROLINE ANDERSON

RESISTING HER RESCUE DOC

ALISON ROBERTS

MILLS & BOON

First Published in Great Britain 2019
by Mills & Boon, an imprint of HarperCollins*Publishers*
1 London Bridge Street, London, SE1 9GF

A Single Dad to Heal Her Heart © 2019 by Caroline Anderson

Resisting Her Rescue Doc © 2019 by Alison Roberts

ISBN: 978-0-263-26966-6

MIX
Paper from
responsible sources
FSC® C007454

This book is produced from independently certified FSC™ paper
to ensure responsible forest management.
For more information visit www.harpercollins.co.uk/green.

Printed and bound in Spain
by CPI, Barcelona

A SINGLE DAD TO HEAL HER HEART

CAROLINE ANDERSON

MILLS & BOON

For Ali, without whose skill and perseverance with my
knotted muscles none of my recent books would have
ever been written, and whose extraordinary frankness
and generosity in sharing her cancer journey
have made it possible for me to write Livvy's story.
I can't thank you enough for all you've done for me.
I just wish I could give you your happy ending. xxx

CHAPTER ONE

'Wow, LOOK AT that glorious view!'

Stifling her impatience, Livvy glanced back across the scree slope to the valley floor stretched out below them, the late spring grass a splash of vivid green. In the distance Buttermere lay like a gleaming mirror, the bleak slate hills behind it rich purple in the sun.

And between her and the view—admittedly glorious—was Matt, dawdling his way up the winding, rocky path and driving her nuts because it was the last day of their team-building exercise in Cumbria and there was a trophy at stake.

They'd been there since Friday, four teams all in some way connected to the emergency department of Yoxburgh Park Hospital; Sam and Vicky from the ED, Dan and Lucy from Orthopaedics, and Ed and Beth from Paediatrics, which had left her and Matt as the Trauma team.

She'd only started at the hospital a few weeks ago and she'd met him a few times fleetingly when he'd come down to the ED, but ever since they'd arrived at the lodge and sat down together to decide who would be in each team, she and Matt had seemed a natural fit.

'Are you OK with that?' she'd asked at the time, and he'd nodded, his grin a little cheeky.

'Yeah, suits me. You're small enough that I can pick you up if you dawdle.'

'I don't dawdle, and you'd better not!'

'Don't worry, Livvy, I think I can just about keep up with you,' he'd said drily, and he had, seemingly effortlessly. They'd tackled all manner of challenges, and he'd been witty, mischievous, not above cheating and game for anything Sam threw at them.

Until now. Now, with everything to play for, he was stopping to admire the view?

Yes, it was beautiful, and if they had time she'd stop and drink it in, but they didn't because so far the four teams were neck and neck, so the first to the summit of Haystacks would take the crown. And Matt was trailing.

Deliberately?

'Are you dawdling on purpose or just studying my backside?' she asked, hands on hips and her head cocked to one side, and he stopped just below her, a smile playing around that really rather gorgeous mouth that she was itching to kiss.

He took a step closer, curling his hands around her hips and sending shivers of something interesting through her. They were standing eye to eye, and his mouth was so close now...

His smile widened, crows' feet bracketing those laughing eyes the colour of the slate that surrounded them, and he shook his head slowly from side to side.

'Cute though it is, and it has been worth watching, I'll admit, I was actually studying the scenery then.' The smile faded, replaced by awe. 'Stop and look around you, Livvy, just for a moment. It's so beautiful and you're missing it—and anyway, it's only supposed to be fun!'

She sighed, knowing he was right, but still impatient. 'I know, but we can't let Sam catch us now, we'll never hear the end of it. We can look on the way back when we've won.'

He shook his head again and laughed. 'You're so competitive. Just be careful, that edge is unstable. Why don't you let me go first?'

She laughed at him and took a step backwards out of reach. 'What, to slow me down? No way. And besides, I'm always careful,' she threw over her shoulder as she turned, and then she took another step and the ground vanished beneath her feet...

'Livvy—!'

He lunged for her, his fingers brushing her flailing arm, but she was gone before he could grab her, her scream slicing the air as she fell. And then the scream stopped abruptly, leaving just a fading echo, and his blood ran cold.

She was below him, lying like a rag doll against a rock, crumpled and motionless, and for a moment he was frozen.

No. Please, God, no...

'Livvy, I'm coming. Hang on,' he yelled, and scanned the slope, found a safe route that wouldn't send more rocks showering down on her and scrambled down, half running, half sliding across the shale. Fast, but not too fast. Not so fast that he'd put himself in danger, too, because that wouldn't help either of them.

As he got closer he could see her shoulders heaving, as if she was fighting for breath, and then as he got to her side she sucked in a small breath, rolled onto her back and started to pant jerkily, and his legs turned to jelly.

She was breathing. Not well, but she wasn't dead...

He took her hand and gripped it gently. 'It's OK, Livvy, I'm here, I've got you. You're OK now. Just keep breathing, nice and slow. That's it. Well done.'

Her eyes locked on his, and after a moment her breathing steadied, and he felt his shoulders drop with relief.

'What—happened? Can't—breathe...'

'Just take it steady, you'll recover soon,' he said, his voice calm, his heart still pounding and his mind running through all the things that might be damaged. Starting with her head... 'I think you've been winded. Stay there a minute—'

'Can't. I need to sit up.'

He gritted his teeth. 'OK, but don't do it if you think you've got any other injuries.'

'No. Haven't,' she said, and she struggled up into a sitting position and propped herself against the rock that had stopped her fall.

'Ah—!'

'OK?'

She nodded, shifting slightly, her breathing slowing, and she closed her eyes briefly.

'Yeah. That's better. The path just—went.'

So she remembered that, at least. '"I'm always careful",' he quoted drily, and she laughed weakly as relief kicked in.

'Well, nobody's—perfect,' she said after a moment, and then her eyes welled and he reached out a hand

and brushed the soft blond hair back from her face with fingers that weren't quite steady, scanning her face for bruises.

'Are you OK now? You scared me half to death.'

She met his eyes with a wry smile, and for once the sparkle in her eyes wasn't mischief. 'That depends on your—definition of OK. I'm alive, I can breathe—just, I can feel everything, I can move, so yeah—I guess I'm OK. Do I hurt? Oh, yeah. These rocks are hard.'

'I'm sure. Don't move. Let me check you over.'

'You just want to get your hands on me,' she quipped, her breath still catching.

'Yeah, right,' he said lightly, trying not to think about that right now because however true it might be, he could see she was in pain. He simply wanted to be sure she didn't have any life-threatening injuries and then maybe his heart could slow down a bit. 'Why don't you let me do my job?' he added gently, trying to stick to business.

'Yes, Doctor.'

'Well, at least you can remember that. How many fingers am I holding up?'

'Twelve.'

He tried to glare at her but it was too hard so he just laughed, told her to co-operate and carried on, checking her pupils, making her follow his finger, feeling her scalp for any sign of a head injury.

Please don't have a head injury...

'My head's fine. It's my ribs that hurt.'

So he turned his attention to her body, checking for anything that could be a worry because she'd hit that rock hard and a punctured lung could kill her. He squeezed her ribcage gently.

'Does that feel OK?'

'Sort of. It's tender, but it's not catching any more when I breathe and I can't feel any grating when you spring them, so I don't think I broke any ribs,' she said, taking it seriously at last. 'I thought I had an elephant on my chest. I had no idea being winded was so damn scary.'

'Oh, yeah. I've only ever been winded once, when I fell out of a tree. I must have been six or seven, but I remember it very clearly. I thought I was dying.'

She nodded, then looked away again, just as they heard a slither of shale and Sam appeared at their sides.

'How is she?' he asked tightly.

'Lippy and opinionated but apparently OK, as far as I've checked. She was winded. At least it shut her up for a moment.'

Sam chuckled, but Matt could see the relief in his eyes. 'Now there's a miracle.'

'Excuse me, I am here, you know,' she said, shifting into a better position, and Sam looked down at her and grinned.

'So you are. Good job, too, we don't need to lose a promising young registrar, we're pushed enough,' he said drily, and sat down. 'Why don't you shut up and let him finish so we can get on?' he added, and Matt laughed. As if…

'Any back pain?' he asked, but she just gave him a wry look.

'No more than you'd expect after rolling down a scree slope and slamming into a rock, but at least it stopped me rolling all the way down,' she said, trying to get to her feet, but he put a hand on her shoulder and held her down.

'I'm not done—'

She tipped her head back and fixed him with a determined look. 'Yeah, you are. I'm fine, Matt. I just need to get up because there are rocks sticking into me all over the place and I could do without that. You might need to give me a hand up.'

He held his hand out but let her do the work. She'd stop instinctively as soon as anything felt wrong, but he was horribly conscious that he hadn't ruled out all manner of injuries that might be lurking silently, but that was fine, he had no intention of taking his eyes off her for the rest of the day.

She winced slightly, but she was on her feet.

'How's that feel?'

'Better now I'm off the rocks. Did you see what happened? Did I step off the edge, or did it crumble?'

He snorted. 'No, it crumbled. I told you the edge was unstable, but did you listen? Of course not. You were in too much of a hurry. When you weren't walking backwards, that is.'

'Only one step—'

'I'll give you one step,' he growled. 'So, are you OK to go on?'

'Of course I am. You seriously think I'm going to give up now just because of this?'

'You might as well. I don't get beaten,' Sam said, getting to his feet, and she laughed in his face.

'We'll see about that,' she retorted, stabbing him in the chest with her finger, then she took a step and yelped.

Matt frowned. 'What?'

'My ankle.' She tried again, and winced. 'Rats. I

can't weight-bear on it. I must have turned it when the path gave way.'

'Well, that's just upped my chances,' Sam said with a grin, and Matt rolled his eyes.

'You two are a nightmare. Right, let's get you off here and have a better look at that.'

Livvy flexed her ankle again and regretted it. She was so mad with herself, and she was hideously aware that it could have been much, much worse. If it had been her head against that rock instead of her chest...

After all she'd been through, that she could have died from a moment's lack of concentration was ridiculous. She'd meant what she'd said about being careful. She was always careful, meticulous with her lifestyle, fastidious about what she ate, how much she exercised—she woke every morning ready to tackle whatever the day brought, because *whatever* it brought she had at least been granted the chance to deal with it, and she never stopped being aware of that glorious gift.

And now, after the physical and emotional roller coaster of the last five years, she'd nearly thrown it all away.

Stupid. Stupid, stupid, stupid.

'OK?'

She nodded, her teeth gritted, because her ankle was definitely not OK and the rest of her body wasn't far behind. She was going to have some stunning bruises to show for this. What an idiot.

They carried her carefully across the loose rock slope to where the others were waiting, clustering round her and looking concerned as they set her on her feet, and she felt silly and horribly embarrassed.

And annoyed, because she'd been really looking forward to climbing up Haystacks and there was no way she was going up it now, and she couldn't see how she could get down, either, so one way or another she was going to miss out on the climb and coincidentally cause the others a whole world of aggravation.

Either that or just sit there and let them pick her up on the way back.

Whatever, they'd be worried about her, Matt especially since he'd seen her fall, and she felt awful now for scaring him. Scaring all of them, and putting a dampener on the whole trip.

'Sorry, guys,' she said humbly. 'That was really stupid.'

'It was an accident. They happen,' Dan said calmly, but Matt just snorted and turned away. Because he was angry with her? Maybe, and she felt like the sun had gone in.

'Want me to look at it?'

'It's fine, Dan. It's only a sprain and anyway I'm not taking my boot off.'

'OK. Just keep your weight off it.'

'I can't do anything else,' she said in disgust, and lowered herself gingerly onto a handy rock.

'So what now?' Matt asked, still not looking at her.

She followed the direction of his gaze and traced the rough path that seemed to wind endlessly down until it met the track that led to the car park. Funny, it didn't look so beautiful now. It just looked a long, long way away.

'We'll carry her down,' Sam said.

'No, you won't. You've got to finish the challenge!' she protested, but Sam shrugged.

'Well, we can't leave you here, Livvy.'

'Yes, you can. I'll be fine. I'm not ruining anyone's day just because I was an idiot. Please, all of you, go on up and I'll wait here. I might even work my way down. If I take my time I'll be fine. I can go down on my bottom.'

'No,' Matt chipped in, turning round at last, his expression implacable. 'I'll take you back. Our team's out, anyway.'

'Are you sure?' Sam asked him, but she shook her head, really unhappy now.

'Matt, I can't let you do that. You were looking forward to it!'

He just smiled, his eyes softening at last. 'It'll keep. It's millions of years old, Livvy. It's not like it's going anywhere. I can climb it another time.'

'But—'

His tone firmed. 'But nothing. We're teammates, and we stick together, and it's what we're doing. End of.'

She rolled her eyes. 'Are you always this bossy?'

'Absolutely. Ed, can I borrow the car?'

Ed nodded and delved in his pocket and tossed him the keys. 'Mind you don't crash it. Annie'll kill us both.'

'I'll do my best,' he said mildly. 'Go on, you guys, go and have your climb and I'll take Livvy back and come and get you when you're done. Call me when you hit the track.'

'Will do—and no more stunts, Henderson, we need you in one piece!' Sam said as they headed off, leaving her alone with Matt.

* * *

He laughed and shook his head in disbelief.

'I can't believe I'm so stupid.'

She looked up at him, her face puzzled. '*You* are?'

'Yes, me. I've spent the last three days trying to work out who you remind me of, and it's just clicked. You're Oliver Henderson's daughter, aren't you? It's so blindingly obvious I can't believe I didn't see it. You're the spitting image of him.'

'Do you know him?'

He perched on a rock in front of her so she didn't have to tilt her head. 'Yes, I was his registrar, years ago. He's a great guy. I'm very fond of him, and your mother. How are they both?'

'Fine. Doing really well. He's about to turn sixty, but he doesn't look it and he's got no plans to retire and nor has Mum.'

'I'm not surprised. They're very dedicated.'

'They are. Dad just loves surgery, and Mum would be bored to bits without the cut and thrust of ED, so I can't see them retiring until they're forced, frankly! So, when were you at the Audley Memorial? I must have been at uni or I'd remember you, unless you're much older than you look.'

He chuckled. 'I'm thirty-six now and I was twenty-seven, so that's—wow, nine years ago.'

'So I must have been twenty then, which explains it, because I didn't come home a lot in those days. I had a busy social life at uni, and it was a long way from Bristol to Suffolk.'

'Yes, it is. Give them my love when you speak to them.'

'I will. I'll call them later today.'

'So, how are we going to do this?' he asked quietly, getting back to the core business, and she shrugged.

'I have no idea. I can't hop all the way down, but I can't walk on it either, so it looks like the bottom shuffle thing.'

'Or I can carry you,' he suggested, knowing she'd argue.

'How? Don't be ridiculous, it's not necessary. And anyway, I weigh too much.'

He laughed at that, because she hardly came up to his chin and, sure, she was strong, but she definitely wasn't heavy, he knew that because he and Sam had already carried her to the path. He got to his feet.

'Come on, then, sling your arm round my neck and let's see how we get on with assisted hopping.'

Slowly, was the answer. He had to stoop, of course, because she was too short to reach his shoulder otherwise, and after a while they had to change sides, but she said it hurt her ribs, which left only one option.

He stopped and went down on one knee.

'Are you proposing to me?' she joked, and it was so unexpected he laughed. Ish.

'Very funny. Get on my back.'

'I can't!'

'Why?'

'Because I'm not five and I'll feel like an idiot!'

He straightened up, unable to stifle the laugh. 'You just fell off the path!' he said, and she swatted him, half cross, half laughing, and he couldn't help himself. He gathered her into his arms, hugged her very gently and brushed the hair away from her eyes as he smiled ruefully down at her.

'I'm sorry. That was mean.'

'Yes, it was. I feel silly enough without you laughing at me.'

'Yeah, I know. I'm sorry,' he said again, and then because he'd been aching to do it for days and because she was just there, her face tipped up to his, her clear blue eyes rueful and apologetic and frustrated, he bent his head and touched his lips to hers.

It was only meant to be fleeting, just a brush of his mouth against hers, but the tension that had been sizzling between them since they'd arrived on Friday morning suddenly escalated, and when her mouth softened under his he felt a surge of something he hadn't felt for two years, something he'd thought he'd never feel again.

Not lust. It wasn't lust. That he would have understood. Expected, even, after so long. But this was tenderness, yearning, a deep ache for something more, something meaningful and fulfilling, something he'd lost, and it stopped him in his tracks.

What was he doing?

He pulled away and cleared his throat.

'Come on, let's get you down to the bottom and I'll go and get the car and come back for you. And I *will* carry you, because frankly it'll be easier for both of us and if I don't get you off this mountain safely your father'll kill me.'

He turned his back on her, knelt down again and told her to get on, and after a moment's hesitation, when he could almost hear her fighting her instincts, she leant into him, wrapped her arms round his neck and let him hoist her up onto his back.

He wrapped her legs round his waist and straightened up with a little lurch, and she gave a tiny shriek that morphed into a giggle.

'This is ridiculous,' she said, and he started to laugh.

Her arms tightened round his throat. 'Don't mock me.'

'I'm not mocking you, I promise,' he said, stifling the laugh, and she loosened her arms around his neck and rested her head against his with a sigh.

'I'm so sorry I messed up your day,' she murmured in his ear, and the drift of her warm breath teased his skin and the feelings he'd thought he'd suppressed roared into life again.

'Don't be,' he said gruffly, trying not to think about his hands locked together under her bottom. Her undoubtedly very, very cute bottom. 'It was just an accident. So, tell me, why trauma?' he asked to distract himself. 'Why not general surgery, like your father?'

'That's probably Mum's influence, and surgery's still an option, but I'm undecided about it, and trauma's a nice high-octane job.'

He chuckled. 'High-octane, sure, but I'm not sure I'd call it nice, especially the surgery. It can get pretty gory.'

'So why did *you* choose it?'

'I don't know. Probably your father's influence. I always wanted to be a surgeon, and when I was his registrar we had some interesting trauma cases and it just reeled me in. Yes, it's gory, but it's very gratifying when you can offer someone who's been badly injured a better outcome.'

'I would have thought you'd have been in London, then. That's where a lot of the trauma cases are. More scope?'

He felt his heart hitch. 'Yeah, well, I've done London, and frankly in the year and a half I've been in Yoxburgh there's been plenty to keep me busy.'

More than enough, and nothing to do with his job. Not that he was going into details. He didn't want to let reality intrude on a weekend that had been like a breath of fresh air after the roller coaster of the last two years, but that was all it was, a breath of fresh air, and it was going nowhere, he knew that, because there simply wasn't room in his life for a relationship, however appealing. And anyway, there was an embargo on personal stuff this weekend, so he changed the subject.

'Are you OK there? I'm not hurting you?'

'No. It's a bit sore, but it's better than walking. How about you?'

'I'm fine. We're nearly there, anyway. Not long now.'

Frankly, it couldn't be soon enough because, apart from being racked with guilt, she was swamped with feelings that were so unexpected she didn't know how to deal with them.

It shouldn't have surprised her that he'd given up his chance of a climb to get her safely back down, because over the last three days he'd proved himself to be tough and determined and a brilliant team player.

Not that he didn't know how to have fun. They'd had plenty of that, and she hadn't laughed so much in ages.

They'd been teasing and flirting for most of the time, too, but she hadn't expected him to act on it and his gentle kiss just now had brought all sorts of unexpected feelings rushing to the surface. Not to mention his hands locked together under her bottom, propping her up. They must be numb by now, and she had another pang of guilt.

'Are you sure you're OK, Matt?'

'I'm fine,' he said, and then they hit the track and he unlocked his hands and braced her as she slid down and put her feet on the ground.

He flexed his hands and shoulders and she watched the muscles roll under his damp T-shirt as he turned to her. 'I won't be long. Will you be all right?'

She lowered herself to a rock and dragged her eyes off his shoulders. 'I'll be fine. There's no rush. I'll just sit here and look at the view,' she told him with a wry smile.

Mostly of him, as he turned away and headed down the track towards the farm at the end where the car was parked.

She studied him, his strong, firm stride, the straight back, his arms hanging loose and relaxed from those broad shoulders. Broad, solid, dependable. And sexy.

Very, very sexy.

Would they see each other again once they were back? She didn't think so, despite this sizzle between them all weekend, because there was something about him, some reserve in his eyes, and when he'd kissed her he'd pulled away.

Would he have done that if he intended to follow through? Probably not, and she still didn't feel ready for a relationship anyway after all she'd been through, but if nothing else they were good friends now and she'd known from that first day that she could rely on him.

He had a rock-solid dependability, carefully hidden under a lot of jokes and laughter, and if she had to be in this fix, she couldn't have asked for a better person to help her out of it.

She just wished she hadn't made it necessary.

* * *

'We need to get this boot off.'

He'd propped her up on a sun lounger on the deck outside the lodge, and he was perched on the end by her feet, wondering how to remove it without hurting her.

'They're pretty old,' she offered. 'I don't mind if you need to cut it off.'

He shook his head. 'I don't think I will. I'll take the lace out and see how we get on.'

He unthreaded it, peeled back the tongue as far as it would go and slid his fingers carefully inside. 'How's that feel?'

'Not too bad. A bit easier now you've undone the lace.'

'Let's just see what happens if I try and ease your foot out. Yell if I hurt you.'

She gave a stifled snort. 'Don't worry, I will,' she said drily, and he looked up and met those gorgeous clear blue eyes and saw trust in them. He hoped it wasn't unfounded.

'Right, here goes,' he said, and gently cupping his hand under her ankle to support it, he eased the boot away.

She made a tiny whimper at one point, but nothing more, and then it was off and he lowered her foot carefully onto a pillow. 'How's that feel?'

Her breath sighed out. 'Better. Thank you.'

'Don't thank me, I haven't prodded it yet,' he said drily, and began to feel his way carefully around the joint, testing the integrity of the ligaments.

'Ow.'

'Sorry.' He prodded a little more, feeling carefully

for any displacement, but if there was it was slight. 'I don't think it's fractured, and it doesn't feel displaced, so I think it's probably only a slight ligament tear. You need an X-ray, though.'

'It can wait till we get back, can't it?'

He nodded. 'I think so. There's not much else going on with it, I don't think, but we'll get Dan to look at it when he comes back just to be on the safe side. In the meantime I'll get you some ice and I can strap it, if you like. That should help.'

'Please. And I could kill a cup of green tea—oh, and a banana, if there's one left,' she said, throwing a grin over her shoulder as he headed for the kitchen, and he gave a grunt of laughter.

'I get the distinct impression you're milking this,' he said drily as he walked away, and he put the kettle on, discovered there were no ice cubes, wetted a couple of tea towels and put them in the freezer, and raided the first-aid kit for some physio tape.

'Better?'

She nodded. 'Much.'

It was, hugely better, which wasn't difficult. Her boot had been pressing on the outside of her ankle, and removing it had made a lot of difference. So had the cold pack and the strapping that, considering he was a trauma surgeon and not a physio or an orthopaedic surgeon, was looking very professional. It still shouldn't have happened, though, and she sighed.

'What?'

She shrugged. 'Just—I'm cross with myself. And sorry, because I really thought we had a good chance

of winning until I took my eye off the ball, and now
I've blown it and ruined your last day.'

He frowned, his eyes serious. 'It's hardly ruined.
You're alive, Livvy, and you might not have been. If
your head had hit that rock instead of your ribs, it
could have been a very different story. I'd take that as
a win any day. And it doesn't matter about my climb,
or the challenge.'

'Yes, it does, and I still feel guilty. If you'd teamed
up with someone else you might have won, but now
I've let you down.'

'No, you haven't.'

'Yes, I have! I'm the weak link in the chain, Matt.'

He rolled his eyes. 'You're not weak! There's nothing weak about you.'

'I didn't look where I was going on a narrow rocky
path with a crumbling edge. That's pretty weak from
where I'm standing.'

'You're sitting. Well, lying, really, technically speaking.'

She was, still propped up on the sun lounger with
her ankle wrapped in the thawing tea towel in a plastic bag, a cup of green tea in her hand and a packet of
crunchy oat cookies on the table between them because
apparently the bananas were finished. Ah, well. She
took another cookie and bit into it.

'You're a pedant, did you know that?' she said mildly
around the crumbs, and he chuckled, his frown fading.

'It might have been mentioned. How's your ankle
now?'

'Cold.'

'Good. How about your ribs?'

'Sore. I might move the ice pack.'

'Here, let me.'

He picked up the makeshift ice pack, turned it over and gestured to her to pull up her T-shirt. She eased it out of the way and he winced.

'Ow. That's a good bruise. Let me feel that.'

'Why, because poking it is going to make it feel so much better?' she said drily, but he just gave her a look that was getting all too familiar and tugged up her T-shirt a little further. And then he frowned and ran his finger across the top of her abdomen from side to side along her scar. Well, one of them.

'What happened? Another accident?'

'Yes, but not my fault, before you say it. I was in a car crash when I was nineteen months old. I had a ruptured spleen and a perforated bowel.'

'Ouch.' He turned his attention back to her ribs and prodded them gently and rather too thoroughly. 'Well, there's nothing displaced,' he said, and she rolled her eyes.

'I could have told you that. I don't have a fracture, Matt.'

'How do you know? It's not possible to be sure.'

She sighed. 'Because I'm inside my body and you're not?'

One eyebrow shot up, his eyes locked briefly with hers and then he let his breath out on what could have been a laugh and tugged her T-shirt back down, and she realised what she'd said.

Colour flooded her face and she groaned. 'Sorry—I didn't mean that quite the way it came out.'

'No, I don't suppose you did.' He got to his feet and picked up his mug, hefting the ice pack in his hand and avoiding her eyes. 'This thing's thawed. I'll get you another one, then I'll make some more coffee and sort my stuff out. Do you want another drink?'

She shook her head, half mortally embarrassed at her off-the-cuff remark, and half tantalised by the idea of Matt's really rather gorgeous body so intimately locked with hers.

'No, I'm fine.'

She heard the door close behind her and stifled a groan, then dropped her head back against the sun lounger and closed her eyes.

Why had she said that? She'd never be able to look him in the eye again. Idiot. Idiot, idiot, idiot!

But her body was still caught up in the thought, and she didn't know whether to laugh or cry...

CHAPTER TWO

SHE DIDN'T MEAN it like that.

Obviously she didn't mean it like that, but the idea was in his head now, the thought of his body buried deep inside hers flooding his senses and driving him crazy.

He closed the kitchen door, put the tea towel back into the freezer, switched the kettle on again and then dropped his head against the cupboard above and growled with frustration.

What was *wrong* with him today? First the kiss, now this?

For the first time since Juliet, he wanted a woman. Not just any woman, but Livvy, apparently, and the thought wouldn't leave him alone.

All he could think about was peeling away her clothes and kissing every inch of her, touching her, stroking her skin, feeling the warmth of her body against his, the hitch in her breath as he touched her more intimately, the heat as he buried himself inside her—and he didn't know how to deal with it.

Should he be feeling like this? It had been two years— two years and a week, to be exact—but was that long enough? He didn't think so, but his body didn't seem to agree with him.

What do I do, Jules? Where do I go from here? I'm not ready for this...

He heard a sound in the living room and opened the door. Livvy was limping across the room, hopping from one piece of furniture to the next and then leaning heavily on it as she hobbled.

'Where are you going?'

'I thought I'd go and lie down for a bit, then maybe pack?'

'Let me give you a hand.'

'I can manage.'

Stubborn woman.

'Of course you can, but only until you run out of furniture.'

He reached her side, took her arm and slung it round his neck and wrapped his other arm round her waist, being careful of her ribs.

'OK?'

She nodded, and as she took a step forward there was a sharp crack and she gasped.

'Was that your ankle?'

'Mmm. Ouch.'

They looked down and she flexed it gingerly. 'Oh. It feels better—like something was hung up.'

'Try putting some weight on it, but carefully.'

She did, and nodded. 'Better. It's still very sore, but that definitely feels better.'

'OK, well, don't push your luck and don't try and weight-bear on it unnecessarily until you've had it X-rayed. Let's get you to your room.'

When they reached the side of the bed he let go

carefully and she eased away from him, taking all that wonderful warmth and softness with her. Just as well. Except that instead of sitting down, as he'd expected, she looked up at him, slid her arms round him and hugged him, bringing all that warmth and softness back into intimate contact with his starving, grateful, desperate body.

'Thank you,' she murmured.

His arms closed around her without his permission. 'What for?' he asked, his voice a little strangled.

'Just being you. You've been great the last few days. It's been so much fun—well, till I wrecked it.'

'You didn't wreck it.'

She tipped her head back and their eyes met. 'Yes, I did. Stop being nice, Matt. I know I was an idiot.'

He laughed softly and kissed her without thinking.

Just a brief kiss, nothing passionate or romantic, but still the sort of kiss you'd give a lover, a partner. Someone you were intimate with. And he wasn't intimate with Livvy, and wasn't going to be. He wasn't ready yet, and he had other commitments that had to take priority. Would always have to take priority.

So he straightened up, trying to distance himself when all he wanted was to topple her backwards onto the bed and make love to her, but her eyes had widened, and after an endless moment she reached up, pulled his head gently back down to hers and kissed him.

Properly, this time, her lips parting, her tongue tangling with his, reeling him in, sending his senses into freefall.

He wanted her.

Every cell in his body was screaming for it, for her, for the heat, the passion, the closeness. He could feel her body pressed against his, feel his roaring to life, the ache, the longing in both of them as he kissed her back with all the pent-up need of two years of loneliness and putting himself last.

And then abruptly she let him go and sat down on the bed out of reach.

'Is that your phone?'

Phone?

The ringtone was almost drowned out by his pounding heart, but it dragged him savagely back to reality.

'Um—yeah. Yeah, it is.'

He pulled it out of his pocket, slightly dazed, took a step back and turned away, clearing his throat and groping for a normal voice.

'Hi, Sam. Are you done?'

'Yes—we've just reached the track. How's Livvy?'

Kissing me...

'She's fine. I don't think it's broken. I'll come and get you.' He put the phone back in his pocket and turned back to her without meeting her eyes. 'That was Sam,' he said unnecessarily. 'I'm going to get them. Will you be OK?'

'Of course I will. You go. I'll see you later.'

He nodded, his heart pounding, his body screaming for more, his head all over the place.

What was going on with him? How could he want her so badly?

He had no idea, but he didn't have time to deal with it now, and maybe never. Stifling regret, he picked the keys up and walked out.

They loaded the car after lunch, did a final sweep of the lodge for missed possessions and set off on the six-

hour drive back to Suffolk. She was in the front beside
Ed to give her room to stretch her foot out, and Matt
was behind her with Sam and Beth, with Lucy, Dan
and Vicky in the rear.

She sighed quietly, and Ed shot her a searching look.

'Are you OK?'

She nodded. 'Yes, I'm fine. Well, apart from feeling guilty for getting the best seat and ruining everyone's day.'

'You do a lot of that. Feeling guilty. You don't need
to, at least not around me. It took you and Matt out and
distracted Sam enough that Beth and I won, so I've
got no beef with you,' he told her with a grin, then his
smile gentled. 'Livvy, why don't you just close your
eyes and rest? You've had a tough day.'

She nodded, wishing again that she hadn't fallen,
that she hadn't kissed Matt again in the bedroom and
made things awkward, that she was sitting beside him
and taking advantage of the last few hours they had
together, instead of being in the front with a damaged
ankle and a feeling that she'd overstepped the mark
with that kiss.

Would he want to see her again? Maybe, maybe not.
If his phone hadn't rung, what would have happened?
Would they have made love? Maybe, and that surprised
her because she didn't do that sort of thing. It hadn't
even been on her radar for the last five years, but she'd
never fallen into bed with someone she knew so little
and certainly not after only three days of casual flirting, but maybe he didn't do that sort of thing either, because when Sam had called him, he couldn't get out fast
enough. Had she read him wrong all weekend?

Highly likely, judging from his reaction, although he'd

been with her all the way when they'd been kissing—or she thought he had. His body certainly had been, but maybe not his head.

Well, it didn't matter, the moment was gone, the bullet dodged, and it was just as well because there were things he didn't know yet—things she'd have to tell him before this went any further. If it was even going to, and she wasn't sure she was ready for that.

Probably just as well his phone had rung, then.

What was wrong with him? Why was he reacting like this?

She was right in front of him, so close that the scent of her shampoo, so familiar now, was drifting over him and taunting him just like it had all weekend.

How could he want her like this? He didn't even know her—and three days under Sam's embargo of any personal information or discussion of life back home or in the hospital hadn't helped with that at all. She was still an unknown quantity. And if he knew nothing about her apart from that she was Oliver's daughter, she also knew nothing about him, about his life, his family, his motivations, his commitments.

He could have told her, could have broken the embargo and spilled his guts, but he hadn't wanted to. If he was honest, he'd enjoyed the freedom of simply being himself, without all the baggage that went with it, but there was no way he could take it any further than a mild flirtation without her knowing a whole lot more about him. It wouldn't be fair, it wouldn't be honest, and there was a world of difference between being frugal with the truth and denying the most important things in his life.

And anyway, he had nothing to offer her, nothing that wouldn't be an insult.

He rested his head back and closed his eyes, but she moved her head and the scent drifted towards him again and there was no escape.

Halfway back they stopped for a drink and a leg stretch. Ed and Sam swapped places, and yet again she wasn't next to Matt, who was now right in the back, as far away from her as he could get. Why hadn't he offered to drive? Was he avoiding her? Maybe, after that excruciatingly embarrassing remark she'd made, not to mention the way she'd kissed him afterwards. She still couldn't believe she'd done it, it was so unlike her to take the initiative, and she'd probably embarrassed the life out of him. Oh, well, they'd be back soon and she'd see then if she was right or not.

Finally Sam pulled up in front of her house and Matt climbed out, retrieved her rucksack and helped her into her house, then paused on the doorstep looking troubled.

'Will you be OK on your own?'

So he *was* avoiding her, or he'd offer to stay with her. Sucking up her disappointment, she straightened her shoulders and plastered a bright smile on her face. 'Yes, I'm fine. I've got friends round the corner if I get stuck.'

'You're sure? No headache, no abdominal pain, no spinal issues? Numbness, tingling anywhere?'

She sighed. 'Matt, I'm *fine*,' she said patiently, and he gave a brief nod.

'OK. Get checked over tomorrow, won't you—or sooner if…?'

He hesitated a moment, his eyes locked with hers, and for a fraction of a second she thought he was going to kiss her, but then he smiled wistfully and reached out and touched her cheek, brushing it lightly with his knuckles. 'It's been a lot of fun. Thank you, Livvy. Take care.'

And with that he turned and walked down the path and got back into the car, and Sam pulled away, leaving her staring after them as they turned the corner and disappeared.

She closed the door with a sigh, hopped into her sitting room, lowered herself carefully onto the sofa and put her foot up.

So that was the end of that, then. So much for hoping something more might come of it. He could have stayed, or offered to come back after Ed had dropped him off, but he hadn't, and all she could do was accept it. Not that she was looking for a relationship, in any way, but it would have been nice to be asked. Nice to be more than just *fun*.

Unless he was...?

Oh, idiot. He was married. Hence the guilt in his eyes, the reluctance, the harmless dalliance that didn't break any vows but just made it a bit more *fun*.

That word again.

She rested her head back, closed her eyes and swallowed her disappointment. She was tired. Tired, confused and sore. That was all. And it wasn't as if anything had really happened...

Her phone rang, and she answered it.

'Hi, Dad. How's things?'

'Fine. How are you? How was the weekend?'

Confusing...

'Great. I'm just back, actually. It was fabulous. Well, until this morning on the way up to Haystacks when I fell off the edge of a path and twisted my ankle.'

'Ouch! Are you all right? How did you get down?'

Fast, but that wasn't what he meant and she wasn't telling them she could have tumbled all the way down to the bottom of the scree slope if it hadn't been for the rock. 'Carefully,' she said with a wry laugh. 'Two of the guys helped me back to the path, and then Matt carried me down. You know him, he's one of your old registrars. Matt Hunter? He's a consultant trauma surgeon at Yoxburgh, and he was my teammate.'

'Matt? Wow,' he said softly, something slightly odd in his voice that puzzled her. 'How is he?'

Even more puzzling. 'He's fine. Why?'

'I just wondered. I haven't seen him since his wife died.'

She felt a slither of cold run down her spine. 'His wife *died*?' she said, her voice hollow, because she'd just worked out he was married, but he wasn't, or at least not any more...

'Yeah. Juliet, and they had two tiny children. She had a brain haemorrhage while we were at a conference, and she didn't make it. I'm sure I told you about it. It must have been two years ago.'

That was Matt? She felt sick. 'You did, I remember. Oh, that's awful. I didn't know it was him. So he's got two little children?'

'Yes, a boy and a girl. They were just babies, really. I suppose Charlie must be nearly three now, and I should think Amber's about to start school, but it was desperately sad. He's a really nice guy—friendly, funny, easygoing, but rock solid and utterly reliable. I'm sure he's a brilliant father.'

Her heart ached for him. 'I'm sure he is.' And it explained the thing she hadn't been able to identify that lurked in the back of his eyes, and the fact that, embargo or not, every night he'd disappeared for a few minutes.

To check the children were OK, and talk to them?

And it also explained why he'd left her this evening rather than come in, and why he'd looked torn about it. Not because he was married, but because he had two little people who would have been missing him.

'So he seemed OK to you?' her father was asking.

Had he?

'Yes, absolutely fine—or I thought so. He didn't say anything about it, but Sam had banned us from talking about home or work. It was all about having a clean slate and not making pre-judgements about each other, but I would never have guessed all that in a million years.'

'No, I don't suppose he'd show it, anyway. He probably wanted to leave it at home. I hear he's an excellent surgeon. He showed huge promise nine years ago, so I'm not surprised he's a consultant now. I think he was only about thirty-four or so when Juliet died, but he'd done a spell with the Helicopter Emergency Medical Service, and by the time she died he was a specialist registrar in a major London trauma unit, poised and ready for a serious consultancy. It's a massive career change for him to move to sleepy Suffolk, but it's obvious why he's done it. I know his family are in the area. Give him our best wishes when you see him again, and tell him we often think about him.'

'I will. So—talking of fathers,' she said, changing the subject because frankly she needed time to let all that lot settle, 'how are the plans for your sixtieth coming on?'

He laughed ruefully. 'I have no idea. Your mother's sorting that out, but I believe we're having a marquee at home and a catered buffet and dancing. Jamie's doing the playlist so goodness knows what the music'll be like, and Abbie and your mother have chosen the menu but I have no idea what's on it. To be honest I'm trying not to think about it because I don't feel that old, so I'm in denial.'

She chuckled softly. 'Well, if it's any consolation, Dad, you don't look it, either, so I'd enjoy your party and go with the flow. So what have you guys been up to over the weekend?'

He let himself in quietly, and found his mother dozing in the family room. He closed the door softly, and she stirred.

'Hi, Mum. I'm home.'

Her eyes blinked open and she smiled. 'Oh, hello, darling. I must have dozed off. Did you have a lovely time?'

He stooped and kissed her cheek and dropped onto the sofa beside her. 'Great, thanks to you. How've they been?'

'Fine, if a little wearing. Have you been worrying?'

He laughed softly. 'Not really—not about them, more about being so far away. All the what-ifs. You know…'

'Yes, of course I know. I knew you would be, but we've all been fine. They've been as good as gold all weekend. I've only just put them to bed but I'm sure they won't mind if you wake them. I would have kept them up for you but they were shattered. They've been really busy. Amber's drawn you hundreds of pictures, and Charlie's helped me in the garden, and we've been to the beach and made sandcastles with the Shackleton tribe, and we went there on a play date this morning as well, which was nice. They're lovely people.'

'They are. And it was a godsend that Annie let Ed take their eight-seater car. Getting around up there wouldn't have been nearly so easy without it, but poetic justice, he and his teammate won the challenge, which was good.'

'Not your team?'

He smiled wryly. 'No. My teammate hurt her ankle, but to be honest just being so far away from the kids was enough of a challenge. It was beautiful there, though, and I'm really glad I went. Anyway, I don't want to hold you up, I expect you want to get home, don't you?'

'Don't you want me to stay tonight? If I know you, you'll want to be in early tomorrow.'

He shook his head, nothing further from his mind. 'No. Tomorrow I want to get the kids up and spend at least a little time with them before I drop them at nursery, so feel free to go, Mum. You must be exhausted. I know I am.'

She smiled gratefully. 'Oh, well, in that case...'

She kissed him goodnight and left, and he carried his luggage up, peeped round the corner at Charlie lying sprawled flat on his back across his bed, and went into Amber's room. She was snuggled on her side, but the moment he went in her eyes popped open and she scrambled up, throwing herself into his arms as he sat on the bed.

'Daddy!'

'Hello, my precious girl,' he murmured as she snuggled into him. He buried his face in her tangled hair and inhaled the smell of beach and sunshine and pasta sauce, and smiled.

It was so good to be home…

Her ankle felt better the next day.

Still sore, and she was definitely hobbling, but whatever that crunch had been it was better rather than worse. She went to work in her trainers because they were the only shoes that fitted comfortably, and the second Sam caught sight of her she was whisked into X-Ray to get it and her ribs checked out.

'All clear,' he said, sounding relieved. 'Right, you can go home now.'

'No, I can't. I'm here to work.'

'Seriously?'

'Seriously. I'm fine.'

Sam sighed, shrugged and gave in. 'OK, but sit when you can, take breaks and put it up whenever possible. You need a bit more support on it, I think. Is that strapping adequate?'

'It's fine. It's really good. Matt knows his stuff. It feels OK.'

He rolled his eyes. 'If you say so. I'm not convinced I believe you, but we're short-staffed as usual so I'm not going to argue, but you're in Minors—and the moment it hurts—'

'Sam, I'll be fine,' she assured him, and he shrugged again and left her to it, so she went and picked up the first set of notes and found her patient, all the time wondering if Matt would be called down to the ED and if so, if he'd speak to her.

He wasn't needed, but he appeared anyway just after one, to her relief, because after the initial rush in Minors it had all settled down to a steady tick-over and she had far too much time to think about him and what her father had told her.

She was standing at the central work station filling in notes when she felt him come up behind her. How did she *know* it was him? No idea, but she did, and she turned and met his concerned eyes.

'Hi. I didn't expect you to be here,' he murmured. 'How's the ankle?'

'Better, thanks. Your strapping seems to be working. It's my mind I've got problems with. Sam's put me in Minors,' she told him, and she could hear the disgust in her voice.

So could he, evidently, because he chuckled softly.

'Yeah,' he said. 'I rang him and asked how you were, and he told me you were cross you were out of Resus.'

She laughed at that, because it was sort of true. 'I'm not really cross, and I know someone has to do Minors, but it's gone really quiet and now I'm just bored.'

'Shh, don't say that, you never say that,' he said, his eyes twinkling, and he glanced at his phone. 'Have you had lunch?'

'No. My fridge was pretty empty, and I don't fancy chocolate or crisps out of the vending machine.'

'Well, now might be a good time to make a break for it.'

'Except I can't get to the café easily. Walking from the car park was bad enough.'

'Soon fix that,' he said, and, glancing over his shoulder, he made a satisfied noise and retrieved an abandoned wheelchair.

She stared at it in horror. 'You have to be joking.'

'Not in the slightest. Sit down or I'll put you in it.'

He would. She knew that perfectly well after yesterday, so with a sigh of resignation she sat in the wheelchair and Jenny, one of the senior nurses, nodded and grinned.

'Well done, Matt.'

'Don't encourage him—and call me if you need me, Jenny. I won't be long. And I can push myself,' she said, reaching for the wheels.

'No, you can't, it's not that sort of chair,' he pointed out, and whisked her down the corridor, out of the side entrance and into the park.

Five minutes later they were sitting on a bench under a tree, armed with cold drinks and sandwiches. He patted his lap. 'Put your leg up. I want to have a look at your ankle,' he said, and she sighed.

'If you insist,' she said, but the moment her ankle settled over that disturbingly strong thigh she could have kicked herself. She should have put it on the wheelchair, because his hands were on it and it was distracting her, and she didn't want to be distracted. She wanted to talk to him about what her father had said.

But he was probing it now, gently—or sort of gently, and she was distracted in a different way.

'Ouch!'

'Sorry. It feels swollen still. Are you sure you should be working?'

She rolled her eyes and ripped open her sandwich.

'You're as bad as Sam. You just want to fuss and cluck over me like a pair of mother hens.'

'That's why we're doctors—an exaggerated sense of responsibility for the health of the nation. It's nothing personal.'

Tell it to the fairies. His hand was resting on her leg now, his thumb idly stroking over her shin, and she wasn't even sure he was aware of doing it. She solved the problem by removing her foot from his lap and propping it on the wheelchair like she should have done in the first place, and took a deep breath.

'I spoke to my father last night and passed on your message,' she told him tentatively, 'and he asked me to send you their best wishes and said they think about you often. He spoke very fondly of you.'

'Oh, bless them. They've been amazing to me. I haven't seen them for ages, not since...'

He trailed off, but he didn't need to finish the sentence because she knew.

'He told me,' she said softly. 'About your wife. I'm so sorry. I had no idea.'

His smile was wry and a little twisted. 'I think that was rather the point. No preconceptions. No baggage. And a dead wife and two motherless little children is a lot of baggage in anyone's language.'

She winced at the frank, softly spoken words and looked away. 'I can imagine. I'm really sorry. I wish I'd known. I wouldn't have behaved like I did and I certainly wouldn't have kissed you like that. I didn't mean to offend you or overstep the mark.'

His hand reached out, his fingers finding hers. 'I wasn't in the least bit offended and you didn't overstep the mark, Livvy. There was no mark, and there was nothing wrong with your behaviour. And anyway, I kissed you first, and I shouldn't have done that, either. It was the first time I'd left the kids and gone any distance from home since—well, since then, and I just wanted to be *me*, you know? Not that poor guy whose wife died and left him with two tiny children, but just a man, someone who could be taken at face value.

'I'm sick of being different, sick of people making concessions and tiptoeing round me and worrying about upsetting me. I nearly told you, but then I realised I didn't want to because it would change everything, and I didn't *want* it to change. I was enjoying myself, having simple, uncomplicated fun with no strings, no expectations, just a man and a woman working together to achieve a series of goals and having fun on the way. And it was fun, Livvy. I wouldn't have changed any of it. Well, apart from you hurling yourself down the scree slope. That wasn't great.'

She felt her eyes fill with tears, and blinked them away, because she'd felt the same, the freedom from the burden of people's sympathy, everyone watching their words so they didn't upset or offend or reopen the emotional wounds or poke the sleeping tiger. That was why hardly anybody at the Yoxburgh Park Hospital knew her medical history, and why she hadn't told Matt.

'I wouldn't have changed any of it, either. Well, except that bit. You're right, it was fun, but I guess we're back now.'

He sighed quietly, then gave a wry huff of laughter. 'Yes, we're back. I know that. Amber insisted on sleeping with me last night, and Charlie woke up at four, crying because he'd wet the bed, so he ended up with me as well. Definitely back. And you know what? It feels *good* to be back, and I really missed them, but I'm very, very glad I went away, too, and I'm glad you were there with me.'

She smiled at him. 'I'm glad, as well. Still, it's over now.' Odd, how that made her feel sad. Why should it? It wasn't as if anything had really happened. Just a couple of kisses, some shared banter, the odd hug. How could she miss that so much?

'It doesn't have to be over,' he said, after a long pause. 'I'd still like to see you—not in a serious way, I'm not in the market for anything more than the odd snatched lunch break or a very occasional drink or a quick bite to eat, but it would be great to have that time with you. Not that you're probably interested in such a trivial offering—'

'Of course I'm interested,' she said promptly, surprised that she was. 'I'm not in the market for anything serious, but I'm happy to spend time with you as and when we can. And I don't expect anything, Matt. I really don't.'

He nodded then, his eyes softening into a smile. 'Thank you.'

'Don't thank me. I'm relatively new here, I don't know many people yet and I have plenty of time on my hands. Spending a little of it with you will be a pleasure. And talking of time, I ought to get back, but I'm glad I've seen you so I could pass on my father's message. He spoke very highly of you, and he said your wife was a lovely person.'

A shadow crossed his eyes again, and he nodded. 'She was. Thank you. That means a lot. He was a brilliant mentor and a good friend to me, and I owe him so much. Say hi for me when you speak to him.'

'Say it yourself. I'm sure he'd love to hear from you.'

He nodded. 'Maybe I will. Right, I'd better take you back before I have Sam on the phone asking why I've abducted one of their registrars, but give me your number first.' He keyed it into his phone, and then hers jiggled in her pocket. 'Get that?'

She nodded and smiled. 'I'll send you my father's email address so you can contact him. And call me when you can, anytime you've got a gap in the chaos and you want to meet up.'

His eyes searched hers. 'It's going to be very random, Livvy. Are you sure you're OK with that?'

She nodded, although she wasn't entirely sure what he was really offering in those random moments. Friendship? Or more? An affair? Although that might take more than the occasional coffee break, even if you were desperate.

And she wasn't that desperate, she really, really wasn't.

Was she?

CHAPTER THREE

EVEN THOUGH SHE knew he wasn't offering much or often, his 'random' turned out to be more elusive than she'd expected. Or hoped, anyway.

Maybe he'd been right to imagine that it might not be enough for her. She'd thought it would be fine, but oddly it wasn't, and even though she hardly knew him, she realised she was missing him, missing the flirting and the banter and just his presence.

By Thursday, although he'd been down to the ED at least twice that she knew of, she still hadn't seen him to speak to, but he sent her a text to ask how her ankle was, with a smiley emoji reply when she said it was better, but still nothing else. Nothing about meeting up at any time.

Sure, he'd just been away for the long weekend and was giving the children all his available time, and she knew a patient he'd seen yesterday had needed hours in Theatre because of the horrendous damage to his limbs after he'd been caught in farm machinery, and she'd seen him then, but not to speak to.

They'd instigated the major haemorrhage protocol and she'd been called in to help, but Matt, James and Sam were all there. Joe Baker, the interventional radiologist, was called down to get another line in while they tried to get control of the bleeding in their patient's limbs before he was rushed to Theatre with Matt and Joe at his side, but Matt had had no time to spare her as much as a glance. She'd heard he'd had to take the man back to Theatre today, but she hadn't heard the outcome and he might still be in there, which would explain why he hadn't contacted her.

And anyway, she kept telling herself, he was only talking about a quick coffee or the odd drink, not a relationship. And she'd managed without one for the past almost five years, so why did it suddenly matter now? She had a life. She had new friends here in Yoxburgh, old friends just thirty-five miles away in Audley, and, besides, it was the summer and if all else failed she could go for gorgeous walks along the river bank or by the sea, or get out in the front garden and weed the gravel. Goodness knows it was high time.

Which was why that evening, after a long day at work, she changed into shorts and trainers and a tatty old T-shirt and tackled it. If nothing else it would distract her from a man who was clearly far too busy to fit her into his chaotic life, and it certainly wasn't a moment too soon because the little bit of garden behind the hedge was a mess.

The weeds had flourished in the glorious early summer weather, rooting themselves firmly down in the supposedly low-maintenance gravel, and she was wrestling with a particularly stubborn weed when she heard footsteps approaching.

'Oh, get *out*!' she growled, and the footsteps stopped.

'Well, that's a warm welcome.'

She jackknifed up, lost her balance and stepped back

without thinking, and pain shot through her ankle. Her leg folded as she yelped, and he caught her and took the weight off it, holding her firmly back against his chest.

'Are you OK?'

She straightened up and turned to face him, carefully this time, her heart thudding a little as she met his eyes. 'Yes, I'm fine or I was, until you made me jump.'

He stifled the smile. 'Sorry. Here, let me,' he said, and taking the little fork out of her hand, he shoved it into the ground beside the weed, levered gently and lifted it out, its roots intact.

'There you go. One late weed. Am I forgiven?'

'Only if you take the rest of them out.'

He humphed and lobbed it into the garden waste bin.

'So, what brings you here?' she asked, cursing the fact that she was hot, sweaty, covered in dirt and quite definitely not at her fragrant best. 'I'm sure it wasn't my weeds, although don't let me stop you.'

He chuckled. 'No, not your weeds. I tried to ring you, but you didn't answer, so I thought I'd call by, just in case.'

Her heart skipped a beat. 'Just in case?'

He smiled. 'In case you were in and had a few minutes to spare.'

She looked down at herself. Yes, she had time to spare, but... 'I can't go anywhere, Matt. Look at me!'

His eyes tracked over her. 'I am,' he said, his voice warm. 'And I wasn't planning on going anywhere. I just thought it might be nice to have a coffee with you here, if you can drag yourself away from the weeds for a few minutes?'

Drag herself away? Wouldn't take much dragging. 'Sure. Come on in.'

She picked up her tools and gloves and led him back inside along the hall, through the dining area and into the kitchen.

'You're still limping. I hope that's not my fault.'

It was, because he'd made her jump, but she wasn't going to tell him that. 'I said it was better, I didn't say it was cured. Coffee?'

She turned but he was right behind her, his hands coming up to steady her as she winced again and shifted her weight off her sore ankle.

'Steady,' he murmured, and she could feel the warmth of his hands cupping her shoulders, the cool drift of his minty-fresh breath, and their eyes locked.

Was he going to kiss her? Please...

No. He dropped his hands, took a step back and looked away, and she swallowed her disappointment.

'Um—yes, please, white coffee, no sugar.'

She washed her hands, put the kettle on and opened the cupboard, and he settled himself on a dining chair and looked around.

'It'll have to be decaf, I'm afraid,' she told him.

'That's fine, whatever you've got. I've had quite a lot today, anyway. It's been a tough day.'

'Really? What happened?'

He sighed and scrubbed a hand through his hair. 'We lost the farmer. I'd taken him back to Theatre twice to try and salvage what I could of his limbs, but he'd lost so much blood so quickly before they could get him out that his brain was deprived of oxygen and today his organs shut down and we turned off the life support.'

She stopped, spoon in hand. 'Oh, no. Oh, Matt, I'm really sorry to hear that. Did he have a wife?'

'Yes, and three children. Telling her was—well, I

think she was expecting it, but even so. He was only thirty-six. Same age as me. That was tough.'

It must have been, especially having once been on the receiving end himself, but she imagined that would give him a better understanding of the impact of it. Would that make it easier, or harder?

'Nice house, by the way,' he said as she poured water onto the coffee. 'How long have you been here?'

'Since I took over from Iona Baker's locum when she handed in her notice after her maternity leave. I was working in London but I wanted to come home to Suffolk, and the job came up so I took it, and Sam put me in touch with Ben Walker, one of the obstetricians. It belongs to his wife and I moved in in April but unfortunately I'm only renting it. I gather they only let it to hospital staff.'

'Yes, Ed said he lived here for a while before his grandfather died. It's interesting.'

It was. It had started life as a typical Victorian semi, but the dining room had been opened to the hall and the kitchen, and a door led out via a conservatory to the back garden, so the whole room felt light and airy.

It wasn't everyone's taste, but she loved it.

'It is interesting, isn't it? It's a pity Daisy won't sell. I sold my flat in London and I'm waiting for it all to go through, then I'm going to buy something, but I'm not sure where. Maybe here, maybe Audley, although if I want to go home I can always stay with my parents so I'm a bit undecided, but there's no rush. I love this house and I'm quite happy here for now.'

And then the conversation died, leaving them standing there in a slightly awkward silence while his coffee brewed and her green tea steamed gently beside it.

'Matt…'

'Livvy…'

He laughed softly and gestured to her. 'You first.'

'I was going to ask you why you wanted to see me.'

He frowned slightly. 'I told you—I thought we could have a coffee.'

'No. I meant—generally. Why you wanted to make time to do this.'

His frown deepened, his eyes concerned and a little confused. 'I thought we had this conversation on Monday?'

'We did, but—I'm not really sure I know what you want from me. I've spent days trying to work it out, and I'm still not convinced I know the answer. It could be so many things. Friendship, an affair, friends with benefits—?'

'Friends with benefits?'

He stood up and walked over to her, stopping just inches away, hands rammed in his back pockets, a quizzical look in his eyes, and she shrugged helplessly.

'Well, I don't know—I told you I can't work it out.'

His soft laugh rippled over her and made her skin tingle. 'Oh, Livvy. There's nothing to work out. I don't *want* anything from you, I just thought it would be nice to spend time together. And I think we both know it's probably more than simple friendship, but if that's all you want to offer me, I'll happily accept it, and there's no hurry. I just want to see you. I feel we hardly scratched the surface over the weekend, and there's so much more to you that I don't know, and I want to know more. I want to spend time with you, just be with you and hang out. No agenda. No pressure. Just see where it goes.'

He looked down at the floor, then up again, his eyes sombre now as he spoke again, his voice low.

'I can't offer you a relationship, not one I can do justice to, but I'm lonely, Livvy. I'm ridiculously busy, constantly surrounded by people, and I'm hardly ever alone, and yet I'm lonely. I miss the companionship of a woman, and I'd like to spend time with one who isn't either simply a colleague or my mother. A woman who can make me laugh again. I spend my days rushed off my feet, the rest of my time is dedicated to my children, and don't get me wrong, I love them desperately, but—I have no downtime, no me-time, no time to chill out and have a conversation about something that isn't medicine or hospital politics or whether the kids want dippy eggs or scrambled.'

His mouth kicked up in a wry smile, and he shrugged, just a subtle shift of his shoulders that was more revealing than even his words had been, and she forgot the coffee, forgot her foot and her common sense, and walked up to him, put her arms round him and hugged him.

'Scrambled, every time,' she said, her voice slightly choked, and it took a second, but then he laughed, his chest shaking under her ear, and he tilted her head back and kissed her. Just briefly, not long enough to cause trouble, just long enough to remind her of what he did to her, and then he rested his forehead against her and smiled.

'Me, too. Preferably with bacon and slices of cold tomato in a massive club sandwich washed down with a bucket of coffee.'

'Oh, yes! I haven't had one of those for ages!'

He laughed and let her go. 'I'll cook you brunch one day,' he said, and it sounded like a promise.

'Is that a promise?' she asked, just to be sure. 'Not that I'll hold you to it, and I'm not in a position to do a relationship justice either for various reasons—work, health...'

'Health?'

She shrugged, not yet ready to tell him, to throw *that* word into the middle of a casual conversation. 'Amongst other things, but—whatever you want from me, wherever you want to take this, I'm up for it.'

'Is that what you want from this? An ad hoc affair?'

She held his eyes, wondering if she dared, if she had the courage to tell him, to let him that close, to open herself to potential hurt. Because she'd have to, if this was going any further.

But there was nothing in his eyes except need and tenderness, and she knew he wouldn't hurt her. She nodded. 'Yes. Yes, it is, if that's what you want, too.'

His breath huffed out, a quiet, surprised sound, and something flared in his eyes. 'Oh, Livvy. Absolutely. As long as we're on the same page.'

'We're on the same page,' she said, and he nodded slowly and dipped his head, taking her mouth in a lingering, tender kiss. And then he straightened, just as it was hotting up, and stepped away with a wry smile.

'Is that coffee ready? I don't have very long and certainly not long enough for where that was going. I begged yet another favour from my sainted mother and I don't want to take her for granted.'

She nodded and turned back to pour it with shaking hands, then felt his fingers curl over her shoulders as he moved in behind her and rested his head against the side of hers, doing all sorts of things to her heart rate.

'That's yes to brunch, by the way,' he murmured, his voice deep and husky. 'It *is* a promise. Goodness knows when, but soon.'

Heat raced through her, and she pressed the plunger down, filled his mug and handed it to him with a shaky smile.

'Here. Shall we go in the back garden? It's a bit of a jungle but it's such a lovely evening.'

'Sure. I love a jungle and it'll make a refreshing change from mine. It's hardly got a stick in it.'

She led him through the conservatory and they sat on the swinging bench at the end in the dappled shade under the wisteria, wrapped around by the whisper of a light sea breeze through the leaves and the quiet creak of the chains as he rocked the bench with a little thrust of his foot, and he sighed.

'This is lovely—it reminds me of the garden we had in London, cool and green and shady. So tranquil, like a little oasis in the madness.'

'It is. It's my favourite place. Work's so busy, and here I can just chill out and be me.'

He nodded. 'I know just what you mean. My current garden was wildly overgrown so I had it landscaped over the winter, but until the trees and shrubs grow back and the beds fill out it just looks barren, and I hate it.'

'It'll grow,' she said encouragingly, and he smiled.

'I know. I'm just impatient, and I really miss our London garden. It became my sanctuary, and when we moved I lost that place where I could go and find solitude. The nearest I get to it now is on the balcony and that's not exactly private, but I've pretty much given up on that. The only place I ever get any privacy is in the bathroom, and that's only if I lock the door, and unless they're asleep the chances of one of the children banging on it and demanding my attention are super-high.'

His mouth tipped up in a wry smile, and she laughed. 'Are they that bad?'

He shook his head. 'No. They're lovely, but they're just always *there*. Don't get me wrong, I love them to bits and I couldn't bear it if anything happened to them, but sometimes I just want to run away and hide.'

She searched his eyes, finding humour but also a little despair. 'Feel free to come here whenever you want,' she said softly. 'You're always welcome to join me. Or I can give you a key and you can let yourself in.'

He smiled, just a slow, slight tilt of his mouth, and then he lifted his coffee to his lips and took a long swallow. 'Thank you.'

'Any time. So, tell me about your children—or are they off limits?'

He smiled a tender, slightly rueful smile and tensed his thigh, giving the swing another push and making the chains creak again. 'No, they're not off limits,' he said fondly. 'Amber starts school in September and she's massively excited and more than ready for it, and Charlie—well, Charlie's just a little boy. He's either running or he's asleep but I expect he might grow out of that. He's not three till August.'

She felt her eyes well. 'It must be so tough being a single parent. How do you cope? How *did* you cope?'

'I don't know. I don't think I did, really. When Juliet died—' He broke off, then gave her a crooked smile. 'It was tough. It's still tough, but it's getting easier, and my mother's been amazing and so have Juliet's parents and her sister, Sally. Without them I couldn't do it, which is why I took the job up here, because Sally's only ten miles away, her parents are a little further, and my mother lives literally round the corner from my house. And I've got friends here. Ed and I go back years, but still… Don't get me wrong, it's a great job and I love it, but it's not where I was heading.'

'No, my father said that. I think he'd imagined you heading up a major trauma centre.'

He smiled wryly. 'Yeah, me, too, but it's not really compatible with family life, or at least not on the way there. Maybe once I'd made it. And maybe that's the only good thing to have come out of this, that I've found a job with virtually no commuting time, that gives the children regular, meaningful contact with other members of the family and me enough job satisfaction that I don't feel in the slightest bit cheated. Well, maybe a bit, professionally, but that's a small sacrifice and nothing compared to what we all gain as a family from us being here, and frankly there have been times when I wasn't even sure we'd all make it through.'

Oh, Matt…

He glanced at his watch and swore softly. 'I need to go. I'm sorry.'

'Don't be,' she murmured, her heart aching for him. 'It's been lovely to see you. I'm glad you came.'

His mouth kicked up into another crooked grin. 'Me, too. I'm still sorry it can't be longer, though,' he added, and the slight disappointment she'd felt at his short visit faded away.

'It's fine, Matt. I understand. And remember, you can come here at any time.'

'Thank you. For that, for understanding, and for the coffee. It means a lot.' He got to his feet, setting the swing rocking gently. 'Don't move, I'll let myself out. You stay there and enjoy the last of the evening sun.'

He leant over, his hand cradling her cheek, and touched his lips to hers in a tender, lingering kiss that wasn't nearly long enough. Then he was gone, leaving her mulling over his words.

There have been times when I wasn't even sure we'd all make it through...

How on earth had he coped? How had the children coped? Poor, tiny little things. She thought of her parents, of how much they loved each other, how close they all were as a family, and then she imagined one or other of them dying and their whole world being torn apart.

Something wet landed on her arm, and it took her a moment to realise that it was a tear. She scrubbed it away, sucked in a deep breath and headed back to the front garden. A bit of hard physical work was just what she needed, and her ankle would just have to get over itself.

She didn't see him again until the following week, and when she did they hardly had time to acknowledge each other because by the time he came down to the ED she was assisting James Slater as he opened the chest of a teenager with stab wounds.

'Perfect timing,' James said bluntly, and she heard the snap of gloves and then Matt was there, gently shouldering her out of the way and taking over, his hands finding the bleed instantly.

'OK, the pulmonary vein's been nicked and this

lobe is trashed. Can I have a clamp and some more suction, please?'

She'd seen him in action before but not like this, wrist deep inside the chest of a dying boy—except the boy didn't die, because he stopped the bleed, and found another and stopped that, too, and then turned his attention to the other wounds in his abdomen.

'He needs opening up. Has anyone had time to look at his back?'

'Yes, it's clear,' James said, and he nodded.

'Right, I need to transfer him to Theatre. Can someone alert them, please?'

'Done it, and I've got PICU on standby,' a nurse said.

'*PICU?* How old is he?' he asked, sounding startled.

'Fifteen,' James growled.

Matt swore softly under his breath and stepped back from the bed. 'OK, let's pack that and get a sterile dressing over it for the transfer, and then we'll see how it goes.'

Once he was satisfied the boy was ready to go he stepped back and stripped off his gloves and the blood-splattered plastic apron, turning towards the door and meeting her eyes for the first time. His face softened briefly into a smile that barely reached his eyes.

'Hi. Thanks for your help. Sorry, I'm a bit rushed. I'll catch up with you later. Right, let's go.'

All business again, he headed out of the door, one hand on the trolley, and James thanked her and sent her back to the patient she'd left when the boy had been brought in. She picked up where she'd left off, but her mind kept straying to Matt and the boy he was trying to save.

Would he be able to? Would the poor kid make it through?

Please, please don't let him die...

He didn't die, to Matt's surprise.

He almost did. He had a couple of goes in Theatre and they'd had to restart his heart once, but now he was in PICU, still critical but at least with a fighting chance of being more than another tragic statistic.

He left the hospital late after he'd talked to Ryan's desperate mother and went home to his children, gathering them up in a massive cuddle on the sofa, blinking hard to shift the tears that welled unexpectedly in his eyes.

'Tough day?' his mother asked, and he gave a grunt of humourless laughter.

'You could say that. It could have been worse, though.'

She nodded, as if she'd understood the subtext. 'I'll make you a cup of tea.'

'Decaf, please. And can you stay? I might need to go back in.'

'Yes, darling, of course I can.'

He sighed, let go of the children, who were squirming in his arms and trying to watch the television, and followed his mother into the kitchen area.

'I don't know what I'd do without you,' he mumbled, and wrapped his arms around her from behind, resting his head against hers. 'You've been a star, Mum.'

'No, I've been a parent. That's what we do, Matt, that's what families are for. We pick up the pieces. You know that.'

'I do, but you've had more than your fair share of it.'

She shrugged, her shoulders shifting against his chest, and the kettle clicked off and he dropped his arms and let her make the tea.

It was only four years since his father had died, and she'd been amazing, nursing him through the final stages of cancer with humour and compassion, and when he'd gone she'd picked up the pieces of her life and carried on, and then, two years later, she'd put her own grief aside and picked up the pieces of *his* life and his children's when Jules had died and left them all devastated.

So soon after losing her husband, that must have been incredibly tough for her, but she'd done it without question, dropped everything and come to him.

Foolishly he'd refused to take any time off work, so after the funeral he'd put the children in nursery and sent his mother home, but they'd been too distraught so after three days she'd come back to look after them in the family home, but that had meant he was never alone so he was bottling up his grief, snapping at everyone and shutting down his emotions because he was afraid of what would happen if he let go.

So after a few more days she'd brought them back up here because he thought it would be better for them to have a calm, orderly life, with him appearing every weekend pleased to see them, rather than be in their own home with him coming back in the evenings crabby and angry and needing to fall apart.

He'd taken time off then, a couple of weeks when he'd hardly got out of bed, just lain in the sheets that still smelt of Jules and cried until his chest ached and his eyes were raw and his heart felt as if it had been torn in two.

But they'd missed him desperately, and he'd missed them, too, so he'd finally pulled himself together and changed the sheets, cleaned the house and his mother had brought the children back to London and stayed, and when the job in Yoxburgh had come up, she'd helped him get the house ready to put on the market, shown the buyers round it and packed up all their things for storage until the new house was ready.

All except Juliet's things.

He'd done that, working on autopilot, and he hadn't dealt with them until the week before he'd gone to Cumbria. Now they were packed in boxes in his study, ready for the children to look at when they were old enough.

He hadn't felt ready until then, just as he now wasn't ready for what he felt with Livvy, either, but it seemed to be happening, some slow awakening of his senses, a thawing of a part of him that had been numb for two years.

Was it wise? Probably not.

Disloyal?

No, not that. Jules wouldn't have wanted him to be lonely, but he still had unfinished business with her. If only he'd had time to say goodbye, but by the time he'd got to the hospital she had been in a coma and it had been too late.

Had she known he was there? He hoped so, hoped she'd known how much he loved her, how much she'd given him over the years, how much he had to thank her for—

'Matt?'

He blinked, his eyes coming back into focus,

and took the tea from his mother. 'Thanks,' he said gruffly. 'Sorry, I was miles away.'

'I know,' she said, her eyes so full of compassion and understanding it nearly unravelled him. 'Come on, let's sit down with the children for a few minutes until their film finishes and then you can put them to bed—unless you'd like me to do it?'

He shook his head. 'No. I'll do it. Oh, damn. Don't you have book club tonight?'

She smiled ruefully. 'I do, but it doesn't matter. I haven't finished the book.'

'Do you ever?'

She laughed. 'Sometimes.'

'Go anyway. I'm sure it doesn't matter. Where is it?'

'Only round the corner. Joanna's house—Annie's mother, and Marnie will be there, too. Maybe I will go, if you're sure you're all right?'

'I'm fine, Mum. You're only seconds away, so I'll call you if I need to go back in.'

'That wasn't what I meant,' she said, and he had to look away. He cleared his throat.

'So, what have they had to eat? Let me guess—pasta.'

'No. Actually, no, for once. I made them a chicken tagine with couscous. They loved it. I've saved you some, but you'll probably think it's a bit mild.'

'I'm sure it'll be lovely. I'm starving. Thank you—for everything.'

His mother flapped her hand at him and headed back to the sofa with her tea, and he followed her, sat down on the other sofa and watched the end of the programme with his precious children snuggled up on each side of him while his tea cooled, forgotten.

Livvy saw him on Monday in Resus, over a week since he'd come to her house, and they went for coffee after his patient was transferred to Interventional Radiology with Joe Baker and he was off the hook for a few minutes.

She'd been on edge since their conversation that Thursday and for some reason the time had seemed to stretch interminably, so she was ridiculously pleased when he asked her to join him. Maybe he'd take the opportunity to arrange a time to see her properly, when they could be alone.

He picked up a banana, asked for a cappuccino and Livvy ordered a pot of green tea and found a bag of mixed nuts and seeds, her heart jiggling in her chest.

Would he suggest it?

'Do you ever drink coffee?' he asked as they sat down, and she shook her head.

'Not usually. I'm not a huge fan.'

'But—green tea?' he asked, pulling a face. 'Is that for health reasons?'

Again, not the right time, and not enough time to discuss it properly, but it settled her heart down again. 'Partly. It's good for you,' she said, without going into any further details. 'And anyway, I love it.'

He laughed. 'I can't imagine why. I think it's vile, but each to his own. I emailed your father, by the way,' he added. 'I've been meaning to contact him for ages and I've never got round to it, so thanks for jogging me. Anyway, he replied and said it would be nice to see me again, so I might run up there sometime if I get a minute. I could maybe take the children one weekend.'

She nodded. 'They'd love that, but don't plan it for this coming weekend. It's Dad's sixtieth, and they're throwing him a party on Saturday night. Actually,' she said, thinking about it and wondering if it would provide that opportunity she was waiting for, 'you ought to come with me.'

He shook his head. 'No, I can't do that.'

She felt a little stab of disappointment. 'Oh. I suppose you'd have to get someone to look after the children and it's very short notice. That's a shame.'

He shook his head again. 'I wouldn't, as it happens, because they're having a sleepover with their cousins at Juliet's sister's house, but there's the small matter that I haven't been invited.'

'Yes, you have—by me,' she said, taking away that excuse with a smile. 'You can be my plus one. I'll even drive you so you can drink—unless you don't want to come?' she added, suddenly wondering if she'd overstepped the mark. Again.

'Won't you be staying over?'

She shook her head. 'I don't have to. I was going to, but I'm sure they can use my room for someone else. Seriously, Matt, why not? It'll be a great party. Unless you're working?'

'No. No, I'm not working, but it just feels a bit cheeky.'

'Rubbish, you'd be more than welcome.'

He frowned, but he didn't say any more, just glanced at his phone and sighed. 'I need to go. I've got a patient to check on and then I've got an outpatients' clinic.'

'Yeah, I should go, too. But please think about it.

I'm sure they'd be delighted if you came. I know they'd love to see you.'

And she'd love him to come, if she could only persuade him...

He laughed, his eyes creasing. 'You don't give up, do you?'

She smiled wryly. 'No, but just tell me this. If he'd asked you himself, would you have said yes?'

'Probably. Well, after I'd talked to you and made sure you were OK with it.'

She laughed. 'Why wouldn't I be OK with it?'

'I don't know, but it doesn't do to make assumptions,' he said softly, surprising her.

'Matt, you should know me better by now,' she scolded gently. 'I'm more than happy if you want to come. Think about it and let me know.'

He nodded. 'OK. And that's not a yes, by the way.'

'Of course it isn't,' she said, but she couldn't stop her smile and he rolled his eyes, laughed and walked her back to the ED.

CHAPTER FOUR

HE DIDN'T GET a minute to see her in the next few days, but her invitation was never far from his mind and he still didn't know what to do about it.

He hadn't been to a party since Jules had died, mostly because he hadn't had the time or the inclination, but this was Oliver's sixtieth, a milestone party for a man to whom he owed so much, for all sorts of reasons. Did he want to go with Livvy?

Yes, he realised. He did—but was it wise? Their relationship was so new, so unformed that he wasn't even sure they *had* one. Their only conversation about it had ended with talk of an ad hoc affair, and he certainly wasn't ready to go public with that, especially not with her parents, of all people.

Except, of course, because it was so new, they probably wouldn't think anything of it other than that their daughter was his colleague and so it was entirely reasonable that they should go to the party together. They didn't need to announce to anyone that they were starting a relationship—if you could call something so hit and miss a relationship.

She didn't seem to want more than that, though, which was fine by him because he couldn't give her more anyway, but one of the reasons she'd given was health issues, and that intrigued him. What health issues? She hadn't said, and he hadn't seen her in the sort of situation when he felt he could ask. Maybe on the way to the party, or the way back?

And the party was a way of getting to see Bron and Oliver again, a way to thank Oliver personally for what he'd done for him, but also a chance to see more of Livvy, and spend more than fifteen snatched minutes with her over a cup of green tea, for heaven's sake!

He sent her a text.

Is the invitation still open?

Seconds later her reply pinged back.

Yes, of course. It's black tie—is that a problem?

No problem. What time shall I pick you up?

It starts at seven thirty. And I'm driving. I'll pick you up.

He laughed. Yes, she'd offered, but he wouldn't hold her to it. For a start it just felt wrong, and more importantly he never went anywhere without being able to get away under his own steam—just in case. Except Cumbria, and he would have hired a car or caught a train or got a taxi if necessary. And that was exceptional. Audley was about thirty miles up the road, less than an hour away. And he didn't need alcohol. He'd had enough to last a lifetime in that lonely fortnight after Jules had died, and he was fine without it.

Besides, if he was with her and she was dancing in

some slinky little number that was going to trash his mind, he needed to be stone-cold sober or he might well make an idiot of himself in front of her parents.

I'll drive you. Call me old-fashioned. :)

There was a pause—a long one. Because she was busy? Quite likely. It was half an hour before she came back to him.

Not going to argue. I hate driving at night! Pick me up at six forty-five. X

He was late.

Only a couple of minutes, but it was enough to stretch her tight nerves just a little tighter.

She'd been ready ages ago, dithering over whether her new dress was all right, if he'd like it, if she should wear her hair up or down, could she wear heels—only low ones but still, her ankle wasn't quite right yet—and how much make-up? She hardly wore any usually, but tonight—

And the dress. She'd loved the dress the moment she'd seen it, and it could have been made for her. The left shoulder was bare, with diagonal pleats across the bodice that started at the waist and ran up to the right shoulder, ending in a delicate waterfall of chiffon like a floaty little cap sleeve that covered the top of her arm. It was pretty, elegant, fitted her like a glove and was a perfect match for her eyes, but she'd spent the last few years hiding herself away in loose, casual clothes and it was—well, fitted, for want of a better word. And dressy.

She'd told herself off for being ridiculous. It was beautifully cut, and it was a glamorous party, so why shouldn't she be dressy? So she'd twisted her hair up and secured it with a sparkly clip, put on her normal going-out make-up and the wedge-heeled sandals and gone downstairs to wait, her nerves as tight as a bow-string because tonight might be the night, and she felt like a teenager going to her first prom.

She was watching from the bay window of her little sitting room when he arrived, and as he rounded the front of the car and stepped onto the kerb, she felt her mouth dry.

What was it about formal dress that made men look so good? Not that Matt didn't always, but tonight he looked stunning as he strode up the path and waved to her through the window. Even sexier, if that was possible, and her pulse hitched.

She hesitated at the front door, ran a hand over her dress, wondering again if he'd like it, hoping he would, telling herself it didn't matter when she knew it did, then finally she opened the door, and he smiled again as he stepped inside and dropped a kiss on her cheek, his eyes warm.

'You look amazing,' he said, his voice low and soft and a little rough at the same time, and she felt the tension ease a little. Well, no, that tension. The other tension, the tension that was all about how gorgeous he looked and how much she was looking forward to spending all that time with him on a—was it a date?—ratcheting up a notch or six.

'Well, I thought I'd lash out on a new dress,' she said, her voice oddly breathless. 'He's only going to be sixty once.'

His voice deepened a fraction and his eyes never left her face. 'I wasn't talking about the dress.' Then his eyes dropped, and he scanned her slowly and smiled. 'Although I have to say it really suits you. You look beautiful, Livvy. Absolutely gorgeous. He'll be so proud of you.'

She felt soft colour sweeping up her throat, and felt suddenly shy. She was never shy! What was he doing to her?

'Thank you,' she said, fighting down the unexpected blush and scanning him blatantly just for the fun of it. 'You don't look so bad yourself.'

He grinned. 'That's because you're used to seeing me in scrubs. It's just the tux. Same old me underneath, I'm afraid.'

'Yeah, that must be it, all in the tailoring,' she said, making a joke of it while she dragged her tattered composure back into shape and tried not to think about what was underneath the immaculately cut suit. She picked up her bag and a soft cashmere wrap in case it was cold later, and turned back to him.

'Shall we go?'

He gestured to the front door and gave a little mock bow. 'Your carriage awaits. I even washed it.'

'Good grief. That's going above and beyond.'

He chuckled and opened the car door for her and helped her in, lifting her dress clear of the sill so it didn't get dirty, even though the car was gleaming.

So thoughtful. So—perfect? And so unavailable...

No. Not unavailable. Just not permanent. There was a difference, and she was looking forward to exploring it.

'I take it you know the way to their house?' she asked as he slid behind the wheel, and he laughed softly.

'Yes, I know the way. Sit back and relax.'

Livvy walked through the open front door of the Victorian house on the park that was her family home, and Matt followed her in, hanging back a little.

Her father was there greeting his guests, and he looked fit and well and nothing like sixty. He hadn't changed, not in the two years since he'd seen him, and very little in the nine years since he'd first joined Oliver's team as a baby registrar, and he saw the love in his eyes as he pulled his daughter into a hug and kissed her cheek.

'Hello, darling. You look beautiful,' he said warmly, and then he looked up and his eyes widened.

'Matt! Come in! How good to see you!'

'You, too. Happy birthday,' he said, holding out the bottle of champagne he'd brought him, and Oliver thanked him and took it, then wrapped him firmly in a hug that spoke volumes before he dropped his arms and stepped back, his eyes warm and filled with compassion. 'Oh, it's so good to see you again. Livvy said she was bringing someone, but she wouldn't say who, and I'm so glad it's you. It's been much too long,' Oliver said warmly, then slung an arm around his shoulders and wheeled him down the hall. 'Come and see Bron, she's in the kitchen. Bron, look who Livvy's brought!'

Her eyes lit up. 'Matt!' She set down the tray of canapés, wiped her hands and enveloped him in a hug. 'Oh, Matt, it's *so* good to see you again. I'm so—'. She broke off, hugged him harder and let go, her eyes suddenly over-bright. 'How are you? How are the children?'

'We're fine,' he said firmly. 'Really. They're growing up fast. Amber starts school in September, and she's
well and truly ready for it, and Charlie—well, Charlie's
just exhausting. My poor mother's run ragged, but she
loves them to bits and they love her, and—you know,
we're getting by. Still, I'm not here to talk about me, I
want to hear all about you two, but I guess you're busy.'

She laughed. 'Just a little, but there are lots of people
you'll know. Here, grab a tray of canapés, wander out
into the garden and pass them round and find yourself
a drink and I'll catch up with you later. I want to see
pictures of the children.'

He chuckled, took the tray from her and headed out
to the garden as instructed. There was a marquee in
the middle of the lawn and it was teeming with people, some of whom he'd worked with. Ross Hamilton
was there, one of the general surgeons and a contemporary of Oliver's, talking to Jack Lawrence, the ED
clinical lead. They would have heard about Jules, and
he wondered if they'd feel they had to say something,
or if they'd just avoid him. He'd had a lot of that and
he suddenly wished he hadn't come—

A hand slipped into the crook of his arm with a little squeeze. 'Sorry, I got caught by some old friends
and I've been looking for you everywhere—where did
you go?'

He looked down at her with a smile, glad that she
was back by his side, noticing how the cornflower
blue of her eyes seemed to be made even brighter by
the dress, which matched them exactly. The dress that
was playing hell with his blood pressure. The dress he
wanted to peel slowly off her and—

'Your father took me into the kitchen to see your

mother, and she handed me this tray of canapés and put me to work.'

'Typical.' Livvy laughed up at him, and he felt as if the sun had come out. 'So, who do you remember, and who do you recognise and can't place?'

He smiled but he could feel it was a little crooked. 'To be honest, I'm happy just hanging out with you, Livvy. I've hardly seen you for days—'

'Matt!'

He turned to find Ross and Lizzi Hamilton had come up behind him. He'd met Lizzi several times, and the first thing she did was hug him wordlessly.

'Good to see you,' Ross said, his voice a little rough as his hand engulfed Matt's and shook it firmly. 'So, how are things? I gather from Oliver that you're working with Livvy in Yoxburgh?'

'Not with her, but she's a trauma doctor so we meet in Resus pretty often.' Not often enough, if he was honest, but it was better than nothing, which seemed to be the alternative.

They chatted for a bit while he force-fed them canapés, then they moved on and he turned to Livvy. 'I need a drink, I haven't got one yet and I could murder a glass of something cold and wet and alcohol-free.'

'Come.' She slipped her hand through his arm and led him into the huge conservatory where a bar had been set up, and took the tray of canapés from him to put it down by the glasses. 'So, what do you fancy? Fizzy water? Cola, tonic, juice, elderflower cordial, a fruit punch—guaranteed non-alcoholic? Or there might be some alcohol-free beer.'

'That sounds good.'

She whipped the top off a bottle and handed it to

him, picked up a glass of sparkling water, put a handful of the canapés in a paper napkin and steered him back down the garden to a vacant bench tucked under the eaves of the old coach house. A glorious fragrant rose smothered the red-brick wall, and the delicate scent surrounded them as they sat down.

Livvy sighed. 'Oh, that's better. I should have realised it was too soon to wear heels,' she grumbled softly, and he rolled his eyes and sighed and took one of the canapés.

'You don't say. What are you trying to do—twist it again?'

'All right, all right, I know it's stupid, but they're only low wedges and I wanted to look nice.'

'Nice?' He laughed under his breath, and shook his head at her. 'Livvy, you couldn't fail to look nice, especially in that dress. And you look more than nice. Much, much more.'

He felt his smile fade, driven out by something unexpectedly powerful, and he could see an echo of it in her eyes, an unfulfilled yearning, a need that hadn't been met. Yet.

Not now!

He looked away quickly and turned his attention back to the colourful and glamorous crowd.

'It's a good turn-out.'

'It is. I'm glad. They've got dancing later in the marquee.'

He felt his heart thud. 'Will you be able to dance?'

She laughed. 'If I take my shoes off, and anyway, I'll have you to hold me up. I'm not going to be jiving.'

'Well, not with me, anyway. I draw the line at making a total fool of myself but don't worry, I won't stand on you and I will hold you up.' Although it might kill him to hold her that close…

'Good,' she said, and then she slipped off her shoes, scooped them up and got to her feet again.

'Come on, my brother and sister are here and they want to see you again.'

'Hold on, let me remember their names. Is it Jamie?'

'Yes, and my little sister's Abbie. Did you know she had a crush on you?'

He groaned and rolled his eyes. 'Seriously?'

She laughed up at him, her eyes sparkling, and he had a desperate need to kiss her. He stifled it fast.

'Seriously,' she was saying. 'She was only sixteen then. I'm sure she's outgrown it. She's twenty-five now, lives with her boyfriend and she's a doctor.'

'It seems to run in the family.'

'No, Jamie broke the mould. He's an architect. Here they are. Hi, guys. Remember Matt?'

The group parted to let them in, and he smiled and shook hands and then contented himself with watching Livvy.

It was no hardship.

They chatted until the music started, and then he and Livvy ended up on the dance floor. Her ankle was giving her a bit of grief, so he held her, as promised, and the feel of her in his arms and against his body trashed his last shreds of detachment. He didn't care who saw them together, what they thought—didn't care about any of it.

All he cared about was holding her, but the music stopped at midnight, hauling him back to reality, and they ended up in the kitchen, clustered round the table, with just the family left.

Jackets had been abandoned long ago, bow ties were hanging, top buttons and cufflinks well and truly undone, and with everyone else gone he could finally relax.

He was sitting beside Livvy at the table, and Bron was busy with the kettle while Oliver piled the last of the canapés onto a plate and put them on the table next to a cheeseboard.

'Coffee, Matt?'

'Oh, please, Bron, nice and strong. I need something to keep me awake. I'm too old for this malarkey.'

'I don't know, the young have no stamina,' Oliver said, rolling his eyes.

'Maybe we've just had less champagne,' Abbie said drily, and everyone laughed.

Bron put the coffee down in front of Matt, and Oliver caught her and pulled her onto his lap. 'That was a great party, darling. Thank you,' he said lovingly, and kissed her.

'Oh, yuck, get a room,' Jamie heckled, laughing, and Oliver joined in the laughter.

'It's my birthday' he said, 'and I'll kiss my wife if I want to.'

'Quite right,' Livvy said. 'You ignore him, Dad.'

'So, Livvy,' Bron said, settling back against Oliver's shoulder and looking perfectly content, 'tell us all about this trip to Cumbria.'

'Oh, it was great—well, right up until I hurt my ankle.'

'Yes, how *did* you do that?' Abbie asked, and Matt snorted and everyone's eyes swivelled to him.

'What?' Abbie asked.

He shrugged. 'Ask her,' he said, unable to stifle the smile, and then he caught her eye and they both started to laugh.

'What?' Abbie said again, joining in the laughter, and he shrugged again.

'Oh, it was silly, really. She was nagging me for not going fast enough, worried we weren't going to be first to the top, and I told her to be careful because the path was unstable, and she said, "I'm always careful", and then it crumbled and she fell down a scree slope. Luckily she hit a rock.'

'Luckily?' Oliver said, frowning at her in concern. 'You never said anything about a rock, Livvy.'

'That doesn't surprise me,' he said drily. 'It was about forty or fifty feet down, right at the top of the slope, really. If it hadn't stopped her...' He felt his smile fade. 'Well, it was a long way to the bottom, put it like that, and the rock broke her fall and fortunately nothing else.'

His laughter was long gone, driven out by the remembered horror, his fear that she was dead, his relief when she started to breathe again.

'She was badly winded, but that was all. That and a few colourful bruises and the ankle, of course, but I didn't know that at the time so it was a bit worrying. She was very lucky. And she was all for us going on up and her making her own way down when she couldn't put any weight on it and could have cracked a rib and got a pneumothorax or a ruptured spleen or—'

'I don't have one any more.'

'Yeah, but I didn't know that at the time, and you still have lungs.'

'Anyway, I knew I was all right.'

'Yeah, of course you did, because you have X-ray eyes,' he said drily. 'So, needless to say, I ignored her and took her down, protesting all the way, but that's Livvy, I guess, she just won't give up fighting. More guts than sense.'

'Oh, we know all about that,' Oliver said softly, his eyes flicking to Livvy, and she laughed and changed the subject abruptly, as if she was suddenly uncomfortable.

'So, Jamie, what are you working on now?' she asked, and they moved on to talk about architecture and gradually he felt her relax again.

Why? What had Oliver said that had made her tense up like that? Something about her fighting, something significant, something that clearly had affected all of them. Her health issues that she'd been so evasive about? He had no idea what, but he wanted to know.

Later. He'd ask her later.

The party broke up shortly after one when everyone started yawning, and as they paused in the hall to say their goodbyes, she saw Matt and her father deep in conversation and her curiosity was piqued.

'You don't have to thank me, Matt,' her father was saying, his voice soft, but he shook his head.

'I do. Without you...'

Without him, what?

'It was little enough, I was just glad to be able to help, we both were. I wish we could have done more. And it's great to see you again. Stay in touch this time, eh?'

'I will. And thank you so much for a great party. It's

been good to see everyone again. I'm so glad Livvy brought me.'

'So am I, and I'm glad you enjoyed it. Drive carefully, now, she's very precious to us.'

'I'm glad to hear it,' she said, linking her arm through Matt's and wondering what that had all been about. 'Come on, it's time to go. At their age they need their beauty sleep.'

'Cheeky minx,' her father said with a chuckle, and he wrapped her in a firm, warm hug, cradling her against his solid chest as he had done so very many times in her life.

'Love you, Dad,' she said, suddenly welling up, and his arms tightened a fraction before he let her go.

'Love you, too. Take care of her, Matt.'

'I will.'

Their eyes met, her father sending him some warning message, and she tutted at him.

'I can take of myself, Dad. I'm fine.'

She hugged her mother, kissed her brother and sister goodbye and hooked her arm through Matt's.

'Right, let's go.'

She settled back against the leather, wriggled her feet out of her shoes and glanced across at him. 'Can I ask you something?'

'Only if I can ask you something, too.'

'Me first,' she said, and he gave a resigned laugh.

'Go on, then. Fire away.'

'What did my father do that you thanked him for? It sounded fairly significant.'

'Ah.' He let out a soft huff of breath—almost a laugh, but somehow not, and there was something about it that chilled her. 'It was the day Jules died,' he told her quietly, and her heart sank.

Oh, no...

'We were on a conference in Birmingham and I'd gone up by train, but it was Sunday when it happened and the trains weren't running because of engineering works, so he dropped everything and drove me to London.'

'I didn't realise that. I knew he was with you.'

'Yes. He was amazing. I've never forgotten that, and I've never really thanked him, not properly, so it was good to have the chance because his support made a huge difference.'

She reached out a hand and laid it on his arm, feeling the tension, and guilt racked her. 'I'm so sorry I asked. I can't even imagine what it must have been like for you, but I'm glad he was there and you didn't have to make the journey alone. It must have been awful.'

'It was. And I was very glad he was there, too. So, my turn now.'

'Your turn?'

'To ask you a question.'

'Ah. OK. Fire away,' she said, although she thought she knew what was coming, but fair enough, she'd made him dig out his demons and it was high time she told him.

In the dim light from the instrument panel she saw him glance across at her, then back to the road before he spoke, his voice soft.

'What did your father mean when I said about you having more guts than sense, and he said he knew all about that?'

She gave a forced little laugh, her heart beating faster. 'Nothing. He was just being silly.'

Matt shook his head. 'I don't think so. He didn't sound silly, he sounded deadly serious, as if it was really important. Significant even, to quote you.'

She nodded slowly. He had sounded serious, because he had been, and for good reason. She swallowed, knowing the moment had come, knowing there was nothing she could do but suck it up and tell him.

'Talk to me, Livvy. You said you have health issues. Is that what he was talking about? Are you sick?'

'No. I'm not sick, but I had cancer nearly five years ago.'

'Cancer?'

For a moment he was silent, but then he let his breath out in a long, slow whoosh and pulled over, stopping the car. The interior lights came on automatically, and he twisted round to look at her, his face shocked. 'You had cancer? When you were—what, twenty-four?'

She held his eyes and nodded.

He swore softly, and reached out a hand and cradled her jaw tenderly, his thumb stroking lightly over her cheek in a gentle caress that nearly unravelled her. 'That's tough. That's really tough. How are you now? Are you OK? Are you still having treatment?'

'No—no, I'm fine, they took it out, it's gone and I'm OK. But I've re-evaluated my life and I'm careful with my diet and stuff.'

'Hence the horrible green tea,' he said, and she saw his mouth flicker into a smile that didn't reach his eyes.

She laughed. 'Hence the horrible green tea— although I do actually like it.'

He gave a soft huff of what could have been laughter, and leant over and feathered a gentle kiss on her lips.

'We're a right pair, aren't we?' he murmured, and then he straightened up and restarted the engine. 'I'd better get you home, Cinderella, before you turn into a pumpkin.'

'I think that was the carriage,' she pointed out drily, and he chuckled, put the car into gear and pulled away.

CHAPTER FIVE

'ARE YOU COMING IN?'

He hesitated, not sure it was a good idea but not sure he could resist.

Not sure he *wanted* to.

'OK, but only for a moment.'

He followed her through the house to the kitchen, and she turned, one hand reaching out to the kettle.

'Coffee?'

'Yeah, please, if you've still got decaf.'

He shrugged off his jacket and hung it over the back of a dining chair, then turned it round and sat and watched her as she spooned the coffee into the cafetière and took out a teabag for herself.

'I might go and change out of this dress while the kettle boils,' she said, heading for the stairs, and he felt an arrow of disappointment.

'That's a pity,' he said, without engaging his brain.

She stopped with her hand on the newel post and looked at him with a puzzled frown. 'Why is it a pity?'

'Because I've been fantasising about taking it off you ever since you opened the door to me,' he said softly, throwing away the last shred of his common sense, and her eyes widened, her lips parted and he watched, mesmerised, as her chest rose and fell a little faster.

So beautiful. So very, very lovely...

Her arm fell back to her side, and she took a step towards him. 'Funny, that,' she said, a tiny smile flickering on soft, moist lips that he was aching to feel with his own. 'I've been thinking the same about your shirt.'

Their eyes locked, and his breath left his body in a rush.

'Livvy?'

He wasn't sure who moved first, but then she was in his arms and he was holding her close and breathing in the scent of her, so warm, so vibrant, so alive.

She'd had cancer. How? Why, when she was so young?

He lifted his head, tilted her face up to his and touched his mouth to hers.

She moaned softly and parted her lips, and he did what he'd been aching to do all evening. He cradled her face in his hands and plundered her mouth, revelling in the taste, the texture, the heat of her breath as she gasped, the press of her body against his, firm and toned and yet still yielding, pliant, all woman.

And he wanted her in a way he'd never thought he'd want again.

He lifted his head and stared down into her eyes, searching them for any sign of doubt, any flicker of hesitation, but there was none.

'I want you,' he said gruffly, and she whimpered and closed her eyes.

'I want you, too—so much, but unless you've got a condom stashed in your wallet...'

Disappointment hit him in the gut, and he tilted

his head back with a groan of frustration. 'No. No, I haven't. I didn't think we'd— Not so soon.'

She dropped her arms and eased away. 'Then we can't. I can't risk getting pregnant—I mustn't.' And then she dropped the bombshell. 'I'm on tamoxifen.'

'Tamoxifen?'

It was like a bucket of cold water, and he felt the heat drain away, leaving only shock and the need to hold her. He shut his eyes, letting it sink in, and folded her close again.

'You had breast cancer.'

It wasn't a question. The fact that she was on it was enough. But—breast cancer at twenty-four? That was seriously not good news. And it was an oestrogen-responsive cancer, or she wouldn't be on tamoxifen, not at all, and certainly not after five years. Which had a knock-on effect on all manner of things.

He lifted his head, staring down into her eyes, seeing the shadow of fear there behind her bravado, trying to imagine what she must have gone through. Was still going through, because tamoxifen wasn't a picnic...

'Oh, Olivia... Come here.'

He wrapped her in his arms again, cradling her head against his shoulder, and pressed his lips to her hair. 'Forget the coffee. Let's just go to bed.'

'But we can't—'

'Yes, we can, it's fine.'

'Matt, it's not fine, I can't get pregnant, I really can't—'

'Shh, I know that,' he murmured, soothing the panic he could feel rising in her. 'Trust me, Livvy. I'm not going to do anything. I'm too tired to do you justice, anyway. I only want to hold you.'

'Hold me—?' A tiny sob rose in her throat, and he watched her swallow, fighting it back down. And then she nodded, took a step back, gathered up the hem of that beautiful dress that had tormented him all evening and led him up the stairs, past the bathroom and back towards the front of the house.

She obviously hadn't been expecting him to go in her bedroom because there were clothes all over the place, shoes scattered, the bed rumpled.

He didn't care. He wasn't there to check out her housekeeping skills, and as she stood in the middle of the room, looking racked with doubt, he closed the curtains, turned on the bedside light and walked quietly back to her.

'What's wrong?' he asked softly, taking her hands in his, and she shrugged.

'Nothing. I'm being silly. It's just that I don't know how you'll react when you see me naked...'

'Livvy, I'm a surgeon,' he pointed out gently. 'I've done my share of breast surgery, I know what to expect. I also know it'll take guts to show me, and I know you've got that in spades, but maybe you're just not ready yet to share something so intimate with me, but you don't need to if you don't want to, not tonight, and maybe never. That's fine. I'm not asking you to get naked if you don't want to. You can wear whatever you like. All I want is to hold you. Nothing more. I'm not here to judge you, and nothing's going to change the way I feel about you. You can trust me, and if you're not ready to do that yet, either, if you'd rather I went home, then I'll go. It's up to you.'

He held his breath, waiting, and finally she lifted her head and met his eyes.

* * *

Why did everyone think she had guts?

Right then, she felt like the biggest coward in the universe, because she didn't even have the courage to take her clothes off in front of him and it wasn't like he'd be shocked by her scars. They weren't even bad in the great scheme of things. But they were *hers*, and she wanted him to want her and he might not, and that made it different.

Maybe later, further down the line, when she knew him better…?

But if she let him go, if she bottled out now, would he ask again? And how would she feel if he didn't?

Gutted.

She held his eyes, trying to read them, looking for pity, but it wasn't there. Compassion, yes, and understanding, but something else, too, something warm and very masculine that sent a tiny shiver of need through her.

'Don't go.'

His eyes flickered with something unreadable. 'Sure?'

She nodded and sucked in a deep breath. 'Yes. Yes, I'm sure,' she said firmly—more firmly than she felt, but obviously enough to convince him because he smiled then, his mouth tilting slightly, then heeled off his shoes and put them neatly side by side.

His trousers were next, folded carefully over the back of the chair, then he unbuttoned his shirt systematically, button by button, his eyes never leaving hers.

Was he doing it to torture her? Because if so, it was working.

He laid the shirt over the trousers, stripped off his

socks and tucked them into his shoes and then, in snug jersey shorts that left much too little to the imagination, he walked slowly towards her, and she felt her mouth dry.

'You look a little over-dressed,' he said softly, and then waited while her heart started to beat faster and her courage wavered.

Now what? Because it was one thing *her* seeing her scar and it reinforcing, every day, the fact that she was alive and well and here to tell the tale. It was quite another to show it to someone else. Even someone who knew what to expect. Especially someone whose reaction mattered so much to her.

But she trusted him, and if she was going to be with him he had to see it, so she might as well get it over with. She screwed up her courage again and held his searching gaze.

'So, I thought you wanted to take my dress off?'

His lips parted, and then he laughed softly and closed his eyes for a moment.

'It'll be a pleasure,' he said, his voice a little rough and gravelly, and took that last step towards her.

'Be careful with it,' she warned, and he laughed again and shook his head slowly.

'I'll be careful,' he promised, and she knew he was talking about more than the dress.

Although the dress did seem to be an issue. He frowned as he studied it. 'You might need to give me a clue. I have no idea how it comes off.'

That made her laugh, too, releasing some of the tension, and she obligingly lifted her left arm and pointed to the concealed zip at the side. 'And there's a tiny hook and eye at the top.'

'I've got it,' he said, and gripping the tab, he slid the zip carefully down, inch by inch, until it reached the bottom, his fingers brushing her skin in passing and making her quiver.

'Over your head, or down past your hips?' he asked, and her heart lurched.

'Hips,' she said, knowing what was coming next because the dress had inbuilt support so the only underwear she had on was a pair of barely there silky shorts. As he lifted his hands the breath jammed in her throat, trapped there by the pounding of her heart, and then he surprised her.

'Turn around,' he said softly, his hands settling on her shoulders and nudging her gently in the right direction.

She turned, confused, and then felt his fingers take hold of the right shoulder and ease it carefully down her arm. She pulled her arm free, and the dress caught on her hips for a moment, then slithered off and puddled round her ankles, leaving her all but naked.

She had an overwhelming urge to cross her arms across her chest, but she swallowed her fear and kept them still.

Trust him...

'Step out of it.'

If she could make her feet move. She lifted one, then the other, her legs shaking slightly, and he eased the dress away. She heard it rustle as he put it down, and then he was back, his hands curving over her shoulders, his fingertips resting on her collarbones, his thumbs sweeping lightly over the back of her neck.

She felt his breath against her nape, then the touch of his mouth, warm and reassuring. 'So let's see how this clip works,' he said, and then his hands were in her hair, freeing it so it tumbled down around her shoulders, and she heard him sigh softly.

'That's better. I love your hair,' he murmured, sifting it through his fingers, and then gently, without exerting any pressure, he turned her back towards him.

'Come here,' he said softly, and drew her into his arms, folding her gently against that broad, reassuringly solid chest. She felt the brush of the soft, dark hair that sprinkled his pecs, the warmth of his skin on hers, smelt the scent of his body overlaid with cologne, warm and slightly musky and enticing.

'That's better,' he murmured, and for a long time he did nothing except hold her. Her heart was pounding—or was it his? His, maybe, strong and steady, and she felt hers settle, but then he lowered his head and trailed a line of kisses over her cheek and down across her shoulder, lifting her hair out of the way, tunnelling his fingers through it and kissing the side of her neck behind her ear, sending flames licking through her.

Then he let her go, slid his hands down her arms and linked his fingers with hers as he took a step back and looked slowly down, and she closed her eyes and waited, her heart racing now.

'Look at me,' he murmured, and she opened her eyes and stared straight into his. They were dark, darker than she'd ever seen them, the colour of wet slate, his pupils flared, and his chest was rising and falling with every breath.

'You're beautiful, Olivia,' he said, his voice raw, 'absolutely beautiful,' and her heart turned over. Nobody had ever said that to her before—well, only her parents and that didn't count, not in this way. Not in the way he'd said it, and she felt her eyes fill.

'Come here,' he murmured, and she took a deep breath and stepped into his arms.

'That feels so good.'

His voice was a low murmur, his breath drifting against her skin as they lay tangled together in her bed. He scattered tiny, nibbling kisses over her face, and Livvy closed her eyes. She could feel the need in him, in the rise and fall of his chest, the pounding of his heart, the hard jut of his erection against her body. She moaned and moved closer, their legs meshing, but that just made the ache worse. 'I want you.'

'I want you, too, but we can't.'

'I know. I'm so cross. Why didn't we think ahead?'

He laughed unsteadily, his hand cradling her face, his thumb stroking her cheek rhythmically, soothing her. 'Because we didn't have an agenda,' he said. 'And because I guess we're both out of practice and it didn't even occur to us that this might happen so soon, even though we'd had that conversation. I'm sorry. I just didn't expect it, and I didn't realise—I just thought you might be on the pill or something.'

She nodded. It certainly hadn't occurred to her, and she was kicking herself for that because she'd expected him to have thought of it.

'I can't take the pill, and even if I could, I wouldn't need to be on it. There hasn't been anyone, not since...'

'Not at all?'

She shook her head. 'No. The guy I was with then really couldn't handle it, our relationship wasn't strong enough, so I ended it, and since then I haven't been ready—physically, emotionally. But I'm ready now, and we can't, and that's my fault.' She laid a hand against his cheek, feeling the tingle of stubble, the hard line of his jaw, the clench of a muscle. 'I'm sorry.'

'You have nothing to be sorry for,' he said gently, sifting his fingers through her hair now, his eyes on hers. 'Nothing. And there's no hurry.'

His mouth found hers again, and she felt heat race through her like a wildfire, reaching every part of her and making her whimper. She reached for him, her hand sliding down his chest, but he caught her wrist and stopped her.

'Uh-uh,' he murmured. 'You can't do that, Livvy. I'm hanging by a thread as it is and when we do this, I want to do it properly, not when we're both tired and we can't follow through.'

His fingers traced her cheek, and his smile was gentle and a bit wry. 'I think it's time we went to sleep, don't you?'

He reached out and turned off the light, then gathered her up against his chest and kissed her again, a tender, gentle kiss, cooling the heat but filling her with a different sort of warmth that brought tears to her eyes.

She settled against him, her head on his shoulder, and as she lay there she could hear his heartbeat slow, taking hers with it as she drifted peacefully into sleep.

He woke shortly before seven and got up, pulled on his clothes and brought her a cup of green tea, kissing her awake.

She blinked and stared at him. 'You're dressed! What time is it?'

'Seven. I need to go. I'm going to be conspicuous

enough going home in these clothes, but the later I leave it the worse it'll be because there'll be more people about.'

'You'll just meet all the runners and dog walkers getting out before it's too hot,' she told him, and he had a horrible feeling she was right, but it had to be done and, anyway, the children would ring him soon and he needed to be able to talk to them without distractions or they'd be curious. Or Sally would, and he wasn't ready to tell Sally about this—whatever this was—when he was still coming to terms with it himself.

Besides, he needed to go shopping.

'Look, I have to go. Why don't you get up when you're ready and have a shower and then come round to mine? I'll feed you brunch.'

'Scrambled egg club sandwich?'

He chuckled and kissed her again. 'Of course. Bring some green tea, I don't have any and they might not have any in the little shop. Do you know where I live?'

She shook her head.

'I'll text you my address when I get home. It's on the clifftop near Ed and Annie, on the way to the harbour. Ring me when you leave.'

'OK. I'll see you later—about nine?'

'Sounds fine.'

And it would have been, if he hadn't bumped into Ed. He'd been walking their dog along the clifftop, and he crossed the road and paused on the drive as Matt got out of the car.

'Morning! Another gorgeous day.'

He stifled a groan and patted the dog, who was nudging his hand. 'Isn't it a bit early to be so cheerful?'

'This is early?' Ed said with a laugh. 'The kids have

been up an hour, and I always walk the dog first thing, you know that.' He eyed his clothes pointedly. 'Good party?' he added with all the subtlety of an express train, and Matt sighed.

'Yes, thanks. Bit of a late night, though.'

'So how *is* Livvy? I take it she's got over her fall?' he asked.

How the hell—? Unless it was just a random punt...

'She's fine. She's coming over shortly for brunch so I can't hang about, I need to go shopping.'

'She's nice. I like her,' Ed said casually, but there was nothing casual about it and he had to stop himself from rolling his eyes. 'She's also very kind and soft-hearted,' he added quietly. 'Don't hurt her, Matt.'

He stopped trying to get away and turned to face his old friend. 'Why would you think I'd hurt her?'

Ed shook his head, his eyes serious now. 'I don't know, but your car was outside her house fifteen minutes ago and you're not exactly dressed for a lazy Sunday morning, so I'm guessing you spent the night with her.'

He held on to his temper with difficulty. 'How is that in any way your business?'

'It isn't. I know that, but I care about you, Matt, and I care about Livvy, and I'd hate to see either of you get hurt. Just be sure you're ready for this before you get in too deep—unless it's just casual sex, but I really hope not. You've had a tough time, and I'm glad you're moving on, but I'd hate to think you were using her to do it.'

'I'm not *using* her,' he said firmly, slamming the car door and walking off before he said something he'd regret, but his friend's words had struck a chord, and he went into the house and closed the door with a shaky sigh.

Was Ed right? Was he using her? No. Surely not. That wasn't how it felt at all, but how did it feel?

Crazy, immense, confusing.

And hugely important, somehow. So the other thing, then. Was Ed right about that, about him getting in too deep, too soon? And too deep for who? Him, still mourning the loss of Jules, or Olivia, still dealing with the aftermath of cancer?

Both of them, probably, but Ed's less than subtle warning had come too late, because he was in it up to his neck now and there was no way he could walk away from her even if he wanted to. And he didn't want to.

What about the children?

What about them? They weren't part of this—this whatever it was. Arrangement? It wasn't even that organised.

He went into his bedroom, sent her a text message with his address, then showered slowly, pulled on shorts and a T-shirt, tidied the house a bit and headed out to the nearest express store. It had just opened, and he grabbed food for breakfast and a few other essentials.

Something for him and the kids tonight, salad, more ketchup—and condoms? He hesitated, staring blankly at the display, wondering at the wisdom of it. If he bought them, they'd use them. If he didn't, they'd wait.

Maybe that was a good idea, just until he'd worked out what the hell he was doing and why.

He left them on the shelf and headed for the checkout.

Her phone was ringing as she got out of the shower, and she grabbed her towel, scrubbed her hands dry and picked it up, putting it on hands-free so she could dry herself while she talked.

'Hi, Dad, you're up bright and early. How are you? How's the head?'

He laughed, the sound echoing round the bathroom. 'My head's fine, thank you. How's yours?'

'Oh, fine. I'm tired, but I'm OK. It was a great party.'

'It was, wasn't it? Your mother's good at that sort of thing. So, I take it you got home all right?'

Her heart gave a little lurch.

'Yes, fine, thanks. We got back about two. Matt was very pleased to have seen you both and had a chance to thank you for what you did for him. I knew you'd been there, but I didn't realise you'd driven him to London that day. It must have been awful.'

'He told you about it?'

'Only that, really. Not much at all.'

'No, I don't suppose he did. He probably finds it hard to talk about. Livvy, darling, you will be careful, won't you? Don't let yourself get too involved. He won't mean to hurt you, he's not like that, but he was devastated when his wife died and he can't be in a good place even now, and there are the children to consider as well, and I know that's an issue for you. Just be careful and don't let yourself get in too deep.'

Too late...

'Dad, I'm fine. Don't worry about me, or him, or the children. Neither of us is looking for anything serious and I know it's not going anywhere. Look, I don't mean to be rude but we've arranged to meet up for breakfast and I'm just out of the shower and I need to dry my hair.'

'OK, but take care. I love you.'

'Love you, too.'

* * *

She rang Matt as she left home, and he was just getting the shopping out of his car when she pulled up on the drive outside his house. His very impressive, beautifully presented clifftop house that made her little rented Victorian semi seem very tame.

'Hi,' she said, going over to him, and he bent and kissed her cheek.

'Hi. You OK?'

'Yes, I'm fine, thanks. A bit tired still, but that goes with the territory, I'm often tired. So, what's in the shopping bag?'

'Bacon, eggs, tomatoes, bread and some other bits and pieces. I really need to do a proper internet order if I ever get a minute, but I did manage to get green tea for you so I'm not entirely useless. Come on in.'

She wondered what else he'd bought and if he'd remedied their tragic failure to think ahead. Maybe. She could only hope.

She followed him through the door and into a huge L-shaped living space that ran across the house and from front to back, with stunning views down the drive and across the clifftop to the sea, and her eyes widened. 'Oh, wow. That's amazing. I can see why you bought it.'

He gave a hollow laugh and dumped the shopping on the worktop.

'To be honest, eighteen months ago the sea view was the last thing on my mind, but it ticked all the boxes. It's got four bedrooms, it's literally just round the corner from my mother, who is utterly indispensable to me and the children, and it has the added bonus of a garage I can convert into an annex for her if and when necessary, so it was exactly what I needed, but it was in a shocking state and I poured a lot of money and effort into it without really thinking about anything but the practicalities.'

He smiled wryly. 'And then suddenly I had time to stop and look out of the window and, yes, it's amazing. There's a balcony outside my bedroom and I sit there often, just staring out over the sea, listening to the gulls and the waves breaking on the shore and watching the world go by.'

'I could do a lot of that,' she said wistfully. 'I love the sound of the sea. I'm not sure I'd swap it for my oasis, though.'

'I wouldn't, I love your garden. Mine'll get there one day, I suppose, when everything's grown a bit, but in the meantime I do have a great view so I'm not exactly deprived. And of course ultimately I'll end up with both. So—scrambled, I take it?'

'Of course.' She dragged her eyes off the view and turned to face him with a smile. 'Anything I can do to help?'

He opened the folding doors across the front of the kitchen and they ate their club sandwiches perched at the breakfast bar.

She licked her fingers, pushed the plate away and sighed contentedly. 'That was amazing. I haven't had a club sandwich that good for ages.'

'Is that because it's on your anti-cancer hit list?' he asked, and she laughed and shook her head.

'No, not really. It's not great, and I wouldn't do it every day, but in the grand scheme of things it's not bad. Top of my hit list is sugar because cancer loves it apparently, followed by anything fed with hormones or too much Omega 6, plus high glycaemic index foods like white rice and flour and stuff like that, so no dairy, no cakes, no puddings, nothing with added sugar, although I do eat a lot of fruit. Oh, and loads of fresh veg and extra virgin olive oil and lots and lots of fish, and organic produce as a rule when I can, and I don't drink alcohol any more. And I make sure I exercise and get lots of fresh air.'

'Sounds pretty healthy.'

'It is. I do draw the line at revolting super-green smoothies, though,' she added with a wry grin, and he chuckled.

'I can't *imagine* why. Ugh.'

'Ugh is an understatement. Have you ever had one? They taste like grass mowings.' She put her mug down and swivelled round to face him. 'Can I be cheeky and ask for a guided tour?'

He shrugged and slid off his stool.

'Sure. It's not that exciting.'

Well, it might not be to him, but a sea view like that was her idea of heaven and she was aching to see what he'd done with the rest of the house.

He walked her through the downstairs first—a utility room, cloakroom, another sitting room that opened to the garden, with lots of toy storage and comfy sofas, the walls smothered in children's paintings lovingly pinned up, all named and dated, and then on the opposite wall were framed black-and-white photos of the children, which gave her a pang of longing that she quickly suppressed.

The children weren't part of this, they weren't relevant, only insofar as they governed what time she and Matt could spend together, so she hauled her eyes off them and followed him out of the room.

He took her upstairs next and then, as if to turn the screw, he showed her the children's rooms—a delicate blue, surprisingly, for Amber, and white with a mural of trains stuck on it for Charlie—then the guest room, which his mother used when he was on call, he said, and the family bathroom, obviously tastefully refitted, although the effect was trashed by the addition of about a million bath toys.

She could hear the squeals of laughter, the splashing, the giggles, and the ache in her chest just grew worse.

They're nothing to do with you.

Then finally he led her into his bedroom, and she heaved a silent sigh of relief because this was undoubtedly an adult room.

It was the largest, as she might have expected, with a huge and incredibly inviting bed opposite a wall of glass giving a stunning view of the sea and sky, and it took her breath away.

What would it be like to lie there with him, to make love in that huge bed with the sound of the sea drifting in through the open doors? To sit on the balcony and listen to the keening of the gulls, and then go back to bed and make love again...

'That's amazing,' she breathed. 'What an incredible room. You must get fabulous sunrises.'

'I do, but I see them rather too often at the moment, considering it rises at four thirty at this time of year,' he said drily.

'That's horribly early! Why are you awake then?'

He gave a wry chuckle.

'I'm not. It's Charlie. Sometimes he wakes up needing to wee and won't settle again unless he's with me, but just lately I've been getting the bed to myself most nights, which is a real luxury. I still wake up, though. Habit.'

She laughed, as she was meant to, but her mind was torn between the yearning to hold a little wakeful boy and cradle him back to sleep, and wondering what it would be like to wake up to the sunrise with Matt and make love with the first rays of light gilding their bodies...

And then she glanced across the room at the chest of drawers on the far side, and stopped.

Stopped thinking about the children, stopped fantasising about spending one of those uninterrupted nights with him in that huge and inviting bed, stopped wondering if he'd bought condoms, stopped thinking about his body underneath those shorts.

Stopped thinking altogether, because there on the chest of drawers in a simple white frame was a black-and-white photo of a woman holding a sleeping baby in her arms, and tucked in beside her was a little girl with Matt's eyes and her long dark hair. Amber, of course. She recognised her from the photos downstairs, but the woman... They were both smiling, and Livvy felt as if a giant hand had squeezed her heart.

'That's Juliet with the children,' he said softly, his voice tender. 'It was taken just after Christmas, five months before she died.'

She swallowed and turned away, unable to look at it any longer because it felt such an intrusion into his privacy and grief. Before it had just been a bedroom, and Juliet hadn't had a face, and now it all seemed much more real, the scale of his loss, the agonising grief he must have gone through, still be going through. The children's grief and loss, the loss of their mother, irreplaceable and so much loved.

She didn't belong there…

'I'm sorry—'

'Don't be. She's gone, Olivia. I know that. I still love her, I always will, but she's gone, and I'm getting used to it. It's just taking me a while.'

She nodded, swallowing again, blinking away the sudden, stinging tears. 'Dad phoned this morning and warned me not to get in too deep, said you couldn't be in a good place right now. He was right, wasn't he?'

He gave a soft huff of laughter and turned away from the picture, ushering her out of the door and down the stairs.

'That depends what you call good. I've sold our house in London, found a new home, a new job, a new life. I'm moving on, slowly but surely, so I'm in a better place than I was, that's for sure. I wouldn't want to go back to those early days.'

She shook her head. 'I'm so sorry, Matt. It must have been awful.'

'It was, but I'm getting there. Come and see the garden.'

He opened a door at the end of the hall and went out, and she followed him slowly, wondering what she was doing there and how she'd got into this. And—the garden? That was such an abrupt change of subject…

She stopped. 'Do you want me to go?'

'Go? No, of course not. Why would I want you to go?' he asked, but then he turned and looked at her, and with a sigh he pulled her into his arms and hugged her, and she wrapped her arms around him and hung on.

CHAPTER SIX

FOR A WHILE he said nothing, then he gave a sigh and lifted his head and looked down at her, his eyes troubled.

'It's not just your father who's worried about us. I got lectured today as well,' he said. 'I met Ed on my way home this morning while he was walking the dog. He'd been past your house earlier, seen the car there and knew I hadn't been home, and of course I was in those clothes, so he said he was glad to see I was moving on but then told me rather pointedly that you have a kind heart and I'm not to hurt you by getting in too deep before I'm ready.'

'You won't hurt me,' she said, not altogether sure it was true. Well, she was sure *he* wouldn't hurt her. Whether the situation would hurt her was another question entirely, and one she'd rather not consider because she didn't think she'd like the answer. Although if her reaction to the children's pictures was anything to go by, she had her answer already.

'I hope not. Ed also said he hoped I wasn't using you and I told him I'm not. If I am it's entirely unintentional, anyway, and if you feel I am, then for goodness' sake tell me, because it's the last thing on earth I want to do.'

She lifted her hand and cradled his jaw, feeling the prickle of stubble against her palm, the flicker of a muscle in his cheek. 'You're not using me, Matt. Not in the least.'

He turned his head and pressed his lips to her palm, then gave a wry little laugh and moved, putting a little space between them, although he held on to her hand, folding it inside his.

'Good. I really don't want to, which is why I didn't buy condoms this morning. I didn't want to railroad either you or myself into something rash, and now I'm regretting it.'

She shook her head and gave him a wistful smile. 'Don't regret it. Just be sure you're ready, Matt. There's no hurry and I don't want you doing something you're not ready for, something that will make you feel disloyal to Juliet or that you're cheating her or that I don't measure up.'

He frowned. 'I wouldn't feel that, Olivia, and I wouldn't for a moment compare you to her. We had a good marriage, a brilliant marriage, and I wouldn't for the world have had it end the way it did, but it has, and she's gone, but I'm still here and so are the children, and we're all entitled to a life, even if it's a very different one from the one we'd thought we'd have. She'd be furious with me if I passed up any chance for happiness, however fleeting, and she'd be the last one to want me to be lonely. She would have hated that for me.'

Livvy felt her eyes fill. 'She sounds lovely. You must miss her so much.'

He smiled sadly. 'I do. I miss her every day, but life goes on, and I'm still alive, and since I met you I feel I've come out of the shadows and into the light again, and d'you know what? It feels good, Livvy. It feels really good, and that's all down to you.'

He led her to a faded, weathered bench tucked in a corner between the house and the newly planted shrubs, and patted the seat beside him.

'Come and sit with me. This is a lovely bench, the only thing I have from our London garden, and I don't spend anything like enough time on it any more, but all I can see from it now is emptiness and a lawn that needs cutting, so I look at the trees next door instead.' He grinned wryly. 'You have to tilt your head back a bit, so you can end up with a crick in your neck if you're not careful.'

She smiled and sat down beside him—had Juliet sat on this bench with him? Probably—and she looked at the trees for a moment, then her smile faded and she turned to face him, her mind still on Juliet and his tragic loss.

'I don't want to take you back into the shadows, but can I ask you something?'

He turned his head and met her eyes. 'Of course you can. You can ask me anything.'

'What happened that day? How did you know she was ill?'

He sighed and looked away again, back to the trees that seemed to give him comfort. 'I didn't,' he said quietly. 'I'd spoken to her the night before and she had a headache. The children had been noisy all day, she said, and her head was banging and as they were asleep she was going to get an early night. It didn't sound like anything out of the ordinary, because she'd had the odd headache from time to time, as we all do, so I said good idea, went in to dinner, and I rang her in the morning for our usual catch-up and I couldn't get hold of her.

'It didn't really worry me, I assumed she was busy with the children and she'd ring me when she could, and I had a breakfast meeting scheduled with your father and a few others so I showered and dressed and went down to the dining room, and then I still hadn't heard from her, so I rang again, then I rang her mobile, then the house phone again, and Amber answered.'

'Amber?' she asked, shocked. 'How old was she?'

He shrugged. 'Two and three quarters? Something like that. I could hear Charlie screaming in the background and I thought Jules must be dealing with a stinky nappy or something, so I asked to speak to her and Amber told me Mummy wouldn't get up and she was talking funny.'

'Oh, Matt,' she murmured, feeling sick at the thought. 'So what did you do?'

He shrugged again. 'What could I do? I was a hundred miles away and I didn't know what the hell was going on, I just knew it wasn't good. I couldn't even ring the neighbours, I didn't know their numbers, Jules had all that sort of stuff, so I asked Amber where her mother was and she said she was in bed, and Charlie wanted his bottle and she was hungry, too, so I asked her to take the phone to her mother and hold it by her ear, and Jules made this odd mumbling sort of noise and I knew then that it was really bad. I told her not to worry, that I'd get help and just hang in there, I'd be home as soon as I could.

'Your father was with me by then, and he just took over. He'd heard what I'd said, seen my face, could hear Charlie screaming, and he dialled 999, told them the situation, handed me his phone and told me to direct them to the house, then took my phone off me and talked calmly to Amber while we headed back to our rooms. He packed his things and mine, still talking to Amber while I was on the phone to the police, and then he put me in his car and started driving.'

'So where was your car?'

'At home, because I'd gone by train, but I would have been in no fit state to drive anyway, so he handed me back my phone and drove like the wind while I talked to Amber again, and to the police on his hands-free until they got into the house, then they told me the paramedics were in and they were taking her to hospital, and Amber said a nice lady was there and she was going to get them breakfast, so I told her to be brave and look after Charlie and help the lady to find all their things and I'd see her soon, and then I rang Juliet's mother and told her to get to the hospital, put the phone down and fell apart, and he just kept driving and talking to me, calming me down, keeping me sane.

'He called your mother and got her to come down on the train from Suffolk, and they looked after the children with the police while I went in to see Jules in ICU. She was in a coma, one pupil fixed and dilated, and as I watched the other one blew and I knew she was gone. I never got to say goodbye, and that still hurts. If I'd known when I spoke to her that it would be the last time—'

His voice cracked a little, and she reached out a hand and squeezed his wordlessly, because there were no words she could have used. He blinked and looked up, staring up at the trees and probably seeing something else entirely. Then he hauled in a breath and started again.

'They did brain-stem tests but they were all dire, and in the end your father was the one who broached the subject of organ donation. He knew Jules and I were both doctors, and he knew her, knew what she was like, knew she wouldn't have wanted her body to go to waste, and he was right to raise it with me, because she would have come back to haunt me if I hadn't done it.'

He swallowed. 'I baulked at it at first, and then I thought of the people out there desperate for a transplant, and that maybe it would give them a chance to live a normal life, so I said yes, use everything they could, and I know her heart and lungs went to a teenager with cystic fibrosis, and her kidneys went to two people in their thirties with end-stage renal failure. I don't know about all the other organs, but I just know that in a way Jules is still out there somewhere, giving other people a chance at what she'd lost. That's a huge comfort.'

Livvy felt a tear slide down her cheek and swiped it away. How could he be so strong, so brave? She'd be in bits. He said he had been. Maybe he still was, and maybe her father and Ed were right?

'Anyway,' he added after a long pause, 'your parents were wonderful, and without their kindness and support I don't know how I would have got through that day. They stayed with the children until my mother came, and then I had to tell Amber her mother was never coming home. That was the hardest thing I've ever done in my life—'

He broke off again, and she squeezed his hand, unable to speak.

'So, anyway, that's why I wanted to thank them. For that, and for all the kindness they'd showed us over the years, the welcome they gave Juliet when I was his registrar—all of it. I can't even begin to explain how much it all meant, how much it still means, and I've never really told them.'

She didn't know what to say, so she said nothing, just leant over and hugged him, her eyes squeezed tightly shut, and he wrapped her in his arms and held her for an age. And then finally he lifted his head and sighed.

'Sorry. That was a bit heavy. I didn't mean to spill my guts like that but you did ask.'

She nodded, blinking hard. 'I know. I'm sorry. I should have realised it wasn't a simple question. I didn't mean to make you dredge all that back up, I'm really sorry.'

She felt his shoulders shift in a little shrug. 'It's OK. It's never very far away. So, your turn now, talking of dredging things up. How did you find out you had cancer?'

She sat up, swiped the tears away and laughed at that, because it seemed somehow trivial and insignificant in comparison to what he'd gone through, although at the time it had seemed horrendous and insurmountable and maybe still did, when she let herself think about it, which was why she didn't, because otherwise she'd crumble.

And she wasn't going to let herself do that.

'I felt it,' she told him, trying to sound matter-of-fact, 'this tiny little bump. It was so small, like a little pea, but just enough to feel. I was very thin at the time, I'd been living on fresh air and nerves through my finals, and I was just getting to the end of my F1 year, my first year in the real world, and I was in the shower and I felt this little thing up near my armpit, so I went to see my GP thinking it was just a gland, I was run-down, it was nothing, and he said it needed investigating and referred me urgently, which freaked me out a bit, so as soon as I got my mammogram appointment I contacted the breast clinic and pointed out I worked in the hospital so I was available at no notice if they had a cancellation, and two days later they rang me to say someone had broken down on the way and could I take the appointment, and three days after that they called me back in, did a million more tests and told me I had cancer.'

He swore softly and threaded his fingers through hers. 'And then what?'

She laughed. 'They did a lumpectomy, but the pathologist said they hadn't taken enough margin so six weeks later after it was healed I had to have another op, and then when it was healed again I had radiotherapy. They'd taken four lymph nodes, and they were all clear, so I didn't need chemo. I was very relieved about that because I was dreading it, but anyway, it healed, I was fine, and I got on with it, but it was pretty grim and I took a year out just to come to terms with it because it shakes you, you know? You feel nothing's the same any more, and you suddenly realise who your friends are and who matters and who doesn't, and what things are important and what's just white noise, and you cut all that out of your life. Like Mark.'

'Mark?'

'My ex. He didn't want to know, and if he didn't want to know, I didn't want him there, so I cut him out of my life. I read a ton of books about self-help, diet, fitness—'

'Hence the green tea and the sugar ban,' he said softly, and she smiled and nodded.

'Hence the green tea and the sugar ban and all the other stuff. And you know, I feel better than I ever have? I'm fit, I'm well, my work-life balance is better, I sleep well now, I don't do things that make me stressed or unhappy, and every day I get up and count my blessings—number one being that I'm still here.'

Even if I'm alone because I can't drag anyone with me on this crazy roller coaster, and even if I'll never be able to have a child...

He gave a soft huff of laughter. 'Yeah, I absolutely get that. Life's pretty fragile. You've only got to do our job to realise that, but you can get immune to it and then it comes home to roost and it's quite a wake-up call. It's certainly given me a better insight into how to give bad news because I know now what it feels like to be on the receiving end of it, and it ain't pretty.'

He sighed, and glanced at his watch.

'I need to go soon, I'm having lunch with the children at Juliet's sister's, but we've got time for another drink if you'd like?'

'Are you sure?' She turned to face him, searching his eyes, but they were puzzled.

'Why wouldn't I be sure?'

She shrugged. 'I don't know. Because talking about her upset you, and that's my fault and I thought you might want me to go.'

'No. I wanted you to know, and I wanted to know about you, and I certainly don't want you to go. It's all good.' He slung an arm around her shoulders, dropped a quick kiss on her lips and pulled her to her feet.

'Come on, let's go and get another drink and soak up some of that gorgeous sea view you're raving about, and then we can talk about when we're going to squeeze in another date—assuming you still want to, now you know what a sad case I am?'

She stared at him as if he was crazy. 'Of course I want to! Well, if you do…'

'Oh, I do,' he said, his eyes curiously intent. 'I definitely do.' His mouth quirked. 'But I might need to go shopping.'

She felt the tension shift and the atmosphere lighten, and she smiled back at him.

'I'm so glad you said that.'

He laughed, swore softly under his breath and kissed her, then let her go and stepped away. 'Don't look at me like that! It's difficult enough. Right, let's get this drink before we do something stupid.'

It was so simple in theory, but in practice finding time to get together when both of them were free and his mother could babysit was next to impossible, and it was frustrating him to bits.

He worked mostly days except for when he was on call or on the weekend rota, and Livvy was on a phase of late shifts, so it was Friday before they caught up face-to-face.

He was called down to the ED to look at a young man who'd been slashed by a bottle in a drunken brawl at five in the afternoon, and he found her in a cubicle, applying pressure to the wound while the man gripped her by the wrist and yelled abuse.

'Problems?' he asked her, but the patient answered.

'Stupid woman's hurting me, I want a doctor, not a reg—whatever it says on her badge!' he yelled, and Matt calmly prised his fingers off her wrist, placed a hand on his chest and pinned him firmly to the bed.

'Then you'd better behave. Either you need our help,' he went on, his voice deadly quiet, 'or you leave, but we don't take that sort of abuse from anybody, under any circumstances, and you either apologise to *Dr* Henderson now or I call Security and you leave and take your chances, but you've already lost a lot of blood so I don't fancy the odds. The choice is yours.'

'But she doesn't know what she's doing!'

'Dr Henderson knows *exactly* what she's doing, and right now she's trying to stop you bleeding to death, so the least you can do is be a little co-operative while she does it,' he said tightly. He felt the man slump under his hand, and he nodded. 'Right, let's start again. My name's Matthew Hunter—'

He tensed again. 'It says you're Mister on your badge! That's not a proper doctor, either!'

'Mr Hunter is a consultant trauma surgeon,' Livvy said crisply, 'and I only called him down because he's a soft-tissue injury specialist, so you should consider yourself very, very lucky to have him and start to co-operate before he refuses to treat you.'

He opened his mouth, shut it and let out a huff.

'Better,' Matt said, stifling a smile at Livvy's skilful and cutting intervention. 'Now apologise to her,' he added, and the man grumbled what might just have been an apology, and he let him go.

'Right, if we're all done with the drama let's have a look at this,' he said, snapping on gloves, and Livvy moved out of the way and he lifted the saturated pad and slapped it back on.

'OK, he's nicked an artery, we need to move to Resus.'

'An artery? Isn't that dangerous?' the man said, his eyes widening.

'Only if we let go. You need to pick your fights more carefully.'

'It wasn't me who did it, it was my mate,' the man said, looking worried now and missing his double meaning, and Matt stifled a laugh.

'You need to pick your friends more carefully, then. Right, let's move,' he said, and holding pressure on the leg, he kicked the brakes off and helped shift him through to Resus.

It took nearly an hour for him to repair the leg to his satisfaction, but finally the man was shipped out to the observation cubicles and he had a minute to talk to Livvy alone.

He ushered her out of Resus and into the corridor.

'How can they get in that much trouble in the middle of the afternoon?' he grumbled, and she laughed.

'Tell me about it. Anyway, enough of him. How are you?' she asked, looking up at him with a smile, and his mouth tilted.

'Much better now he's gone and I've got you to myself. What are you doing tomorrow evening?'

'Tomorrow? Nothing.'

'So do you fancy going out for a meal?'

Her eyes lit up. 'That would be lovely. Or I could cook for you?'

He shook his head. 'No. That would make me a liar. I told my mother there was a possibility a couple of people from the hospital were going to the pub,' he said with a wry grin, and her mouth formed a little O, and then she smiled.

'In which case, the pub would be great. Do you want me to meet you there?'

'No. I'll pick you up but I haven't decided where we're going yet. Seafront, river or country?' he asked.

'Ooh, that's tough. River?'

He nodded. 'I know the perfect place. Eight o'clock OK?'

She smiled up into his eyes, and his heart started to beat a little faster.

'Sounds perfect. Is it dressy?'

He shook his head. 'No. We did that last week. This is definitely casual. I'll probably wear jeans and a shirt. Right, I need to get home. I'm already late. See you tomorrow.'

He glanced around to make sure there was nobody watching, then dropped a kiss on her lips, winked and walked away, his heart lighter and his body humming with anticipation.

The house was quiet when he got home, and he found his mother in the family room, picking up toys.

'Here, let me.' He got down on his knees to help her. 'I'm sorry I'm late. How've they been?'

'Oh, fine. I told them you'd go up and see them when you got back, and they were quite happy.' She stacked the last of the toys on the shelves and straightened up. 'So, is this pub thing on tomorrow night, or don't you know yet?'

He got to his feet and busied himself straightening the pile of books on the shelf. Not that they needed it.

'Yes, it is, if that's all right? I was about to ask you. I need to leave just before eight, but I'll make sure they're in bed by then, and I won't be late.'

What was it about mothers? She added another book to his pile, tilted her head on one side, frowned and said, 'Matthew, look at me,' in that voice she'd used since he was about three and she'd caught him raiding the chocolate biscuits.

He gave an inward sigh and met her eyes, wondering what she'd see. Too much, probably.

Definitely. 'You are allowed a life, darling,' she said softly after a long, long moment. 'I really don't mind babysitting so you can go and have fun. And if you like, I'll have them for a sleepover. They haven't been for a few weeks, and Amber was asking about it yesterday. Then you wouldn't need to worry about getting back early, or even at all,' she added, her voice laden with meaning.

He felt his eyes fill for no very good reason, and looked away again. 'Are you sure?'

'Yes, I'm sure. I take it this is Oliver Henderson's daughter?'

How had she known that? Except of course she knew they'd been on the team-building thing together, and he'd taken her to the party. Not to mention babysitting so he could have that sneaky little coffee in her garden—their first date, if you could call it that. Blindingly obvious, really, and he should have realised she'd guess. Unless Ed had been shooting his mouth off...

He nodded. 'Yes. Yes, it is.' He sighed and dragged a hand through his hair and turned back to face her again, the whole situation suddenly overwhelming him.

'I don't know where it's going, and I know it's too soon, but—Mum, she's had breast cancer—'

'Breast cancer?' she echoed, shocked, and he nodded.

'Yes, I know, and she's only twenty-nine now, and she's so matter-of-fact, and so positive and proactive and just—just *so* brave. It's heartbreaking listening to her, because she brushes it aside and says it's fine, but you know it's not fine, she was so young, and—'

He broke off, and his mother took his arm gently. 'Oh, darling. Are you sure it's wise getting involved with her?'

He gave a huff of laughter without a shred of humour because it was so unfunny.

'What, because she might die, too? It's highly unlikely, she says they got it all and she should know, but in any case I can't live my life thinking like that even if it wasn't all right. We all have to die at some point, but that doesn't mean we don't deserve to be happy in the meantime. And there's something about her that makes me happy, and I haven't been happy for two years, Mum. And I want to be, even if it's foolish, even if I'm setting myself up for heartbreak all over again, because I just want to be with her. I need to be with her, and I think she needs to be with me, at least for now, and if I can make her happy, too, then that's all I can ask.'

She studied him thoughtfully. 'That sounds as if you're thinking long-term.'

'It does, doesn't it?' he murmured, examining that thought. 'I don't know. Maybe I am. I just know I want to be with her. I haven't got any further than that yet, but I wouldn't be surprised.'

'And where do the children fit into all this?'

He stared at her, a hollow feeling in his chest. 'I don't know. It's a good question and one I keep asking myself, but I can't answer it right now because I honestly don't have a clue, because I really wasn't expecting to feel like this so I'm totally unprepared for it and I don't know what to do. I have to protect the children, I know that, but what about her? Doesn't she deserve to be happy? Don't I? And I don't know where it's going, I just know she means a lot to me and I can't walk away.'

'Oh, Matthew...'

Her arms went round him, and he hugged her close, his eyes tightly shut, because she of all people knew what might lie ahead. She'd nursed his father till he'd died of cancer, supported him through the chemo, the tests, the new chemo, another one, the palliative operations, the endless cycle of hope and despair, and then she'd buried him, heartbroken and yet relieved that finally his pain was over.

So she knew exactly what might lie ahead for him if it all went wrong, and for the children, and he felt her body shudder as he held her. And then she pushed him away, cupped his head in her hands and kissed his cheek, her eyes brimming with tears.

'You're a brave man, Matthew. You remind me so much of your father. That's exactly what he'd say.'

Then she let him go, sniffed hard and straightened her shoulders and headed for the kitchen. 'I've made a chicken and bacon salad for you. It's in the fridge, and there's some olive ciabatta to go with it, and we went to the farm shop and picked some raspberries. They're in the fridge, too. So, shall I pick the children up at five thirty tomorrow in time for supper?'

* * *

Livvy spent the rest of her hectic Friday night shift dealing with abusive drunks and silly kids who'd over-indulged, and then a girl of fifteen was brought in in a state of collapse after taking something at a party, and Livvy was the first to see her.

She immediately called James Slater, their clinical lead, and she was relieved when she heard the door swish open behind her.

'OK, what have we got?' he asked.

'This is Kelly, she's fifteen, she's got rigid muscles, shallow breathing, heart rate's one-sixty, she was ag-gressive and incoherent on admission, and then she had a tonic/clonic seizure, started foaming at the mouth and lapsed into unconsciousness. She's taken something at a party, but nobody would say what.'

'Looks to me like ecstasy—MDMA,' James Slater said tightly. 'Right, let's get on this. Bloods, please. Let's find out what's going on. Have you given her anything?'

'IV diazepam. Why do they do it?' Livvy muttered, but it was a rhetorical question and, anyway, nobody had time to answer her.

He rattled off a list of tests he wanted done while Livvy got another IV line in, and he nodded.

'Good. Right, let's get some normal saline into her, please, and let's get these clothes off and cool her down before we lose her. And can someone talk to her friends, please, and find out for sure what she's taken? What's her temperature?'

'Forty point one.'

'Right, she's got malignant hyperthermia—'

'She's taken a cocktail,' Jenny said, coming back in. 'MDMA, something else, nobody knows what, all washed down with vodka, and then she's drunk lots and lots of water because someone told her to.'

'Damn. She's got dilutional hyponatraemia as well. Right, let's catheterise her quick, and get her on IV frusemide and try and shift this. And we need to alert PICU, she's going to have to go up there if we don't want to lose her.'

They didn't lose her, although it got worryingly close at one point, and finally she was shipped off to PICU for intensive care and Livvy went to talk to her parents before going home an hour late.

She crawled into bed, checked her phone and found a text from Matt.

Can we make it six tomorrow? Kids are having sleepover with my sainted mother. :)

She felt a quiver of anticipation, her exhaustion forgotten, and replied.

Sorry, vile shift, just got this but six is fine. Looking forward to it. How did you talk her into it?! x

He didn't reply, but then she didn't expect him to, not at gone midnight, but it pinged into her phone at seven the next morning.

She offered—disturbingly! It seems mothers have second sight. I'll see you in eleven hours. M x

Her whole body fizzing with anticipation, she spent the morning in the garden weeding, then cleaned the house, changed the sheets on her bed and went shopping for breakfast items and a few other things. Just in case…

And then she showered, ransacked her wardrobe and wondered what he called casual. How casual? He'd talked about jeans and a shirt, but there were a million different ways of doing that.

It was hot, too, but the pub was on the river, so there might be a cool breeze. Cropped jeans and a pretty top? A skirt? Or her ultimate go-to, a bold print jersey maxi-dress that she could dress up with chunky beads and heels, or wear with beach sandals.

'Stop overthinking it!' she told herself, and put on the dress and the minimum of make-up, left her hair down and slipped on a pair of toe-post sandals. Her toenails were still OK from the previous weekend, and she stood back and looked critically at herself.

The dress, like most of her more fitted clothes, had a bit of detail over the bust to disguise her lop-sidedness, a wrap-over with a twist in this case, and although if she lifted her arm her scar would show, he'd seen it anyway and it was time to stop hiding in the shadows and get over herself.

She stopped fussing, tidied her bedroom, grabbed a cardi in case it got chilly by the water and went downstairs to wait, her heart jiggling in her chest. Was tonight the night? Would he want to make love to her, or was it still too soon? Probably, but her reckless side, the side that wanted to live life to the full and not waste a single minute more, really, really hoped not…

CHAPTER SEVEN

SHE WAS WEARING another long dress, but casual this time, light-years away from the formal gown of last weekend, and she still looked gorgeous. More so, even, because this time he *knew* what was underneath, and he couldn't wait to see it again.

He pulled her into his arms and kissed her, massively tempted not to bother with dinner, but he wanted to do this properly, so he lifted his head reluctantly and nuzzled the tip of her nose with his.

'You've caught the sun.'

'Mmm. I spent the morning weeding the garden and getting some vitamin D.'

He chuckled and let her go. 'So, are you ready?'

'Yup—if I'm OK like this?'

He ran his eyes over her again, just for the joy of it, and smiled. 'Very OK,' he said softly, and she smiled.

'Let's go, then.'

It wasn't far to the pub, just a few miles, but he was right, the view was stunning, and the light breeze off the water made it perfect.

That, and having him sitting beside her on the terrace on a picnic bench overlooking the river. He was wearing dark jeans with a white linen shirt and deck shoes, and he looked every bit as gorgeous as he had the week before. It wasn't the tux, she decided as he put the drinks down in front of them and settled himself beside her, it was him. She caught a waft of cologne warmed by his skin, felt the brush of his thigh, the touch of his fingers as he lifted a strand of hair away from her eyes and tucked it behind her ear, and she wanted him more than she could believe was possible.

It was the first time since Mark, the first time ever since her cancer that she'd got this close to anyone, but she'd never expected to feel so much and now she was impatient.

Later, she told herself, and turned her attention to the menu, poring over it with him.

'Oh, it's too hard, it all looks delicious.'

'We can always come again.'

She smiled up at him. 'Sounds like a plan. So, what are we eating today?'

In the end they both chose the same—a crab and prawn tian with avocado, followed by pan-fried local sea bass served on a bed of samphire with a mixed leaf salad and sweet potato fries on the side. She wouldn't normally have had the fries, but just this once she let herself indulge, and they were delicious.

All of it was, the food simple but beautifully cooked, and in between mouthfuls they talked.

Not about work. He banned that, and she was more than happy to forget about the previous evening's shift, but he told her what he'd done that day with his children, and she could see the love shining in his eyes as he talked about them affectionately.

They'd been to the beach with Ed and Annie and

their children, and they'd built sandcastles and the children had buried him and Ed in the sand and then tickled their feet.

'It was great. Really good day. And no tantrums,' he said with a chuckle, as if that was a rare thing.

'Sounds like you had fun,' she said, hoping she didn't sound too wistful, and he nodded wryly.

'We did, but the beach has its downside. Any time you feel like getting all your orifices filled with sand, come and join us. I'm sure the children will oblige.'

'Gosh, you make it sound so tempting,' she said with a laugh, and it was, in a way. Not the orifices, obviously, but the rest of it, and she felt a pang of longing to be there with them, to be part of it, the chaos and laughter, the warmth, the love. Was he inviting her to join them, or was it just a throwaway remark? She wasn't sure, but maybe it was still too soon. The last thing she'd want was for his children to be hurt, but it didn't stop the longing.

'Are you going to finish your fries?' he asked, and she pulled herself together and thought about him, not his children, not her unborn babies who were just a distant dream, but him, the man. That's what this was all about, and that's all it was about, at least for now and maybe for ever.

'No, you go ahead,' she said, and pushed the plate towards him.

And then at last they were done, the food eaten, the conversation coming to a natural halt, and he turned to her, his eyes searching, and her heart skipped a beat.

'Coffee here, or home?' he asked quietly, the unspoken question hanging in the air between them, and she smiled.

'Home, I think, don't you?' she murmured.

'Sounds good to me,' he said softly. 'Don't move, I'll go and pay the bill.'

'So, your place or mine?'

'Mine,' she said without hesitation, and he nodded, as if he understood her reluctance to go back to his house with all its reminders of his wife and children.

He'd been openly affectionate and flirting with her all evening, so by the time he pulled up outside her house she was tingling with anticipation. She hoped she wasn't misreading him. She didn't think so.

She unlocked the door and he followed her in and headed for the kettle.

'Green tea?' he asked over his shoulder, and she took a deep breath and dredged up her courage.

'I'd rather undress you. I've been fantasising about it ever since I opened the door to you.'

He turned slowly towards her. 'I thought that was my line?'

'Mmm, it was, but that was last week and this is now, so I thought I'd steal it.'

His smile widened, a slow, sexy smile that flooded his eyes with promise. 'I've been shopping,' he murmured, patting his pocket, and she felt the tension ramp up, humming in the air between them.

'So have I,' she confessed, and he laughed and hugged her.

'So what are we waiting for?' he asked softly, and followed her up the stairs.

'I tidied up for you this time,' she said lightly, hoping her voice didn't reflect her nerves, and he chuckled and put his arms around her from behind, nuzzling his face against hers so she could feel the slight rasp of stubble against her cheek.

'Do you really think I care?'

'Well, I've seen your house, it's pretty tidy.'

He turned her round and dropped a kiss on the tip of her nose. 'Not guilty. I have a cleaner, and my mother tidies constantly.'

'Don't spoil it,' she teased. 'I was imagining you were highly domesticated.'

He laughed. 'Hardly. I do what's strictly necessary and I don't waste time on the things that aren't. Like small talk,' he added with that lazy, sexy smile making another appearance.

He feathered a gentle kiss over her lips, then lifted his head again, his expression changed, his eyes suddenly darker.

'You looked lovely tonight, sitting there by the river with the wind in your hair, all sun-kissed and radiant and bubbling with laughter.' He brushed his knuckles lightly over her cheek. 'I want you so much. I haven't been able to think about anything else all week.'

'Me, too,' she said, and cradling his jaw in her hand, she held his searching gaze. 'Come to bed, Matt. I need you. Make love to me,' she murmured, and he closed his eyes and turned his face into her palm, pressing his lips to it for a moment.

She could feel the slight prickle of stubble against her palm, the jump of a muscle under her fingertips, then he lifted his head and met her eyes again.

'It'll be a pleasure,' he said gruffly, his hands reaching for her, but she pushed his hands away and started to undo his shirt.

'My turn first,' she said, and unhurriedly, button

by button, garment by garment, she peeled away his clothes with shaking fingers until he was standing in front of her naked.

Naked, beautiful and very, very ready.

He lifted his hand and touched her cheek, his fingers trailing slowly, slowly down over her throat, dipping under her collar bones, tracing the neckline of her dress. Her heart was hammering so hard against her ribs she thought they'd break, and she took a step back and caught hold of the dress.

'Uh-uh. My turn,' he said, and then frowned and made a face, and she laughed.

'It just pulls off,' she said, putting him out of his misery, and he laughed with her and said, 'Good,' and reaching for the dress he hitched it up slowly, his hands brushing tantalisingly against her legs. He paused to cup her bottom and ease her against himself with a quiet groan, then moved on up her body, inch by inch, past her hips, her waist, her ribs, until finally he peeled it carefully over her head and dropped it to the floor.

And then he stood there and stared down at her, his eyes lowered so she couldn't read them.

Why? Why had he stopped?

She'd expected to feel nervous, but suddenly she was more worried about him now, about what he was feeling, if it was too soon, if he was really ready for what had to be a huge psychological milestone. Hers felt monumental enough. What it was like for him? Had he changed his mind—?

No, if his next words meant anything.

'Do you remember what you said to me in Cumbria,' he murmured, his voice low, 'about you being inside your body, not me?' His finger traced a line down her throat, between her breasts, down to her abdomen, his hand flattening against her, fingers splayed across the lace of her shorts, so near and yet so far. 'It's been driving me mad ever since. It's all I can think about.'

'Well, don't let me stop you,' she said a little breathlessly, and he laughed softly and met her eyes again.

'First things first.'

He reached around behind her, sifting her hair through his fingers for a moment, then his hands moved down and he took off her underwear with gentle, careful fingers, peeling away her bra, then her lacy shorts, dropping them on their other clothes.

Then he straightened up, his eyes trailing slowly over her body before he muttered something and turned away abruptly, and she had a sudden rush of insecurity.

He picked up his trousers and her heart sank, but then he found his wallet and pulled something out, and relief swamped her.

'Oh… For a moment there, I thought you were going.'

'Going?' He gave her a quizzical smile. 'I'm not going anywhere. No way on earth. I was just getting these.'

He dropped the little foil packets on the bedside table, turned back the bedclothes and took her in his arms with a deep groan.

'Oh, that feels so good,' he said, and then his mouth found hers, slow and coaxing, his tongue delving as his hands roamed gently over her body, driving her wild. She threaded her fingers through his hair, running her other hand slowly down over his back, feeling the strong muscles that bracketed his spine, the hot silk of his skin, the contrast as her hand moved round and down over his taut abdomen.

'Livvy—!'

She heard the sharp hiss of his indrawn breath as her fingers circled him, but he didn't stop her, just slid his hand down between their bodies, his knee nudging her legs apart, his fingers gentle and sure and devastatingly accurate.

She clenched her legs together around his thigh, her legs giving way, and he scooped her up and laid her in the middle of the bed, following her down, his mouth never leaving hers. His hand found her again, coaxing, teasing, building the tension until she wanted to scream.

Then he pulled away and reached for the bedside table.

'Let me,' she said, her voice unsteady. She tore the foil wrapper open with fingers that shook a little, pushed him onto his back and straddled his thighs, stroking him teasingly with a fingertip from his collar bones all the way down, down, slowly, tantalisingly, following the narrow line of dark hair—

'Livvy, please, get on with it,' he begged, laughing a little desperately, and she obliged, slowly rolling the condom down, drawing it out deliberately even though it was killing her because she wanted him so much. She wasn't alone. He swore and grabbed the sheet, clenching it in his fists, his eyes tight shut.

'What are you doing to me?' he mumbled through gritted teeth, and she laughed.

'You know *exactly* what I'm doing to you,' she murmured, and then she moved up until she was straddling his hips, chafing against him, watching his control waver as she lowered herself slowly down over him, taking him into her body, giving it time to adjust.

He tilted his hips and she gave an involuntary gasp and rocked against him, and his eyes opened and locked with hers, his hands reaching for her, grasping her hips and holding her still.

'*Don't—move.*'

She rocked again, just gently, and he groaned.

'Livvy...'

'I'm so close...'

He rolled then, taking her with him, their bodies meshed together, legs tangled, his control splintering as he picked up the pace.

His hand slid between them again, his body shifting slightly so he could reach her, his mouth never leaving hers, and she felt the tension tighten unbearably, building until she thought she'd scream, but still she couldn't let go.

'Now, Livvy, please, come with me,' he said raggedly, and as his body stiffened she felt the tightly coiled tension inside her shatter into a million pieces.

She sobbed his name, and then as the avalanche of sensation died away he sagged against her, his head on her shoulder, his breath rasping. She could feel his heart pounding against her chest, feel the heat of his breath, the ripple of shock waves running through them both.

For the longest moment neither of them moved, and then he lifted his head and stared down into her eyes.

'Oh, Livvy,' he said, his voice catching, and he touched his mouth to hers in a tender kiss that nearly broke her heart.

* * *

He had to move.

He rolled away from her, breaking the contact reluctantly, and got to his feet, his legs barely holding him.

'Back in a moment, I need to deal with this,' he said gruffly, and headed for the bathroom, closing the door behind him and resting back against it for a second while his emotions settled.

I love her.

The thought was so profound, so overwhelming, it nearly broke him.

How? How, so soon?

In a daze, he dealt with the condom, washed his hands and face and stood staring at himself in her bathroom mirror.

Had Jules meant so little to him that he'd replaced her this fast? Except he hadn't replaced her, not at all. He still loved her, and he knew he always would, but was it possible he loved Olivia as well?

How could that be? And it was so sudden, so unexpected.

Happiness, yes, he could buy that, but—*love?*

No. It was just the heat of the moment. It couldn't be love. Love took years to grow, to turn into that almost organic state where you could finish each other's sentences and anticipate the other's needs and wishes.

That was love—wasn't it? Not this barely there, untried emotion that he felt for Livvy.

Well, untried, anyway. It wasn't barely there, it was very much present, and he felt as if he'd been punched in the gut.

He opened the door and went back to her and found

her sitting on the edge of the bed. She looked up at him, her eyes wary.

'Are you OK?' she asked.

He found a smile. Actually, it wasn't hard. Not hard at all. 'Yes. Yes, I'm fine,' he said quietly, realising he was. 'Very fine. How are you?'

'I'm very fine, too, thank you,' she said, and her smile was tender and loving.

Her, too?

No. It was just the magic of the moment, nothing more. It couldn't be more.

'Good,' he said, as she got to her feet and came over to him and rested against him for a moment. He lifted a hand and cradled her head against his chest, and then she straightened up and smiled at him.

'I need the bathroom. I won't be long.'

He lay down again, staring blindly up at her bedroom ceiling, his thoughts tumbling.

OK, so it wasn't love, but what was it? He didn't know, and he couldn't work out what he felt.

Not regret, he knew that without a shadow of a doubt. It had been wonderful, amazing, and he'd been more than ready. What he wasn't ready for was the tidal wave of emotion that had swept over him when she'd come apart in his arms.

He heard water running, the door opening, and then she was back, snuggling down beside him and bringing warmth and joy with her.

They didn't speak. There didn't seem to be anything to say, or any need to say it.

He turned his head slightly and pressed a gentle kiss to her forehead, and she tipped her head back and smiled up at him, her lips irresistible.

He didn't even try to resist.

* * *

His kiss was gentle, unhurried, his lips lazily sipping and tasting, the urgency gone now from both of them.

He eased the bedclothes away, his hand tracing a path down her throat, down over her shoulder to her wrist, trailing over the pulse point. He lifted her hand and laid a gentle, lingering kiss on the palm, then threaded his fingers through hers and worked his way slowly back up the inside of her arm, kissing every inch.

He reached her armpit and paused before he reached the scar, lifting his head and meeting her eyes searchingly.

She felt a quiver of resistance and quelled it. This was Matt, who'd just made the most beautiful and tender love to her. She was safe with him.

'Does it feel strange? Would you rather I didn't touch it?' he asked softly, and she shrugged.

'No, it's fine. It's numb, so it's a bit weird—but that's OK.'

He nodded, traced the scar gently with his fingers—checking out the surgery, probably, in doctor mode—then bent his head and feathered slow, tiny kisses along its length, definitely not in doctor mode now but back to the gentle, sensitive lover who seemed to know how to make her body sing, even there.

It was strangely soothing, if a bit unnerving, but then he reached the end of the scar and moved on, his tongue flicking lightly over her nipple, and she sucked in a breath and clenched her legs together as the sensation rippled through her.

'Oh—!'

He paused and lifted his head. 'Is that a good oh, or a bad oh?' he asked, and she laughed a little.

'Definitely good.'

He smiled wickedly and did it again, then treated the other breast to the same torture until she was ready to scream. And then he moved on, his stubble grazing lightly over her skin as he sipped and nibbled his way down over her ribs to her abdomen.

And then he paused and traced a fingertip along the fine, almost invisible line that ran from side to side just above her waist.

"Whoever the surgeon was did a lovely job. Very neat.'

'It is. My father did it.'

He lifted his head and stared at her. 'Your *father*?'

'Yes. He didn't realise he was my father at the time.'

He shifted back up the bed and lay down again facing her, looking even more puzzled. 'We are talking about Oliver?'

'Of course.'

He shook his head. 'I don't understand.'

'No. He didn't, really,' she said with a smile. 'They'd had a bit of a thing at a conference a couple of years before, and they—well, whatever, he was called away in the night and he left a message to say his brother-in-law had been killed and his wife was pregnant and he had to go to her.'

His eyes widened. '*What?* Your father was *married*?'

'Sounds like it, doesn't it? Except he wasn't. It was his sister Clare's husband who was killed, and his sister who was pregnant but it all got a bit lost in the translation so when my mother realised she was pregnant she didn't tell him. Then they ended up working together at the Audley Memorial and she still thought he was married, and although he knew she had a child she still didn't tell him, and then I was rushed in after the accident without any ID, and he was on take, so he operated. He managed to save some of my spleen, repaired my bowel and flushed my abdomen and it was all going well.

'And then, just when he was about to close, he found out I was Mum's child, and he looked at me properly for the first time and realised I must be his. We share the same rare blood group, B negative, and I was the spitting image of his nephew, so he just knew.'

'Wow. So who closed? Surely not him?'

'Yes, he did. He decided he couldn't trust anybody else to do it as well as he would, because he cared more.'

Matt shook his head. 'I can't imagine operating on one of my kids. That must have been such a shock.' His finger traced the line again. 'He's done a truly beautiful job. It really doesn't show.'

'You saw it.'

He laughed and kissed her. 'I'm a surgeon, Olivia, so I do tend to notice these things. So, how was your mother about it?'

'Shocked, worried for him in case it went wrong, relieved when it didn't. She'd been about to tell him because they were seeing each other again and they were in love anyway, so they just got married pretty soon afterwards, and then Jamie and Abbie came along, and they've been nauseatingly happy ever since—or maybe that's me, being jealous because I know I'll probably never experience it.'

He frowned, his face puzzled. 'Why not?'

'Because I don't think I'll ever have my own family.

I can't get pregnant while I'm on tamoxifen because it's too risky for the baby, so I'd have to wait until I come off it and allow time for it to leave my system, and by then it could be too late for my ovaries. Tamoxifen can shut them down.'

'Didn't they ask if you wanted to harvest eggs before you started treatment?'

'Yes, but it meant two months of being bombarded with hormones, my radiotherapy had already been delayed by the second op, and I was freaked out at the thought of all those missed cancer cells mopping up the hormones and invading my body, so I said no and it's haunted me ever since because that might have been my last chance, but it's done now and it's not the end of the world.'

Except sometimes it felt like it, so she tried not to think about it.

He frowned again. 'There are all sorts of ways you can still be a mother, and it certainly shouldn't stop you being happy. You could adopt, or foster, or be a stepmother, or just be with someone without kids. Not everyone wants children, Livvy. There are lots of people who don't, for all sorts of reasons.'

'But I do,' she admitted, opening her heart to him with painful honesty and letting the sorrow seep in. 'I desperately do. I love children, all children, but that's not what it's about, and if I ended up adopting or being a stepmother I'm afraid I might resent the fact that they weren't mine, and that scares me because it wouldn't be fair to them. I just want to be pregnant, to grow a baby inside me. It's almost biological, and sometimes I just feel hollow with the need. And I don't know if

I can, or if I'll ever be able to, or even if I should because of the cancer risk. And that hurts.'

'Maybe you could get pregnant once you're off
tamoxifen. Women do, and surely the cancer risk is
minimal now? You said they'd got it all. What stage
was it?'

'Stage I, and they did get it all, and then took more
tissue to be super-cautious, and I had radiotherapy and
I'm taking tamoxifen, which I hate because it makes
me feel rubbish—I've done everything I can, sorted
my diet, my lifestyle, my priorities—so I'll almost certainly be all right, but pregnancy is years down the
line. I still have hope, there's still a chance, but that's
not for now and maybe not ever, because I didn't take
that risk when I had the chance. It's just something I
have to live with—'

Her voice cracked and she turned her head away.

'Sorry. Ignore me. I'm just having a pity party.'

'Oh, Olivia,' he whispered softly, his breath drifting over her face, and then he kissed her, tenderly now,
making her eyes fill. 'I'm sorry.'

'I'm OK,' she assured him, wishing her voice
sounded a bit stronger, that she hadn't shown him so
much of herself, the bits she never shared, even with
her parents. 'You don't need to feel sorry for me. I'm
alive and well and that's enough to ask for. Alive, and
making a valid contribution. I'm a good doctor, I know
that, and I love it.

'And anyway, there are other things,' she went on,
trying to put a positive spin on it. 'My hobbies, my
family, my friends. I have a good life, Matt, and I'm
fine with it most of the time. Yes, sometimes I have a

bit of a wobble, but it doesn't mean I can't be happy. I'm happy now. You make me happy.'

She wasn't sure who she was trying to convince, him or herself, but his arms tightened around her, holding her closer.

'Good, because you make me happy, too,' he murmured, kissing her tenderly, and then turned out the light, wrapped her gently against his heart and held her, the steady rhythm under her ear soothing as she drifted into sleep.

He lay awake for a long time, feeling the slight rise and fall of her chest against his side, the whisper of her breath against his skin, her words running through his head in a continuous loop.

Such sad words, said in such a brave, determined voice that didn't hide the pain that lay beneath it.

I just want to be pregnant...carry a baby inside me...hollow with the need...haunted me ever since... might have been my last chance...didn't take the risk.

And then the other things she'd said, about being a stepmother.

I might resent the fact that they weren't mine and that scares me...it wouldn't be fair to them.

He'd thought it himself, thought as he'd lain awake in the middle of the night all last week that his priority had to be to keep his relationship with her and his children separate, to keep them apart from each other until he knew where this was going so there was no chance of his children being hurt or confused, but that was before he realised he loved her, before he realised he wanted more. Much, much more.

Well, Juliet's death had taught him that you didn't

always get what you wanted, you got the hand life dealt you, and if the hand he'd been dealt meant he could share only a small area of his life with her, would that be so bad?

They could still be together, still be happy, just not all the time. And if they managed that right, made sure they made time for each other regularly, then maybe that would be enough, for both of them, until they were sure of each other. And maybe then, if she met his children, maybe she'd realise that she wouldn't resent them. Maybe they could become her family?

No. He was getting ahead of himself. It was much too soon to start thinking about things like that.

Wasn't it?

Carefully, so he didn't wake her, he eased his arm out from under her head and shifted slightly away, throwing off the covers. It was a hot night, and he needed air.

Trying not to disturb her, he got quietly out of bed, picked up his jeans and underwear and went downstairs, letting himself out into the garden.

The moon was full, and he sat on her swinging bench at the top of the little paved garden and inhaled the heady fragrance of the wisteria growing over the trellis behind him. It reminded him of Jules, of the night-scented stocks she'd planted in amongst the shrubs just before she'd died, but suddenly it all seemed a long, long time ago, and his life was in the here and now.

With Livvy? He hoped so.

But what about the children? They'd gain so much from her being a part of their lives, and they had so much to give her, but was it fair to expect it from either them or her? And what if she *did* resent them?

No. There was no way she'd do anything other than love them with her whole heart and soul. She didn't have a resentful, selfish bone in her body, he was sure of it. He just had to prove it to her.

He breathed in again, drawing in the scent, letting it fill his lungs. It was beautiful, the silence of the night broken only by the sound of a distant siren and the faint creak of the chains as the bench swung slowly back and forth, and he closed his eyes and let the peace soak into him, but even so his mind couldn't rest and his heart ached for her.

Why did life have to be so complicated?

CHAPTER EIGHT

HE'D GONE.

She hadn't heard anything, no doors closing, no car starting, but there was a silent quality about the house that told her she was alone, and she wanted to cry.

She wished she'd kept her mouth shut. No doubt it had made him realise he should protect his children from her, just in case.

They'd never discussed her meeting Amber and Charlie, and if she was honest she wasn't sure she wanted to, maybe because she'd want it too much, or because she was afraid she'd be resentful of his happiness, but maybe that was irrelevant if he'd decided their relationship couldn't go anywhere further because of the children.

Not that he'd said anything that in any way implied he *wanted* it to go further, and it was far too soon even to think about it, but what if, now he knew she probably couldn't have children, he'd thought she only wanted him because of his ready-made family, a substitute for the babies she could never have?

Had he doubted her motives? She hoped not, because she really didn't have any apart from wanting to be with him. But his children had to come first, and if he'd had the slightest shred of doubt, he had a duty to protect them. She understood that absolutely, but it hurt that he might believe she'd use him—use all of them—like that.

Yes, her heart ached to be part of a noisy, busy family, but she didn't know how she'd feel about someone else's children, if she'd be happy or if they'd just constantly remind her of what she'd missed out on. She hadn't even let herself think about his children, just to make it easier, but she was sure he must have done. They'd suffered enough—and so had she. There was no point torturing herself unnecessarily.

She laughed at that. Torturing herself? What was she thinking? It was him she'd tortured, burdening him with her self-pity, and she felt a rush of guilt.

At least she was alive. She thought about the woman with dark hair who would never see her babies grow up, about the pictures they'd drawn, scattered like confetti over his fridge and the playroom walls, the people who were alive now because of his generosity in donating her organs.

She thought about the life he lived without her, a juggling act between work and home, with his indispensable mother filling in the gaps and having the children for a sleepover so he could have a life, even if it was only one night in however many that he could snatch off from reality.

And she felt sorry for *herself*?

She was flooded with shame, disgusted at her neediness when he needed her far more than she needed him. She was fine. She had a great life. He didn't, not any more, because it had all been snatched unfairly from him when Jules had died. And if sharing her life with him could bring him a crumb of happiness, a fleeting moment of downtime from responsibility on the rare occasions when he could get away, then she would do it without question.

She wanted more of him than that, much more, but she knew she couldn't have it, knew he wasn't ready for it, and if that was all they could ever have she'd take it willingly, because she'd rather have that occasional little glimpse of paradise with him than the drab grey of life without him.

Except now he'd gone, and she didn't know why. Maybe it *was* because of the children, or maybe it was simply that common sense had reared its ugly head and he'd run for cover from a broken, needy woman who didn't know how to keep her mouth shut.

Wise man.

Disgusted with herself, she threw off the bedclothes, pulled on her dressing gown and padded downstairs, and then she realised the back door was open. And she could hear a sound, a familiar, rhythmic creak.

She walked silently into the conservatory and there he was at the top of her little garden, his eyes closed, head tilted back, one foot pushing the bench. Push, swing, push, swing.

He hadn't gone...

She walked up to him, her feet almost silent on the paving, but she must have made a sound because his eyes opened and he smiled and held out a hand to her and pulled her gently onto his lap.

'I'm sorry, I just felt like some fresh air. Did I wake you?'

She shook her head, relief flooding her.

'No, I was just hot—the joys of tamoxifen. Are you OK?'

He smiled again, his eyes unreadable, shadowed in the stark light of the moon, and she felt his thigh tense as he gave the ground another little push, rocking the swing again.

'Yeah, I'm fine. You?'

She nodded. 'I thought you'd gone because of my self-pitying little misery fest.'

He laughed softly and hugged her closer. 'No. I'm still here. You don't get rid of me that easily. Your garden smells amazing at night, by the way. I love it. I wish mine was like this.'

'Give yours time. I'm sure you've got some wonderful plants in there.'

She rested her head against his and closed her eyes, relishing the feel of his bare chest under her hand, the rhythmic shift of his thighs as he rocked the swing, his solid warmth, his gentleness, his strength. She was so glad he hadn't gone, but he'd have to soon, and she wasn't ready for that. Not yet.

'What time are you picking up the children?'

'I'm not. My mother said she'd keep them till lunch if I wanted. She'll probably take them to the beach. Why?'

'I just wondered how long we've got.'

He tilted his head back and looked up at her, his smile sad. 'Not nearly long enough.'

She bent her head and kissed him tenderly, needing to feel his arms around her, his body close to hers because that might be all she could ever have of him.

'Then let's not waste it,' she murmured, and pulled him to his feet and took him back to bed.

* * *

His phone pinged at eight, and he reached out for it, then put it down and pulled her back into his arms with a contented little noise.

'Everything OK?'

'Mmm, it's fine. It was Mum. They're off to the beach with Ed and Annie and all the children before it gets too hot.'

She felt a pang of guilt for keeping him from his little family. 'Shouldn't you go? Your time with them's so limited.'

He tilted his head back so he could look at her, his eyes searching. 'Do you want me to go?'

'No! Well—only if you want to. I just don't want you to feel you have to stay. You see little enough of them, and they're only small and they need you. You should go, really.'

'You're right.' He smiled, kissed her and rolled out of bed, straightening up with a bone-cracking stretch. 'Let's go to mine for breakfast, and then we can wander down to the beach and join up with them later.'

'Really?'

He sat back down on the edge of the bed and took her hand. 'Really. I think it's time you met my children,' he said seriously, and she felt her eyes widen, her heart suddenly beating just that little bit faster.

'Are you sure?' she asked, feeling a little stunned, a little panicked because she'd been sure he'd never let her near them after all she'd said.

'They don't bite,' he said gently, but that wasn't what she was worried about. It was more the possibility that having met them she'd love them instantly, as part of him, and she wasn't sure she wanted to expose herself to that much hurt in case their relationship didn't last.

'Don't you want to keep us apart?'

'No. It's fine.' His smile was warm and a little wry. 'Don't worry, I won't tell them what we've been up to.'

'I didn't think you would for a moment, but what *will* you tell them? And how about your mother? What will she think?'

'She won't think anything. She knows we're together, it was her idea, and they're my children and I'd like you to meet them, unless you really, really don't want to. I'll just tell them you're my friend from work. They already know a bit about you.'

She felt her eyes pop open wider still. 'They do?'

He laughed softly. 'Yes, they do. I told them about you falling down the mountain. Amber was walking along a low garden wall, and it was getting higher and higher as the road went down the hill, and I told her to be careful and she said, "Daddy, I'm *always* careful!", which sounded so like you. So I told them about you.'

She bit her lip, trying not to laugh and failing. 'I can't believe you told them. They'll think I'm an idiot.'

'Oh, well, if the cap fits—'

'You're so rude,' she said, swatting him playfully and laughing, but he just hugged her.

'Don't worry about them, they don't judge, they're just small people. They take everything at face value. And I know my mother would like to meet you.'

To see if she measured up? She chewed her lip, the laughter vanishing in an instant. 'It's not that I don't want to meet them all, I do—'

'Well, that's all right, then,' he said firmly, and

twitched the covers off her. 'Come on, gorgeous. Let's hit the shower.'

'Together?'

He grinned and pulled her to her feet. 'Why not?'

He hustled her through the shower, keeping it brisk and matter-of-fact in the end because otherwise they'd get sidetracked and he wanted to get home now and get on with the day.

Starting with breakfast, and then going to the beach.

They took the food she'd bought back to his house, made a stack of club sandwiches and ate them on his bench while she ran a critical eye over the new shrubs and the ones that had been hacked back.

'I think you just need to be patient,' she said. 'You've got some beautiful things.'

He laughed and shook his head. 'How would I know? I can recognise wisteria and roses. Beyond that, I'm useless.'

'My mother loves gardening, she taught me everything I know. Come on, let's have a look,' she coaxed, and gave him a guided tour of his own garden, pointing out the names of each of the shrubs she recognised, their various merits and flowering season, and after a while he was convinced she was stalling.

Well, he wasn't going to let her, wasn't going to give her any further opportunity to try and talk both of them out of going to the beach so she could meet the children. He'd been thinking about it all night because he knew that until he saw them together, until he saw her reaction to his children and theirs to her, he had no idea what the future might hold for them all, and he needed to know.

And so did she.

She was telling him about the *viburnum tinus* which had been cut back hard when he stopped her in mid-flow, a finger on her lips.

'Enough,' he said, laughing down into her eyes. 'We can do this another time. Let's go to the beach, it's less challenging.'

Really?

Maybe for him, but not for her, which was why she'd been stalling furiously.

By the time they'd crossed the road, gone down the ramp to the slipway and walked along to the Shackle-tons' beach hut, her heart was thrashing in her chest. What would the children think of her? Would they hate her? And would she, as she feared, fall instantly in love with them both? What if she didn't? What if she resented them? If they resented her?

He was walking beside her but a careful distance away, not quite touching, and all of a sudden there was a flurry of arms and legs and a little girl with their mother's dark hair hurled herself at him.

'Daddy!'

'Hello, my little princess!'

He swung her up and round, his laugh echoing through her, and she felt a huge lump in her throat seeing them together, their obvious joy in each other, the love that shone from both their faces. He put her back on her feet and scooped up a boy, smaller than Amber but the spitting image of his mother except for his father's smile.

The lump in her throat got even bigger as she watched him hug and kiss his grubby, sandy little son, and when he put him back down on the ground and turned to her, she had to struggle to find a smile.

'Livvy, meet my children, Amber and Charlie. Guys, this is Olivia, my friend from work. Say hello.'

'Hello, Amber, hello, Charlie.'

In typical little-boy fashion Charlie mumbled what could have been hello and ran off, distracted by two small boys about a year younger than him, probably Ed and Annie's twins. She turned back to Amber, who was studying her seriously.

'Are you the lady who fell down the mountain?'

Livvy bit her lip and tried not to laugh, but it was hopeless. 'Your daddy's been telling tales,' she said, and Amber shook her head, all serious still.

'He told me you were being silly, just like I was on the wall, and you could have hurt yourself a lot worse.'

Her smile faded. 'Yes, I could have done. He's quite right. And he did warn me, and I stupidly didn't listen.'

She nodded sagely. 'He said that, too,' she said, deadpan, and Livvy had to bite the inside of her cheeks. 'Is your ankle better now?'

'Yes, thank you. It's fine now.'

Amber nodded and cocked her head on one side. 'I like your dress, it's very pretty.'

She'd pulled on the jungle-print dress she'd worn the night before, just for speed and because it was so easy to wear—and, to be honest, because he'd told her she looked beautiful when she was wearing it, and that made her feel beautiful.

'I'm glad you like it. It's my favourite dress.'

'My favourite dress doesn't really fit me any more

and Daddy says I need a new one, but he hates shopping,' Amber said sadly.

There was a snort from beside her, and she looked up to see Matt rolling his eyes and laughing. 'I don't hate it, but I am hopeless. Hopeless and completely out of my depth.'

'And Grandma hates it, too, and Daddy says she's always buying things and taking them back because she can't make up her mind. And Auntie Sally's too busy, and I haven't got a mummy any more,' she added, and Livvy sucked in a quiet breath.

'I could take you,' she said before she engaged her filter, and Amber's eyes widened in excitement.

'Really? That would be amazing!'

'Well, that's me off the hook,' Matt said lightly, but his smile spoke volumes and she just hoped he didn't read too much into it.

There wasn't time to speculate, though, because Amber slipped her warm, sandy hand into Livvy's and dragged her over to a group of women clustered round the front of a beach hut.

'Grandma, this is Daddy's friend Olivia,' she said importantly, that little hand still holding hers, 'and she's going to take me shopping for a new favourite dress.'

Four pairs of eyes locked onto her, and not for the first time today she wished she'd kept her mouth shut...

'Oh, that's nice, Amber,' one of them said, getting to her feet. 'How kind of her. Matt, darling, why don't you and Amber go and help Ed with the children? We'll be fine.'

He shrugged, held his hand out to Amber and left her there feeling slightly abandoned and with a definite case of interview nerves.

'Hello, Olivia. I'm Jane, Matt's mother,' the woman said, giving her a slightly sandy handshake and a warm smile. 'It's lovely to meet you at last. Let me introduce you to Marnie, Ed's grandmother, and Joanna, Annie's mother, and Annie who's married to Ed, but of course you know that. And those are their four children on the beach.'

They all greeted her with friendly smiles and welcoming words, but she could see the questions lined up in their eyes.

She glanced across to where Ed and the girls were helping the little ones build a sandcastle, but Matt had his back to her and was clearly not going to be any help at all, and as he reached them Ed lifted his hand and waved at her.

'Hi, Livvy. How's it going?' he called.

She wasn't answering that loaded question under any circumstances, so she just smiled, said, 'Good, thanks,' and turned back to the women, leaving him and Matt to it. She had enough on her plate dodging the bullets she felt were coming her way any minute.

'What a lovely beach hut,' she said, casting about for something neutral, and Annie picked it up seamlessly.

'Yes, it's amazing. It belongs to Marnie but we sort of share it. So, it's lovely to meet you at last. How's the ankle?' she asked, bringing the conversation neatly back to her, and she laughed and rolled her eyes.

'I'm never going to live that down, am I?' she said, and Matt's mother and Annie both shook their heads and laughed with her.

'I was just about to make some drinks. Tea or coffee?' Annie asked, heading for the beach hut's tiny kitchen area, and Livvy followed her as the safest bet.

'I don't really drink either, I'm afraid, unless you have decaf? Or fruit tea?'

'There's a really nice peppermint green tea?'

'Perfect,' she said, and Annie put the kettle on and smiled at her thoughtfully.

Here we go.

'So, you're the person who's put the smile back on Matt's face. I'm so pleased. It's great to see him looking happy again.'

That surprised her. 'I thought Ed didn't approve?'

Annie frowned slightly. 'I don't think it was that. He was worried—about you getting hurt, and Matt getting in deeper than he was ready for. They've been friends for years, ever since they were at school, and he was just worried about him. It's been really tough for him.'

She nodded slowly. 'I know. I knew they were friends, that was obvious, but I didn't realise they went back that far. It sort of explains—well, quite a bit, really. Matt often talks about doing things with you all, but I thought he'd only known Ed since he started at the hospital.'

'Oh, no, since they were both sixteen. They did the same science subjects, and they spent a lot of time together, apparently. I'm so glad he came back here when the job came up. Jane's really been through the mill, too, what with losing her husband to cancer and then supporting Matt after Jules died, and it's been a really positive move for all of them, I think, after such a run of tragedies.'

His father had died of cancer? Oh, no...

Annie straightened up and smiled. 'Still, that's all in the past now, and he's got something to look forward to.'

'I think it's a little soon to assume that,' she said quickly, trying to cut off the matchmaking look in Annie's eyes before it took hold too firmly, but Annie just smiled.

'Well, we'll just have to wait and see,' she murmured, but then the kettle whistled, to Livvy's relief, and Annie turned off the gas, reached for some mugs and made everyone a drink, and—for now at least—she was off the hook.

It was warming up to be a scorching hot day, and by eleven o'clock they'd packed everything up and were heading back towards the clifftop.

'We're having a barbecue,' Ed said, falling into step beside them as they got to the top. 'Want to come?'

'Yeah, that would be great,' Matt said. 'Livvy?'

'Yes, Olivia, please, *please* come?' Amber squealed, and she looked at Ed.

'Did you mean me, too?'

'Well, yes, of course,' Ed said, as if it was a foregone conclusion that she'd be coming if they did. 'Unless you don't want to come?'

'No, I— That would be lovely, but you won't have catered for me.'

He laughed as if she'd said something hilarious. 'We don't cater, Livvy. We throw stuff on the barbecue until people stop eating. You'll be fine.'

'Matt?'

'Yes. Absolutely, yes.'

'Well, in that case—thank you, that would be lovely.'

Amber squealed again and grabbed her hand, bouncing up and down on the end of her arm like a yo-yo, and she had to laugh, but deep in the pit of her stomach was lodged a nugget of fear that meeting all these lovely people had been a huge, huge mistake, one she might well regret for the rest of her life.

She was sitting on the grass in the cool, dappled shade of a birch tree, the leaves whispering in the light breeze coming off the sea, and Annie wandered over and sat beside her, snatching a moment of peace.

She'd brought cold drinks with her, and Livvy took hers and sat back with a sigh.

'Thank you. This shade is just lovely.'

'It is, isn't it? So, how are you getting on in the ED? I still miss it in a way, but I wouldn't trade it for the world.'

She laughed, hoping it didn't sound too hollow. 'I can understand that. Why swap your children for the ritual abuse of a Friday night?'

Annie chuckled. 'I have to say I don't miss that at all. I don't remember a single one that wasn't hideous.'

'No, last Friday was awful,' she said. 'We had a girl who'd taken ecstasy. She's alive, but she's still in PICU and her parents are beside themselves.' She looked across at Annie thoughtfully. 'So, on the subject of daughters, since you have two, any idea where I can take Amber for a new favourite dress?'

Annie frowned. 'I imagine we're talking party dress here?'

'I have no idea. Probably.'

'There's a little boutique near the seafront that has a children's section. It just depends how special, but they aren't outrageous and they have some lovely stuff. I've bought things for Grace and Chloe, and Kate got her wedding dress there when she and Sam got married. Have you met Kate?'

She shook her head. 'No. I'm not a mum,' she said, stifling the little pang, 'so I don't mix in the same circles. I'm just a lowly registrar with a very full-time job.'

Annie gave her an odd look. 'You don't need to be a mum, Livvy. We're all still ourselves.'

Which was all very well, but since the entire day from the moment they'd hit the beach had been all about the children, she'd felt slightly marginalised. Not that anyone had been anything but lovely to her but, still, she felt as if she didn't quite belong—

'Look out!'

She glanced up, saw the ball heading for her and lifted her arms to catch it and throw it back.

'Nice save,' Matt said with a laugh, and kicked it back towards the children.

'It's lovely to see them all together,' she said wistfully. 'You and Ed are very lucky. How long have you been together?'

'Five years?'

'But—the girls...'

'They aren't his—although you'd never know. He adores them, and he's a brilliant stepdad. Their biological father doesn't even know they exist, and frankly that's a good thing, because they don't need him. Ed's a better father he could ever be.'

Livvy looked across the garden to where Ed and Matt were playing football with the children. So Ed was a stepfather, as well as a father, and that was obviously a huge success, but then they'd had their own children, too. If she'd had the sense to harvest some eggs, maybe she and Matt could have been in the same situation, and she could have helped him to bring up his children and her own. Not that she'd be a better mother than Jules, of course not, but she'd have given it everything she had—

But it wasn't going to happen, and there was no point wallowing in it. She'd done enough of that in the last twenty-four hours.

She pulled up a bit of grass and fiddled with it for a moment, then looked up and saw Annie watching her thoughtfully.

'So—where do you and Matt go from here?'

She shrugged. 'Nowhere, really. I'm just taking every day as it comes, and if Matt's in my life for a while that's amazing, and if not, well, I'm sure I'll cope.'

'But he loves you,' Annie said softly, her voice shocked.

She stared at her. 'No, he doesn't.'

'Yes, he does. Of course he does! Haven't you noticed the way he looks at you?'

She felt her eyes fill, and looked away. 'He doesn't love me, Annie. He's still in love with Jules. He always will be. He's just taking the edge off his loneliness, but that's fine. I know that, and so am I.'

She got to her feet, brushing the little bits of grass off her dress and slipping her feet back into her shoes. 'It's time I was going. I've got stuff to do before tomorrow, and I'm on an early shift. Thank you for a lovely day. It's been really nice to meet you.'

Annie stood up and hugged her. 'You, too. And anytime you fancy a coffee or a chat, just come and find me. I'm always around. Maybe you and Matt could come for a meal one evening. Or we could get my mother to babysit and come to you and bring the food. That might be better. I know Matt feels guilty for relying on his mother, and I've got the T-shirt for that one, too, so—whatever, talk to him and come up with a date.'

'But I—'

'Come up with a date for what?'

Matt's arm settled round her shoulders, easing her up against his side as if it was the most natural thing in the world.

Did he love her? Really?

'I've invited you both for a meal,' Annie was saying. 'Whenever you like. Are you giving Livvy a lift home? You can leave the children here, if you like.'

He met her eyes, his thoughtful. 'I was going to suggest you come back with us. The kids could do with a shower to get the sand off, but then Amber's desperate to talk dresses with you. I think she'd like to show you her wardrobe, but I can take you home if you'd rather.'

It was the Amber thing that did it.

Not the warmth of his body against hers, the tender look, the open invitation in his eyes.

Just Amber, a little girl who didn't have a mummy any more.

She'd made her a promise, and she couldn't back out now, even if she did feel a sudden and almost overwhelming urge to escape from all the cosy domesticity and get her defences back in place.

'OK. Just for a little while, then. I can always walk home, it's not far.'

CHAPTER NINE

THE 'LITTLE WHILE' stretched on into the evening, ending with them sitting on the balcony outside his bedroom, sipping ice-cold fizzy water and staring out over the sea.

'Good day?' he asked softly, and she nodded.

'Lovely day,' she said, and it had been, even if it had left an ache of longing in its wake.

'Amber's so excited about you taking her shopping. Are you sure you can cope with it?'

That made her chuckle. 'She's not quite five, Matt. I think we'll be fine. And she's absolutely right, her favourite dress is very beautiful.'

'It's a bit too beautiful, really. She can't wear it nearly as often as she'd like to. If you could find something a bit more practical but just as lovely, then she could get more use out of it.'

'I'll see what we can find. And I'll make sure it's got room for growth.'

'Oh, yes, please, so we don't have to do this again for *years*!' he said with a laugh.

'I can't promise years, Matt, that's unrealistic, but I'll do my best. Annie suggested a little boutique down by the prom. I'll track it down and have a look before I take her.'

He shifted round and studied her thoughtfully. 'You're taking this very seriously.'

'Of course I am. A pretty dress is a *serious thing*, Matt,' she said lightly. 'Ask your daughter.'

His lips twitched. 'No, thank you. I'm in enough trouble for my inability to understand as it is. Frankly, you're welcome to the job.' He reached out and took her hand, touching it to his lips, his voice suddenly serious. 'Thank you for today. I'm sure you had much better things to do than hang out with a bunch of rowdy children.'

'No, I didn't,' she said honestly, because how could she lie to him? There was nothing she'd needed to do, nothing that wouldn't wait. Well, her laundry, but that was a perennial problem and one she could deal with when she got home.

His grip on her hand tightened in a gentle squeeze. 'It's getting chilly out here. Let's go and lie on the bed,' he murmured.

'We can't!'

He smiled. 'Yeah, we can. We can still see the sea, and it's just a bit more private.'

She didn't want to. Not really, not under the eyes of Jules, watching from the top of the chest of drawers, but they went back inside and it wasn't there.

'It's gone,' she said, staring at the space where it had been, and Matt nodded.

'Yes. It's in the playroom, on the wall. I decided Amber needed to see it more than I did, and I'd stopped talking to it—to her. I used to tell her everything, ask her how to cope with stuff, and I realised I've stopped doing that now, because if I want to talk to someone, I talk to you. There'll always be a bit of me that belongs to her, but it's getting smaller every day, and there's another bit of me that I didn't even know existed that you seem to have claimed. I don't know quite how it happened, or when, but it has.'

His smile was tender, and he drew her into his arms and kissed her, just a simple, gentle kiss that made her eyes well with tears.

They lay down, and she snuggled into his side and lay staring out through the huge wall of glass, her eyes unfocused, her thoughts tracking back to last night and her fears.

'Will you tell me something honestly?' she said quietly.

'Yes, of course I will. What is it?'

'You don't think I'm only interested in you because you've got children, do you?'

For a moment he didn't speak and her heart nearly stopped, but then he sighed softly and pressed his lips to her hair.

'No. No, I don't. It did cross my mind for a moment last night, but then I thought about it, and it's just not you. You're much too considerate of others, much too thoughtful and caring—so, no, I don't think you want me for my children, because you're not a user. And besides, I practically had to drag you down to the beach to meet them, so if anything I was more worried that you *didn't* want them, but then when I saw you with Amber I stopped worrying about it.'

She shrugged. 'How could I not want them? They're lovely children. They're a real credit to you.'

He gave a soft laugh. 'I can't take any credit for

that. It's been a joint effort, we've all muddled through somehow, and I'm just happy we seem to have come out of it as well as we have. And this cuts both ways, you know. You could be thinking that the only interest I have in you is that my children would benefit hugely from having a mother, because they would, of course. And I know they've got my mother and Juliet's sister, but it's not the same.'

'No. No, I don't suppose it is, and I'm sure you're right, they would benefit from a mother figure, but it won't be me.'

'Why won't it?'

His question was softly voiced, reaching down into the heart of her pain. She turned her head and met his eyes, sure he'd see the sadness that must be lurking in hers.

'It's too soon for you, and anyway I'm not a good choice, Matt. You should find someone else.'

'Maybe I don't want someone else. Maybe I want you.'

'No, you don't, you just want company. And besides, I still haven't been signed off by the oncology team and the breast surgeon.'

'Stop worrying about your cancer. It was stage I, and it's unlikely to come back, and even if it does, they can do far more for cancer now, and new advances are being made every day. And anyway, I take it you're still having regular screening?'

'Yes, and I will do for a while, I guess. I've got a mammogram in a week and a bit, and then hopefully the oncology team will sign me off and I'll be done, apart from the yearly mammograms, but there's still the joy of another five years of tamoxifen, just to be on the safe side, so even if I decided then that I wanted children, I probably couldn't have them because I'd been on it too long, so you'll never be able to have any more with me, and you might want to, so you should be with someone who can give them to you. You're a natural father—'

'Why would I need more children? I'm more than happy with my two. If I had none, I'd still want you. It's not about the children. It's about us. And you still haven't answered my question.'

'What question?'

'Do you think I'm only interested in you as a mother for my children?'

She stared at him, a little stunned because it had never occurred to her. 'No. No, of course not! I think you're lonely, and we're attracted to each other and I fill a void in your life.'

'You do more than that for me. Much more.'

'No,' she said, her voice gentle but firm. 'No, Matt, I don't, and I can't.'

She looked away, unable to hold his intense gaze. 'I need to go home. It's getting dark.'

She climbed off the bed and he followed her, his bare feet silent as they went down the stairs.

'Let me call you a taxi. I don't like the idea of you walking home alone.'

'Matt, I'll be fine.'

'Yes, you will, because you're going in a taxi.' He pulled out his phone and ordered one, then turned her gently into his arms.

'You mean so much more to me than just filling a void, Livvy,' he said softly. 'Much, much more. I—'

She pressed a finger to his lips and broke away before he could say any more, needing to get away from him because she needed him so much, wanted what he was dangling in front of her so badly that it was a physical ache, and she was sure his next words would have been 'I love you'. And that she really, really didn't want to hear. Not now, with her five-year check hanging over her.

'I'll wait outside for the taxi,' she said, pulling the door open and stepping out, her sandals in her hand, bag over her shoulder, and he sighed and followed her, sitting beside her on the garden wall as they waited for the taxi to come.

'Olivia, don't shut me out.'

'I'm not,' she lied. 'I just don't want to be any more than that to you. I don't want it to get any deeper, I don't want any expectations or promises or talk of the future. I can't deal with it. One day at a time, Matt. That's all. That's all it can ever be.'

He didn't say anything, but she could feel the tension coming off him in waves, and she heaved a silent sigh of relief when the taxi drew up.

He leant through the window, gave the taxi driver her address and paid him before he had a chance to stop her, and then closed the door behind her, his hand lifted in a silent farewell.

As the taxi pulled away, she'd never felt so lonely in her life...

Why? Why was she shutting him out?

He felt an ache in the centre of his chest, an ache he hadn't felt for two years.

Stupid. She hadn't died, she'd just told him she didn't want him as much as he'd hoped, as much as he wanted her. But it didn't add up. None of it added up. She was backing away from him, and at the same time she'd promised Amber she'd help her choose a dress, and she'd spent ages with her, delving through her clothes. He'd heard them talking and laughing in her bedroom, and when he'd looked in they'd been sitting on the floor in a pile of clothes, sorting through them, and they were both smiling.

Why do that? Why lead Amber on if she didn't want to be part of their lives? Why lead him on?

Except she hadn't, and he'd all but dragged her to the beach today. She hadn't wanted to go, and now Amber was looking starry-eyed and it was all going to end in tears.

He swore, silently and viciously, and for the first time in ages he opened a bottle of wine, poured himself a hefty glass and went into the playroom.

Jules was looking down at him, her smile ripping a hole in his heart, and he walked out, went up to his bedroom and was instantly surrounded by Livvy, her scent lingering in the air.

He went out onto the balcony and sat down, just to get away from the reminders of the woman who'd said she didn't want him.

No. She hadn't said that. She'd said she didn't want to talk about the future. She wanted to take it one day at a time.

That's all it can ever be.

Could he do that? Take it literally one day at a time, never looking ahead, never allowing himself to dream?

He gave a hollow laugh, because it was so far from what he wanted that it was almost funny.

Didn't really have a choice, though, did he, not the

way she'd left it? But that was fine. One day at a time, he'd woo her, show her how good it could be, tell her without words how much he loved her, and hopefully he'd win her round, convince her that it would be OK, that there were no certainties in life and you couldn't live in a vacuum just waiting for the axe to fall, you had to get on with it and grab life while you had the chance.

And Amber? Should he let Livvy take her shopping, or should he protect his vulnerable little daughter from any further potential hurt? It was OK for him to take the risk, but his daughter? A tiny part of him, instantly crushed, thought that she would make a brilliant secret weapon, a way to break down Livvy's defences and let them all into her heart, but that was unfair on Amber, unfair on Livvy and so morally corrupt it sickened him that he'd even thought it.

His eyes prickled, and he tipped the wine over the balcony, went back into the bedroom and lay down, resting his head against the stack of pillows where they'd talked about the future that they'd never have.

Well, he'd see about that. It would be tough, but he'd do it. He'd done tough, he understood it, and one thing he wasn't was a quitter.

One day at a time…

She got up at the crack of dawn on Monday morning for her early shift, had a brisk shower and gave herself an even brisker talking-to.

She'd cried half the night, and her eyes were puffy, the whites reddened, and she looked like death warmed up.

She couldn't even blame it on the heat, because it had been cooler overnight, but she could hide it with make-up. Not enough to make it obvious, just enough to take the edge off, and she'd caught the sun so hopefully that would help, too.

Apparently not. Sam took one look at her and raised an eyebrow.

'Heavy night?'

'Ha-ha,' she said. 'I didn't sleep well. So, what's the plan?'

'You're in Resus with me. A car's gone off the road and the driver's impaled on some fencing. If they get him in, we'll need Matt down here, so he's on standby and we've alerted the blood bank. In the meantime, there's a patient who was brought in earlier with a drug overdose who needs monitoring. We're waiting for a bed for him. Otherwise it's quiet.'

'OK,' she said, although it was far from OK because Matt was the last person she wanted to see and for once she wished she hadn't been put in Resus. A nice little day in cubicles would have suited her fine.

In the event, Matt didn't come down, because the man impaled on fencing died at the scene from massive blood loss, so she was spared the ordeal of being professional when all she really wanted to do was throw herself into his arms and cry her eyes out and tell him she'd lied, she did want him, she wanted him desperately.

No! Stop it!

Somehow she got through the day, and she only had another hour till the end of her shift when the PA burst into life. 'Adult trauma call, ten minutes.'

Please, not soft-tissue injuries.

It was, of course. She went to Resus, and Sam briefed the team.

'OK, this is a woman in her thirties, she's fallen out of an upstairs window through the glass roof of a lean-to greenhouse, so multiple injuries and blood loss. She was stabilised at the scene, but we're going to need X-rays to trace all the glass, possibly a CT scan if we can get her stable enough, and she's going to need a lot of soft-tissue work, so I've alerted Matt Hunter, he's on his way down now, and I've got the blood bank on standby and we may need to involve Plastics, too.

'But number one, nobody pull out any glass unless it's obviously very superficial, because we don't want her suddenly bleeding out, and you all need to double-glove and be very careful of the glass splinters. She could be covered in them.'

He went through the team, allocating tasks, and then the paramedics wheeled her in and did the handover.

'This is Sarah Field, thirty-two years old, fallen through a window and landed on her right side on a glass roof and through it onto greenhouse staging. GCS fourteen at the scene, now fifteen, BP one ten over sixty-five, sats ninety-eight per cent...'

She tried to concentrate, but at the front of her mind was Matt, arriving any moment now.

How would he be with her? Distant? Wary?

Professional. Of course he was. He didn't look at her, just at the patient, most particularly her right arm, which was covered with a large pressure dressing.

She was lying on her left side, the least damaged side, and he went round and introduced himself to her, scanning her body quickly as he did so before lifting the dressing off her arm where the glass had sliced a huge flap of skin and muscle almost off.

'I need to take this first, is that OK?' he asked, and Sam nodded.

'We'll work our way round the rest,' Sam said, and looked up at her. 'Livvy, can you take her head and face, please?'

Which put her right next to Matt. Tough. She ignored him, and bent over so the woman could see her.

'Hello, Sarah, my name is Olivia, I'm a doctor. Is it OK if I have a look at your face? There are some little bits of glass that I can lift out, and we need to clean off the some of the little splinters that are on the surface and then we can get a better look at you.'

'OK,' she said weakly, and Livvy started work, carefully lifting away all the visible glass fragments. A nurse was doing the same thing on her neck and shoulder, another working through her hair with a very fine comb, and her clothes were carefully cut away to expose multiple small lacerations.

'There's a flap here on her scalp,' the nurse said, and Livvy leant over at the same time as Matt, and their heads brushed.

He glanced at her, his eyes neutral. 'Sorry—may I?'

She pulled back, leaving it to him, and he issued some instructions and returned to the arm, giving her back her space.

It took nearly an hour, but finally the splinters were out, the wounds were stitched or steri-stripped or glued, and Matt had reattached the blood supply to the flap on her arm, dealt with several other wounds including the scalp flap, and was ready to take her to Theatre to start the delicate reconstruction of her arm muscles.

And finally, after all that time, he looked up and met her eyes.

'Good job on her face,' he murmured. 'Well done.'

She felt a strange little burst of pride, and smiled. 'Thank you. Good luck with the arm. I have no idea how you'll deal with such a huge flap.'

'Want to find out?'

She stared at him. 'What—in Theatre?'

'Why not? You must be about to go off, I know you were on an early, and you're interested, you said you aren't sure if surgery is for you—scrub in and find out. You can assist.'

'But I—'

'But nothing. Come on, I don't want to hang about. Are you in or out?'

'In,' she said, unconvinced about the wisdom of it but fascinated about the surgery, and in the end she was glad she'd gone because it had been a joy to watch him work.

Every tiny nerve, every muscle bundle was carefully lined up and held with the finest sutures, and by the time he'd finished the patient's arm looked almost normal.

'That's amazing,' she said, and he smiled wryly.

'Just doing my job, Livvy, and it was a clean cut. She'll always have a scar, that can't be avoided, but hopefully she'll have full function of all the muscles and nerves, given time. And it's her right arm, so it matters even more. At least we seem to have got all the glass out of her, and once she's come round and she's stable she'll have a CT scan to check for random fragments that we've missed, because she's peppered with it and we're bound to have missed something.' He stripped off his gloves and gown, peeled off his mask and hat and lobbed them in the bin. 'So, what are you doing now?'

She glanced up at the theatre clock. 'I was going to go and see if that boutique had any dresses for Amber, but it might be closed.'

'Are you still happy to do that?'

She stared at him in astonishment. 'Of course I am! I promised her, Matt. I can't go back on that, and I wouldn't want to.'

'So it's just me, then, that you've got a problem with.'

His eyes were unguarded now, and she could see the hurt in them. Hurt she'd caused.

'It's not you, Matt. It's just—I'm always a bit antsy coming up to my mammogram. It brings it all back, makes me nervous.'

'So why not just say that? Why give me all the other excuses?'

'Because I don't want you to be hurt.'

His soft huff of laughter drifted over her silently, but he didn't answer. He didn't need to, because she was hurting him anyway and she could see it in his eyes.

'Go on, go and see if the boutique's still open, and let me know how you get on. I need to go into Recovery and deal with my patient.'

'OK. And thanks again for letting me assist. It was amazing.'

'You're welcome. Call me later.'

'I will.'

It was still open, and the proprietor was wonderful.

'I'm looking for a new favourite dress for a friend's

little daughter,' she explained, 'and she hates pink and she doesn't want anything with a unicorn on it.'

The woman laughed and led her through a doorway to the back of the shop.

'There you are. We have some very pretty summer party dresses for little girls, and there are lots that aren't pink and don't have unicorns,' she said, and showed Livvy a whole rail to choose from.

Some were incredibly fancy and fragile, others much more robust and equally pretty. And as the woman had said, there were lots that weren't pink and she didn't see a single unicorn.

'Oh, they're gorgeous!' she said. 'I'll need to bring her.'

'Of course you will. How big is she?'

'Oh.' She waved her hand up and down, trying to guess. 'So high? I'm not sure. She's five in September, and she's quite slender and leggy. And she needs growing room.'

'OK. I'm sure we'll find something. Do you have a budget?'

She shook her head. 'No. My only criterion is something she can wear more often than the one covered in fine net that she's outgrown and hasn't worn nearly enough to make her happy!'

'That's easy. Bring her when you can.'

'Thursday afternoon? I finish work early then.'

'That's fine. I'll look forward to meeting her. Will her mother be coming?'

Livvy swallowed. 'No, that's why I'm doing this. She doesn't have a mother. She died.'

'Oh, how sad,' the woman said softly. 'We'll have to find her something really special.'

* * *

By the time she'd picked Amber up from Matt's house on Thursday afternoon the little girl was positively fizzing with excitement, and the moment she saw the rows of dresses hanging up her eyes were like saucers.

'They're all so pretty!'

'I've pulled a few out for you,' the proprietor said, handing Livvy half a dozen hangers, and they went into the dressing room and Amber tried them all on.

Some were too tight, some too loose, one too short, but then there was one that fitted perfectly but still allowed room for growth, without a trace of pink or a single unicorn, and yet delicately pretty and made of pure, soft cotton with a cotton lining.

It even had a matching cotton cardigan in the exact same soft slate blue as Amber's eyes, with pearly buttons and a picot edging, and watching Amber's delighted reaction when she saw herself in the mirror, Livvy felt her eyes well with tears.

'I think we're probably going to take this one,' she said to the lady, and she smiled.

'I had a feeling you might say that. It's a good choice. It's machine washable, too, and it's pre-shrunk.' She lowered her voice. 'There is another one, which is in the sale, and if she's about to start school she's likely to get lots of party invitations. It's not as dressy, probably not a "favourite" dress, but I think it might suit her.'

It did, and Amber loved it, too, but her little face was troubled.

'If I have this one, does it mean I can't have the other one?'

Livvy shook her head. 'No, sweetheart. It means you can have a favourite dress for parties and more special occasions, and another favourite dress for when it's not quite so important.'

'I can have both?' she squealed, bubbling over with excitement, and Livvy scooped her up and hugged her. Her little arms snaked around her neck, clinging tight, and then she squirmed to be put down and rushed back over to the mirror for another look.

Livvy turned to the saleswoman, surprised to see tears in her eyes, and she felt the prickling echo of them in her own.

'Well, I think that's a success,' the woman said briskly, and Livvy smiled at her.

'I think so, too. Thank you so, so much.'

'It's the least I could do,' she said, and busied herself with wrapping the dresses in tissue.

'They're beautiful. Thank you so much, Livvy. What do I owe you?'

'Nothing! They're a present.'

'I can't let you do that—'

'Yes, you can. Please. It was a pleasure, just to see the look on her face.'

He let out a little huff of laughter and gave up, pulling her into his arms and hugging her. 'You're a star, do you know that?'

'Absolutely,' she said lightly, but her eyes were glittering and he could tell just from looking at her that she'd found the whole thing very moving.

Such a simple thing, and yet not, because she'd probably never have a daughter of her own, not even a stepdaughter if she stuck to her guns. And that would be a tragedy. He swallowed the lump in his throat and hugged her again.

'I've missed you. We need to make another date.'

'Not yet. I'm working all weekend, and I've got to go to the Audley on Monday for my mammogram.'

'I thought you were working in London before?'

'I was, but after I was diagnosed I switched to the Audley so I could be at home for my treatment. It seemed sensible. But maybe later in the week?'

He nodded. 'I'll ask my mother if she can have the children. How about Friday? I'm not working on Saturday so I can stay over.'

'Friday's fine. I'm not working on Saturday, either. Talk to your mother and let me know.'

The weekend was hellish, but she went over to her parents' on Sunday evening after her shift ended and spent the night with them, then went into the hospital for her mammogram and met up with her mother again for lunch before driving home.

It would be two weeks before she got the result, so she put it out of her mind and tackled her overdue chores. She did a load of laundry and hung it out to dry in the conservatory, blitzed the house, watered the garden and then sat down on the bench with a cold drink just as Matt phoned.

'Hi, how are you?'

'Fine. I've been doing housework, which is deadly dull. How about you?'

He chuckled, which made her smile. 'I'm fine. Amber insisted on wearing her second favourite dress to go round to my mother's for lunch yesterday, and she was distraught because Charlie spilt his drink over it, but d'you know what? It's come out of the washing machine looking as good as new, so I just wanted to thank you again, because it was a brilliant choice and if it had been ruined, life wouldn't have been worth living.'

She laughed at that, wondering how stressed he'd been, visualising the tears and hysteria from Amber.

'Does she know it's OK?'

'Oh, yes. It's back in her wardrobe and she's happy again. So how did the mammogram go?'

'Oh, hellish as ever. I call it the crusher, but it's fine, it's saved my life once, I have no issues with it. My parents send their love, by the way. I spent the night with them and had lunch with Mum today.'

'How are they?'

'Fine.' Apart from worrying about her and quizzing her about her relationship with him, but she wasn't going to tell him that.

'Did they give you a hard time about me?'

She laughed. Apparently she didn't need to tell him. 'Only a little. I told them about taking Amber shopping, and they seemed to think that was a bit serious. I told them it wasn't but they looked as if they didn't believe me.'

He didn't answer that, just grunted, told her his mother could babysit on Friday and then changed the subject to a patient he'd had in a while ago who'd come back for further surgery. 'I've got to take him to Theatre again tomorrow. I wondered if you'd like to scrub in. It could be quite interesting.'

'I'd love to, but I'll have to see how busy it is. I don't suppose James will take kindly to me messing off in the middle of a shift.'

Ludicrously busy was the answer.

Far too busy to leave the department, too busy even

for a proper break, just a snatched sandwich or a gulp of water between patients, and it set the tone for the rest of the week.

Still, she'd see him on Friday, and they spoke in the evening a couple of times.

And then on Friday, she got back to the house to find a recall letter from the breast clinic, and her world went into meltdown.

CHAPTER TEN

SHE WASN'T ANSWERING her phone.

There had to be a perfectly good reason, like she was watering the garden or she'd nipped out to the corner shop or she was in the shower or drying her hair—any one of a dozen perfectly plausible reasons, but he had a cold, sick feeling in the pit of his stomach and he knew—he just *knew*—there was something wrong.

He'd been trying to get hold of her for half an hour. Nobody dried their hair for that long. And the last time his calls hadn't been picked up—

Stop it! She's not dead.

But the fear in his gut was growing, and there was nothing he could do about it because his mother wasn't feeling well so she couldn't babysit, so he had no way of getting to Livvy to see if she was all right.

Unless…

He spotted Ed on the clifftop, heading home with the dog, and he ran out and hailed him.

'Can you do me a massive favour? Can you babysit the kids for ten minutes? They're in bed asleep but Mum can't make it, she's not well, and I can't get hold of Livvy and I'm supposed to have picked her up twenty minutes ago, and I'm a bit worried.'

'Yes, of course I can. Go. Ring me if there's a problem.'

He nodded, dived back in, picked up his keys and drove straight to her house. Her car wasn't outside the front and her bedroom window was closed, as if she hadn't got home.

Odd. If she'd been held up at work she would have called him, or got someone else to.

He peered through the letter box and saw nothing, so he tried her phone again, and he could hear it ringing.

She must have left it behind—except she never left her phone behind. And the door from the kitchen to the conservatory was open.

The garden. She was in the garden.

His shoulders dropping with relief, he drove round to the back of the house, hitched up on the kerb and got out.

'Livvy?'

Silence, apart from a familiar noise, the slight, rhythmic creak of the swing. And she hadn't answered him, even though she must have heard, but at least she was alive. He grabbed the top of the gate, hauled himself up and dropped to the ground on the other side.

Her car was there, neatly parked in the car port, and he ducked under the wisteria into the garden and found her huddled on the bench, her eyes vacant and red-rimmed, and his heart turned over.

'Hey, what's happened?' he asked softly, and she looked up and met his eyes and he felt sick.

He sat down and gathered her up against his chest, her body resisting, shudders running through it, and lying on the floor at her feet was a crumpled letter from the Audley breast clinic.

They found something.

He felt the air leave his lungs in a rush, and he cradled her head against his shoulder and rocked her gently.

'Did you get a recall?'

She nodded. 'They found something,' she said in a tiny voice. 'I have to go back.'

'When?'

'Monday.'

Damn. Why was it the weekend? Why was it always *the weekend?*

'Matt, why are you here?'

He pressed a kiss to her hair, his heart welling over. 'Because I was supposed to be taking you out for dinner,' he said gently, 'but my mother's not well and I've been trying to ring you and you didn't pick up.'

'Oh. Sorry. I forgot,' she said, her voice hollow.

She was in shock, her body cold and stiff, her lips bloodless.

'That's OK. Come on, let's get you some things, you're coming back to my house for the weekend.'

'No. Just leave me—'

'No. I'm not leaving you, Livvy, never again. You're coming back with me. What do you need? Underwear, toothbrush, deodorant, clothes—'

'Tamoxifen,' she said, and then a sob tore its way out of her body and he squeezed his eyes shut and held her.

She didn't give in, though, just crushed it all down as he guessed she always did and lifted her head and sniffed.

'Matt, I'm OK, really. I don't want—I can't—'

'Yes, you can. Come on, get up and we'll go and get you some things together and then we'll go back to mine so we can talk.'

'I don't want to talk. There's nothing to say.'

'There's a lot to say, a lot I should already have said, but that's fine, we've got time. Come on.'

He got up and tugged her gently to her feet, gathered her things together in the bedroom and bathroom, picked up her bag, locked up the house and took her home.

Ed was sitting in the porch by the open door, the dog lying at his feet, and he took one look at Matt's face when he got out of the car and stood up.

'Anything I can do?' he asked quietly, but there wasn't so he shook his head.

'No. Thanks for staying. I can't talk now.'

Ed nodded, told him to call if he needed anything and left him to it.

'Come on, Livvy. Come inside.'

He was going to nag her until she went, so she got out of the car, her body working on autopilot, and he shepherded her into the house and took her up to his bedroom. She crawled onto the bed without a word, and he lay down and pulled her into his arms.

She resisted for a moment, then burrowed into him, clinging to him like a lifeline, too weak to fight it any longer because she needed him so much and it was all going to go horribly wrong—

'Hey, it'll be all right,' he murmured.

'No, it won't. It's come back, I know it has. Why am I here? You don't need this, Matt. You don't need me—'

'Yes, I do. I love you, Livvy, and I know you love me, too.'

Her eyes welled with tears because this was what she'd been dreading, the moment when it all imploded.

'No! No, don't say that. You can't say that. You can't love me, I won't let you.'

'You can't stop me, my darling. I love you, and I don't have a choice about that—and I don't want a choice. I don't want anybody else, I want you.'

'But I could die—'

'Yes, you could. We all could. We all will. I still want you. I still love you, and I always will, for as long as I have you, and that's not negotiable because there's nothing I can do about it. You mean the world to me, and whatever happens in the future I'm here for you. We can do this, Livvy. We can face this together, whatever it is, whatever they've found. It's probably nothing, but even if it isn't, I'm here, and I'm staying.'

'No. That's not fair to you.'

'Life isn't fair. If it was fair Jules wouldn't have died, and my father wouldn't have got cancer, and I wouldn't have a job and neither would you, because we wouldn't be needed. It's not fair, but it's what we have, and we have to make the best of every single moment of it, and that means staying together.'

'But what about the children? What about Amber—?' Her voice cracked, and she felt his arms tighten.

'Let's not worry about them yet, let's get you sorted first and find out what's going on and deal with it, OK? Because it's probably nothing.'

She sat up and sniffed, and he stuffed a tissue into her hand and she blew her nose and lay down again, her head on his shoulder, determined not to cry.

'I keep telling myself that. It's happened before. I had a cyst and they got all excited about it, but—you know, it's just there, the threat, it's always there, and I ignore it and just get on with life and then it sneaks up and bites me when I'm not looking. That's why I was so crabby, because I knew it could happen, but I never expected it—'

'I know. I never expected Jules to die, I didn't expect to lose my father in his early sixties, but that doesn't mean I wish I'd never known them, never loved them. Marry me, Livvy. Let me be here for you. Let me love you.'

Her heart turned over, the longing to say yes overwhelming her. 'No. I can't. I won't. I'm not going to marry you because you feel sorry for me, or because you're lonely, or because you want to atone for not being there for Jules when she died—'

'That's not why I'm asking you to marry me! I don't feel sorry for you. I *hate* what's happened to you, what's happening now, but it's not pity. And I don't want to marry you because I'm lonely, and it's certainly not because I feel guilty about Jules, because I don't. There was nothing anyone could have done. Even if I'd been there, she would probably have died, or at best been in a vegetative state, and she would have hated that. I want to marry you because *I love you.*'

She shook her head, trying not to listen, shutting out the words she couldn't bear to hear because she wanted it so much, wanted him so much—

'Please don't love me, Matt, please. I can't bear the thought of you being hurt.'

'Then don't hurt me,' he said simply. 'Let me in, Livvy. Let me help you, let me be there for you, love me back, because that's all I need. I don't need guarantees, I don't need certainty, I just need you, for as long as I can have you, whether that's six weeks or sixty years.'

She turned her head and stared at him.

'Sixty years?'

'Why not?'

'You'll be ninety-six.'

'Yeah. If I'm lucky. I'm working on the principle I could live that long, so I'm taking care of myself, but I don't expect it, I'm not banking on it, and I'm not putting anything off until tomorrow because it may not be there.'

He stroked her hair, his fingers gentle as he brushed it away from her face.

'I know the future's uncertain, but you're denying us the certainty of happiness for the uncertain possibility that your cancer could come back, maybe now, maybe years down the line, maybe never. I'll take that risk, Livvy. I'll take it hands down over losing you for nothing, because I love you,' he murmured, and then his lips found hers, his kiss tender and—steadfast?

Odd word, but it popped into her head and made her want to cry, because that was just him all over.

'Make love to me,' she whispered, and he got up and locked the bedroom door and came back to her, pulling her to her feet and kissing her again, his mouth coaxing, tender.

He undressed her slowly, and she turned her head and looked out at the darkening sky and silver sea beyond the open doors.

'Aren't you going to close the curtains?'

'No. Nobody can see in. We're too high, and anyway, the lights aren't on.'

He stripped off his clothes and led her back to the bed, his mouth finding hers again, his touch gentle. His body gleamed silver in the moonlight, and she ran her hand over his skin, feeling the texture of it, more alive than she'd ever been because this moment was so precious, and she wanted to store every moment of it, to save it in her memory bank. Just in case...

She cradled his face in her hands, kissing him back a little desperately, and she felt the nip of his teeth on her lip, the heat of his breath as he explored her body, wringing every drop of sensation out of her.

Their lovemaking was touched with sweetness, but also desperation, a poignant tenderness and honesty that unravelled her, and when it was over he lifted his head and gently wiped the tears from her cheeks.

'Now tell me you don't love me,' he said unevenly, and she bit her lip and turned her head away.

'Come on, Livvy. Tell me you don't love me as much as I love you. Go on, Livvy. Say it.'

'I can't say it.'

'Why? Why can't you say it?'

She turned her head back and stared straight into his eyes.

'Because I do love you,' she whispered, and his eyes filled and he gathered her into his arms and cradled her against his heart.

'Thank you. Thank you for being honest with me at last. I love you, too, Livvy. So very, very much. And we can do this, my love. We'll get there, somehow. It'll be all right.'

Would it? She doubted it. She'd given up on miracles a long, long time ago—but then she hadn't had Matt in her life.

Could she let him love her?

Could she let herself love him, and his children?

Maybe he was right and they didn't have a choice, not about any of it.

* * *

He lifted his hand and stroked the hair back off her face. 'Are you OK?'

She nodded. 'I just want it over. I want to know, whatever it is. It's the not knowing that's so hard.'

'I know. Have you eaten?'

'Eaten?' she said, as if he'd asked her if she could fly, and he laughed softly.

'Yes, eaten. I'm starving. Do you fancy a sandwich?'

'Have you got any hummus and celery or peppers or whatever?'

'I think so. Why don't you have a shower while I go and raid the fridge?'

He closed the curtains then and pulled on his underwear and left her to it, padding downstairs in bare feet to see what he could find, and a few minutes later she appeared, her hair wrapped in a towel, wearing the shirt he'd taken off with the cuffs turned back, and looking unbearably lovely.

'That shirt's never looked so good,' he said with a smile, and she smiled back at him, her eyes sad and wounded still but a little less afraid.

'Did you find hummus?'

'I've found all sorts of things. Shall we eat here?'

She nodded and settled herself on the bar stool. 'Matt, I don't think I should stay. What about the children?'

'What about them? You can use the spare room if you want, but I don't think it's necessary. They're going to have to get used to it.'

'No. Matt, no. I can't do this to you—'

'You're not doing it to me.'

'Or them.'

He looked away, his heart sinking.

'Let's just get through the weekend, eh? I'll call the hospital in the morning and clear my diary for Monday. What time's your appointment?'

'Two, but—'

'OK. I can do that.'

'You don't need to come!'

'Yes, I do. I've said I will, and I will. You're not driving yourself all that way. Do your parents know?'

'No, and I'm not telling them, so please don't.'

'OK. That's fair enough, there's no need to spook them. You can talk to them afterwards, when it's all fine.'

'If.'

'When. Here, have something to eat.'

She didn't know what he told the children the next morning, but Charlie just ran around in his own little world, driving cars along the walls and screeching round the garden making aeroplane noises, and Amber sat at the table in a shady corner of the patio with a colouring book and some pencils and watched her out of the corner of her eye.

She was sitting on Matt's bench hoping that the sun would thaw the cold place inside her, and he'd gone in to make them all a drink and a snack when Amber got up and came over to her, wriggling up onto the bench beside her.

'Why are you sad?' she asked softly, and Livvy felt her heart squeeze.

'I'm not sad, sweetheart, I'm just a little worried about something.'

'Are you sure you're not sad?'

'Yes, I'm sure. What are you colouring?'

'A butterfly. Do you want to help me?'

Yes, but was it a good idea? To bond with her, and let Amber get closer to her—just in case…?

'Would you like me to?'

'Yes, please. It's very beautiful. It'll make you feel better.'

It did, oddly. Not the colouring, although concentrating hard on it was nicely distracting, but the quiet company of this gentle and affectionate little girl was very soothing, and they spent a large part of the day sitting side by side over the colouring book while Matt entertained Charlie and kept supplying them with drinks and snacks.

And that night, after the children were in bed and they'd eaten the curry he'd made for them, he took her to bed and made love to her again, and yet again his gentleness made her cry.

'I'm sorry. I just…'

'I know. It's OK,' he murmured, and held her until she fell asleep.

On Sunday they borrowed the Shackletons' dog, Molly, and went for a walk, down to the harbour and along the river wall. Molly was too big for either of the children to hold, so Matt had her on her lead and walked with Charlie, and Amber slipped her hand into Livvy's and skipped along beside her behind them, pointing out the gaunt ribs of old boats that had sunk in the mud at the edge of the river.

'Daddy said they might have been smugglers,' she said, eyes wide, and Livvy found herself smiling.

They had lunch outside the pub overlooking the harbour, with Molly begging shamelessly, and then walked back up to the house and handed her back to her family, and somehow the rest of the day crawled slowly by.

She couldn't sleep that night, and while Matt was asleep she put his shirt on again and crept out through the doors and sat on the balcony, listening to the faint, distant sound of the sea sucking on the shingle as the tide receded. It was soothing and rhythmical, and if she'd thought she could do it without waking him she would have let herself out and gone down there.

But then he would have woken and been worried, and he didn't deserve that, so she sat and stared into the darkness, watching the lights on a ship moving slowly across her field of view, until finally a pale silver light crept over the edge of the sea and the sky began to lighten.

Monday.

She'd thought it would never come, and now it had, she wished it hadn't.

She heard a faint sound and turned, and he was standing there in the doorway, his hand held out to her. She took it and let him lead her back to bed.

She took the whole day off work, but Matt was in clinic until twelve, which meant she was alone in her house all morning, and of course she was swamped with nerves and dread and negative thoughts that wouldn't leave her alone.

'It'll be nothing,' she kept telling herself, but then Matt pulled up at the gate and she walked out of the front door into his arms and burst into tears.

'I can't do this,' she sobbed, but he just held her for a moment until she'd pulled herself together, handed her a tissue and put her in the car, then slid behind the wheel and reached over to give her hand a reassuring squeeze.

They walked into the breast clinic, she gave her name and the receptionist smiled at her.

'I'll just get the breast-care nurse to come and talk to you,' she said, and she felt the blood drain from her face because this was what had happened before, when she had been diagnosed.

'Livvy? Come and sit down, you're white as a sheet.'

He led her to a chair and sat with his arm around her, and then the breast-care nurse came out, all smiles.

'Hi, Livvy. Don't worry, there are just a few little dots in your left breast and the consultant wants a closer look. They look like cysts, like you had before, but he just wants to be sure, OK? We won't keep you long.'

She nodded, and her hand found its way into Matt's and clung like a limpet until she was called in.

Then called again, and then again, because the consultant still wasn't happy that he'd seen enough.

'I'm sorry. Hopefully that'll be it,' the radiographer said, and she went back out into the waiting room and Matt gathered her into his arms.

'OK?'

'Sort of. You know those olive presses they have to squeeze the oil out?' she said, and he chuckled and dropped a kiss on her lips.

'I'm sorry.'

'Don't be. It's not your fault.'

She was then sent off for an ultrasound, and finally the breast-care nurse showed them into the consultant's office and his smile told her everything she wanted to know.

'Hi, Livvy, sorry about that, but it's good news, it's all fine. Just cysts, the one you had before and a couple of new ones. They're all tiny, but the one that was there before hasn't grown, so we'll keep monitoring them, but I'm absolutely certain they're not cancer, so you can relax.'

Beside her she heard Matt's huff of relief, but she wasn't convinced. It couldn't be that easy—

'Are you sure?'

He smiled patiently. 'Yes, Livvy, I'm sure. You're fine. I'm signing you off. I still want an eye kept on those cysts, but as far as I'm concerned your cancer's gone, there's no sign of it anywhere, the oncology team have discharged you—you're done.'

'And the tamoxifen?'

He shrugged. 'You've had it for five years. You could keep taking it, or you could stop. It's up to you, but it's probably not necessary any more. You're at no more risk now than anybody else.'

'And my fertility?'

He shook his head. 'I can't answer that, because it's not that straightforward and everyone's different, but what I would say is make sure you don't get pregnant for at least six months to allow the tamoxifen to clear your system, and I would recommend you never use any hormonal contraception. Apart from that, all I can say is go away and enjoy your life.'

He stood up and shook her hand, and then Matt's, pausing with a puzzled frown.

'I remember you. Matt Hunter, isn't it?'

'Yes. I remember you, too. Good to see you again—especially with good news.'

He smiled. 'Take care of her. She's very special to us.'

His arm closed round her shoulders, holding her firmly against his side. 'Don't worry, I will. She's very special to me, too.'

He led her out of the room, down the corridor and into his arms.

'I'm OK,' she said, and burst into tears.

He held her close, his eyes firmly shut, somehow keeping his own emotions in check, and then when she lifted her head he kissed away her tears and handed her a tissue.

'You have an unending supply of these,' she said, and he chuckled.

'I do. I have small children. I also have shares in the company.'

'Seriously?'

'No, of course not,' he said, laughing, and her lips tipped into the first proper smile he'd seen for days.

'Will your parents be at home?'

'Maybe. It's Monday, they both finish pretty early.'

'Let's go and see. There's something I want to ask your father, and you need to tell them you've been signed off.'

'I do. They'll be relieved.'

No doubt. He knew he was, but it wasn't over yet because he still had to convince Livvy to let him into her life, and if there was one thing he knew about her, it was just how stubborn she could be, but maybe he could marshal an ally.

They were there, and she walked into the kitchen and told them the good news, and the relief on their faces was a joy to see.

They broke out the champagne—the bottle he'd given Oliver for his birthday, Matt noticed—and he and Livvy had a tiny glass each, him because he was driving, her because she didn't drink now, but this was different, and it needed toasting.

Then the conversation moved on, and he caught Oliver's eye.

'Can I have a word? I've got a patient who you've seen in the past, and there's something I want to run by you. Can we go into your study?'

'What was that all about?'

'Oh, nothing much. Just a mutual patient. Sorry we had to rush away, but Mum's still not feeling amazing and I need to get back to put the kids to bed.'

'That's fine. You can drop me home.'

'No. We need to go straight to mine. I'll get you a taxi home, but maybe we can have supper first. Or you could stay?'

'That's becoming a habit.'

'Not all habits are bad.'

He reached out a hand, and she threaded her fingers through his and he lifted them to his lips. 'Feeling better now?'

She rested her head back and smiled contentedly. 'Much. Tired, though. I spent rather too long sitting on your balcony last night.'

'I know. I was watching you. Why don't you close your eyes and go to sleep? I'll wake you when we get there.'

* * *

Amber ran to her when they walked in, wrapping her arms around her hips and hugging her.

'You're here again! Can we do some more colouring?'

'Darling, it's your bedtime and anyway, I expect Livvy might be tired,' Matt's mother said, her eyes concerned, but Livvy smiled at her.

'I'm fine. Really.'

'Really fine?' she asked, and Livvy realised Matt must have told her.

'Yes. I'm *really* fine,' she said, and then watched as Jane's eyes welled with tears.

'Well, that's wonderful. I'm so pleased. Right, if you don't need me, I'll go home and leave you all to it.'

Matt kissed her. 'Yes, sure. Thank you so much for today. I'm sorry we're so late.'

'Don't be.'

She kissed his cheek, then hugged Livvy and left, and Matt told her to find herself a drink and took the children upstairs.

He was an age, even though he didn't bath them, and sitting in the kitchen near the open door she could hear him and Amber talking. She couldn't hear what they were saying, but there was a little shriek of excitement at one point, and he shushed her, and then she heard the door open and Amber say, 'Please let me ask her!'

'No, Amber. It's better coming from me. Go back to bed.'

She heard a little protest, then his deep murmur, then his footsteps running lightly down the stairs. He came into the kitchen, pushed the door to and walked towards her, his face solemn, and she frowned in puzzlement.

'What was that about? What's better coming from you?'

She didn't know what she was expecting—another dress-buying favour, a trip out, a manicure? But he looked too serious for that.

'Something Amber apparently feels very strongly about, but I thought exposing you to her charm offensive would be emotional blackmail, and I didn't think that was fair because, yes, it affects her and Charlie, but ultimately it's between us, and I need you to feel you can be honest.'

He took her hand, and then to her surprise he went down on one knee, and her heart hitched.

'Are you offering me a piggy-back down a mountain?' she asked, trying to lighten it, but he just shook his head and smiled.

'No. I'm offering you a piggy-back through life, Livvy, because whoever we are, whatever's going on, there are always ups and downs, and we need someone to do that for us, to keep us going when the going gets tough, to lift us up when we're down—you could always return the favour.'

'I don't think I could lift you,' she said unsteadily, but he shook his head, his eyes tender.

'You lift me all the time. In the short time I've known you, you've made me happy in a way I thought I'd never be happy again. You've brought me so much hope, so much joy, so much love, and I want you to give me—to give the children—a chance to give that back to you, to give you some of what you've given us. Will you marry me, Olivia? Not because I feel sorry for you, or because I'm lonely, or because I feel guilty, but because I love you, with all my heart, and I can't bear the thought of not having you in my life, in our lives, because you'll make them so much richer. And I know it won't be easy, marriage never is, you have to take the rough with the smooth, but that's what life's about, and I want to share mine with you for as long as we have, whatever happens and whatever it brings us.'

He lifted her hand, holding it flat against his heart, and his eyes were burning with love.

'Marry me, Livvy. I need you, I love you, and I don't want to spend another day without you. Please don't make me. And if that sounds like emotional blackmail, it isn't meant to. It's just the plain, honest truth.'

She couldn't speak. The tears were welling so fast his beautiful eyes were going out of focus, and she could hardly breathe.

'Y-yes,' she said, and then, just in case that wasn't clear enough, she said it again, lifting his hand to her lips and kissing it. 'Yes. Yes, I'll marry you, I don't want to spend another day without you, either. I love you. All of you, so very, very much.'

Behind him the door opened, and Amber ran in and hugged him.

'I *told* you she'd say yes, Daddy!'

Livvy laughed and swiped away the tears that were streaming down her cheeks, and he got to his feet, Amber in his arms, and handed her a tissue.

'I think I might need more than one. Maybe you should buy the company.'

'Or stop making you cry. That might be better.'

'Not if I'm crying with happiness.'

'Maybe not. Amber, say goodnight to Livvy and

then go up to bed, please. It's way past your bedtime and we have things to talk about.'

'Like the wedding?' she said excitedly.

Livvy smiled at her, knowing how much the little girl was going to love helping them plan the wedding. 'We can talk about the wedding later, Amber,' she said gently. 'There'll be lots of time to do that.'

'But can't we do it now?' she pleaded,

'No. It's late and you're tired and it's time for bed,' he said, and Livvy bent down and kissed her, then holding her hand she led her upstairs and into her room, tucked her into bed and kissed her goodnight.

'I'm glad you said yes. I really wanted you to be my new mummy,' Amber told her, clinging to her hand, and she smiled, her eyes welling again.

'I'm glad I said yes, too, and I'll do my best to be a good mummy to you and Charlie.'

'Can I call you Mummy?'

Oh, heavens. Livvy's eyes overflowed, and she blinked hard. 'I think we need to talk to Daddy about that,' she said, wondering if he might have strong feelings about it.

She kissed Amber again, then stood up and turned, to find Matt standing there, his face awash with emotion.

'Night-night, little one,' he murmured, bending down to kiss his daughter, and then he turned and ushered Livvy out of the room.

'Finally,' he said, shutting the door, and taking her hand he led her through his bedroom and onto the balcony, turned her into his arms and stared down into her eyes.

'You see what I mean about the charm offensive?'

'No. She's delightful. She even—did you hear? She asked if she can call me Mummy.'

'I know. And, yes, of course she can, if you don't mind.'

'Mind? Why should I mind? I was worried about you. You don't feel—well, that it's not my place?'

He shook his head. 'No. She needs a mummy, and I'm only too happy that it's going to be you. But don't be fooled. She can be a tiny bit manipulative. Are you sure you don't feel press-ganged?'

She shook her head, unable to keep the smile off her face. 'I don't feel press-ganged. I just feel wanted.'

'Oh, you're certainly wanted, my darling.' He dropped a tiny kiss on the end of her nose. 'You need to phone your parents and put them out of their misery.'

'How do they know—? Oh, you sneaky thing! That's what you wanted to talk to him about!'

'Of course. You have to do things properly. But there's something I have to do first before I let you go,' he murmured, a slow, sexy smile playing around his mouth as he bent his head and kissed her...

* * * * *

RESISTING HER
RESCUE DOC

ALISON ROBERTS

MILLS & BOON

CHAPTER ONE

How annoying was this?

Apart from a large motorbike that forced its way down the centre of the road, traffic on this coastal route into New Zealand's capital city, Wellington, had suddenly slowed and then come to a complete halt for no obvious reason.

Cooper Sinclair was due to meet his colleagues at the city's rescue helicopter base in just over an hour before he started his new job there tomorrow. He had, of course, planned for any contingencies that could have delayed his arrival, but that window of time had been used up by a flat tyre way back near Lake Taupo in the middle of the north island. A few minutes later, when the traffic showed no signs of beginning to move again, he followed the example of someone he could see nearer the brow of this hill, who was getting out of his car to try and find out what was going on.

'What's happening?' he called.

'Accident,' the stranger yelled back. 'Someone's driven off the road and gone down the bank just on the other side of this hill.'

The 'bank', from what Cooper could see, was more like a small cliff with a rocky beach at the bottom of the steep slope. From the top of this hill, or just over its brow, it could have been a drop of over fifteen metres and a vehicle landing on a hard surface like that from even a much smaller distance could be badly damaged with its occupants in real trouble. Turning swiftly, Cooper opened the back of his SUV to extract a small backpack. He tossed his keys to the stranger he'd been speaking to as he ran past.

'Get someone to move my car off the road if it's needed,' he said. 'I'm a paramedic. I'm going to see if I can help.'

'Good on ya, mate.' The stranger nodded. 'I'll keep an eye on your car.'

A small crowd was gathering on the side of the road and, as Cooper got closer, he could see why some people were looking so shocked. The car must have gone off the road with some speed to have buckled and then broken through the metal safety barrier like that. It had careened down the steep bank, carving a path through the undergrowth, and had come to rest, teetering on a low outcrop of rocks with waves breaking around it.

He might not be on duty but it was automatic for Cooper to go into scene assessment mode. To be looking for what extra help was going to be needed and what apparent dangers there were for any responding crews—and the public.

'Stand back,' he told people as he moved through the crowd. 'The edge of this bank doesn't look that stable. Has anyone called the emergency services?'

'I think an ambulance is on its way,' someone told him.

Cooper pulled out his own phone to punch in the three-digit emergency number. They needed more than an ambulance here. Police would be needed to control traffic and spectators. The fire service was needed urgently to stabilise this car with winch lines or something to prevent it getting dislodged by the waves and ending up completely underwater. Even if there were injured people inside the vehicle, it was too dangerous for anyone to try and approach it until it could be secured somehow. Would the hooks and lines from the fire trucks be enough? Maybe they needed to get a crane on the way…

His assessment and planning came to a crunching halt as he got through the rest of the crowd to get a completely clear view of the bottom of the bank. He didn't even finish dialling the emergency services number.

'*Hey…*' he yelled as loudly as he could. 'What the hell do you think you're *doing*?'

'She just took off down there,' someone said from behind him. 'Seemed like she knew what she was doing…'

'She's mad,' Cooper muttered, staring down at the lone figure on the rocky foreshore a good ten metres beneath him.

The tall, slim woman was standing on top of a rock, a short distance from where the car was teetering on other rocks. She was wearing rolled-up jeans and sneakers, and a white T-shirt that was knotted on one side. Right now, her arms were in the air and she was swiftly winding long dark hair into a knot that she somehow secured easily onto the top of her head. Then she leaned forward, holding her arms out to balance herself, obviously looking for a place to step that would take her closer to the car.

'*Oi...*' Cooper's shout was even louder this time and he was moving as he made the sound. 'Get *back*...'

Sure enough, the ground was crumbling on the edge of the drop and he started a slide that was barely controlled as he aimed for a shrub that had branches big enough to hold his weight. Then he climbed over some rocks and kept going, faster than he knew was safe but he had to get down the bank and into a position where he could stop this crazy bystander from creating yet another problem for the emergency services when they arrived on scene. On top of being concerned about the woman's well-being, he was not happy that he was being forced to put himself in danger like this. As soon as he could, he yelled again.

'Stay where you are. *Wait*...'

She took absolutely no notice of him. With a nimble leap, she landed on another rock and then steadied herself as a wave washed over her feet. Then she moved again to land within reaching distance of the back door of the crashed car. That was when Cooper saw what she was focused on—a small face in the window of that door—a child who looked no more than a couple of years old. He saw her grab the handle of the door and try to open it, almost losing her balance as a larger wave curled around her legs. The door didn't open.

Nobody else was following Cooper down the bank. For a few seconds, when he reached the bottom, he lost sight of what the woman was doing as he scrambled over the rocks closest to the base of the cliff but then reached the point where she had been when he'd first seen her and he had a clear view of what she was up to. She had managed to open the driver's door and he could see the shape of an adult slumped forward, ap-

parently unconscious. The rescuer tilted the person's
head back to open the airway, which told Cooper that
she did, at least, have some idea of what she was doing,
but she didn't pause to do anything else in the way of
assessment or treatment for the driver. She slid her arm
between the front seat and the back door, twisting her
body to enable her to reach the lock, and both the confidence and elegance of her movements kept Cooper
standing on his rock, simply watching.

She got the back door open and must have released a
safety belt that allowed her to scoop up the small child
who was now screaming with terror.

'Mummy... *Mummy...*'

The woman was saying something that Cooper
couldn't hear as she wrapped her arms around the child
and turned, looking down to choose both her stepping
point and a moment when a new wave was not about
to break. Cooper moved at the same time, his long
stride taking him to the next outcrop of rocks. Someone needed to see what was going on with the child's
mother and to try and get her out of the car if it was
possible to do so without it being too risky. It wasn't
something he would want to try on his own, so it was
a relief to hear the sound of sirens getting louder on the
road above them. He would make sure this woman and
the kid got back safely to shore and then come back to
plan the next steps that could be taken the moment the
first crews got down the bank.

To his surprise, he found the child being shoved into
his arms by the woman. There was nothing he could
do but take hold of it.

'Take her,' she said. 'I've got to go back.'

'*No*… It's not safe,' Cooper told her. 'Wait for the firies. That car's not stable.'

'That car has a *baby* in the back seat,' she snapped. 'Keep yourself safe. I've got a job to do, here.'

Cooper was left staring at her back, his jaw slack. He was the person who should be doing whatever was needed here. He had years of experience as an advanced paramedic. Qualifications in scene management and dealing with unusual and dangerous situations just like this. Who was this woman? And what was it about her that made him feel as if she really was the person in charge, here? Did it have anything to do with that hint of something like a grin she'd thrown over her shoulder as she'd turned away from him? Or that he was sure he'd heard her say 'Trust me… I know what I'm doing…'?

The toddler in his arms wriggled and screamed so he held her tightly and carried her carefully out of the water. He could see uniformed fire officers making their way down the bank where a ladder was being positioned. He could also see that the fire truck had been parked so that the winch gear at the back could be deployed. It was going to take a lot more than wedges or chocks to stabilise a car that was rocking on its perch with every wave. There was no sign of an ambulance crew yet. One of the fire officers reached the water's edge at the same time as Cooper. He held his arms out to take the child.

'Is she injured?'

'Haven't checked. Her airway's certainly clear.' And children who were crying that loudly were generally not badly injured. It was more likely to be the quiet ones you had to worry about. 'Are there any medics on scene yet?'

'Not yet. Traffic's snarled up badly for miles. They'll deploy a chopper soon, if it's needed.' The fire officer stared past Cooper. 'How many others are in the car, do you know?'

'Apparently there's a baby in the back. There's a crazy woman who's trying to get her out.' Cooper turned his head but all he could see was an undeniably shapely, denim-clad bottom poking out of the back door of the car. Wriggling, as she moved backwards and then turned, a baby's car seat in her arms.

'Good grief…is that Fizz?' Another fire officer had joined his senior colleague and was shading his eyes against the glint of the afternoon sun on the sea, trying to assess what they were about to deal with.

'Trust her to be first on the scene.' The older fireman shook his head, heading into the water to help rescue the baby. 'Why doesn't it even surprise me?'

'Fizz?' This was getting even weirder, Cooper decided. Who had a name like some sort of party drink?

'She's an ED doc,' he was told. 'But give her a chance to get out in an ambulance or helicopter and she's in, boots 'n all. Everybody in this business knows Fizz.' His tone was admiring. 'Don't worry, she knows what she's doing.' But he was watching the handover of the baby seat to the fire officer. 'Uh-oh…'

'Oh, *no*…' Cooper couldn't believe what he was seeing. There were experts on scene now. Equipment to make any further rescue attempts a lot safer. This woman with the odd name and an unbelievable attitude had already saved two children but it seemed that that wasn't enough. She was heading back to the car yet again.

'Fizz!' the younger fire officer yelled. 'Hold your horses. We need to get a cable onto that car, at least.'

Either she didn't hear him or—and this seemed more likely to Cooper by now—she was choosing not to hear him. He wasn't the only person to be appalled by her recklessness and, as he automatically moved to try and prevent another casualty, he found himself part of a group of rescue workers, armed with ropes and tools and protective clothing. There were police officers here now, as well as the fire crews, but he still couldn't see any paramedics arriving.

'Stay back, mate,' one of them told him. 'This isn't a spectator sport.'

'I'm a paramedic,' Cooper replied. 'With specialty training in disaster and scene management.'

And this looked like it was about to become a disaster, on a small scale, anyway. A wave large enough to reach his waist rolled in and one of the firemen lost his footing. The crashed car also lost its grip on the rocks beneath it, tipping and then sliding sideways with a chilling, metallic screech. A second wave rolled right over the top of its roof.

Where was that adrenaline junkie emergency department doctor?

Cooper couldn't see her anywhere and, just for a heartbeat, he was aware of something that felt like... grief?

He didn't even know this woman and she had taken stupid risks here, so if she was injured or had been killed—perhaps knocked out and then pinned underwater by the car—everybody would know it was her own fault but...

But how incredible a person was she? Cooper had met a lot of courageous people in his lifetime, both as his colleagues and amongst the patients he had treated, but this woman stood out as being something quite astonishing. Fearless. Concerned only about people other than herself.

Or maybe it was something much deeper than that. Much darker. A flashback to a moment in time he could never undo and would never forgive himself for. A moment that he could have used to try harder to stop someone doing something foolhardy. A moment that could have meant he wouldn't have lost the person who'd been everything to him.

A chain of people was in the water now and a plastic basket stretcher was being carried towards where the car had settled, but Cooper was ahead of them and he could see that the driver's door had stayed open as the car had been washed sideways. He could see movement as the foam of a wave cleared. The doctor was still alive...but she was inside the vehicle and it looked like she was struggling to release the catch of the safety belt.

Cooper had a cutting device on his multi-tool that was in a pocket of the first-aid kit he kept in the small backpack but he'd left that back on the beach before he'd climbed that first rock. Because he'd known he wouldn't be able to treat anybody until they were out of the sea. Not that he spared more than a split second of thought to how useful that device would be right now. In fact, he wasn't thinking anything particularly coherent. If he had been, he'd never have done what he did right then, which was to take a deep breath, reach down to take hold of the car door and pull himself beneath the surface of the water.

It was useful to have the outline of the door as a guide because it took more than a second to be able to see past the sting of salt water in his eyes. And it kept him from being washed away by the swirling current of the waves coming past. The car was more stable now than it had been on top of the rocks but it was still moving. How long had it been since the first wave had rolled over its roof and started to fill the interior? How long had it been since this mysterious woman had taken a breath of her own? Her hair had come undone from its knot and was now floating around her head, making her look like a mermaid and probably obscuring her vision as she wrestled with the seat-belt catch.

Cooper caught her hand and pushed it away from the catch. Then he held the bottom and felt for the release button. Pressing it down hard didn't seem to be enough, so he held the button down with one hand and took hold of the upper part of the strap with his other hand and pulled. Hard.

He felt the driver of the car slump towards him as the belt was released and he caught her under her armpits, pulling her free of the vehicle and then pushing up through the water. He just had to hope that she didn't have any kind of spinal injury but there was no way she could have been left in the car long enough for a more careful extrication process because she would have drowned.

He wasn't even sure that she was breathing now as he lifted her head clear of a breaking wave but there were others taking over. Taking the woman from his arms and putting her into the rescue basket to carry her towards the shore. Beside him, his fellow rescuer had already emerged from beneath the surface and she was dragging in great gulps of air as she tried to catch her breath.

'Thanks…' she managed. 'I was having a…bit of trouble…there.'

Not that she looked at all bothered by the fact that her 'bit of trouble' could have actually put them both in danger. She wasn't looking directly at him, either, as she pushed her hair back from her face and swiftly braided it to get it under control but he could see that her whole face had a glow about it—as if it had been so exciting, she'd do it all over again in a heartbeat.

Wow…there was something inspirational in that kind of passion. But Cooper had always known that, hadn't he? She reminded him of…

No. He wasn't about to go there. Even the nudge in that direction was discomforting, which was probably why his tone was distinctly sharp when he spoke again.

'It's lucky I didn't have to rescue you as well,' he said. 'I can't believe you did that.'

The reprimand in his tone was wasted on her. She didn't seem to even be listening. She was watching the progress of the fire officers who were carrying the driver back to shore.

'I need to see if she's okay.' She started moving. 'I'm just hoping…she didn't start drowning while I was fiddling with that belt.'

'There was still some air in there, between waves.' Cooper automatically reached out as the woman beside him stumbled on a rock. To his surprise, she caught his hand and held it as they both made their way back to shore as quickly as they could. His brain registered how that wet T-shirt was clinging to her body and he knew that image was going to resurface at a later, and less inappropriate, moment.

They were both soaking wet and should have been freezing given the water temperature and the slight breeze adding a chill factor but, oddly, the only thing that made Cooper realise he might be cold was the extraordinary warmth of that hand he was holding. It wasn't until she let go, as they leapt out of the last wash of the waves, that he started to shiver.

The toddler and the baby in the car seat were nowhere to be seen so they must have been taken up the bank already. Perhaps the police officers on scene were caring for them in the warmth of one of their vehicles. They needed to get the female driver into shelter as well but it looked as if she wasn't stable enough for what would have to be a slow journey up the steep slope.

He watched Fizz crouch beside the woman. She had her cheek near the victim's face and a hand on her abdomen. 'She's breathing…just.' She looked past the group of fire officers nearby. 'Doesn't look like we've got an ambulance on scene yet, does it?'

'No.' Cooper could see his own backpack not that far away. 'But I'm a paramedic. I've got a kit. I'll grab a stethoscope, shall I?'

It was the first really direct look he had received from her. She had brown eyes, he noticed. Really dark orbs that were assessing him with lightning speed.

'Get my kit, too, would you?' she said. 'It's over there on top of that flat rock.'

Cooper moved instantly. It felt as if he'd passed an

unspoken test of some kind, he realised as he grabbed both backpacks and turned back. Not that it should have made any difference at all to this situation but instinct told him that it would not be an easy thing to gain this woman's approval. Absurdly, Cooper actually felt a beat of pride in himself that he was being accepted as a temporary colleague.

He was a big bear of a man, this unexpected assistant that she had. Well over six feet in height and broad-shouldered.

Felicity Wilson believed that he was what he said he was. He'd clearly known what he was doing when he'd taken over getting this woman out of her crashed car and the way he'd told her to stay back until the car could be secured safely was pretty much what most people in the emergency services would have told her.

How could anybody have stood back when you could see that tiny face in the window, though? And yeah… Fizz knew she had a bit of an issue with impulsiveness when it came to dangerous situations but how good did it feel when taking that risk actually worked?

It would feel even better if she could make sure the mother of those children made it out of this disaster alive.

He had big hands as well, this man, but they were clever and nimble. He was opening pockets within the backpacks and extracting all the kinds of things that were going to be needed. Fizz stole the occasional glance as she looked up from doing a rapid primary survey on her patient, who was groaning but not conscious enough to open her eyes or speak to them coherently. She lay in the plastic rescue basket the fire service had provided.

Currently, those officers were setting up a canvas wind shield around them and watching what was happening. Two of them had taken off their heavy jackets and had passed them to the medics. Fizz felt swamped by the size of the garment but she wasn't about to let it hamper her movements.

'I'd put her GCS at less than ten. She's tachycardic at one twenty-four,' she told the man helping to stabilise her patient. 'Tachypnoeic with a respiration rate of thirty-two and… I'm not sure I'm getting any breath sounds on the left side. Hard to tell with the noise of the waves.'

'Pneumothorax?' The fire-service jacket looked like it was the perfect size for this man. And he looked as if he was well used to a uniform and the authority it conveyed. He had found the small oxygen cylinder in a side pocket of her first-aid kit and was attaching a mask. 'Is she hypoxic?'

'Let's get some oxygen on.' Fizz nodded. 'Got some shears?' She cut at the woman's clothing when he placed the tool in her hands and then slipped the elastic of the oxygen mask around their patient's head to keep it in place.

'Look at that…' The marks of deep bruising from the seat-belt injury were already visible in dark red patches. Fizz palpated the side of the woman's chest. 'Definitely some rib fractures.'

Her partner had his fingers on the woman's neck. 'Carotid pulse palpable but weak,' he told her. 'Looks like her jugular venous pressure is raised, too.'

Fizz nodded. She could see the veins on the neck

were visibly distended. She needed to have another listen to the chest and to check whether the tracheal line
was deviated, which could confirm that air trapped in
the woman's chest was developing into the emergency
that a tension pneumothorax represented.

Her partner was setting up for an IV, she noticed.
He had his own roll that contained cannulas, alcohol
wipes, Luer plugs and tape. He also had a litre of saline and a giving set ready to go. And he'd got a blood-
pressure cuff on their patient's arm already.

'Blood pressure's eighty-five over fifty,' he told her.
'Can't see any external bleeding. I'll check that her pelvis is stable in a tick.'

Fizz nodded but didn't say anything for a moment.
She had her stethoscope on her patient's chest. Right
side then left side. Yes…she was sure there were no
breath sounds on the left but was it air or blood that
was stopping the lung functioning?

'I'm missing my ED ultrasound,' she muttered.

'The portable ones we carry in the ambulance now
are great. Love them.'

She gave him a glance that probably looked startled
but she knew that it was only the most highly trained
paramedics that got to use equipment like portable ultrasound machines or ventilators. This guy not only
knew what he was doing but he was very likely to be
very good at it as well. It only took the briefest eye
contact but she knew that he could tell exactly what
she was thinking. His gaze was steady.

I am good at what I do, it told her. *You can trust
me…*

'What's your name?'

'Cooper. Cooper Sinclair.'

He wasn't local. Fizz would have noticed this man amongst all the emergency services personnel she had worked with in the last few years. Noticed and remembered him. It wasn't just his size that made him stand out. He had a strong Scottish accent. Not that where he came from or why he was here was of any interest to her right now.

'What do you need there, Doc?' A senior fire officer had come close. 'Ambulance is just arriving on scene now but it'll take them a minute or two to get their gear down the cliff. They want me to ask you what you need.'

'The usual,' Fizz responded. 'Life pack, oxygen and the kit. I'd like to get her airway secured before we move her.'

'Her name's Sonya Greene. We got her bag out of the car and found her driver's licence. She's thirty-two years old.'

The same age as she was. With two very young children. 'Somebody tracing next of kin?'

'Cops are onto it. I'll go and help get that gear down to you.'

'You going to intubate?' Cooper asked as the fire officer stepped back, talking into his radio.

'I'll need to decompress the chest before intubating.'

He nodded. 'Positive pressure ventilation could make a pneumothorax a lot worse.'

'I think it's getting worse, anyway. Does that look like tracheal deviation to you?'

His head came very close to her own as he leaned over to get into a position to be able to see the line of their patient's neck and chest. Fizz could feel his body heat, which struck her as odd because she knew how cold they both had to be, despite the thick jackets over their wet clothes. She made a note in the corner of her brain that they should probably wrap some foil sheets around themselves at the first opportunity. But she wasn't going to mention it just yet. Somehow, she knew that this Cooper was not going to be any more interested in his own protection from hypothermia at the moment than she was.

'Yeah,' he said. 'Tension pneumothorax?'

'That's what I'm thinking.'

The new medics on scene arrived moments later.

'Want me to get an IV in, Fizz?' one of the paramedics asked.

'We're good for the moment. You've got that, haven't you, Cooper?'

'Yep.'

It was someone else's turn to look startled. Fizz gave him a brief nod. 'Cooper here is an advanced paramedic, Jack,' she told the new arrival. 'I was lucky he was here. We nearly didn't get to save this woman. And right now, I need to decompress her chest and I want to do a finger thoracostomy rather than a needle decompression. Can you draw up some local?' She looked at the second crew member. 'Could you get the monitor on, please? I'd like to know what her oxygen and CO_2 levels are.'

All four of them were kept very busy for the next fifteen minutes but Fizz was satisfied that it was safe to transport their patient by that point. The chest decompression had dealt with the breathing emergency and both the pulse and breathing rate had dropped to an acceptable level. Blood pressure was coming up and the airway was controlled.

'Good job.' She nodded, as the paramedics secured their patient in the basket for the journey up the steep bank. 'I'll come with you in the ambulance and get a police officer to get my car back into town.'

There were plenty of fire officers ready to help lift the basket stretcher and pass it up the chain of people on the bank. Fizz shoved things back into her pack and zipped it shut. She could tidy and restock it at the hospital. Cooper was collecting his own kit.

'Thanks for your help,' she told him. 'Couldn't have done it without you.'

'It was a pleasure.' Cooper smiled at her and, to her surprise, Fizz found her breath actually catching in her throat.

Wow...that was some smile...

'Yeah...thanks, mate.' Jack, the paramedic, was slipping the straps of his large pack over his shoulders. 'You here on holiday or something?'

'No. I'm actually starting work here tomorrow. At the Aratika Rescue Base?'

'Oh, wow...choppers?'

'And the rest.' Cooper's shrug was modest. 'Coastguard work. Police operations. Specialist Emergency Response Team stuff.'

The glance Jack threw over his shoulder, as he went to catch up with the progress of the stretcher, was impressed.

Fizz had to admit she was pretty impressed herself. The members of that team on the rescue base were an elite group of people. She'd love to be an official, full-time member of that team herself but she loved her hospital work too much to give it up. Right now, she had arranged her life to give her the best of both worlds, by devoting her spare time away from ED shifts to the base and she got to work with some amazing people in both arenas.

It looked as if a new and very interesting person had just arrived in one of her worlds.

'Guess I'll be seeing you around,' she told Cooper. 'I try to be available to help on as many shifts as I can with the base.'

'Good to know,' he said. 'I'll be able to find out the end of this story. I hope it's a happy ending.'

'I specialise in happy endings wherever possible.' Fizz threw him a grin as she headed towards the bank. The stretcher was more than halfway up already. They would be on the road and heading for the biggest emergency department in the area within a few minutes.

She turned her head once more as she stepped onto the first rung of the ladder that was now secured to the bank.

Cooper wasn't that far behind her.

'Hey,' he called.

'What?'

'Just wanted to say that your name suits you. See you around, Fizz.'

She didn't say anything in response. She didn't look back again as she climbed to road level and then into the back of the ambulance. It was time to put the big, Scottish paramedic right out of her mind and focus on keeping her patient stable until they reached the hospital and got her to Theatre, if necessary, as quickly as possible to sort out that chest injury.

Fizz knew she would see him around sooner or later.

Hopefully, it would be sooner…

CHAPTER TWO

'IT'S A FANTASTIC LOCATION.'

Cooper was standing in front of the glass wall that made up this central, third-floor office area of the Aratika Rescue Base. He could see the helipad directly below them with people working around two bright yellow aircraft. It looked as if one of the helicopters was being refuelled and someone—presumably a pilot—was walking around the other one, doing a detailed external check.

'They're Kawasaki BK117s, yes?'

'With every bell and whistle you could wish for.' Aratika's manager, Don Smith, sounded proud. 'We've got a backup Squirrel in case both the BKs are out at the same time and there's no way of getting to another job by road or sea, but that's actually never happened during my time here.' He rapped his knuckles on the window sill. 'Touch wood. If I needed saving I'd want it to be a BK showing up. They're awesome rescue aircraft.'

'They're exactly what we used at the base in Scotland. Love working in them.'

'You'll be very familiar with the layout, then, which

is a bonus. How many years have you got under your belt now? Ten?'

'Close enough. I got into helicopter work as soon as I could after I graduated as a paramedic. It was always my burning ambition. Ever since I saw a crew at work when I was a teenager, up in a mountain range in Scotland.'

But it hadn't been the overwhelming relief of seeing the helicopter arrive at that accident scene that had instilled an unwavering determination to be like the members of that crew. It hadn't even been the astonishingly technical level of care that had been provided for the victim of that horrendous fall that had made him feel like he was in an episode of some high drama medical television series. No...what had stayed with Cooper and made him so determined to be like those heroes had been the way *he* had been cared for. The absolute compassion in the way they had done their best to support him as he'd dealt with the horror of his brother's death and the respect they had shown to both himself and to Connor—even after they knew there was nothing more they could do for him.

'And you've added a string of other accomplishments as well.' Don's words cut into the memory that had flashed into his mind. 'I have to say your CV was pretty impressive. Urban and Land Search and Rescue qualifications, with mountain experience. Disaster management. Coastguard training...'

Cooper shrugged modestly. 'I like to keep busy. And I like the challenge of learning new stuff. Or being in a new environment—and from what I've seen of New Zealand so far, it's got a lot to offer.'

He knew how impressive his CV was but there was

a downside to the kind of ambition that had driven him to achieve so much in his career already. It came from a single-minded devotion to that career that had meant there'd been no room for anything else in his life. Here he was in his mid-thirties—all of twenty years since his determination to be the best rescue worker ever had been conceived—and there'd been nothing to hold him back from shifting his life to the other side of the world for a fresh and interesting challenge.

No long-term relationship to consider. No family ties that were binding. No desire for family ties like that, for that matter. Cooper Sinclair lived for his work and, yeah…the downside was that it could be lonely sometimes, but he wouldn't have that impressive CV or be as good at this job as he knew his references recorded if he'd let a personal life interfere with where he was heading. Or maybe that should be where he'd already arrived. Was that why he'd come in search of new challenges in a new country? Because he'd been running out of ideas of how to take his skill set to an even higher level?

He shifted his gaze to a parking area off to one side of the helipad, where there were four-wheel drive emergency vehicles, huge command centre trucks and even rescue service motorbikes parked.

'You're well equipped to respond by road. And did I read that you take charge of any major incidents?'

Don nodded. 'We get dispatched to work with police and the fire service as command for any multiple casualty incidents or disasters. We also have single-crewed vehicles available at all times for first response if the local ambulance service is overloaded or they need advanced paramedic assistance for patient care. Those staff members are in addition to the helicopter crews. That's where we're starting you off for orientation.'

Cooper's eyebrows rose even though he tilted his head to acknowledge the challenge. But Don smiled.

'Don't worry. We're not throwing you in the deep end by yourself just yet. You'll be double-crewed until you are comfortable with protocols and destinations, etcetera. In fact…' Don checked his watch. 'Let's head downstairs. Shift changeover will be happening and there'll be a good crowd to introduce you to, including the guy who's going to be crewed with you for the moment. I expect they'll all be having breakfast right now.'

'Sounds great.' Cooper took one more look at the stunning view of Wellington harbour in front of him with the skyline of the city visible to one side, past the cranes and ships of a busy port and rugged, forest-covered hills in the distance to the other side. 'I still can't get over this view,' he said as he followed his new manager. 'You must have one of the best offices in the world.'

'Can't complain,' Don agreed. 'But this location was chosen for more than the view it gives us upstairs. It provides the fastest access to pretty much everywhere we need to go. We've got a straight run into the central city, or over to the west coast, we've got the coastguard base two minutes away when they need a medic, and if we're heading to the mountains or further north, the choppers just head straight for those hills, which is well away from the flight paths for the airport. That's where the name came from. Aratika means a direct, or straight, path in Maori.'

'Great name.' Cooper let the door swing shut on the view behind him.

There was an enticing smell of frying bacon coming from the kitchen area of the staffroom on the second floor of this big, modern building and, due to the change of a night shift to a day shift, there was a large enough group of people to present a challenge in remembering all the names coming at Cooper. Paramedics, pilots, ground crew, which included mechanics and people that serviced and restocked gear—even an older woman who seemed to have the role of a housekeeper—Shirley. It was Shirley who was cooking the bacon at the moment.

'Welcome to Aratika,' she said to Cooper, with a warm smile. 'Can I interest you in a bacon sandwich?'

'Thanks…maybe later.' Cooper wasn't ready to relax enough to eat yet but everybody here seemed just as welcoming as Shirley, so far. It was disconcerting, a moment after thinking that, to find someone staring at him, their jaw dropping.

'No way…' He looked back at the newspaper spread on the table in front of him, flipping back to the front page.

'That's Joe,' Don told him. 'He's the one you'll be double-crewing with until you're comfortable with how things work around here. Joe? This is Cooper Sinclair.'

'And unless he's got an identical twin brother…' Joe looked up again as he got to his feet. 'I've been looking at a picture of what you were getting up to yesterday afternoon. You just couldn't wait to get to work, huh?'

'Oh?' Cooper's smile froze halfway. It was a just a throwaway comment on behalf of his new colleague. There was no was Joe could know that he'd touched a deep nerve.

That Cooper *had* had an identical twin brother…

Joe gestured at the newspaper. 'You're a hero already.'

Cooper hadn't seen any newspapers yet today. Or any television last night, for that matter. By the time he'd got through the traffic jam the accident had created and located the central city hotel that would be home until he found something more permanent, he'd been too wrecked to do anything but sort out his wet clothing, find something to eat and then crash for the night. At least he'd been able to contact Don and apologise for missing his orientation meeting at the base and it had been a relief to find that his new manager hadn't been fazed.

'Tomorrow's another day,' he'd said. 'Can't fault you for getting involved in an accident scene. Would have been disappointed if you hadn't.'

Joe was looking just as laid back as he held out his hand. 'Good to meet you, Cooper. Look forward to working with you.'

Cooper shook his hand. 'Likewise.'

Don was reaching for the paper. 'Front page? Oh... Nice photo...'

Someone had taken it from the top of the cliff with a good zoom lens. There he was, with that crying toddler in his arms, facing back towards the shore. Just a little out of focus in the background behind him, he could see Fizz heading back to where the car was teetering on the rocks, a splash of foam catching the sunlight dramatically in mid-air like a halo around both the vehicle and the woman.

'Looks like you were enjoying yourself, mate.' One of the pilots had stepped closer to look over Don's shoulder.

'I wouldn't say that, exactly,' Cooper murmured,

but he had to admit there was a hint of something other than professional concern in his expression and he knew why as well.

That had been the moment when he'd been processing the way Fizz had dismissed his bid of taking charge of the situation. When she'd turned back to go and get the baby. When she'd cracked a version of what had become an old joke—*Trust me... I'm a doctor...* He'd been gobsmacked but undeniably impressed. Maybe that was the reason for that hint of a lopsided smile on his face and yes...it did look as if it could be interpreted as him getting an enormous amount of satisfaction out of what he was doing. It was just as well, he thought, that the picture hadn't been taken a bit later, when they'd been holding hands as they'd hopped rocks to get back to shore—their wet clothes plastered against their skin.

He'd been right about that particular image coming back to haunt him. It had happened when he'd stood for a long time under the spray of that very welcome hot shower. It had come back with even more punch when he'd slid, naked, between the crisp sheets of his bed. If she ever got tired of being some kind of action woman, Fizz could probably easily get a job as a model. Tall and slim but with curves in all the right places. That long dark hair, dark eyes and olive skin that made him think she could have Mediterranean ancestry. Greek or Italian, maybe?

'I heard about that job. I was in the ED when it came in.'

Cooper turned towards the speaker, relieved to have his runaway thoughts reined in so abruptly. It was a petite woman with blonde hair who was about his own age. What was her name again? Oh, yeah... Maggie.

'Do you know if the patient was still stable on arrival? I think her name was Sonya. And if the kids were okay?'

'Yep.' Maggie nodded. 'I was around for a while. I'd gone in with a kid from up north who was in status asthmaticus and I wanted to hang around until he was stable. I'm pretty sure the kids were fine. They got checked out and there were relatives to take care of them, including their father from what I gathered. They put a chest drain in the mother, took off about a litre of blood and fluid, gave her a blood transfusion and then took her off to Theatre. I don't know what they needed to do to patch her up, though. You can ask Fizz next time she's here. She went with her to Theatre.'

'Fizz?' Someone else, a bacon sandwich in hand, paused to peer at the picture. 'Oh, for heaven's sake… that's her in the background, isn't it?'

'She was the first on scene,' Cooper said. 'I was yelling at her to stay back until the car could be stabilised but she didn't take a blind bit of notice.'

'Sounds like Fizz.' But Joe was grinning. 'You'll find she behaves better when she's in uniform.' His grin broadened. 'Sometimes.'

The familiarity in his tone gave Cooper an odd beat of something he didn't want to try and identify but could be related to envy, perhaps? Just how well did Joe know Fizz? And why was he even wondering about whether she was single or not? For heaven's sake, he'd only just arrived in a new city to start a new job and a new life. Hooking up with someone hadn't even entered his head as part of his immediate agenda. To contemplate the remote possibility of hooking up with someone he'd only spent a matter of minutes with, not to mention someone who'd pretty much ignored him to start with, who'd bossed him around like a minion after that, and had probably forgotten his existence the moment she'd walked away was…well, it was stupid enough to make it easy to dismiss in the same instant it had grazed his mind.

Don's smile was tolerant enough to suggest that he, too, not only knew Fizz well but could excuse her lack of compliance with safety instructions. His expression reminded Cooper of a fond parent who made allowances for a wayward child. The attitude to the young doctor was intriguing. What did she have that made everybody who knew her prepared to forgive what came across as a maverick streak—something that was not usually acceptable in the emergency services community?

Don had already moved on from his amusement in relation to how well Fizz behaved herself when she was officially on duty. 'Speaking of uniforms, we need to get Cooper here kitted out. Although…' His gaze took in the black T-shirt, dark trousers and steel-capped boots Cooper was wearing. 'Just a team T-shirt might be enough for the moment. And some overalls for a chopper callout, maybe. If there's room, he could go as third crew at some point soon. He definitely needs a pager, though. Preferably before your shift is due to start.'

'Come on…' Joe signalled that Cooper should follow him. 'I'll introduce you to Danny downstairs who's in charge of uniforms and pagers and suchlike and then we'll find you a locker. The grand tour can wait until after breakfast if things stay quiet for that long.'

Even as he finished speaking, a loud beeping was

heard and one of the pilots reached for his pager. Two of the paramedics, including Maggie, reached for theirs seconds later. All three staff members got to their feet and headed for the stairway that led to ground level.

Maggie wagged her finger at Joe as she went past. 'That was your fault,' she told him. 'You said the "Q" word. Karma's going to get you soon, as well, you know.'

'She's right.' Joe sighed. 'We'd better sort your pager out first, Cooper. We'll be the next taxi in the rank before long. Let's get you that pair of overalls until we sort your full uniform out properly.'

'Phew...' Felicity Wilson let herself sink into the armchair in the corner of the emergency department staffroom of Wellington's Royal Hospital. 'I thought we were never going to get a break.'

'It's been full on, hasn't it? Thanks for staying on, Fizz, but you can get away anytime now. We're fully staffed for the afternoon shift and we've caught up on the backlog.'

'I'll just have my coffee and catch my breath.' Fizz smiled at her colleague, Tom—one of the senior consultants here. 'I've already ditched my plans to attend a four-wheel drive club meeting. They're just planning the next run, which is a sand forest gig that I've done before. I might wait until the CT scan results come through on that six-year-old kid that fell out of the tree. I hope he hasn't got anything more than a mild concussion to go with his broken arm.'

'Young Micky? He's been a frequent flyer in here since he was a toddler when he fell off the couch and broke his collarbone. Apparently that was his first attempt at flying.' Tom shook his head. 'You have to feel sorry for his mother.' His glance at Fizz was accompanied by a grin. 'I'll bet your mother had that worried look a lot of the time when you were growing up.'

'I wasn't accident prone.'

'But you're into dangerous pastimes. You probably jumped out of trees with a homemade parachute instead of falling out of them.'

'Actually, no… I was quite a boring kid. Very well behaved.'

Tom shook his head. 'So what happened? You grew up and just got a taste for things like hang gliding and off-road driving?'

Fizz shrugged. 'Something like that.' Yeah…she'd got a taste for an overdose of adrenaline, that was true. Who wouldn't, when you discovered that it could blow anything else that you were feeling into oblivion?

Things like grief.

And having no faith in the future.

Mind you, it was such a long time ago that she'd discovered the potency of adrenaline as a mood-altering medication it was just a part of her history. A life-changing part, admittedly, especially when she'd eventually found a way of incorporating that kind of excitement into the job she loved so much. At least people were more likely to be impressed when you were putting yourself in danger in order to save other people and not just for personal escape masquerading as enjoyment.

'And you always just happen to be where the action is happening. That picture of you in the paper a few days ago… Unbelievable… And you just happened to be driving right behind the woman who ran her car off the road?'

'I saw it happening. Some idiot on a motorbike was trying to pass when he didn't have room and she had to swerve. Her wheel caught in the gravel on the side of the road and she just lost control and went straight through the barrier.' Fizz shrugged. 'Hey…what can I say? Apparently I'm a trauma magnet.'

'I guess it keeps life interesting.'

'Yep…' Fizz took a sip of her coffee, her mind slipping back to that incident the other day. To the adrenaline rush of getting that child and the baby out of that car. To that moment of fear when she'd been underwater and realising that she wasn't going to get that safety belt undone and that, at any moment, the car could get displaced enough to trap her underwater.

She was no stranger to situations that were scary. She had chosen them, way back, when it hadn't actually seemed to matter that much if she didn't survive. By the time she'd got through to the other side of the darkest period in her life, she had every desire to survive but she still didn't shy away from situations that she knew might be a little too risky, because she knew how good that rush of relief was when they were over. That sheer exhilaration that the odds had been beaten and you were still alive? It was definitely a kind of drug, that feeling.

Addictive…

And every time it added to her confidence in being able to rely on herself. It confirmed her belief that being totally independent was the only safe way to exist and it was okay, because life was still good. Better than good, in fact.

'Anyway… I'd better get back.' Tom drained his mug and then rinsed it out under the tap. 'You in tomorrow, Fizz?'

'No. Day off.'

'As in a real day off, or are you doing a shift at the rescue base?'

'Rescue base,' Fizz admitted. 'But you know what they say about a change being as good as a holiday, right?'

Tom was laughing as he left the staffroom. Fizz sipped her coffee again, her gaze drifting towards the big table in the centre of the room and to the pile of magazines and newspapers on one end of it.

It had only been a couple of days since she'd been in the background of that front-page picture. Was the paper still in that pile? Not that Fizz kept mementoes like that but, now that Tom had reminded her, she just wanted to have another look at that photo.

It wasn't until she'd found the paper on the bottom of the pile that Fizz realised why she'd wanted to see it again. There was something about the man who was the hero of this image that was pulling her back.

Attracting her…

And it had been a long time since she'd been aware of that particular kind of tingle. Had her self-imposed break from men gone on long enough to have run its course? Was she missing male companionship—not to mention great sex—enough to make it worth the risk of having to deal with someone who started wanting something more than she was prepared to offer?

More than she was capable of offering?

Maybe the attraction was simply there because they'd shared a dramatic incident and he'd been the one to tip the balance and make the good result of that rescue possible. Fizz could still feel echoes from that touch of his hand when he'd pushed hers aside to deal with unclipping that seat belt. And when he'd gripped hers to help her keep her balance when they'd been scrambling over those slippery rocks on their way back to dry land. How safe had that physical attachment to that big, solid man made her feel? Not that she needed anyone to make her feel safe but it hadn't been unpleasant, that was for sure.

She could remember how deft his hands had been when he had been working with her to save that woman's life on the beach. And that hint of laughter curling through a rather gorgeous accent when he'd said that her name suited her. It wasn't just Cooper Sinclair's accent that was gorgeous, either. Fizz stared at the photo. She'd noticed how big he was that day but she hadn't taken any particular notice of his features—those intelligent eyes, that strong nose and chin. A mouth that looked ready to curl into what would probably be a cheeky smile at any moment.

Okay. The attraction wasn't just to do with the situation they had both found themselves in. And it wasn't just that she was over being celibate. This Cooper was something special. He was also a foreigner who might only be in the country for a limited amount of time, which could be a real bonus. If—and, given the impression she already had of him, it might be quite a big if—he was single, it was possible he might be interested in a friendship. One of those friendships that had benefits, even, and were as close to a conventional relationship as Fizz was prepared to allow.

She cast a somewhat furtive glance over her shoulder but she was still alone in the staffroom. Carefully, she ripped off the front page of this old newspaper and then folded and tore around the edges of that photograph. Then she folded the image until it became a small square that she slipped into the pocket of her scrubs tunic.

It was an odd thing to do but…she might want to have another look at it later. When she wasn't in danger of being interrupted.

CHAPTER THREE

'HI, COOPER, HOW's it going?'

'Hey, Maggie... I didn't know you rode a bike.' Cooper shut the door of his SUV, which he'd parked in the corner of the staff parking area at Aratika Base, well away from any rescue vehicles and especially the big trucks that might need to exit the park quickly.

'It's what helped me get a job here, I think.' Maggie tucked her helmet under her arm and fell into step beside Cooper as they headed for the ground-floor entrance on one side of the helicopter hangar. 'We can rotate sometimes if we need a change or there's a gap that needs filling in the roster—that's why Joe's on the road crewing with you at the moment. He'll probably be back on the choppers next week.' Maggie used her security card to open a steel door. 'I love spending a few shifts on a bike. If there's a major snarl-up in traffic due to a crash, a bike is the best way to get on scene fast. We can respond first and do what we can before the police can clear a way in for an ambulance or find somewhere for a chopper to land.'

'I haven't ridden a bike for a few years. Maybe I'd better brush up on my skills.'

'Good thinking. I see you've got an SUV, though. Do you do some off-road four-wheel driving?'

'Not yet. Could be a fun thing to get into here. There must be some great places to go.'

'I've been out with Fizz. She belongs to a big four-by-four club and they have days where they get onto some farms with steep gullies and rivers to get across. Or they get into a forest near a beach so there's sand dunes and things to deal with. It's a bit hair-raising but pretty exciting.' Maggie was leading the way into the ground-floor locker room. 'It's also a great way to pick up driving skills. I should do more of it. Oh… I had a chat to my other flatmates, Laura and Jack, last night and told them you might be interested in our spare room. They're keen, so come and have a look after work today, if you like.'

'That would be fantastic. I'm not into hotel living. A few days has been more than enough.' Cooper put his gym bag into his locker and shut the door. He was already wearing his uniform and the overalls for helicopter or other callouts were hanging on his hook at the end of the row on the wall.

'It's a cool old house. Big villa. It's in the Aro Valley, which isn't too far from here. Less than a fifteen-minute drive even if the traffic isn't great.'

'Sounds great.'

'We're all either paramedics or nurses so, with our shift work, it means it's not that much of an issue that we've only got one bathroom. We're hardly ever all there at the same time. There is one thing you should probably know, though…'

'What's that?' Cooper had been distracted by someone coming through the door of the changing room.

Fizz…

He hadn't seen her since the day before he'd started work on the base and that was nearly a week ago. Long enough for him to have got over that odd reaction and the even crazier notion that maybe there was a possibility they could hook up.

'Hi, Maggie…' Fizz was walking with a confidence that said she knew exactly where her locker was. That she was completely at home here, in fact. 'And…um… Cooper, isn't it?'

'Yeah…'

Had she had trouble remembering his name? The effect of the hesitation was not dissimilar to having a bucket of cold water thrown at him. So much for thinking that there might have been a mutual spark of attraction there.

'Cooper Sinclair,' he added. 'We never did get properly introduced, did we? Your real name isn't actually Fizz, is it?'

'Don't go there.' Maggie laughed. 'Her real name is Felicity and she hates it. You won't be popular if you try using it.'

There was a slight flush of colour on Fizz's cheeks and she barely held eye contact with Cooper for more than a heartbeat. As if she was a little flustered, perhaps? He might not really know this woman at all, but instinct told him that being flustered was out of character for this woman. Interesting. And, no, he wasn't going to make himself instantly unpopular by using a name she didn't like but, for the moment, he was certainly going to keep any interaction between them completely professional. Because instinct was also telling him that if he came on too strong, he would get a very firm knock back.

'I heard you went up to Theatre with our patient from that accident the other day,' he said. 'Sonya?'

'I did.' Fizz was opening her locker but it wasn't to find any uniform items. She was already wearing the black T-shirt with the rescue base's logo of a helicopter flying above a path leading straight towards a mountain range and she had it tucked into the standard issue black pants that brushed the top of her steel-capped boots. With her hair firmly drawn back and tamed into a long braid, she looked ready to leap into a car or a helicopter and respond to any emergency. She hung her big shoulder bag on a hook in the locker, having extracted a stethoscope, notebook, pens and a couple of muesli bars as she continued talking to Cooper.

'She lost a lot of blood when we got a chest tube in so she needed a transfusion. They did a thoracostomy in Theatre and found some small arteries that were still bleeding so they got repaired, along with the lung damage.'

'Is she still in hospital?'

'No. She went to the intensive care unit, got extubated the next day. The chest tube got taken out forty-eight hours later and she was discharged yesterday.'

'Wow...good to hear.' Cooper was impressed. Not just that their patient was recovering so quickly from both the injury and the surgery but that Fizz had clearly kept a very close eye on her progress. 'Do you always follow your patients up that closely?'

'Try to...'

Fizz slung her stethoscope around her neck and looked even more ready to respond to anything. She also looked as if she either had no interest in continuing this conversation or couldn't think of anything to say. There was a moment's silence that could have become awkward if Maggie hadn't broken it.

'Cooper might be moving into the spare room at my place,' Maggie told Fizz. 'Except he doesn't know about Harrison yet.'

'Harrison?' It was a relief for Cooper to turn towards Maggie and stop wondering why there was any awkwardness in the atmosphere. 'Is he a flat pet?'

Maggie laughed. 'Kind of. One of the housemates is Laura, who's an ED nurse at the Royal, and she's a single mum. Harrison is five. He's no trouble and they share the biggest room in the house that's got an ensuite bathroom. It just depends on how you feel about kids.'

'I'm fine with kids,' Cooper said. His mouth curved into a grin. 'I like them. As long as they're not mine, that is.'

'You don't like your own kids?' Fizz shut her locker door with a decisive clunk and shot him a glance from beneath raised eyebrows.

'Don't have any,' he responded. 'And don't intend to in the foreseeable future, anyway.'

Maggie let out an audible sigh. 'What is it with the men around here? Nobody seems to want to settle down and have a family. Not just the men, either,' she added. 'Seems like half the staff here are single. Look at me—I'm thirty-five. If I don't get on with something soon, it's never going to happen.'

'Ah…but would you want to give up this job?' Fizz slung her arm around Maggie's shoulders as they both walked towards a steel staircase. 'Imagine how boring it might be to be stuck at home with a few rug rats. You won't catch me doing that…'

'You're only thirty-two, aren't you? Just you wait, Fizz. Your biological clock will start ticking one of these days.'

Fizz laughed. 'Doubt it. And if it does, I'm going to ignore it. Life's too much fun just the way it is.'

Cooper was just behind them as they headed up to the first floor and the staff area. The contrast between these two women was quite startling. Maggie was very attractive with her curly blonde hair and blue eyes. He'd been out as third crew on a helicopter call-out with her on his second day here, so he'd seen her at work and knew that her intelligence and skills more than made up for any lack of height or brute strength. She rode a Harley-Davidson motorbike, which gave her an edge that should have added to her attractiveness, and it sounded like she was looking for someone special in her life.

Maggie should be exactly the type of woman that would be perfect for Cooper—if he was looking, of course—which he wasn't.

But when Maggie was standing beside Fizz, she seemed to become pale and it wasn't just her colouring against Fizz's dark hair and eyes and olive skin. It was as if her personality paled as well, to the point of being almost insipid? Cooper knew that wasn't the case, it was just that Fizz had an extraordinary kind of glow about her. She was a maverick, all right. Clearly she wasn't about to bow to any social pressure any more than she was inclined to automatically follow orders regarding safety. She wasn't looking for a conventional future of finding a partner and settling down to raise a family. Instead, she was throwing herself at life and extracting all the fun she could out of it. And if that meant throwing caution to the wind and doing things that were reckless, then so be it.

She was a bit wild.

And that wasn't just attractive, it was undeniably exciting. It felt as if the aura around this woman was touching his own skin. Making it tingle oddly. No wonder he'd been aware of awkwardness between them— he was creating it. Not that Cooper was going to allow even a hint of his reaction to show. The fact that Fizz had barely remembered his name was quite enough for self-protection barriers to have been engaged instantly. He wasn't about to make an idiot of himself in front of his new colleagues. *With* one of his new colleagues, in fact, even though her presence on the base was intermittent.

Oh, man…

It was a relief to get into the staffroom with the group of friendly, familiar faces. Enough people to dilute how powerful the presence of Cooper Sinclair was when he was breathing the same air that Fizz was. He was too big. Too cute. Too…*everything*…

It was disturbing, that's what it was.

'Fizz…how are you, love?' Shirley was calling from where she was standing in front of the stove. 'It's poached eggs on toast this morning. Can I tempt you?'

'Oh, yes, please, Shirley. You're an angel. I went for a run this morning and there was no time to do more than grab a couple of these muesli bars.' She held out her hand to reveal her snacks.

'Keep those for later. Sit down and I'll bring you some eggs. Maggie? Cooper? You up for eggs?'

'No, thanks,' Maggie said. 'I've had my breakfast.' She went towards the big pine board on the wall behind the dining table, where Don was pinning up a notice. 'Is that the new roster?' she asked.

'I'd love some,' Cooper said to Shirley at the same time. 'I went running this morning, too, and I'm starving.'

Oh, no… If Shirley had asked Cooper first, then Fizz might have lied and said she'd already eaten breakfast as well. But now he was sitting beside her at the table and, any moment now, they'd be eating a meal together, albeit a snatched one before their shift was due to start. Joe was also sitting at the table, along with Andy, one of their pilots, and a couple of paramedics from the night shift. She was more than familiar with sitting down with team members from this rescue base. It shouldn't feel any different with the inclusion of someone new. But it did. And Fizz knew why.

It was entirely her own fault that she was feeling a bit…well, weird, around Cooper Sinclair. She'd looked at that newspaper clipping a few times too often, hadn't she? Remembering his voice and that cute Scottish accent. The sheer, solid size of him that made her feel quite small and feminine, which was no mean feat for a girl who'd reached nearly six feet by the time she was sixteen. She'd remembered too often how it had felt to have him holding her hand as well and that had morphed into imagining a whole lot more by the time she was lying awake in her own bed in the early hours of the mornings. The idea that a friendship might be possible, a really close friendship, had become more and more attractive.

It was embarrassing, that's what it was. She was a thirty-two-year-old woman, for heaven's sake, and she was having a bit of a *crush* on someone? She'd actually felt herself blushing when she'd gone into the locker room this morning and had seen him for real again and not just in a rather crumpled photograph. And Felicity Wilson *never* blushed. She needed to get a grip and keep any interaction between herself and this new team member strictly, and utterly, professional until she could get her head around this.

It was just so different.

Not that Fizz was a stranger to interactions with men. She'd experienced a wide spectrum, in fact—from having been head over heels in love at one point in her life to having to fight off determined advances from extremely undesirable people at the other end of the spectrum—but *this* was different.

She wasn't in any danger of falling in love, of course. That state of mind—which was pretty close to being crazy, given how it could take over your life—had been a one-off and had died at the same time that Hamish had. Any relationship in the years since that life-changing event had...well, it had just happened. Had come from a friendship that involved doing things together, preferably extreme sports, and sex just became part of the friendship. A bonus that got added in later, when and if it seemed like a good idea.

That was why she was feeling so flustered right now, wasn't it? Because she wasn't even friends with Cooper Sinclair yet but she was already thinking about how nice it would be to touch him? To *be* touched?

She needed to take a big step back. Fast. It had to be Cooper who took that first step towards friendship. Chasing men—like falling in love—was another thing that Fizz never did, but she'd given off some pretty strong signals already, hadn't she? Like voicing her approval of Cooper's statement that he had no intention of having kids by letting him know that she felt the same way. Had he sensed the underlying message that a friendship between them could work well because neither of them was interested in something long term or permanent? That neither of them would be harbouring secret plans for a potential future?

The eggs arrived, on thick pieces of buttered, sourdough toast, sprinkled with fresh parsley.

'Wow…' Cooper eyed his plate after thanking Shirley. 'This looks amazing.' He glanced sideways at Fizz. 'I've never come across an ambulance station or rescue base that has its own cook before.'

'Shirley isn't employed here,' Fizz told him. 'She's a volunteer. Everybody puts into a kitty for a grocery fund.' She ate the first bites of her breakfast in silence but then spoke again. This was good. Just a friendly sort of conversation.

'She's a bit of a legend is our Shirley. Her son's life got saved by a helicopter crew years and years ago and she wanted to thank people so she started baking cakes and bringing them in for morning tea, and organising fundraisers and so on.' She lowered her voice, although Shirley was now stacking dishes into the dishwasher and the clatter meant that she couldn't possibly know she was being talked about.

'After her husband died a few years ago, her involvement here just grew. She started being here in the mornings to cook breakfasts and now she does a roast dinner on a Sunday. I've only been lucky enough to be on a Sunday duty a couple of times but I can tell you that Shirley does the best roast beef and Yorkshire puddings you're likely to get outside England.'

Fizz turned her attention back to her plate but she could feel Cooper's gaze on her face. A thoughtful kind of gaze. Good grief...he could just *look* at her and it felt like a physical touch? This was definitely odd.

'Is that typical of people in this country? That kind of generosity?'

'Well, Shirley's one in a million, of course, but I think it is true to some extent,' she told him. 'And I think that we get to see it more than others in this job. The ambulance service or first response in isolated areas is always run by volunteers who give up a lot of their own time for training and being on duty. I can't count the number of times I've arrived on scene on a callout to find local people going above and beyond to do what they can to help. It's part of what I love about doing this—why I signed up to volunteer.'

'You don't get paid to be here?' Cooper sounded surprised.

'It's one of my hobbies,' Fizz told him. The admiration she caught in his expression was more than a little disconcerting. Okay, she wanted him to be interested in her as a friend but as an equal, not someone on a some sort of pedestal. Finding it so hard to break that eye contact was even worse. How could something become so intense within the space of a single heartbeat? Somehow, she needed to lighten the atmosphere.

'I get a free uniform.' She managed a smile as she dragged her gaze free. 'And great breakfasts. And sometimes cake for morning tea as well.' She wiped up the last of her egg yolk with a crust of the bread and then jumped to her feet, picking up her plate, as her gaze scanned the other people scattered throughout this space. She raised her voice slightly.

'Where do you want me today, Don?'

'You're crewing with Maggie. Aratika One. We'll send you out for anything that's called in as status one. I might send Cooper out with you as third crew if he's on base—if that's okay with you. He's still getting up to speed with all our protocols.'

'Sure.' Fizz nodded, letting Shirley take her plate from her hands. Smiled, even, although her heart had just sunk a little.

She didn't want to work with Cooper Sinclair.

No, that wasn't true. She did want to work with him, she just didn't want him to know that he was messing with her head more than a little. How mortifying would it be if he guessed how often she'd thought about him since their little adventure on the beach? More than that, it was disturbing that she was feeling this way. She didn't want to be hoping for something that might or might not happen. Fizz needed things to be normal. If something happened, great. If it didn't, it didn't matter. It was when you started hoping, or worse—planning, that you left yourself vulnerable to disappointment. Heartbreak, even.

Maybe even a friendship with this man wasn't a good idea.

A friendship with 'benefits' was absolutely not a good idea.

'He needs to go on the next job that involves the

coastguard, too,' Don added. He turned towards Cooper. 'You haven't met anybody there yet, have you?'

'No.' Cooper was taking his empty plate to where Shirley was still busy clearing up.

'Come with me. I've got a copy of their standard operating procedures in my office. You might want to have a browse if you get any downtime today. You've done a training course for boat rescues, though, haven't you?'

'Yes. I did a holiday season with a coastguard unit in Cornwall a few years back.'

Fizz watched the two men head for the stairs. Hopefully, there wouldn't be much in the way of downtime today. The sooner she had the distraction of being whisked away to assist on a job where somebody was critically injured or ill, the better. It wouldn't matter if Cooper was there, either. Once she was focused on a patient, there was no way she would have any head space for anything other than what needed to be done to save a life or at least make someone a lot more comfortable.

She jumped as she heard Shirley's voice right behind her.

'Oh my,' the older woman said. 'He's a bit of a looker, our new lad, isn't he?'

'Oh?' Fizz feigned surprise. 'I hadn't noticed.'

Shirley's breath came out in snort that said she didn't believe a word but she bent to start wiping the table. 'I wonder if he's got a kilt,' she murmured. 'Imagine that…'

'I'd rather not.' Fizz didn't have to feign the sincerity in her voice. Her fingers felt for the pager clipped to her belt, tapping it gently. Willing it to start beeping and advertise an incoming call. With a bit of luck, it would happen very soon, so she'd be out of the building by the time Cooper came back down those stairs.

It was hard to concentrate on the standard operating procedures of the coastguard that related to the safety of extra personnel on board.

Cooper was too aware that Fizz was present in the staffroom as well. Right at the far end of this large space, mind you, because she was having a game of pool with Andy the pilot as they waited for a call to come in, but he was still aware of her.

What had it been about, the intensity in the look she'd given him, just before she'd hurriedly finished her breakfast and almost jumped to her feet to get away from the table? It was confusing, that's what it was.

She'd barely been able to remember his name when she'd seen him again and then she'd given him a look that had made him feel like there was some sort of deep, significant connection between them.

Cooper might not believe in that nonsense about 'love at first sight' but he certainly knew that 'lust at first sight' existed. This didn't feel like a simple mutual sexual attraction, though—he was quite familiar with what that felt like. This felt…different. Unpredictable, perhaps. A bit wild. Dangerous, even…

Rather like Fizz herself.

The first call that came in was for someone to be first on the scene at a traffic accident on the main road that led into Wellington from the north. Joe and Cooper got dispatched and fought their way through the stalled traffic to find a car that had been clipped by a truck and had then gone into the path of another car in the neighbouring lane. The truck driver was uninjured and angry that someone had cut in in front of him like that.

'I had nowhere to go. You can't just stop a ten-ton truck like it's a dodgem car, you know?'

The driver and passenger of the third vehicle involved had only minor injuries—a bumped elbow and a mild whiplash that would need checking out at an emergency department. The driver of the other car was still trapped in his vehicle but he was conscious and said he felt fine. He also smelt strongly of alcohol.

At this time of the morning? Cooper and Joe shared a glance.

'Must have been a good night out,' Joe murmured. 'Let's see if we can get a collar on him. Once an ambulance gets here, I think we can make ourselves available again. There's nothing that's going to need advanced management here and it's going to take a while.'

A fire service truck had managed to get through the traffic jam with the help of the police and its crew were getting their cutting gear ready to free the trapped driver. Traffic on the other side of the road seemed to have come to a standstill as well and there were horns being sounded by frustrated commuters who just wanted to get to work.

Despite the noise around him, Cooper could still hear the chop of rotors overhead and looked up to see one of Aratika's bright yellow rescue helicopters airborne and rapidly gaining height. Was Fizz on board this time—being taken away to help with a serious emergency?

Joe noticed the direction of his glance. 'Don't worry, mate. I'm sure you'll get the chance to go and play later.

Fizz is the biggest trauma magnet we've got. It's just a matter of getting your timing right.'

A blip on a nearby siren had cars edging sideways and an ambulance managed to get close enough to the scene to allow its crew to start unloading their gear. Before long Cooper and Joe would be free to make their skills available where they might be really needed.

Cooper smiled. 'As they say…timing is everything.'

And perhaps fate was giving him a chance to take a good look at this instant attraction. To think about it and realise that it really wasn't a very good idea to go any further down that particular track. Fizz was like no other woman he'd ever met and it was quite possible that he could get chewed up and spat out without even seeing it coming.

Due to the crumpled, jammed doors on the driver's side, Cooper had to climb into the other side of the car, the moulded, plastic cervical collar in his hands. He needed to put this on to protect the driver's neck until it could be cleared from injuries, because a crash that had mangled this car enough to trap him had also had a real potential to cause a neck injury. The fact that this patient was drunk meant that he might not be so aware of any warning signs, like pain.

'Don't need that thing,' he told Cooper. 'I'm fine, man…'

'It's just to be on the safe side,' Cooper said. 'Especially for when we get you out of here. Keep as still as you can. I know it's not the most comfortable thing, but it'll keep your neck safe. I'm going to sit behind you while they cut the car up and hold your head to be extra sure it doesn't move, okay?'

The firies covered both Cooper and the driver with

a sheet of plastic to protect them from shattering glass as they cut into the mangled metal and then peeled it away to give access to the patient.

The noise of the pneumatic gear was far too loud to be able to talk, or even think particularly coherently for a minute or two. It was a small space of time in which Cooper focused on keeping this patient's neck as safe as possible. And, just for a moment, it occurred to him that he should really keep his *own* neck safe as well. Not physically, but emotionally.

Fizz could be a challenge he might regret going anywhere near.

But Cooper could feel a smile tugging at one corner of his mouth.

That was precisely why he'd come to the other side of the world, wasn't it? For a new challenge?

CHAPTER FOUR

IT WAS ONLY a glance.

It only lasted a split second.

But it was…annoying.

Fizz finally latched the central buckle of her harness together as the skids of the helicopter lifted off the ground. And, yes, she should have had it fastened a few seconds prior to that but she'd been leaning to pull a pair of gloves free from their box so that she could put them on in transit and be ready to hit the ground running at the other end of this short flight.

It wasn't that Cooper had said anything. Or even caught her gaze. But she had seen the tilt of his head and just knew that he was watching. Waiting for her to buckle herself in safely.

Had she really decided that it was a bit disappointing, only minutes ago, that it seemed like she wouldn't even be on base at the same time as Cooper for the whole of her shift today? That she'd have to wait a whole week to see him again, unless she was on duty in the ED when he came in with a patient? Now not only was she heading to an emergency with him in the same helicopter, Cooper was her partner instead of third crew. Maggie had cracked a tooth this afternoon and made an appointment with her dentist for when the shift ended but this job had meant that she might not get back in time. It had been Don's suggestion that Cooper take her place.

'You reckon he's up to speed, Joe?' he'd asked, out of Cooper's earshot.

'I reckon.' Joe had nodded. 'Give him a go. I'm willing to bet he'll cope with anything you can throw at him.'

So here he was. Sitting in seat beside her in the cabin of this helicopter. Being the safety-belt police.

'Did the whole page come through for you, Cooper?' Fizz knew her tone was a little too crisp. 'You up to date on what we're going to?'

'Car through a shop window.' He nodded. He was pulling on a pair of sterile gloves himself. 'Victim hit by the car and then pinned under shelving that came down. Crew on scene are calling for backup for a possible pelvic fracture.'

Fizz nodded. 'If it is a pelvic fracture it could be a time-critical injury and land transport would take far too long with this being rush hour.'

Cooper's head was tilted as he peered down through the window. 'We're heading north, yes?'

'Yes.'

'The road certainly looks crowded.'

'We're heading for Upper Hutt,' Fizz told him. 'One of the four cities that make up Wellington's metropolitan area. The main road north hugs the coast. This one goes inland.'

'There's a lot of forest down there.'

'That's Rimutaka Hill in that direction.' Fizz leaned into her safety harness, stretching towards Cooper to point through the window on his side. 'Beyond that is the Tararua Forest Park. Brilliant for tramping if you're into that kind of thing.'

'Love it.' Cooper nodded. 'How 'bout you?'

Fizz couldn't help her lips curving into a grin. 'I got winched down once in a rescue. It was brilliant.'

Cooper's eyebrows rose. 'You're winch trained?'

'Not exactly. I'm hoping to be before too long, but that time I got taken down in a nappy harness. The patient had a major chest injury that needed a bit of surgery.'

Suddenly, Fizz had to look away from Cooper. Because she was remembering the kind of intimate body contact that was involved when you were strapped to someone else like that. Imagining how different it might have been if Cooper had been the paramedic taking her on that exciting descent into a small clearing in the forest. The thought was gone as soon as it came, but it was enough to ring an alarm bell. Just how had she lost her focus to that extent? A momentary loss of control, maybe, but it was a reminder of why it was disturbing to be experiencing this crush or whatever it was. Her brain hadn't been hijacked by that kind of detour since…well, since she'd fallen in love with Hamish, probably.

It couldn't be allowed to happen again.

'Andy? Have we got any update from the scene?'

'Fire service are still working to stabilise a wall that's been damaged. No update on patient status. We're going to land on a football field that's about two hundred metres from the scene. ETA two minutes.'

Fizz gave a single nod, drawing in a deep breath. Focus was not an issue now. Someone could bleed out internally from a pelvic fracture if one of the main blood vessels had been damaged and the ambulance road crew that had responded to the incident would not have the skills or gear to deal with that kind of critical emergency. She had her harness unfastened the moment the skids were on solid ground again. She shoved one trauma pack towards Cooper and then grabbed a second one herself. She was moving fast, even as she looped the straps over her arms, and she was jogging by the time she spotted a police officer signalling from the edge of the field, but she knew that Cooper was keeping up with her pace. She could feel the solid shape of him so close behind that she would be able to see him if she turned her head just a little.

She didn't. Fizz kept her gaze firmly on where she was heading.

Man, this felt good.

The police officer leading the way to the scene was shouting information over his shoulder as they ran.

'Victim's a fifty-six-year-old male. He was in the direct line of the car when it came through the window at speed. Elderly driver apparently stood on the accelerator instead of the brake.'

'Is he conscious?'

'No. But the paramedics there don't seem to think he's got a head injury. His legs are in a bad way.'

'How far now?'

'Just around this corner. You'll see the crowd.'

Cooper could already see the reflection of flashing lights in the windows of buildings they were passing. He could feel the tension that was always there when you were approaching an emergency situation. There was nothing like this moment in time to make him feel so focused. His brain could work faster, his senses were all on high alert and he had enough experience to be confident that he could deal with whatever was waiting for them.

Them…

This wasn't just about being on the periphery of the action in this new job while he got himself up to speed on any protocols that were a little different from what Cooper was used to and to allow his colleagues to get to know and trust his abilities.

He was the paramedic partner to the doctor on duty right now. Another set of hands, skills and knowledge to complement those of the more highly trained medic. A vital member of this small team. And it *felt* like a team. Maybe it was because they had worked together once already, at that accident scene, but it felt like more than that. It felt like the most natural thing in the world to be loping along beside this woman, heading for what could be a challenging emergency situation. There was a sense of connection—a kind of recognition—that might be disconcerting on a personal level but it was exciting on a professional one. Cooper knew that Fizz would tackle anything. And that she was skilled enough to improve their odds of being successful.

Not only would she tackle anything, mind you, she'd head straight in without giving her own safety enough thought. Cooper actually grabbed her arm as a group of emergency service personnel stepped aside to let them onto the scene.

'Watch out,' he said. 'There's glass everywhere.'

There was. The car had gone through a plate-glass

window and shards of it were still clinging to parts of the frame, looking like the points of vicious spears.

Fizz yanked her arm free. Or maybe she was just continuing to move forward and was too focused on what lay ahead to bother acknowledging the warning. They were beside the car that had crashed into this building now. Cooper could see the backs of people crouched over someone on the floor. He could see broken shelving that had been lifted clear and pieces of timber that were propping up a damaged wall. He could also see the hazards like tins of canned food that were rolling around when they got knocked and wet patches on the floor from broken bottles of liquid. He still had his arm out when Fizz slipped a little on a wet patch but she clearly didn't need, or want, any assistance with her balance this time.

Fair enough, but that wasn't going to stop Cooper keeping an eye out for any other hazards. Or doing whatever he could to mitigate them.

The local ambulance crew looked relieved to have backup. They relayed all the information they had as Fizz and Cooper smoothly took over the management of what was clearly a critically injured patient and they were there to assist as much as they could. Fire officers were working around them to try and clear debris and make sure the area they were working in was stable, providing background noise to the urgent communication taking place between the members of the medical team.

'Blood pressure's dropping...systolic's down to ninety-five.'

'I'd like another line in. We're going to need a blood transfusion.'

'Multiple fractures to both legs...'

'I can't get a femoral pulse...'

'Pelvis is unstable. Let's get a pelvic binder on...'

'Cooper? I want to get control of his airway. Can you draw up some drugs for me, please? For an RSI?'

'Sure.' Cooper unrolled the kit to find, draw up and then administer the anaesthetic agents required for the rapid sequence intubation. He was right beside Fizz, his fingers on the neck of their patient to provide cricoid pressure as she carefully inserted the laryngoscope into the mouth and then tilted it until she had a clear view. He had the bougie ready to put in her hand and then the tube to slip over the top for her to position in the trachea. And then it was time to pull the guide device out.

'I have the bougie—do you have the tube?'

'I have the tube.'

Cooper attached the bag mask and delivered a breath as Fizz unhooked her stethoscope from around her neck to check the correct placement of the breathing tube by listening to lung sounds. She looked up and gave a single, satisfied nod as he handed the bag mask to one of the paramedics to keep up the ventilations.

'All good,' she said.

An understatement, Cooper decided. That whole, intense procedure had been completed in no more than about thirty seconds. And that was partly because they had worked together so well.

It wasn't just their physical skills that meshed so well, either. Cooper got the impression that Fizz felt the same kind of connection and confidence in him that he did in her—that sense of recognition—as if they already knew each other?

'I can't get a femoral pulse,' Fizz said a moment later as she checked their patient again. 'Have you got a BP?'

'Still dropping. Unreadable.'

'He's got a significant haemorrhage going on. You familiar with the REBOA procedure, Coop?'

Some distant part of his brain registered the fact that she'd shortened his name—as if she knew him so well he needed a nickname—but it didn't shift his focus.

'The insertion of the balloon catheter to occlude the aorta and stop internal haemorrhage?'

'Yep.'

'I've read about it. Seen video. It's not something that was part of our protocols.'

'There's not many places that do it.'

Fizz caught his gaze and held it for a moment, a query in her eyes. He knew she was asking if he felt comfortable assisting her in what would be an advanced invasive procedure. His single nod was subtle but sufficient.

'We'll give him another unit of blood, but if his pressure doesn't come up, I think that's our next step.'

It was Cooper who took the next set of vital signs as the second unit of blood was pushed as fast as possible by someone squeezing the bag with both hands.

'Systolic of eighty-five,' he reported.

It looked like Fizz let out a breath she'd been holding. 'Okay…let's get going. The sooner we can get him to Theatre the better. Can we get a stretcher in here, please?'

With so many people available it was a quick task to package their patient on the stretcher and then carry him back to the helicopter. As the clamshell doors closed on the cabin and they took off, Cooper checked his watch to realise that they'd been on the ground for less than twenty minutes. They would have this critically injured person in the emergency department—maybe even in an operating theatre—well within the golden hour of dealing with major trauma.

He'd been impressed with Felicity Wilson the first time he'd seen her in action but right now he was blown away. It had been a privilege to work with her and he couldn't wait to do it again. On a professional level, he had never worked with anyone that made him feel part of such a tight team and facing future challenges together was an exciting prospect.

It was another incentive to keep their relationship solely professional. This was an opportunity to work with someone who could push his professional boundaries and help him improve his skills and knowledge. Who would be stupid enough to risk that by acting on an attraction that could potentially wreck what held the promise of being an extraordinary working relationship?

'He's good.' Fizz had dropped into Don's office when they'd finally got back to base. 'I'm happy to work with him as double crew any time and I'm sure any other HEMS doctor would agree.'

'Good to know.' Don nodded. He closed his laptop and slid it into a bag. 'High time I headed home. I was just waiting to hear how the job went.'

'It was a good challenge. We almost got to do a REBOA procedure for haemorrhagic shock.'

'Wow...that doesn't happen often.'

'It was probably a good thing for our patient that it didn't need to happen today. Having the capability to carry blood products with us made the difference there.' Fizz was following Don down the stairs. She could hear the murmur of voices in the staffroom and wondered if Cooper was still here.

She hadn't been entirely truthful in the assessment she'd given the base manager about Cooper's performance. He wasn't simply 'good' at his job. He was… well, he was something special. Fizz couldn't think of anyone else she had ever worked with where it felt like half the communication was almost telepathic. Like that rapid sequence intubation. Whatever she had needed had been available without having to ask for it—as if she'd had an extra pair of her own hands, or that they'd been working as a team for years and years.

It almost made up for that annoying streak of taking responsibility for her safety, like the way he'd tried to steer her away from the broken glass she had been quite well aware of. She didn't need to be protected. Didn't *want* to be…

Except that, deep down, it was rather nice to have someone looking out for her, wasn't it?

As if they cared? Or was it because Cooper thought she was feminine and therefore fragile? That was why it was so annoying, of course, but it was disturbing at the same time, because this Scotsman was big enough to make Fizz *feel* feminine and, if she was honest with herself, she kind of liked that as well.

He was still in the staffroom. The night shift crew members he had been talking to responded to a callout as Fizz entered, however, and Don headed home, after telling Cooper he was going to take him off being in a third crew, supervised position on the team.

'You've had the tick of approval from both Fizz

and Joe,' Don told him. 'And I know how high their standards are.'

Cooper grinned at Fizz as they found themselves alone in the room. 'Thanks,' he said.

'What for?' Oh, man... She was going to have to get used to that smile but it wasn't going to be easy. It did something really weird to the pit of her stomach.

'Giving me a tick.'

'You earned it.' Fizz glanced at her watch. 'What are you still doing here? You should have clocked off an hour ago.'

'So should you.'

'I was finishing up my paperwork. It's been a busy day.'

'And I was restocking the kits. It was a good chance to get properly familiar with the storeroom and Danny was happy to stay on for a while and help. He's a nice guy.'

'Mmm. Weren't you going to see that room in Maggie's house this evening?'

Cooper looked surprised that she'd remembered. 'I had a text from her, asking if we could put it off until tomorrow. She got held up at the dentist.'

'Hope her mouth isn't too sore. Which reminds me... I'm starving...' Fizz headed towards the bench and the large biscuit tin that lived in one corner. 'I wonder if any of Shirley's cookies are left.' She prised the lid off the tin. 'Ooh...even better—it's cake... Carrot cake, my favourite...' She turned her head as she opened a drawer and reached for a knife. 'Want a piece, Coop? *Ow...*'

The sound had Cooper on his feet in a split second. 'What is it?'

'Nothing.' Fizz ripped a paper towel from the nearby roll. 'I just nicked my thumb.'

'Let me see...' Cooper was right beside her now, holding out his hand.

'No...it's just a little nick. It's nothing.'

Except the blood was soaking through the paper towel. She needed another one. Cooper was ripping one off the roll and folding it into a small square.

'You need to put some pressure on it.'

'I *know* that.' Fizz gave him a withering glance. 'I did go to medical school, you know.'

He had one hand circling hers, the other waiting with his pressure pad for her to give him access to her injured thumb. Dammit...he wasn't going to give up, was he? She didn't want someone caring about her like this. Looking out for her to make sure she was safe and jumping in to take care of her if she was injured. *Protecting* her...

It could be that Cooper was taking the first step towards a relationship that was more than simply professional. Towards a friendship that she already knew she would welcome. She had decided, only this morning, that she would step back and wait for him to make that first move—because she wanted it *too* much?

But...this was weirdly nerve-racking. Scary, even.

Because Fizz knew that the attraction she felt for this man was not due to having been single for so long. Or that they'd met each other by sharing a dramatic incident. She recognised, on more than one level now, that Cooper Sinclair was special. That there was something between them that was very different from anything she had ever experienced before—even with the man she had chosen to marry.

Her nerves made it easy to back away from that attraction. To tap, instead, into the annoyance of having someone treat her as if she was in need of protection.

'I'm a big girl, Cooper,' she snapped. 'I can look after myself. I don't need you telling me to watch out for anything. Or watch me to make sure I put a safety belt on. I don't need you to look after my damn thumb, either. If I'm stupid enough to do something careless, I'm quite capable of dealing with the consequences.'

His gaze was steady. He didn't look at all put out by her snapping at him. 'I know that,' he said quietly. 'But we're part of a team, Fizz, and team members look out for each other. It's not a weakness to let other people help, you know. And, yeah…maybe I go overboard a bit sometimes but that's just the way I am. I…ah…lost someone once and it wouldn't have happened if there'd been a bit more attention to some basic safety. I'm not about to let it happen again but it's no reflection on how capable I know you are, believe me.'

There was something about that sincere tone of his voice that was making it difficult to keep hold of that annoyance. Or perhaps it was what he was saying—that the death of someone he'd worked with had affected him deeply because he'd cared about his colleague that much? She had sensed that he was a nice person from the first moment she'd met him. Big. Solid. Totally dependable. The kind of person you'd be lucky to work with or have as a friend.

Or maybe it was more to do with that steady gaze from eyes that she hadn't looked at this closely before. Hazel eyes, with a warmth to their golden brown that made her think of…good grief…teddy bears? Yes… she could swear that she'd had a beloved bear when she was very young that had had eyes of exactly that colour. She'd gone to sleep cuddling that bear every night for many years...

Somehow, that awareness of the colour of Cooper's eyes had made her let her guard down. He had gently pushed her hand away, had a look at the cut on her thumb and was now applying pressure to the wound himself.

'It might take a few minutes,' he murmured. 'It's quite deep but I don't think it needs a stitch. We just need to stop it bleeding.'

'Mmm...' The sound was a little strangled. Fizz stared down at her thumb because she didn't dare look up at Cooper again. She hadn't been this aware of the sheer size of him since he'd been holding her hand that day they'd first met, to help her keep her balance on those rocks. It was something deeper than being made to feel feminine, wasn't it? It was almost as if there was a much younger Fizz still inside. A child who cuddled teddy bears when she went to sleep. Who needed her hand held sometimes.

It actually brought a lump to her throat, along with a swirl of something like confusion. Fear, almost...and that was enough for her gaze to flick upwards again. What was it about this man that was so different?

She found that same steady gaze on her own.

'Almost there,' he said softly. 'Another thirty seconds or so should do it.'

Fizz knew she should break that eye contact. She should also pull her hand away from his and look after her injury herself but she did neither of those things and that was undoing.

She couldn't move. She couldn't look away. She was

powerless against the strength of a pull she'd never felt before. An attraction so fierce that what she wanted right now—the *only* thing she wanted right now—was for Cooper Sinclair to bend his head and kiss her.

Was she willing it to happen? Was that why she could see the way his eyes darkened as he seemed to catch her unspoken desire and reflect it back at her? Why his head started to drift down?

He seemed to catch himself with a jerk. It was Cooper who broke the eye contact. Fizz could feel him carefully peeling the wad of paper towel from her thumb. When he spoke, his voice was a little raw.

'I think it's stopped,' he told her. 'We're all good.'

Fizz nodded as she stepped back. 'I'll go and find a plaster,' she said.

Her voice sounded a little odd as well. Shaky, almost, and she knew why. Cooper had got it wrong, hadn't he?

It hadn't stopped.

Whatever it was between them was just getting started and Fizz had the feeling that, if it went any further, it would be a lot harder to stop than any blood loss from a small cut.

She would be playing with fire to give in to this attraction. This was the second time today that she'd had a momentary loss of control, even though she'd thought she'd taken heed of the warning the first time. If it was this hard to fight the pull towards this man when they barely knew each other, how hard would it be to control if it got unleashed?

The thought was a little terrifying.

But it was also more than a little exciting.

It wasn't a physically dangerous situation but, oddly,

it seemed to offer the promise of just as much of an adrenaline rush.

And Felicity Wilson knew only too well that she had a little bit of an issue with seeking out the thrill that came with the release of that particular hormone. She had it more under control these days, mind you. She'd harnessed it, to enhance her life instead of using it to escape things that had threatened to destroy her life.

This crush, or attraction, or whatever it was, was simply the rush of a different variety of hormones, wasn't it? It was purely physical. She wasn't falling in love with this man. For heaven's sake...this was only the second time she'd seen him. She'd been dating Hamish for half their time at medical school before they had both realised how much in love in they were.

Fizz put two plasters on her thumb just to be on the safe side. As she reached to put the small first-aid kit back on top of the fridge, she slid a sideways glance at Cooper. He'd cut a slice of the cake and put it on a plate, along with a fork and a neatly folded paper towel as a serviette.

Good grief...he ate cake like he was at an afternoon tea with his grandmother? With a fork? Fizz had never eaten cake with a fork in her life. It didn't fit with her impressions of Cooper's sheer masculinity and it was another dip in what was becoming an emotional roller-coaster.

To be feeling such strong emotions was not normal. Fizz took her friendships with men as they came. If they went further than simply friendship it was great but if they didn't that was no problem. Of course she enjoyed the chemistry of physical attraction and the satisfaction of great sex but she didn't let it take control at a level that could disrupt her life.

She didn't do planning for a future in a relationship or hope that it would become something significant because that was the best protection there was from disappointment or heartbreak. But she had wanted that kiss, hadn't she? She'd been hoping for it enough to consider how exciting it would be to play with fire.

It was confusing, that's what it was. And the best way that Fizz could find to balance that disturbing level of attraction was to try and find something to build a barrier. Something undesirable about Cooper. Like his over-protectiveness. Or the fact that he could do something as prim and proper as eating cake with a fork. That was kind of old-fashioned. Stuffy, even. Right now, Fizz was tempted to go and cut a slice of cake for herself and stuff it into her mouth using nothing more than her hand, right in front of Cooper. To let him know just how stuffy she considered him to be. How strait-laced and old-fashioned. Had she really entertained the idea of a friendship with benefits with him? He probably wouldn't dream of having that kind of casual relationship.

She turned, in fact, to do exactly that with the cake, only to be faced by…by that *smile*… The one that gave him crinkles at the corners of his eyes and made his whole face light up.

'Here you go,' Cooper said, pushing the plate along the bench in her direction. 'Enjoy…'

CHAPTER FIVE

'Fizz... I'm so glad you're still here.'

'Laura...' Fizz was startled to see her friend and workmate in the emergency department of the Royal as she came out of an office, a medical journal that she'd been wanting to read in her hands. 'What on earth are you doing back at work? You finished an hour ago.'

'It's Harrison. I think he's broken his arm.'

'Oh, no...' But Fizz was confused. 'Where is he?'

'Cubicle Three. He's with Cooper. He drove us in. I came looking for you because I was hoping you might be able to see him. You know how he is with strangers—especially men.'

'I know.' Five-year-old Harrison was small for his age and could be easily frightened. 'But he's okay with Cooper?'

'Amazingly so. I was a bit worried when he moved into the house because...well, he's so big, isn't he? But there's something about him, isn't there? And kids pick up on that sort of thing. It's only been a week but you'd think they'd known each other for years. And he'd just got home when Harry fell. He looked after him right from when it happened.'

Fizz pulled back the curtain to Cubicle Three and, for a heartbeat, her breath caught in her chest.

Cooper Sinclair was sitting on the bed. Harrison was sitting on his lap, leaning back into the crook of one of Cooper's arms. It made him look even smaller than Fizz knew the little boy was. It also made him look as if he'd never been so well protected and Fizz could easily imagine exactly how that felt.

She knew what it was like to have this big man looking after you. Not that she'd seen Cooper since last week, when he'd insisted on taking care of her cut thumb. Part of her had been hoping she'd see him in the emergency department—part of her had been relieved that she hadn't. She'd known what it would be like to make eye contact with Cooper again. How potentially awkward it could be if they were both thinking about the same thing. Sure enough, even the briefest contact as her gaze dropped straight from the man to the child in his arms was enough to confirm she'd been right. Laura had no idea how correct she was. There certainly was something about Cooper Sinclair.

It was still hanging there in the air.

The kiss that hadn't happened.

'Hey… Harry… What have you been up to?' Fizz was smiling reassuringly but she was taking in how pale his face was and the way he was holding one arm against his chest. An arm that was buried in a cushion that had been tied around the hand and wrist.

'I fell over,' Harry whispered.

'He was swinging on the gate.' Laura moved around Fizz to stand as close as she could to Cooper. She reached out to stroke Harry's hair. 'It came off its hinge, didn't it, sweetheart? And you fell onto the foot-path and hurt your arm.'

'Simple FOOSH,' Cooper added. 'Colles' fracture. We improvised with a pillow splint and then it didn't hurt so much, did it, buddy?'

'Thank goodness Cooper was there,' Laura said. 'It's funny, isn't it? We deal with a lot worse than this in here all the time but when it's your own kid, it's so different.'

'Can I have a peep?' Fizz touched the edge of the cushion protecting the injured arm.

Harrison seemed to shrink back further into Cooper's arms and Laura leaned in give him a kiss and reassure him.

'It's okay… Fizz is the doctor today and she just needs to have a look to see what to do next to fix up your arm.'

'But it's going to hurt…' Harrison was clearly trying hard to be brave but tears were imminent.

'How 'bout I undo the bandage, just a little bit?' Cooper's voice was a gentle rumble. 'Just to let Fizz have a peep.'

'You know Cooper won't hurt you,' Laura added. 'He's looking after you, isn't he?'

Harrison nodded but his lips were wobbling.

Fizz watched Cooper very carefully start to unroll the bandage he'd used to secure the soft cushion around Harrison's wrist. It had been the perfect splint, with the filling of the cushion moulding into the classic dinner fork shape of the Colles' fracture and supporting the arm and hand on either side so it couldn't move any further. Both Cooper and Laura were focused on Harrison and Fizz could feel…something. Some kind of bond… A trust between the three of them?

Cooper had only been living in the shared house for a week. Surely there couldn't be anything going on between him and Laura already, could there?

It was an unprofessional thing to be thinking about right now. Even more unprofessional was the flash of something like envy that came as an afterthought. Jealousy, even? No…but maybe regret that she'd let an opportunity disappear. Why on earth had she waited for Cooper to kiss her that night instead of just making it happen herself? What had that been about? She might never find out what it might have been like now.

The thought was gone as instantly as it had arrived. If Cooper had wanted to kiss her, he would have. She was not about to chase someone who wasn't interested. Or chase anyone, for that matter.

'Can you wiggle your fingers for me, Harry?' she asked.

'No.'

'Did you try, buddy?' Cooper was stifling a smile. He held out a giant hand so that it was side by side with Harrison's tiny one. 'Like this…' He wiggled those long fingers slowly, as though he was playing an imaginary piano.

Oh, help… Fizz could actually feel the tingle on her own skin, as if those fingers were touching it. This was getting ridiculous.

But Harrison was moving *his* fingers now. And his thumb, which was enough to reassure Fizz that his median nerve hadn't been damaged. The colour of his hand was good, too, so there were unlikely to be any major complications from this fracture.

'We need to take an X-ray of your arm, Harry,' she told him. 'It's a special photo of the bones inside it. And then we're going to put a cast on it, which is like a hard sleeve and it will stop your arm moving so it can get better.'

'I know what a cast is. Sally at school had one. It was pink.'

'Do you want a pink one?'

'No...pink is for girls.'

'Not necessarily,' Fizz said firmly. 'If you want pink then that's cool. It won't be a coloured one for a few days, though. We put a big, white one on first because your wrist is quite swollen and it needs time for that to go down. Now, how 'bout you and Cooper here have a chat about what colour it's going to be later on, while I have a talk to Mummy for a minute before you go up to X-ray? Is that okay?'

Both Harrison and Cooper nodded. Laura followed Fizz through the curtains.

'We'll get the X-ray and, if it's a straightforward fracture, we'll realign it and get a cast on in no time.'

'Pain relief?'

'Did you give him any paracetamol?'

'Yes...after Cooper suggested it. Honestly, my brain turned to mush.'

'I think we'll use some intranasal fentanyl for the re-alignment. It's fast acting, lasts long enough and you'll only have to wait another thirty minutes or so after-wards before you can take him home.'

'That's a relief. Poor Cooper's not getting much of a free evening. I don't like imposing on him but Maggie and Jack were both out.'

'He looks happy enough.'

'And he's so good with Harry. I can't believe how lucky we are to have got him as a flatmate.' Laura's eyebrows rose as she took in the expression on Fizz's face. 'What?'

'Nothing… I was just thinking about how good he is with Harry.'

If Fizz was honest, she was really thinking about what he'd be like as a partner. As a father, even.

He'd be perfect, probably.

Every woman's dream. Every woman other than herself, that is. Someone like Laura, perhaps?

Laura was still staring at her and comprehension flooded her face. 'Oh, no…it's *nothing* like that… Good grief, Fizz. How could you even think of something like that? Not in a million years…'

Fizz's smile was apologetic. She knew that Laura's relationship with Harrison's father had been traumatic enough to have made her shy away from any relationships with men.

'I have no idea.' She sighed. 'Ignore me. It's just that…like you said, there's something about him…'

Laura's expression had changed. A corner of her mouth curved upwards. '*You* like him, don't you, Fizz?'

Fizz shook her head. 'Not like that. Any more than you do. Now…let's get this show on the road, shall we? If Cooper's happy to stay, he could carry Harry up to X-ray, otherwise let's find a wheelchair. The sooner we get onto it, the sooner we can all get home.'

There was no question of abandoning Laura and Harrison in the emergency department, even though Cooper knew they would be extremely well looked after. They even had a personal physician who was a family friend.

It had been evident from the moment he'd come in here with the child in his arms that Harrison was nervous of strangers so it was amazing that he'd accepted *him* into his life so willingly over the last week.

It felt like a privilege to be trusted more than other people and Cooper wasn't about to break that trust by leaving his new flatmate and her kid here by themselves. So he carried Harrison to X-ray and back to the fracture clinic and he helped Laura reassure him that it would be no time at all until his arm was comfy in its new cast. The pain relief was effective and the procedure to straighten the small arm was straightforward, and then it was just a matter of observing him until the cast had dried enough to be solid and for the sedation to wear off.

'You stayed late for us,' Laura said to Fizz. 'Thank you so much.'

'It was my pleasure.'

'And you gave up half your evening,' she said to Cooper. 'I can't thank you enough.'

'It was no problem.'

'You must be starving. How 'bout I cook something when we get home? For you, too, Fizz. I owe you both.'

'You don't want to be cooking,' Fizz said firmly. 'Harrison's going to need all your attention when you get home and you'll be wanting to get him settled. I'll bet you're exhausted after all this.'

'But...'

'I'll drive you home,' Cooper offered. 'We could pick up some takeout food on the way.'

Laura looked at Cooper and then at Fizz, her expression thoughtful. 'I've got a better idea,' she said. 'I'll

drive myself and Harry home and you two can go and
get some dinner. My treat.'

'Oh, no… I'm sure Cooper's got better things to do
with the rest of his evening.'

Fizz was giving Laura an odd look and, for a moment, Cooper was bemused. Was there something
going on here that he wasn't privy to? The way Fizz
was avoiding his gaze and looking slightly flustered
reminded him of when he'd seen her in the locker room
at the base the first day they had been there together.
When he had thought it interesting that his presence
seemed to be unsettling for her for some reason.

That thought morphed instantly into remembering the end of that day. When he'd been putting pressure on that cut on her thumb. When he'd come within
a heartbeat of kissing her. He could have sworn that
she'd wanted him to but something didn't quite fit. It
just seemed out of character for this strong, confident
woman, in the same way that being flustered seemed
unlikely. If Felicity Wilson wanted to be kissed, Cooper was quite sure that she was more than capable of
initiating that herself. He also had the impression that
a simple kiss would not be enough for someone who
thrived on the thrill of adventure. She would probably
want more. A lot more.

That thought was enough to send a spear of sensation through Cooper's body and drive most coherent
thought away. He knew this was probably not sensible but there was an opportunity here, if he was game
enough to throw caution to the wind and take it.

'Actually, I don't,' he found himself saying aloud.
'I'd love to get some dinner and I'm sure you know the
restaurants around here a lot better than I do.'

'Go down the waterfront,' Laura encouraged. 'There's lots of awesome places and it's not far to walk from here.'

Fizz caught Cooper's gaze, finally, and it looked like she was trying to decide whether to accept some kind of challenge.

He could understand that. For himself, this felt like he was holding a match and contemplating striking it against the side of the box but knowing, at the same time, that this particular match had the ability to self-ignite. Also knowing that the ensuing conflagration held the possibility of getting dangerously out of control.

The eye contact went on for a split second too long. Long enough for Cooper to know they were both thinking of the same thing.

That almost kiss…

He saw the movement of Fizz's throat as she swallowed. Then her chin tilted as if she was confident of coping with whatever challenge she might choose to take and one corner of her mouth curved into a half-smile.

'I *am* starving,' she said. 'And I could show you one of my favourite restaurants if you like pub grub, Coop.'

'My all-time favourite.'

The smile widened. 'Give me five minutes. I'll just get changed out of my scrubs.'

Five minutes was enough to carry a still drowsy Harrison back to Laura's car and strap him into his car seat.

'You sure you don't want me to come with you?'

'I'm sure. Go and have a lovely dinner with Fizz.'

Laura reached into her shoulder bag and pulled out her wallet but Cooper shook his head.

'Don't be daft. You're not paying for my dinner.'

'It's just to say thank you.'

'There's no need,' Cooper said firmly. He was smiling as he turned away before Laura could protest any further. Whether she'd intended to or not, his new flatmate had pretty much set him up on a date with Fizz, hadn't she? Maybe it was him who should be thanking her…

Fizz drank beer rather than wine and somehow that didn't surprise Cooper.

She also chose a meal that needed to be eaten without cutlery and would, no doubt, get messy.

Cooper found himself grinning as he ordered the spare ribs as well. This was already more interesting than any date he'd been on in a very long time.

Not that either of them were admitting this was anything more than a meal between colleagues and potential friends, mind you. The conversation as they'd walked from the hospital to the section of the city near the harbourside that was brimming with restaurants, cafés and nightclubs had been no more than the polite sort of 'getting to know someone' queries and responses.

Cooper had told Fizz he'd been born and raised in Edinburgh, had gone to an English university and had never had any ambition to be anything other than a paramedic after he'd given up his small-boy dream of being an astronaut. He had learned that Fizz was a fifth-generation New Zealander and that it was a percentage of Maori and not Mediterranean blood that had given her that amazing olive skin and those dark eyes. She had grown up in a small, rural town not far from Wellington but was now loving her waterfront apartment that was close to this restaurant. She also told him that she had gone to medical school in the south island city of Dunedin, which she said had the reputation of being the most Scottish city in the world outside Scotland.

'You really should visit Dunedin one day,' she said, as she clinked her tall glass of lager against his. They had found a quiet corner in this quirky gastro pub and were perched on stools on either side of a small butcher's block table. 'Especially if you start getting homesick for Edinburgh.'

'I won't get homesick,' he assured her. 'I'm loving being on this side of the world.'

'It's a long way to have come for a new job.' Fizz wiped a streak of foam off her top lip as she gave Cooper a curious glance. 'Why here and not somewhere in Europe or America or Australia, even?' There was a mischievous glint in her eyes. 'Are you running away from an ex-wife?'

'Nope.' Cooper held her gaze. They were moving onto much more personal ground, apparently. 'I just came for the adventure. Never been married. How 'bout you?'

'Yep. I got married.' Her tone was offhand. And then she shrugged. 'Once was enough.'

Cooper's glass of lager stopped halfway between the table and his mouth. He really hadn't expected to hear that. And, to be honest, he was a bit shocked as well. What kind of bastard had she been married to that would make her dismiss the possibility of ever going down that road again?

'How long did it last?' he asked.

'Two days,' Fizz responded.

Cooper's glass hit the table at the same time as his bark of laughter emerged. He opened his mouth to make some quip about not having given it much of a go but then he saw the way Fizz's face had suddenly stilled and he actually felt a chill ripple down his spine.

'Oh, my God…' he said slowly. 'What happened?'

Fizz was silent for another long moment and then she spoke without looking up. 'It was the second day of our honeymoon. We were on an island off Fiji and Hamish decided he was going to try parasailing. Off the back of a jet boat, you know?'

Cooper nodded but said nothing. He was still reeling from realising just how far he'd managed to put his foot in his mouth.

'They hadn't done the harness up properly. I was sitting on the beach and trying to take photographs when he fell. They reckon he broke his neck as he hit the water.'

'I'm so sorry… That's…just horrible.'

'Yeah…' Fizz turned her head. Was she hoping their food would arrive quickly so that she could change the subject? 'Well, ten years is a long time. I learned how to manage alone and I got my life back together.'

'More than back together from what I can see,' Cooper told her. 'I found out that you're a legend amongst the emergency services here even before I got into town properly. And I've seen you in action and I know how good you are at your job.'

'It's everything to me,' Fizz said quietly. 'My career.'

'Me, too.'

The moment of silence between them this time acknowledged a shared passion. A connection. But Cooper could feel the frown on his face and Fizz noticed it at the same time.

'What?'

'You surprise me, that's all.'

'In what way?'

'Having a tragedy like that would make a lot of people more cautious.' Like he had become himself? 'Unless you were even wilder ten years ago than you are now?'

Fizz's lips quirked. 'You think I'm wild?'

'You take risks. I'm not sure that you take enough time to assess how dangerous something is before you decide to do it.'

'I assess. I just do it fast. And in some situations you don't really have a choice. You're talking about me getting those kids out of the car in the surf, aren't you? Would you have stood back when you saw that little girl crying at the window?'

'No...'

'Of course you wouldn't. Oh...that looks like our food arriving.'

A huge platter of barbecued pork ribs went onto the centre of their rustic wooden table flanked by bowls of warm water with lemon slices floating on the top to wash sticky fingers. For several minutes they both concentrated on eating like cavemen, ripping delicious shreds of sauce-drenched, slow-cooked meat off the bones.

'Good, isn't it?' Fizz dropped another bone onto an empty plate. She sucked some sauce off her fingers before she reached for another rib.

'The best.' Cooper had to drag his gaze away from

Fizz licking her fingers. He'd known he was playing with fire, coming out like this with Fizz, and right now he could feel the heat as a solid force. He had to reach for his beer again in the hope of cooling himself off.

'To be honest,' Fizz said, 'I wasn't remotely wild ten years ago. I was a complete nerd. I only met Hamish because we were both nerds who turned up to the study group that got organised the first day we were at med school.'

The mention of the husband she'd lost was more effective in turning down the heat than a gulp of beer. Was the fact that she would never try replacing him the reason that she was never going to get married again? Had she loved him so much she hadn't even embarked on another meaningful relationship in the last ten years? The idea of competing with a ghost for any sort of attention was daunting. Cooper knew how strong a presence a ghost could have and how much they could influence your life.

'I find that hard to believe,' he admitted. 'I get the impression that you're a complete adrenaline junkie.'

'I am.' Fizz nodded. 'And you know whose fault it was that I became one?'

'Whose?'

'Hamish's.'

She'd shocked him again, hadn't she?

Fizz had seen the moment he'd realised that the fact she'd been married for only two days wasn't some kind of joking matter. That it had been a tragedy.

The atmosphere between them had been very casual up to that point. They had simply been two colleagues going out for dinner and it was a good chance to get to know each other better.

Except they both knew there was more to it than that, didn't they? There were undercurrents between them that were strong enough for Laura to have picked up on. Strong enough to have led to her impulsive idea of doing a bit of matchmaking by pushing them together for dinner. And there was a sense of something very different about Cooper that was attracting Fizz even more strongly than it was warning her to stay away.

And here she was, talking about something that she never talked about. To anyone. Something far more personal than the kind of conversation they'd started this evening with. She'd said quite enough already, telling him about her honeymoon tragedy, but it seemed like there was more that Fizz wanted to say. Why? Did she want Cooper to understand why she was the way she was? To take on board the fact that there were reasons why she would never be the kind of person he might be looking for to share his life? Except...he had given the impression that he wasn't looking for someone to settle down with when he'd said he wasn't interested in having his own children. And why else did people go looking for a permanent relationship?

'I was so angry with him,' Fizz said softly. 'We'd had everything so carefully planned, you know? We'd waited until we were through med school and our first junior years before we got married. We were going to wait another five years before we started a family. He was going to be a cardiologist and I was going to go into general practice so I could go part time when the kids were young. And then he went and got himself killed and it felt like someone had taken my life and screwed it up and thrown it away.'

Cooper was nodding slowly. The set of his mouth implied a genuine understanding of what that felt like. The expression in his eyes confirmed that he really did understand and empathise.

'Things were rough for a long time,' Fizz added slowly. 'Really rough...'

His eyes darkened. He knew what that was like, too, didn't he? Not that Fizz wanted this conversation to get any heavier than it already was. Or to think too much about that time herself. Even after all these years and her increasing professional understanding of mental health issues like depression, she could still feel the sense of shame that had dogged her for not being able to pull herself out of that dark space quickly enough. For having to pretend to be the independent, capable person everybody believed she was until it became a reality.

'And then I went away for a weekend,' she added hurriedly. 'And I saw some people parasailing and that tipped me over the edge. I couldn't understand why anyone could be stupid enough to do something like that for pleasure, so you know what I did?'

She could see the movement of Cooper's Adam's apple as he swallowed—as if it wasn't easy.

'You decided to try it yourself?'

Oh...help...

It felt like he knew her so well already. The idea that someone could 'get' her so easily was undeniably powerful. Fizz could feel it sucking her in. Making her say things she would never have confessed to anyone else.

'I didn't care if I died and I was too angry to be

scared until my feet left the ground and then I was absolutely terrified. But then it happened.'

'The rush?'

Fizz nodded. 'The rush. For the first time in about a year, I actually felt alive again. As if life really was worth living.'

'So you did it again.'

It wasn't a question. It seemed like Cooper understood more than why she had done something so scary the first time. He would probably understand the rest of it, too. The way she had tapped into that power of being brave and independent to gain confidence that she could look after herself. That she could not only get out of that dark space and find life worth living again but that she could protect herself from ever having to go through something like that again. The idea that someone else could understand that much about what had shaped her life was a bit of a rush all in itself.

'I tried everything,' she confided. 'I think the best ever rush was bungee jumping. Have you ever tried that, Coop?'

He shook his head.

'Did you get that base newsletter this week? Did you notice that there are registration spaces still left for the high country and mountain rescue training weekend in Queenstown in a couple of months' time?'

'Yeah…' Cooper looked puzzled. 'Don suggested I go. I've already done some mountain rescue training in Scotland and he'd like me to extend that so I can do some in-house training for the base. But what's that got to do with bungee jumping?'

'As far as I know, Queenstown is the birthplace of bungee jumping,' Fizz told him. 'The best place, anyway. You could do it while you're down there for the course.'

'Are you kidding?' Cooper looked horrified. 'You could go blind from a retinal detachment doing something like bungee jumping. It's crazy.'

'There's the white-water jet boat rides through rapids, too. Queenstown is like the adventure tourism capital of the world.' Fizz could feel her smile widening. 'And there's a very cool drive into an old gold-mining site that's an adrenaline rush all by itself.' She could feel an impulsive bubble that was about to burst. 'Hey… I could come along, too, and cheer you on. I'd love to do some training in the mountains.'

'Training in the mountains might be good for you. You'd have to learn a lot of safety rules.' But Cooper was smiling.

'A bit of adventure tourism might be good for *you*,' Fizz countered. 'You can die from something totally random that could happen at any moment, you know, so you kind of have to make the most of every moment you've got. If you go around avoiding everything to try and stay safe, you could end up not really living at all.'

The remains of their meal had been totally forgotten. The atmosphere between them was suddenly charged. As if challenges had been issued. Or an invitation?

Cooper signalled a waitress and paid for their meal. They walked outside and across the road but then paused. Fizz needed to go in one direction to her apartment. Cooper needed to head back towards the central city to flag down a taxi if he didn't want to walk all the way home. The vibrancy of restaurants and bars, with their bright lights and music, was behind them and the dark waters of the harbour were in front of them, with small boats bobbing on their moorings and a glimmer of moonlight on the ripples.

Neither of them moved.

Because neither of them wanted to say goodnight and walk away?

Cooper seemed fascinated by the harbour view, staring at it for a long moment. And then he turned to stare at Fizz and the eye contact sent a shiver down her spine.

'Thank you for sharing your story,' he said quietly. 'Am I wrong in thinking that it's not something you normally tell people you've just met?'

'I've never told anyone. Not about the adrenaline junkie stuff, anyway.'

He was shaking his head. 'I've never met anyone like you. And, yeah… I do think there's something wild about you but it feels good to be around you. As if that adrenaline high somehow rubs off a little bit.' He was smiling now. 'Maybe you're right. Maybe it would be good for me to try something like bungee jumping. Just once.'

Fizz let her breath out in a huff. 'But you're not going to, are you?'

'Probably not.'

'You're a wimp.'

'I'm safety conscious.'

'You're…' But any other teasing remark died on Fizz's lips as she still held his gaze. 'You're…' It was her turn to shake her head. 'I don't actually know,' she admitted, in a whisper. 'What *is* it about you, Cooper Sinclair?'

'I was asking myself the same thing about you. But I think I've figured it out now. It's the way you embrace life and get the most out of every moment.'

Fizz felt like she was falling into those eyes, which was crazy because she was still looking up. He was *so* tall. So solid and safe. She could feel herself leaning a little, even though she could swear she hadn't moved. Or maybe she had and that was why Cooper put his hands on her shoulders to steady her.

Her mouth felt suddenly dry.

'I don't do relationships, Coop.'

'I'm not looking for one,' he said. 'Especially not with someone I work with.'

'Good.' Fizz dipped her head in a single nod. 'That's that, then.'

'Yeah…'

But neither of them was breaking that eye contact. This had become another 'almost kiss' and this was what that sense of challenge had been about as they'd ended their meal, wasn't it?

A challenge to take a risk. Flirt with the danger of something that could go pear-shaped and make life difficult for both of them when they had to work together. But it was also about living for the moment and making the most of every one of them, and wasn't that what Cooper found attractive about her? And kissing this man held the promise of being a moment like none other in Fizz Wilson's life.

She could feel the heat of Cooper's hand on her shoulders seeping through her clothing and branding her skin. All she had to do to initiate this kiss would be to stand on tiptoe and tilt her face. All Cooper would have to do was to bend his head.

It seemed like they both decided to move at exactly the same time so their mouths met with a little more force than Fizz had been anticipating but that was as thrilling as the touch of Cooper's lips and, within a heartbeat, it wasn't enough. She lifted her hands to cradle his head and pull it even closer. To tempt his tongue to dance with hers. The force of desire that was being unleashed was like nothing Fizz had ever experienced and she felt like she was melting when Cooper's hands slid down her back to circle her buttocks and pull *her* closer.

The strength in those hands... Her feet came off the ground and it was the most natural thing in the world to wrap her legs around his waist, feeling one of her shoes falling off as she did so. She felt Cooper's arms come around her back to hold her safely and then he was turning in a circle, as if this was some kind of dance step. She could feel the huff of his surprise that became laughter beneath her lips but they didn't stop kissing.

The cheer that came from a group of young men heading into a nearby bar was a reminder that they were in a public place. Cooper loosened his hold. Fizz slid down to get her feet back on the ground.

'Oops... Sorry 'bout that.'

'I'm not.' There was still a hint of laughter in his tone.

Fizz ducked her head. She wasn't sorry, either, but she kept her gaze on ground level so she didn't reveal quite how *not* sorry she really was. 'Where's my shoe?'

'Right here, Cinderella.'

She stood on one foot as she slipped her shoe back on. 'I think it's time to go home.'

'That's probably very sensible.'

Fizz turned and took a step. And then another.

And then she turned back and held out her hand. She didn't say anything by way of invitation to come home with her but she didn't need to. Cooper returned her smile and reached out to take her hand. He was already moving in the same direction.

CHAPTER SIX

THEY WERE PRACTICALLY RUNNING, hand in hand, by the time they reached the harbourside apartment block where Fizz lived. By tacit agreement, they decided that waiting for the elevator to take them to the fifth floor was going to take too long, so they took the stairs—two at a time.

Both Cooper and Fizz were thoroughly out of breath by the time she slid her key into the lock and pushed her door open. Cooper pushed it shut behind him with his foot. He couldn't turn to use his hand because Fizz had turned and stopped, right in front of him—so close that her body was touching his and she was already reaching to drape her arms around his neck. Even as he heard the door click shut behind him, Cooper's lips were already on hers. He'd caught her hands and was now holding them above her head as he pressed her against the wall and kissed her as thoroughly as he'd ever kissed any woman in his life.

The heat of her mouth. The *taste* of her. The way she was arcing her body against his as if she wanted to feel every possible square inch of him that she could. Cooper let go of her hands a short time later, unable to resist the urge to touch more of her. When he reached the hem of her shirt and slipped his hands beneath to find the silky-soft skin of her belly, Fizz groaned into his mouth and pulled away. She wriggled against him, taking hold of her shirt hem herself and pulling it up, over her head, to drop it on the floor.

No, she didn't simply drop it. Fizz hurled it to one side and then turned her attention to the T-shirt Cooper was wearing beneath his leather jacket, grabbing the hem and hauling it up. Cooper's breath caught as he felt her hands brush his skin, his nipples hardening so fast it was painful enough for his breath to escape in a sound of astonishment.

Fizz paused instantly. She brought her face close to Cooper's, her lips and then her tongue brushing his before she spoke in a hoarse whisper.

'Too wild for you?'

'Are you kidding?' Cooper's breath came out in a groan this time. Then he scooped Fizz into his arms, one arm around her back, the other catching her behind the knees. 'Which way?' he demanded.

'Straight ahead.' Fizz was laughing. 'Last door on the left.'

The curtains were not drawn on the large window in her bedroom. City lights nearby and the sparkle of moonlight on the harbour in the background gave more than enough illumination for Cooper to aim safely for the centre of the large bed, where he dropped Fizz hard enough to make her bounce against the mattress.

She was still laughing as she unbuttoned her jeans and started wriggling out of them.

'You've got a wild streak yourself, Coop. That was a bit caveman, wasn't it?'

'Maybe you inspire me.' Cooper was shedding his

own clothes. He climbed onto the bed, looming over Fizz as she lay there wearing only her underwear now. Slowly he lowered his head so that he could kiss her again—this time as gently as he could. The flames of a passion that was barely controllable were licking all around them but he wanted to slow this down and make it last as long as he possibly could.

Fizz didn't do relationships. For all he knew, this could be a one-off and, if that was the case, Cooper intended to take a leaf out of her book and enjoy every single moment of it.

Dear Lord...

The very first impression that Fizz had ever had of Cooper was that he was a great big bear of a man. The sheer size of him should have been intimidating, especially given that his bulk was pure muscle. She had never been as aware of that muscle and the strength behind it as when he'd picked her up as if she weighed nothing to carry her to her bedroom. To get dropped like that, with enough of a gap beneath her to make her bounce on her mattress, should have been a warning that she was actually powerless against this man.

Totally vulnerable, in fact.

And yet...even when he was looming above her and she could feel the heat coming from his skin and the musky scent of arousal all around them, Fizz still felt safe. Well...as safe as anybody could feel when it was obvious she was about to jump off a precipice into a kind of sexual experience she just knew would be nothing like anything she had ever experienced before.

Maybe because she wasn't trying to control this.

How could she? In one instant, she was ready to explode with the power of her desire and wanted nothing more than for Cooper to speed this up and take them both over the edge but then, in the next instant, he was pulling back and touching and kissing her with a tenderness that broke her heart but was so compelling she never wanted it to stop.

It was a roller-coaster ride like no other.

A ride that had all the excitement of the kind of adrenaline rush that a brush with danger could deliver. But it was so much more than that. So much deeper.

It was like the thrill of danger while being wrapped up in the safest place imaginable. Within the circle of strong arms that could protect you from anything and gentle hands that could coax a thrill into pure ecstasy. It tapped into longings that Fizz would never admit to having, even to herself. And she didn't need to, because this kind of closeness, despite being only temporary, was enough to satisfy any unspoken longing.

Once wasn't enough for either of them so it was no real surprise when Fizz eventually caught a glimpse of her digital clock and found it was nearly three a.m.

'Oh, no...'

'What?' Cooper lifted his head from the pillow at her tone.

'I have to be on base at six a.m.'

'Me, too. Hey...maybe we'll get crewed together.'

Fizz wriggled out of the circle of Cooper's arms enough to be able to prop herself up on one elbow.

'People can't know,' she warned.

'They might notice,' Cooper said. 'If we're, like... on the same helicopter together.'

'I don't mean work. I mean what happens out of

work stays out of work, okay? I don't want anyone thinking I jumped on the new guy two minutes after he arrived. That's hardly professional. You never know, I might want to apply for one of the full-time HEMS positions one day.'

'I think the truth is more like we jumped on each other.' Cooper smiled. 'And it's been two weeks, not two minutes.'

'And that makes it okay?'

'I reckon.' Cooper was smiling again.

'What are you looking so pleased about?' Fizz frowned. 'I mean it, Coop. I don't want people talking about us. Speculating that this is anything more than what it is.'

'Which is?'

Fizz sighed. 'An inexplicable but apparently irresistible attraction between two adults who are entitled to do what they like as long as they're not hurting anyone else.'

'Ah… That sounds like an eloquent description.'

'Why are you still smiling?'

'Because…' Cooper reached out to brush a long lock of Fizz's hair back from her face and tuck it behind her bare shoulder. 'I thought it might be a one-off kind of thing for you and I'm happy that you're not using the past tense when you're talking about it. You said "happens" out of work, not "happened".'

'I don't do one-night stands,' Fizz told him. 'That's tacky.'

'But you don't do long term, either.'

'Define long term?'

'A relationship.'

'No, that's true.' Fizz lay back against her pillow

with another sigh. 'I don't do relationships. They imply a shared future. Making plans. I did that, once. I have the T-shirt. The one that says *"It doesn't matter what anybody promises you even when you trust them to keep those promises—the future's not a given, and it can disappear in the blink of an eye"*. And it can make your whole life feel like it's disappeared along with it. I'm not about to go through that again. Ever.'

'So...' Cooper sounded thoughtful. 'If this wasn't a one-night stand and it's not the start of a relationship, what is it?'

'Does it need a label? It is what it is. Living for the moment and enjoying something while it lasts. Moving on with no regrets when it stops being fun.' She rested her head against his shoulder. 'That's not a bad thing, is it?'

'Hell, no...sounds like every man's dream.'

'Because you don't do relationships, either?'

'I didn't say that, exactly. I said I wasn't looking for one.'

'But you've had them before? You're not like some international playboy type? Breaking hearts left, right and centre all over the world by delivering fabulous sex and then moving on?' Not that she believed a word of what she was suggesting. Cooper Sinclair was in no way a playboy type. He was too solid. Too sincere.

His laughter was a deep rumble in his chest that Fizz could feel as much as hear.

'Fabulous, huh?' His hand moved to slide across her body, brushing her breasts gently. Fizz should have been sated to the point of total exhaustion but the tendrils of sensation that his touch created told her that she was wrong. She might have had enough for one night but, overall, she hadn't had nearly enough of being with this man. 'And there I was, thinking that *you* were the fabulous one.'

'Hmm… Are you trying to avoid answering my question?'

'About relationships? No. I've moved around too much for anything to get serious. I'm nowhere near ready to settle down. Or maybe I've just got a short attention span. I'm always looking for a new adventure. A new challenge.'

A beat of something like anxiety caught Fizz. She had no idea how long it might take for the novelty of this new and astonishing type of physical adventure to wear off because she'd never experienced it before. How long would someone with a short attention span want it to continue before they were off looking for a new challenge?

'As long as they're safe, huh?' Fizz murmured. 'I wasn't a bit surprised that you carry condoms in your wallet, you know.'

'You wouldn't take risks with sex, would you?' He sounded worried.

'Of course not.' Fizz could feel her eyes starting to drift shut. 'I don't take stupid risks, you know. They're always well calculated.'

'Hmm…'

'You really got affected by that guy, didn't you?'

'What guy?'

'The one you worked with that you told me about. The partner who didn't follow the safety rules and got killed?'

'Ah…yeah, you could say that. He wasn't someone I worked with, though.'

Fizz was on the verge of falling asleep. 'Who was he, then?'

'My brother,' Cooper said, very quietly. 'My twin brother.'

The possibility of sleep vanished in an instant. Fizz felt her whole body tense, becoming alert as if a sudden danger had presented itself, but holding very still, as if it was trying to decide between fight or flight as a response to something shocking.

Fizz chose neither of those reactions. Instead, she turned her head to press her face against Cooper's chest. To feel his heartbeat beneath her cheek and the softness of his skin beneath her lips.

'I'm so sorry,' she whispered. 'I can only imagine how hard that must have been for you.'

'I think you know better than most people,' Cooper responded.

His arm pulled her a little closer and then they both lay there in silence. They should be trying to catch some sleep before they needed to go to work. Cooper needed to get home and be able to go to work in his own vehicle so that people wouldn't guess he'd hooked up with a work colleague so soon after arriving at a new job.

But this was a connection that Fizz didn't want to break.

For her own sake as much as for Cooper's.

No wonder it felt like he 'got' her more than other people did. He knew exactly what it was like to lose someone you were that close to. Someone you'd believed would be a huge part of the rest of your life.

This was a connection that was way more powerful than sharing a passion for their careers. Or the fact that sexually they were apparently a perfect match. This went so much deeper. Soul deep, in fact, because they both knew what it was like to have your world destroyed and have to pick it up again, piece by tiny piece. To come out of that process with the kind of scars that made it feel that it would be impossible to ever get that close to anybody else, ever again.

To have that in common made this even more perfect. Neither of them was looking for anything serious because they both had barriers that were too strong to let that happen. They could, however, enjoy each other's company. Enjoy working *and* playing together. Living for the moment and enjoying every single one of them.

She didn't break the silence between them by asking questions about what had happened to cause such a tragedy. If Cooper wanted to tell her, he would. Right now, he seemed content to simply hold her close. She could hear his breathing slowing and his muscles softening. Maybe he was already asleep. Her alarm was set so Fizz decided she could do that, too. Sink into a couple of hours of sheer bliss, sleeping in the warmth and safety of Cooper's arms.

Content in the conviction that this might have been the first time they had been together like this but it wasn't going to be the last. Not if she had any choice in the matter, anyway.

How did Fizz pull that off?

Cooper was onto his second cup of Shirley's excellent coffee before he'd began feeling like he was totally on top of his game but Fizz looked as if she'd enjoyed a solid eight hours' sleep instead of the two and half they'd finally managed. Her face positively glowed and her eyes sparkled.

It had been a mad dash in the early hours of this morning so that he could get home and shower and then take his own vehicle to the base, as if nothing untoward had happened last night. As if he hadn't experienced the most mind-blowing sex of his entire adult life. He could still feel the physical connection between himself and Fizz—a kind of hum in the air that got more powerful the closer their bodies were to each other's, like when he walked past where she was sitting to put his coffee mug into the dishwasher.

'Have you had enough to eat, love?' Shirley asked.

'More than enough, thanks, Shirley. And you make the best porridge I've ever tasted.'

'Oh, go on with you…' Shirley flapped her tea towel in his direction but her cheeks were pink with pleasure. 'I don't have a drop of Scottish blood in me but I do know to soak the oats overnight.'

Cooper walked back past Fizz, who was reading the newspaper at the table and not taking any more notice of him than she normally would. Nobody here could possibly have any idea what had happened between them last night and if Fizz wanted to keep it a secret, that was fine by him. It made it all the more exciting, in fact.

He paused this time, however. To look over her shoulder and read the headline on the front page of the paper. It wasn't that he was particularly interested in the news, he was simply enjoying that electric hum in the air between them and wanted to test that crescendo effect. And, yes, as soon as he got a whiff of the scent of Fizz's hair, it went off the Richter scale.

Even better, when he saw Fizz closing her eyes in a long blink and taking in a breath as if she was smelling a particularly pleasant perfume, he knew that she was just as aware of the hum as he was.

It was Maggie she turned to speak to, however.

'How's Harrison this morning?'

'He was still asleep when I left. Poor little guy, he was a bit miserable last night when they got back from the hospital. Laura's taken a couple of days off work until he can get his light cast on and goes back to school. It's a stress she really doesn't need, so I said I'd do dinner tonight for everyone.' Maggie glanced up at Cooper. 'Will you be home?'

'I can't think of any reason I wouldn't be.'

One of Maggie's eyebrows rose and Cooper's heart sank a little. Had she been aware of him creeping back into the shared house this morning? Laura might well have told her that he and Fizz had gone out to dinner together. But Maggie was smiling as she turned her gaze back to Fizz.

'You're welcome, too, of course. I'm thinking tacos. And Mexican beer.'

'Count me in.' Fizz reached for her pager as the warning signal of an incoming call sounded in the staffroom.

Cooper's pager sounded at the same moment and, for the first time this morning, they made direct eye contact with each other that lasted more than a split second.

With a beat of what had to be relief, he realised that the hum had been switched off as effectively as if someone had pulled a plug from a socket. The awareness of being so close, along with the memories of that unbelievable physical connection they'd discovered, had been dismissed. This was work, and he was lucky enough to be crewed with Fizz, who was one of the best in this business. That tiny instant of eye contact before they both headed towards the helipad told him that Fizz was in exactly the same frame of mind. A totally professional space where anything personal that could interfere with their performance was simply not allowed. Didn't exist, even.

The call was to a small coastal community isolated enough for the first response emergency team to have been the local fire service. The house was so close to the beach that the damp sand was the obvious place to land.

'Tide's well out but we'll need to keep an eye on time,' Andy warned them.

One of the fire officers was waiting for Cooper and Fizz as they scrambled through sand dunes and tussocks on the edge of the beach.

'Sorry to call you all the way out here,' he said. 'There may not be much you can do.'

'Oh?' Fizz frowned. 'What's going on?'

'It's tricky. Ken—who runs a grocery store in the nearest town—made a delivery for them this morning and he was the one who called for help.'

They were almost out of the dunes now, heading for a small house that looked like a typical New Zealand bach, or holiday house, with bleached wooden cladding and a corrugated-iron roof.

'So what's the problem?' Cooper asked.

'It's a young couple living here. Tim and Sarah Poulson. He's terminal. Pancreatic cancer. Apparently he's got a legally drawn-up "Do Not Resuscitate" order but Ken decided it's not right and something needs to be done. The local doctor got called but both he and the district nurse are tied up with a woman having a baby at the moment. The doc said if Tim's as bad as Ken seems to think he is, then maybe some extra help *is* needed.'

Fizz could now see a van parked in front of a fire engine on an unsealed road behind the tiny house and a man who was pacing back and forth, flanked by another two fire officers. She caught Cooper's glance as they got closer.

This was not like any job she'd been to before. She couldn't just rush in, geared up to save a life, because that clearly wasn't going to be possible. Even prolonging the life of this patient might not be the right thing to do. Disconcertingly, Fizz felt a little unsure of how to tackle this job.

Cooper didn't seem the least bit unsure. He went straight to the pacing man and put a hand on his shoulder.

'Ken?'

'Yeah... Thank goodness you got here so fast. He can hardly breathe, man...and it's...pretty horrible.'

Cooper nodded. 'Thanks for letting us know. We've got this now, okay? You don't need to worry. We'll do whatever's needed to help.'

Ken rubbed his forehead with his hand. 'Thanks... I... I couldn't just leave them like that, you know?'

'I know.' Cooper patted his shoulder. 'It's okay. You did the right thing.'

'But there's nothing more you can do, Ken,' one of the fire officers put in. 'Time you went home now, eh?'

Ken turned to stare at the front door of the house.

'It's okay,' Cooper said again. 'We've got this.'

Did they? Fizz followed Cooper through a garden of seaside plants, decorated with driftwood sculptures, and onto a porch that had a veranda festooned with windchimes made of shells. Normally, she would lead a crew into any scene she'd been called to, but this time she stayed half a pace behind Cooper because he seemed so calm. Confident. In complete control.

He took off his backpack of gear and left it on the veranda before tapping lightly on the door. Fizz followed his example with her pack. A quick glance over her shoulder, as she did so, showed her the delivery van was leaving and that the fire officers were all staying near their truck. She and Cooper were being left to deal with this situation alone.

'Sarah?' Cooper's call was quiet as he stepped inside. 'Air Rescue here. I'm Cooper and I've got Fizz, who's a doctor, with me.'

'Oh, no…' A young woman, probably only in her early twenties, appeared at an internal door. Her long blonde hair was hanging loose and her pale face was streaked with tears. 'I told Ken not to call anybody. Please…we just need to be left alone…' She covered her face with her hands and started sobbing.

Without hesitation, Cooper stepped forward and took her into his arms.

'It's okay,' he said softly. 'We're here to help you. And Tim, if he needs it, of course, but *you* as well. Have you got someone here supporting you?'

She shook her head. 'We…we decided that we wanted it to be…to be just the two of us when it came to the end…' She tried, and failed, to stifle another sob.

'But Ken told me it wasn't right. That I had no right to just...to just let Tim suffer like this...'

Cooper kept his arm around Sarah's shoulders. 'Where is he?' he asked. 'We can check him for you. We can see if he's in any pain and do something to help that.'

'He's been on a morphine pump for weeks now. And fentanyl patches. He was awake a while ago and we watched the sun come up together and he said he wasn't in any pain but...he's not awake now and his breathing sounds awful...'

The main room of this small house had sliding doors that made the whole wall glass and it provided a view across the sand dunes and out to sea. The doors were open a little and the wash of the waves breaking created a gentle background song. A big bed had been positioned in the centre of the room where Sarah's husband, Tim, was propped up on pillows.

'These are his notes.' Sarah handed a file of papers to Fizz. 'The doctor visited yesterday and the district nurse helped me with all the medications. His DNR paper is in there, too. He really doesn't want to be... to be...'

'I understand.'

It was clear to Fizz that this patient was going to die very soon. His breathing did sound very distressed but a gentle examination after she'd quickly scanned all his notes told her that Tim was as comfortable as possible. It was the rattle of accumulating fluid that was making his breathing sound so upsetting for Sarah and she had medication that could help with that.

Cooper came close as she was drawing up the medication into a syringe. 'I'm going to call Andy and tell him we may be here for a while,' he said quietly. 'I don't want to intrude but I don't think we can leave Sarah without support.'

'Of course not.' It could be a matter of minutes but it could be hours. Cooper had to be aware of the kind of costs involved in keeping a rescue crew out of action but, if he was, he wasn't going to let it stop him doing what he felt was the right thing to do.

And he knew exactly how to handle this situation. He helped Sarah adjust Tim's pillows and to wipe his face and put salve on his lips.

'This is the most beautiful place,' he said quietly. 'So peaceful.'

'It was Tim's family's bach,' Sarah told him. 'When he knew he was going to die, this was where he wanted to be. Where he'd had so much fun on summer holidays when he was a kid. It was where we met... I was staying with friends up the beach a bit when I was fifteen. He was seventeen and...and...' She had tears rolling down her face. 'And I don't know what to do now... I thought I would but I don't because it's just too hard...'

'Okay...' Cooper's voice was calm. 'Come and sit on the bed, beside Tim. Lie down beside him if that feels right. Hold his hand. Or cuddle him. Talk to him. He can probably hear you but, even if he can't, he'll know you're here with him.'

'Really?' Sarah's whisper was another sob but Cooper nodded.

'I think so.' He took her hand and helped her climb onto the bed.

'The thing Tim needs right now is to be held by someone who loves him.' Cooper's voice was so gentle that Fizz felt the sting of tears in her eyes. 'It's what he needs and it's what you need, too, Sarah.'

Sarah had her head on the pillows beside Tim's and she was wrapping her arms around her husband.

'We're going to leave you alone,' Cooper added quietly. 'If that's what you want.'

'It's…it's what I promised but…but I'm scared…'

'I know.' Cooper touched her arm. 'But we'll be close. If you need anything at all, just call, okay? We'll hear you.'

The danger of her tears escaping had Fizz out of the room before Cooper. This wasn't her. She dealt with life-threatening emergencies and she had dealt with death on many occasions. And, yes, of course she felt sad when she lost a patient. Devastated, sometimes. But she didn't dissolve into tears. Ever. She'd decided years ago that she'd simply used up her lifetime supply of them when Hamish had been killed. Having to blink away the extra moisture in her eyes in this moment was…well…it was strange enough to be disturbing.

She wandered away from the road, where the fire truck had been joined by a police car now. Round the corner of the house, she could sit on a driftwood log that was just one side of the glass doors of the main room. She could see the beach and the soothing curl of the breaking waves and would hear if she was called for some reason, but she could also stay out of view of where Tim and Sarah were sharing such an intense and tragic farewell.

That was why she was in bits, Fizz decided. It was all just too close to home. A young couple being forced apart for ever, with all their hopes and dreams for the future being torn away at the same time.

There was room on the log for Cooper when he came to find her a few minutes later.

'Andy's on a park a few miles up the coast. If he's needed for an emergency, he'll take off back to the city but come and get us later.'

Fizz nodded. 'I don't think we'll be here all that long.'

'No.'

There was a wealth of things being left unsaid in that short word. The acknowledgement that a young life was ending. That there was nothing they would be able to do to help with all the grief and disruption to lives that was happening and would continue for a very long time. But Cooper had already done so much to help. The depth of his understanding of exactly what to do in such an intense situation had blown Fizz away. She still felt curiously overwhelmed and just a little bit wobbly.

'How did you know,' she asked quietly, 'how to handle that so well?'

Cooper was silent for a long moment. Then he took a deep breath and let it out in a slow sigh.

'I told you my brother died. My twin brother, Connor.'

Fizz nodded. She kept her gaze on Cooper's face but he wasn't looking at her. He leaned down and picked up a shell from the ground in front of them.

'We were sixteen,' he told her. 'Away for the weekend for some hiking and a bit of climbing in the Cairngorms, which is a gorgeous mountain range in the eastern highlands of Scotland. Connor got a bit carried away and took a risk with a ridge. Long story short, he fell and was critically injured. Chest and abdo injuries but mostly it was his head. He was unconscious from the moment he fell. There were other people nearby and they called for help and the next thing I knew, a helicopter was there and paramedics were trying to save Connor's life.'

There was another moment of silence in which Fizz could actually feel the depth of emotion Cooper was dealing with here. She wanted to take hold of his hand but he was still playing with that shell. Instead, she leaned a bit closer, so that her shoulder was touching his.

'I was standing there, watching them,' Cooper continued quietly. 'And, even though I knew nothing about anything medical, I could see that it wasn't going well. I'd seen enough TV shows to know what a flat line on a monitor screen meant, even if it wasn't there all the time. I could feel my world just falling away and I was going with it, into the most terrifying black hole that ever was.

'And...and then one of those paramedics came and put his arm around me and he explained what was happening and how hard they were trying to help Connor, and...it was a lifeline. Something I could hang onto so that I didn't disappear completely into that black hole. They were amazing, those guys. They got Connor to hospital alive and took me in the helicopter with them and made it seem like I was doing a really important job as well, just being with my brother and talking to him. Touching him. They told me he could probably hear me. That he would know I was there...'

Cooper dropped the shell and rubbed his face with his hand. 'That was when I decided I was going to become a paramedic,' he said. 'I thought, if I could ever offer that kind of lifeline to anyone in such an awful situation, it would be a really worthwhile thing to do.'

Fizz nodded. 'You did exactly that for Sarah,' she told him. 'You were…amazing…'

She caught Cooper's gaze as she spoke and suddenly she was completely caught. She couldn't look away. Because she could see so much of what he was feeling in his eyes? The kind of grief he understood so well. How much he cared for others. The sheer enormity of how kind this man was…

It was Cooper who broke the eye contact. 'I might just go and have a peep around the door,' he said, getting to his feet. 'Sarah won't know I'm there but I'd like to know that she's coping. It's romantic that they wanted to be alone together for this but…well…we both know how hard it can be, don't we?'

Fizz stayed where she was. Without thinking, she reached down and picked up the shell that Cooper had been toying with when he'd been telling her about his brother. She curled her fingers around its sharp edges.

It wasn't just Cooper's physical size that made him seem so solid, it was his personality. That kindness and caring made him completely trustworthy.

A human rock.

Weirdly, Fizz felt the sting of gathering tears for the second time that day. The second time that decade, probably.

This time it wasn't because of memories of grief. Maybe it was because of that feeling of longing a human rock could provoke—the desire to cling? Fizz had learned a long time ago not to cling to anything or anyone but how comforting would it be to have someone you *could* cling to if you needed to?

Whoever captured Cooper Sinclair's heart in the future would have a human rock for the rest of her life. Fizz could only hope that she would know how incredibly lucky she was.

Having lost of track of how long she'd been sitting on the log, the quiet call from Cooper startled her.

'Fizz?'

'Yes?' She still had the shell in her hand as she got to her feet. Without thinking, she slipped it into her pocket.

'He's gone. Sarah says it was very peaceful in the end. The police can take over and they're going to give her as much time as she needs before they make any arrangements to transport Tim, but we need you to do the official paperwork.'

'Of course.'

'The firies are going to take us to where Andy's got the chopper parked after that.' Cooper offered a lopsided smile. 'Have you had a ride in a fire engine before?'

'Can't say I have.' The next few minutes were not going to be easy. Having a moment of relief being offered was welcome. 'Working with you is just one big adventure, isn't it, Coop?'

'We've just got started, babe,' he murmured as they headed back to the door of the beach house. 'The best is yet to come.'

CHAPTER SEVEN

COOPER WASN'T THE only one who could provide a bit of adventure.

Not that Fizz had initially had that intention when she'd offered to take him sightseeing when one of their days off coincided a couple of weeks later.

'I thought you might like to visit Featherston, which isn't too far away and is a great example of a small New Zealand town. I happen to know where there's a really good place to have lunch.'

She knew every street of the town, in fact.

'This is where I grew up,' she told Cooper as they drove around after an excellent pub lunch of fish and chips. 'In that house right there.' She stopped the car as they both gazed at the small weatherboard cottage. It was disappointing to see that the garden was so over-grown. 'My grandfather built it. My mother was born there.'

'And she inherited the house? Is that why you grew up there?'

'No.' Fizz pulled away again, heading for the town's main street. 'My grandparents brought me up. Well, my nan did, mostly. Grandpa died when I was about ten.'

Cooper's glance was sharp. Cautious. Was he worried that he might say or do something inappropriate? Did he expect to feel mortified very soon—the way he had when he'd misunderstood why her marriage had been so short-lived?

'My mother's not dead,' Fizz reassured him. 'I'm just not actually that close to her. She got pregnant far too young and decided she still wanted to have a life. She'd pop home occasionally and promise that she'd come and get me as soon as she'd got herself settled somewhere but it never quite happened. As far as I know, she's living happily with her third husband somewhere in Australia. I was the one who inherited the house but I sold it to pay my way through medical school.'

She glanced sideways at some of the newly refurbished buildings they were passing on the main street. 'I should have kept it. Property prices have had a very healthy increase since people realised that it was in easy commuting distance of Wellington but... I guess it felt like there wasn't much keeping me here. Especially after Nan died.'

She didn't let a silence develop to where Cooper might start feeling sorry for her. Or to start feeling sorry for herself, for that matter. It wasn't pleasant to remember those crushing childhood disappointments. Those promises her mother had always made but never kept. Visits that she was going to make. Holidays that they were going to take together. A new home to go to with a new husband so that they could all live together happily ever after.

'Hey...' Fizz stamped on the ancient echoes of being let down. 'How 'bout we do something a bit more exciting before we go home?'

Cooper gave her a slightly wary look. 'I know what "exciting" means in your vocabulary. Does this involve the need for protective clothing of any sort?'

'No.' Fizz threw him a grin. 'You don't even need to get out of the car if you don't want to.'

'Where are we going?'

'Somewhere cool. With a bit of a breeze probably, which will blow a few cobwebs away.' Like the ones that seemed to be hiding in the corners of her old home town. And her heart. 'You up for it?'

His glance was thoughtful now. As if he was weighing up what she'd said. 'Why not?' He finally nodded. 'It's always good to blow cobwebs away.'

There was indeed a stiff sea breeze when they arrived at Ocean Beach after a picturesque drive mainly though farmland. She showed him the quaint, weathered little holiday houses that stretched along part of the beach and then took him on a track she'd been on before with the four-wheel-drive club. The road got rough enough at times to make Fizz focus hard on her driving, especially when there was a steep drop on the beach side as they wound their way around the edge of a hill. There was a deeply rutted track through trees with puddles big enough to send up a wall of muddy water and rocky streams to navigate, which bounced them around and made them both laugh with the fun of it all.

Finally, Fizz parked on the rock-strewn black sand, amongst all the driftwood, and got out of the car to breathe in the salty air and watch the wild waves crashing onto this deserted shore.

Cooper got out as well.

'Where are we exactly?'

'That's Palliser Bay out there.' Fizz pointed out to sea. 'And the South Island is that way, only it's a bit too far to see from this point.'

Cooper turned his head, taking in the endless beach, the rugged green hills of the farmland nearby and the distant peaks of the Rimutakas in the background.

'It's gorgeous,' he said. 'Reminds me of Scotland.'

'Are you homesick?'

'Not at all. There's nothing there for me now.'

He turned back towards the sea but Fizz was still looking at him. She was curious, she realised. She wanted to know what he'd meant by that or, rather, how he felt about that. She had been shocked to learn about his twin brother's death and how terrible it must have been for Cooper. On top of the case they were attending to at the time, it had been such an emotional day Fizz had needed a bit of time to process it all. Even now, she could feel a lump forming in her throat. She stepped over a pile of sun-bleached branches and went to sit on the trunk of an entire driftwood tree with its roots still intact.

Cooper came to sit beside her a couple of minutes later. 'You okay?' he asked. 'You've gone kind of quiet.'

Fizz caught his gaze and, instantly, she was reminded of how she'd seen him that first day. As a human rock. Trustworthy. As trustworthy as Hamish had been and he'd been the first person, apart from her grandparents, that she could trust to keep his word.

'I was just thinking about the last time we were near a beach together,' she said quietly. 'I've been wondering quite a lot about how Sarah's coping.'

'Hopefully she's got family and friends who are helping her.'

'Mmm.'

'Did you?' Cooper slung his arm around her shoulders in a companionable gesture. 'Have plenty of support when you needed it? When Hamish died?'

It felt so natural to tilt her head to find the comfortable hollow beneath his shoulder. 'I think I pushed people away,' she admitted. 'They were all there for the funeral, of course. Even my mother. And Hamish's parents were great and... I know they didn't blame me for the accident but it felt like I reminded them of what they'd lost every time they saw me. That they'd never see their son become a father. Or see their grandchildren grow up. They just kind of faded out of my life, I guess. And my friends stopped trying after a while.'

She'd told him about what had made her become an adrenaline junkie but she'd skated over that dark period. It was another thing she'd never told anybody.

'Sometimes,' she added quietly, 'what you're feeling is so powerful it sucks you in and it makes you push away anything that tries to pull you out. If you push often enough and hard enough, most people will go away eventually.'

'Not the people who really love you,' Cooper said. 'You might think you've pushed them away but they're always ready to come back.'

'You sound like you're speaking from personal experience.'

'Perhaps. I didn't push people away. I think I was the one who got pushed. Until I felt I had to hide so I didn't make everything worse.'

Fizz tilted her head to look up at Cooper's face. 'I don't understand.'

'You know how you told me that when Hamish died,

it felt like someone had taken your life and screwed it up and thrown it away?'

She nodded.

'It was the same for me. Only it was even worse for my mother. She never got over losing Connor.'

'They didn't *blame* you, did they?'

'No more than I blamed myself. We all knew that Connor was headstrong, and sometimes he just wouldn't listen, but the "if onlys" were hard to get past. If only we hadn't gone climbing that weekend. If only it hadn't been raining earlier. If only I'd paid more attention to what he was doing instead of trying to light a fire to cook the breakfast sausages over. If only we hadn't looked so much like each other...' Cooper blew out a breath. 'Every time my mother looked at me, I knew she was seeing Connor. Sometimes she'd actually go pale and then collapse with grief all over again.'

Fizz had found Cooper's hand and she threaded her fingers through his. Had Cooper never been able to express his grief at losing his brother because he'd been trying to protect his mother? She could believe that about him. He would protect anybody he loved to the nth degree. But how sad was it to have felt the need to hide his own emotions like that?

'It got so that it was easier to avoid being at home,' Cooper added. 'It was such a relief to get away to university and then to have my career to focus on.'

Had he become even better at hiding his emotions by focusing so completely on his study and career? Fizz knew how well that worked. She barely thought about any of those heart-breaking regrets these days—like never being able to create the kind of family she'd desperately wanted as a child. A 'real' family.

'Your parents must have been very proud of you, taking up a career that was going to save lives.'

'My dad died just before I graduated. And Mum seemed to fade away over the next few years. Every time I went to visit, she was thinner and sadder and there didn't seem to be anything I could do or say that would help. Her doctors couldn't find any way to help her, either. I think she just gave up on life.'

Fizz squeezed his hand but didn't say anything for a long moment. Curiously, it felt like something was shifting in her chest. A piece of her heart? As if a door was being opened somewhere when she had believed that the key had been lost long ago, because the connection to this person was so strong she couldn't keep Cooper out.

This friendship was special.

It felt…

Well, it felt a bit like family. One of those 'real' ones.

There was a lot to be said for the philosophy of living in the moment, making the most of every one of them and not trying to think too far into the future.

That day off a week or two ago, when Fizz had taken Cooper to see the small town where she'd grown up and then taken him on that wild drive to that beautiful beach, was a shining example of that philosophy.

They'd made the most of that day. Looking back, it had been an extraordinarily intimate conversation, unlike any Cooper had ever had. Was that because he'd never had a friend like Fizz? Someone that could understand how profound the effect of losing someone so close could be? He'd had no idea how much of a release it could be, just telling someone about something, either. He'd never spoken to anyone about how hard it had been after Connor had died but, then, he'd never had someone like Fizz to talk to, had he?

It had certainly brought them closer and Cooper was making the most of every moment he had with Fizz, along with all the other good things his new life was offering him. Within the space of just a few short months his old life in Scotland was feeling like a lifetime ago.

He knew his way around this quirky, hilly city well enough to be able to speed to any emergency he was dispatched to if he was crewing one of the vehicles, and he'd discovered how lucky he'd been to find a place to live in such an interesting part of town. The atmosphere of the rambling old house he was sharing with Maggie, Jack, Laura and Harrison was relaxed enough for no comment to be made when he was out very late, or quite often didn't come home at all.

The Mexican night with tacos and beer had been such a success that it had become a weekly thing, with each flatmate taking turns to provide the meal for whoever wasn't on a night shift. Cooper found opportunities to kick a ball around the back yard with Harrison, whose broken wrist was completely healed now, and there were always occasions to share the kitchen or some housework, along with work stories, with Jack or Laura. Maggie was rostered on the same shift at the rescue base often enough for a real friendship to be developing but, if she'd guessed that Cooper had something going on with Fizz, she wasn't saying anything.

That 'something' that had started as a fierce and irresistible sexual attraction was quite a different 'something' now. It had changed the day of that case when they'd stayed to support Sarah as her husband had died in her arms. And it had changed again that day on the beach when they'd shared how hard life had been after losing the people closest to them. There seemed to be a level of trust now, on both sides, that might have otherwise taken a much longer time to develop.

In its turn, that level of trust had taken their sexual connection to a new level. Cooper didn't have to remind himself to make the most of every moment when it came to the intimate time he and Fizz managed to find at least once or twice a week when their rosters co-operated. It was, without a shadow of doubt, the best sex he'd ever had in his life and he suspected that that had a lot to do with Fizz's philosophy on life.

There was no pressure to put a label on what they had found with each other and there were no expectations that whatever it was was 'going somewhere', which had got in way of a lot of previous relationships for Cooper. He'd been dumped in the past because a relationship was apparently 'not going anywhere', or he'd had to walk away from someone himself because of the building pressure to take a relationship seriously enough, but that wasn't going to happen with Fizz. He was with someone who was in exactly the same place he'd always been as far as relationships were concerned, even if he'd never really analysed that reluctance to commit.

Maybe he could see his attitude to commitment changing at some point in the future but he certainly wasn't ready to settle down yet and take responsibility for someone else's happiness. He was even less ready to consider having a family and taking responsibility for the health and safety of vulnerable children.

He'd told Fizz that his parents hadn't blamed him for

his brother's death any more than he blamed himself and that was true but it didn't mean that there wasn't an element of blame to be found. He'd been the older brother. Only by thirty minutes, admittedly, but he'd been expected to be the responsible one. To take care of Connor and make sure he didn't do anything stupid.

He hadn't managed that very well, had he?

Even now he would have that terrible recurring dream sometimes. When he was shouting at Connor to tell him to come down off the rocks because they were too slippery and it was too dangerous but no sound could emerge, no matter how much effort he was making to force the words out. Even worse was reliving that moment when he got close enough to touch his brother's crumpled body at the base of those rocks and to feel the fear and grief exploding within his chest as if it had just happened all over again.

Whoa… Cooper shook that thought off with practised ease, taking note of what had prompted it so he could try and avoid it in the future. Thinking about having a family and children of his own, that's what it had been. He'd told Fizz that he wasn't looking for a relationship because he wasn't ready to settle down. Given how his brain had just hijacked him with no more than a passing thought of having children of his own, Cooper had to wonder whether he would ever be ready to settle down like that.

He'd also told Fizz that enjoying something like this while it lasted and then moving on with no regrets when it stopped being fun was every man's dream and he'd meant every word of that as well. And now he was living that dream and it *was* perfect.

The fact that he was on the same page as Fizz at the

moment, as far as settling down or having kids went, was a good thing.

It meant that they could just carry on. Enjoying every moment.

Work was pretty close to perfect, too. Cooper wasn't sure if Fizz had said something to Don or that someone else had noticed how well they worked together as a team but he was finding himself crewed with Fizz on one of the helicopters every time she was on base, and that was another aspect of his life that he was making the most of. The challenge of keeping up with how fast this young doctor thought and worked was a joy and there were always new things to learn. Fizz was learning from him as well. He was helping her prepare for her upcoming winch training course and, because she'd also signed up for the high country and mountain rescue course in Queenstown, he was sharing some of his knowledge in that area as well.

'We've only got a couple of weeks before we head to Queenstown,' he reminded her as they were airborne on the way to an incident that was a thirty-minute flight away from Wellington. A slightly hysterical call to emergency services had said a large vehicle—maybe a truck or a bus—had gone off the road and into a gully but the crew were still waiting for information on how bad it was and how many people were involved. They had been dispatched because the location was isolated and there was the potential for serious injuries and an unknown number of victims, but it could turn out to be less than serious or even a hoax. 'Did you read that article I sent you the other day?'

'The one about hazards? Yeah… I had a quick look.'

'So, what are they?'

'The hazards?' Fizz raised an eyebrow. 'Weather, mainly. Storms, lightning, risk of hypothermia. Oh, and there's avalanches and rockfalls, of course. And river crossings and white water. Hey…do we get to do an actual river crossing on this course, do you think? Where you can tackle a swift current by linking arms?'

'I think we might. We're expected to take quite a lot of outdoor clothing.'

'Layers.' Fizz nodded. 'I read that bit, too. Light-weight clothes that can wick moisture away from the body, insulating items for the middle like a top made of merino wool and then a waterproof layer on top. I might go to one of those tramping supplies shops after work today and get some new thermal stuff. Want to come with me?'

'Sure.'

'We could go somewhere for dinner afterwards.'

Fizz wiggled her eyebrows this time, as she held his gaze, and Cooper had to stifle laughter. It was just as well Andy couldn't see into the cabin of this helicopter or he'd know instantly that he and Fizz were a lot closer than simply friends or colleagues. The longer it took for anybody to guess, the better, as far as Cooper was concerned. It was nobody's business but theirs and it didn't interfere with how they worked together. If any-thing, it just seemed to be making them a tighter team.

Yep. Things were pretty much perfect on so many levels.

CHAPTER EIGHT

COOPER AND FIZZ could hear Andy talking on a different frequency as he flew them towards this new emergency of a large vehicle accident and then his voice came through the headphones built into their helmets.

'Okay, guys… First police and fire vehicles are on scene. It's a school bus that's crashed.'

Cooper and Fizz exchanged a brief glance. This was serious. It could be the worst job they might ever face. It wasn't a long glance but it was enough for a silent message of support and strength to be transmitted and received in both directions. They were in this together. They could cope.

'Nobody knows how many kids are on the bus,' Andy continued, 'but it was heading to school so it could be full. It's down a steep gully. Broke a few trees on the way down, which probably lessened the impact, but it's on its side and access is difficult. They're trying to get ladders down and make sure the bus is stable.'

Cooper saw a reflection in Fizz's face of his own increase in adrenaline levels and focus. This could be a Mass Casualty Incident that would be a real challenge to handle, especially when the victims might be young children.

'Comms said they've called for more backup for scene control. As you're qualified in disaster management, Cooper, they're putting you in as scene commander. You know where the vest is?'

'Roger that.' Cooper was already leaning towards the window, waiting for his first sighting of the scene. Getting an aerial view would be an advantage in deciding how to manage this disaster. As they circled the scene, coming down to land on the road a few minutes later, Cooper could already see how chaotic it was.

There were cars backed up in both directions and people running to where the bus had gone off the road on a bend, crowding the firies, who were trying to do their job. An ambulance was having trouble getting past the cars and closer to the scene, thanks to a tractor that was blocking it.

On foot, and moving swiftly towards a police officer who was trying to move people back from the edge of the road, Cooper realised that this crowd was mostly made up of the parents of the children in that bus. Women were crying. There were toddlers and babies in the crowd and the farmer who'd arrived on his tractor was arguing with the policeman.

'It's my kids down there. You can't tell me I can't go down and help.'

People turned to stare at Cooper and Fizz as they arrived. They could all read the lettering on his fluorescent vest that designated him 'Scene Commander'. Cooper knew his physical size helped give him authority in situations like this but he also knew it was more about confidence and giving frightened people the reassurance that he knew what he was doing.

The ambulance and its crew had finally got close

enough to park and open its back doors. Cooper quickly spoke to the chief fire officer, surveyed the scene and then gathered the paramedics and police officers.

'They're going to get access to the bus any minute now and they'll start bringing the children up. From what they can see so far, they don't think there's major injuries. The kids were all wearing their safety belts. We'll use the space beside the ambulance as the triage area. Dr Wilson will assess any serious injuries and we'll get another chopper on the way if it's needed. Given their age, everybody will need another check at the nearest hospital but we may be able to use road vehicles for transport, including the parents' cars.'

He turned to speak to the group of frantic adults and urged them to step back and give all the emergency service personnel room to work. Police officers reinforced his message and people were listening now. Some went to shift their cars and make sure there was room for more emergency vehicles to get through.

Cooper turned back to brief the paramedics on what their roles would be, but when he saw Fizz at the top of one of the fire service ladders he shook his head and strode towards her.

'No,' he said. 'Not this time, Fizz. Stay up here.'

'But…'

'No "buts".' He shifted his gaze to the fire officer beside them. 'There's no one unconscious in the bus, is there?'

'Not that we can see.'

'What about the driver?'

'She's been keeping them calm. She's trapped by her lower legs under the dashboard but she adamant that all the kids are taken out first. And she's told them all to stay still and keep their safety belts on until someone comes to get them, which is just as well what with the broken windows and sharp metal around. The smashed tree branches are another big hazard, like I was just telling the doctor, here.'

'She could be bleeding badly,' Fizz said. 'So could one of the children. I need to get down there…'

The fire officer was peering down the slope. 'First one's on its way up.'

'I need you here,' Cooper told Fizz, 'to assess each one of these children as they get brought up.'

He could see her frustration. She was determined to get down that slope. Her adrenaline levels were high and what Fizz wanted to do was to get into that wrecked bus as fast as possible.

Cooper kept his voice calm. 'You outrank me in medical matters,' he told her, 'but I'm the scene commander here and it's my responsibility to manage this scene as safely as possible. We've got people who know what they're doing, handling the extrications.'

'You're telling me I'm not allowed to go down there?'

Cooper nodded. 'Not unless there's a good medical reason for it. And, even if there is, I'm going to be the one who takes that risk, okay?'

He saw the flash of rebellion in her eyes but, as he held her gaze, Cooper also saw the moment that she accepted his authority and that felt like an even bigger step towards total trust. Tightening the bonds that were there between them as a professional team. Fizz's focus shifted as soon as a fire officer appeared at the top of the ladder, a small, sobbing child held against his chest. It was Fizz who reached to take the young girl, who barely looked old enough to have been heading to school.

'Come with me, sweetheart,' she said. The child wrapped her arms around Fizz's neck and buried her face against her shoulder. 'It's okay…' Cooper heard Fizz say gently as she moved towards the ambulance and the blankets that had been laid on the road as a triage area. 'You're safe now…'

'Jenny…?' A woman with a baby in her arms broke away from the group that was now gathered at more of a distance and ran towards Fizz. 'Oh, my God… Are you hurt?'

It took over an hour to get more than twenty young children safely out of the bus and up to road level, where Fizz was checking each one as thoroughly as she could. A dislocated elbow and a greenstick arm fracture seemed to be the most serious injuries amongst many bumps and bruises and a few grazes and lacerations, but, once each one was bandaged or splinted and comforted, they were taken to the nearest hospital for observation and another check-up. Cooper used a second ambulance that arrived to take the eight-year-old with the elbow injury and his mother to hospital and the well-splinted arm fracture got transported in a police car, much to the small boy's excitement.

The first girl who'd been rescued, Jenny, was still on scene as the final victim of the accident was brought up the side of the gully. Cheryl, the bus driver, was Jenny's grandmother and she was far more worried about the children she'd been driving than the badly broken ankle that had kept her trapped.

'They're all okay, Mum,' her daughter reassured

Cheryl. 'And that's thanks to you making sure they always wore their safety belts.'

Fizz looked up from the IV line she had put in Cheryl's arm. 'How's the pain now?' she asked. 'On that scale of zero to ten?'

'About a four, I guess. A lot better, anyway.' But Cheryl was twisting her head sideways. 'Jenny? Are you sure you're okay, darling? Nothing hurts?'

'I got a big scratch, Nana, that's all. It's better now.'

'I can't believe it happened. There was something wrong with the brakes. I was trying to slow the bus using the gears but the wheel caught the gravel. *Oh...*' The sound was a sob. 'I could have *killed* someone.'

'But you didn't, Mum.' Her daughter was trying to lean close to comfort her mother but the crying baby in her arms was making it impossible.

'Here...let me help...' Fizz took the baby. She cuddled the six-month-old infant against her shoulder and patted its back. 'Hey...what's all this fuss about, huh?'

Jenny reached up to pat the baby as well. 'He's my little brother,' she told Fizz. 'His name's Patrick.'

Cooper had been splinting Cheryl's ankle as Fizz had managed the pain relief. Now Andy was helping him to secure their patient on the stretcher, ready to move her to the helicopter. He found himself glancing in Fizz's direction more than once. The baby had settled in her arms and Jenny was leaning against her legs. Andy was also looking at Fizz as he straightened up after fastening the last safety belt.

'Suits you.' He grinned.

Fizz grinned back. 'I don't think I've ever dealt with so many children in one go. I'm exhausted.'

Baby Patrick's mother smiled as she took her baby

back. 'Thank you so much. You were wonderful with all the kids. Where will you take Mum?'

'To the Royal, in Wellington,' Cooper told her. 'We can fit you all in if you want to come with her.'

'No…don't do that, love,' Cheryl said. 'Patrick sounds like he's hungry. And you need to keep an eye on Jenny. I'll be fine…'

'Jenny should get another check-up at your local hospital,' Cooper told her. 'Like we've advised for all the other children.'

'I'll get in as soon as I can, then, Mum. I know you'll be well looked after with these guys.'

Finally back at base, after handing Cheryl over to the staff at the Royal's emergency department, Fizz flopped onto one of the sofas in the staffroom.

Andy sat at the table to open a packet of sandwiches and Cooper went to make coffee.

'We've got a heap of paperwork to get sorted,' he sighed. 'A patient report form on every one of those kids.'

'I'll ring the hospitals they got taken to, later,' Fizz said. 'I'd like to make sure I didn't miss anything. That was full on, trying to check so many small people.'

'You did great,' Andy told her. 'You're a natural with kids, Fizz. You'll make a great mum one of these days.'

'No, I won't.' Fizz made it sound like no big deal. 'I'm never going to have kids.'

Cooper spooned coffee into mugs. He couldn't agree more with Andy but he also remembered Fizz's response to Maggie's comment that day that her biological clock would start ticking before too long. He could still hear an echo of that dismissive laughter and the declaration that she would simply ignore any ticking of that clock because life was too much fun as it was.

But he'd seen her with that baby in her arms today and he'd seen the way she'd cuddled him and pressed a kiss to his head. Was her determination not to have children herself part and parcel of the same barrier that meant she didn't 'do' relationships?

How sad was that?

And not just for Fizz, Cooper realised as he stirred those mugs of coffee for longer than was necessary. He was aware of a wash of sadness that was far more personal.

Living for the moment was all very well but maybe it wasn't as perfect as he'd thought such a short time ago. It gave whatever their unlabelled connection was a shelf life, didn't it? It couldn't keep going the way it was because it would just morph into a relationship, especially when other people found out about what was going on between them. The question, even if unspoken, of whether or not it was serious or had a future would be hanging over them and Cooper could be quite sure that that would be the point where it stopped being fun for Fizz. When she would move on with no regrets and he would be expected to do the same.

Except that Cooper didn't want to move on. Maybe he wasn't ready to settle down and raise a family but he was nowhere near ready to call it quits on the time he got to spend with Fizz.

He carried a mug of coffee over to her and she thanked him with a smile and a glance that held his for a heartbeat. Like that silent communication in the helicopter earlier, it was so easy to read and respond to the message.

We did well today, didn't we?

We sure did.

We're just the best team, ever...

Absolutely...

But Cooper couldn't return that smile. That unexpected flash of sadness he'd just had had become something that felt more like…fear?

Maybe it had only been a matter of weeks but he couldn't imagine his life without this woman as a central part of it. He knew it was probably a forlorn hope but he didn't want Fizz to move on.

Ever…

His heart felt like it was squeezing itself into a knot and Cooper had to turn away before that ability to communicate with no words gave Fizz any idea what was going through his head right now.

Not just through his head. The realisation was in his blood. Getting sent to every cell in his body.

He loved her.

He was *in* love with Fizz.

He had, without doubt, found the person he wanted to spend the rest of his life with.

And the moment she knew that, their time together away from work would be over. There would be no more shared meals or moonlit walks around the waterfront. No more of those delicious hours in her bed and the reminder of how mutual that pleasure was in those private glances the next time they were together. Even working together would be different because that trust she had in him would be broken.

Cooper took his own mug of coffee towards the table, sitting down opposite Andy. He reached for the day's newspaper that he hadn't had a chance to look at yet, but the words were no more than a blur as his brain scrambled to find a solution to what was suddenly a very pressing problem.

Then his vision cleared. The answer was quite simple, really.

He just couldn't let Fizz find out how he felt. He was good at hiding strong emotions. Losing Connor had taught him that because his mother had been unable to cope with her own emotions so he hadn't been about to make it all so much worse by talking about or revealing his own. As he'd said to Fizz, he'd been pushed away and he'd had many years to hone the skill of hiding. And, yes, part of him knew that he might be making things worse in the long run by staying as close to Fizz as possible for as long as possible, but what choice did he have?

He couldn't walk away. Not voluntarily, that was for sure. And…maybe, if they could keep this going long enough, Fizz would get used to it. Change her mind, even? She was starting to really trust him, wasn't she? Maybe she would come to realise that they were perfect life partners. It wasn't as if he had a desire for his own kids any more than she did. Or even marriage, for that matter.

Cooper just wanted Fizz in his life. And in his bed.

Preferably for ever…

There was something different about Cooper today but Fizz couldn't quite put her finger on what it was.

He seemed a bit quieter as they walked around an exclusive outdoor clothing outlet that evening.

'How 'bout this? A merino blend camisole.' For thermal underwear it was quite pretty and lacy. 'Too girly?'

'Buy it.' Cooper nodded. His grin was pure cheekiness. 'That way, when we're crossing rivers or building shelters in the forest, I can imagine what you've got on under all those other layers. It'll keep me warm with no need for my jacket.'

Oh… That glint in his eyes was enough to make Fizz feel overly warm herself. Suddenly, she wanted to get this shopping expedition over with. To get home and get Cooper into her bed.

But there was still something nagging at the back of her mind when they headed to the checkout counter a little while later. A young couple was in the queue ahead of them and the guy had a baby in his arms about the same age as the baby Fizz had cuddled this morning. The baby was peeping over his father's shoulder and seemed fascinated by Cooper. It wasn't until the baby giggled that Fizz glanced sideways and caught the faces Cooper had been making to amuse the infant.

Had that huge job today with the school bus affected him more than she'd realised? Thinking back, Fizz remembered an odd moment, when they'd got back to base and he'd made her a coffee. For just a second, she'd had the impression that he was quite sad about something. Had working with so many children triggered memories of time with his brother, perhaps? Memories could often catch you unawares, sometimes at very inappropriate times. Not that it had happened for Fizz recently, mind you, but she could sympathise.

She also remembered the way he'd been with Harrison when Laura's young son had broken his wrist.

The thought that this big, gentle man would make the most amazing father was followed by another realisation that almost took Fizz's breath away.

That's what Cooper was really searching for, wasn't it?

He might think he'd come to the other side of the world simply for more adventure and career challenges but he didn't actually realise what it was he was looking for, did he? He just knew that there was something missing from his life.

He'd said that there was nothing left for him in Scotland now because his family was all gone. But he needed a family of his own, didn't he? A wife who would adore him as the rock in her life. Children that he could protect and keep safe to his heart's content.

Except that he blamed himself, at some level, for his brother's death, didn't he? There was a barrier there that he probably wasn't even aware of because the men she'd known hadn't usually tried to analyse that kind of thing, so she couldn't help but wonder if the same could be said of Cooper.

Fizz couldn't share that desire. For her, children were the ultimate planning for the future. Even before they were born, they brought with them so many hopes and dreams for the years to come. The promise of family and for ever. The promise that Hamish had given her and that she'd believed. But it had been a promise that had died along with the man who'd made it. You could only keep yourself safe from heartbreak if you didn't buy into hopes and dreams like that.

But perhaps she could help Cooper.

And why wouldn't she? He was just the loveliest man she had ever met and, hopefully, when their time together had run its course, she would still have a friend for life—one that she already cared about a great deal. Cooper was not just gorgeous, he was clever and kind and...pretty close to perfect, really. He deserved to have everything good that life had to offer, especially after having lived through the worst that it could also offer.

He'd said he'd never had a serious relationship because he'd moved around so much but Fizz suspected that it was because he didn't want to get that close to someone when he knew what it was like to lose them. She got it. More than anyone else could, probably. Fizz was content with her own decision to not have a family in her future but she understood now—in this moment of insight—that there was a real need, deep down, for Cooper to love and be loved. Somehow, he needed to break through the barrier that was holding him back. To find the courage to take that leap of faith in the future.

But how could she help him?

She put her purchases down to have them scanned and picked up the shop's catalogue. There was a montage of pictures on the cover that must have been shot around Queenstown. Climbers modelled all sorts of gear in front of a mountain range. There were kayakers being thrown around in some impressive white water and even a shot of a tandem bungee jump off a bridge over a gorge.

And that could be the key, Fizz decided.

Was part of the barrier Cooper had between himself and the future he deserved tied in with his overzealous attention to the safety of others? What if she could show him that it was possible to take a risk, purely for the enjoyment of the adrenaline rush? That the world didn't necessarily fall apart. Even if it didn't totally break through that barrier, it would be a good start, wouldn't it? A physical push that could lead to emotional freedom?

Fizz handed over her credit card and turned to grin at Cooper as he stood waiting for her.

'I can't wait to get to use this clothing,' she told him. 'Queenstown, here we come…'

CHAPTER NINE

LIFE JUST DIDN'T get much better than this.

Fizz had the window seat on the plane that was coming in to land at Queenstown's airport so Cooper had to lean close enough to catch the scent of her skin in order to soak in the view of impressively craggy mountain ranges against an endless blue sky reflected in the huge lake beneath.

For a moment, the sight of mountains did what they always did and caught at Cooper's heart with a memory of his brother, but it wasn't a painful reminder. If anything, the remembered flash of excitement in his twin's eyes that had always lit up with the challenge of a steep track or some rocks to scramble over was simply added to his own anticipation of this weekend's training course.

There were interesting subjects to be covered and Cooper was keen to learn new skills in tracking and being able to recognise the smallest clues or signs that someone had gone through an area. The refresher course in search methods and the psychological aspects of the kinds of behaviour that lost people could demonstrate would be useful and the day outdoors in the back country was even more exciting. They would be practising bushcraft and survival skills like river crossing and would even create and then sleep in an emergency shelter.

It was exactly the kind of weekend that Cooper loved more than any other because it combined his thirst for new knowledge and challenges with his passion for being prepared to help anybody in any situation. He would happily take on the role of in-house training for other members of the team at the Aratika Rescue Base and he was hoping to find an active search and rescue team in the Wellington area so he could make himself available to help whenever possible.

Best of all, he was in the company of a person who shared his passion. Maybe Fizz had different reasons for being here and her desire to learn more about search and rescue was largely due to her love of adrenaline-producing situations, but right now the motivation was irrelevant. Cooper was already addicted to being in the company of this woman who could make him feel so alive, and they were going to be sharing something new and exhilarating in the next couple of days that could only bring them closer.

If circumstances conspired to bring Fizz a little closer, would she realise how perfect they were for each other and change her mind about allowing a true relationship into her life?

Fall in love with him, even?

She certainly seemed to be delighted to be with him and it had been her idea to come south a day early when they discovered that their rosters made it possible.

'We'll go and have a bit of fun,' she'd suggested. 'I'll find an adrenaline rush for you that you won't be able to resist.'

Fizz almost had her forehead pressed against the window as she stared down at the extraordinary landscape beneath the plane. A bump of turbulence distracted her and she turned to catch Cooper's gaze for a heartbeat. Instantly, her face came alive with her smile and the sparkle in her eyes.

'Gorgeous, yes?'

'Oh, yeah…' But Cooper kept watching Fizz as she turned back to make the most of the view as the plane descended.

He was thinking back to their conversation about this high country and mountain rescue training weekend, so many weeks ago, when they'd gone out to dinner the night Harrison had broken his arm. When he'd told her that it might be a good thing for her to have to learn a few safety rules. When she had told him that a bit of adventure tourism might be good for *him*.

Would it impress her if he did embrace some adventure? Prove that he wasn't overly safety-conscious because he disapproved of chasing that adrenaline rush? Maybe it would make a real difference to show Fizz that he really did understand the forces that were so much a part of her life and that he was prepared to share them. That this didn't have to be simply a weekend of adventure together. It could, in fact, be the beginning of a lifetime of adventures.

Cooper sat back in his seat and tightened his seat belt as the turbulence increased. When Fizz caught his hand to hold it he wondered if the rough air was bothering her but then she gave his hand a squeeze and he caught her grin. She was loving every moment of this ride, probably more so because of the turbulence.

He was going to make the most of every moment

as well, Cooper decided, and he was definitely up for whatever kind of fun Fizz was planning to challenge him with for the rest of the day. Zip-lining, skydiving, white-water rafting—he wasn't going to point out any dangers in these extreme forms of pleasure seeking. He also wasn't going to think about the possibility of their connection ending any time soon because it was no longer fun for Fizz.

Cooper was going to make sure she'd never had so much fun in her life.

The wall of pamphlets in the tourism office made the choice overwhelming.

They'd picked up a rental car, left their bags at their motel near the location of the course venue and then they'd come straight into town so that they could squeeze as much as possible into this day of freedom before the course started tomorrow, and Fizz was on a mission.

She was going to push Cooper Sinclair's boundaries—enough to put him out of his comfort zone. Enough to challenge his preference to keep people physically safe. And to keep himself emotionally safe.

'So...what's it going to be? The famous jet boat experience in the gorge? Skipper's canyon? Skydiving or bungee jumping?'

'This cruise on the *TSS Earnslaw* looks great.' There was a twinkle in Cooper's eyes that told her he was teasing her. 'What a beautiful old ship.'

'You can do a cruise on Lake Wakatipu when you're old and grey and want to eat cake with a fork.'

Fizz looked away to reach for a different brochure. Or was it that she didn't want to reveal the odd frisson that that teasing glance had given her? A delicious ripple of sensation that had nothing to do with how physically attractive this guy was, or how much she respected his intelligence, for that matter. It was simply about how much she enjoyed his company. How good it felt to be around him.

'How about mountain biking?' she suggested. 'Look…you can take the gondola up to the top of that peak and then ride all these trails down.'

'I'll bet the view is amazing from that restaurant at the top of the gondola. Maybe we could aim to go there for dinner.'

'Okay…but only if we go and do something really exciting first. Choose something, Coop.'

'I choose that.'

Fizz followed the direction of his gaze to the large poster on the wall. Climbers on a sheer cliff face with a waterfall right beside them and the view of the valley beyond that made it clear they were a very long way up the side of a mountain.

'I'm not that experienced at climbing.'

'You don't have to be.' A young man came out from behind the desk. 'Even children can do the easier runs. You're clipped in at all times. Every hold is a rung that's secured into the rock. Every bridge has cables so you're never in danger of falling. I've done it myself and…' He blew out a breath. 'It's wild, man…you really should do it.'

Cooper was grinning at her. 'What do you reckon? Want to give it a go?'

'Do *you* want to give it a go?' It might be safe but Fizz was sure that it would be an adrenaline-producing activity. Probably downright terrifying at times. And how would Cooper feel about rock climbing on a mountain, anyway? Wouldn't that bring back potentially overwhelming memories of the way his brother had died?

But he was holding her gaze now and there was something in it that Fizz didn't recognise. Something that was nothing like as light as his usual glint of mischief but not as heavy or serious as when they were working together in some emergency situation, either. It looked almost like a question. Or a promise?

'I'll give anything a go,' he said. 'If it's something you want to do.'

'Really?' Fizz gave up trying to process what seemed different about that gaze.

This was perfect—exactly what she'd been hoping to encourage Cooper to do, and if it did push him a bit further than she had intended by being an activity with powerful associations with his past, maybe that was even better. She could help him through it. Show him that there were no barriers that could prevent him having the kind of future he deserved, and that he would have a friend for life who would always encourage him to chase any dreams.

She turned to the young man beside them. 'Sign us up.' She smiled. 'Can we do it this afternoon?'

What had he done?

Cooper stared at the countryside in front of him. He was sitting in the front passenger seat of a four-wheel-drive vehicle. Fizz was in the back alongside a pile of gear and their guide was driving them closer and closer to what should have been simply a picture-postcard scene of a waterfall cascading down a ravine between rocky cliffs.

He could have chosen anything that would have been enough of an adrenaline rush to impress Fizz with his risk taking and would have taken no time at all—like a jet boat ride or a rafting trip through a stretch of churning white water, perhaps. Or a bungee jump that would have been over in a matter of seconds. But no…he'd picked an adventure that was going to take hours and present challenge after challenge that would probably be emotional as much as physical.

They were going to climb right up to the top of this spectacular waterfall, climbing sheer cliffs, crossing the ravine over multiple bridges and even going behind the rushing water at some point. Mountain climbing. Something Cooper hadn't been remotely tempted to try since his brother's death.

What *had* he been thinking?

He glanced over his shoulder, wondering if Fizz was having any second thoughts about his choice of activity, but she was staring ahead through the windscreen and the expression on her face was anything but doubtful. She had that glow, like she'd had when they'd been bouncing through that turbulence, coming in to land earlier today. Like she'd had that first day he'd met her. When she'd emerged from underwater where she'd been trying to free the woman trapped in that car and she'd been braiding her hair to get it under control, and she'd looked as if putting herself into danger to save someone else had been so exciting she'd do it all over again in a heartbeat.

And he'd found something inspirational in that kind of passion. Because…because she'd reminded him of

Connor, hadn't she? The person he had loved the most in all the world. The more reckless twin who had always thrown himself at life with such determination and had got so much joy out of his exploits. The one who'd always pushed Cooper to be the best—and bravest—version of himself that he could be.

Maybe the choice of this challenge had been subconscious. Confused, perhaps, because he would be doing it with the person who had so quickly become what he'd never thought he'd have in his life again—someone he loved so much that their safety and happiness seemed more important than his own.

The beat of fear that Cooper was aware of as he turned back to see that the mountain was even closer didn't have anything to do with the challenge they were about to face. It was more about how he would cope if he lost Fizz. Or if he could never tell her how he really felt about her—that she was the one person he wanted to be with for the rest of his life. And, even if he didn't say anything out loud, was it possible to feel like this about someone and not let it show?

There was no time to think about anything other than what lay immediately ahead of them when the jeep stopped a few minutes later. There was gear to put on, including a helmet, gloves and a nappy type of harness that had two lengths of synthetic rope attached with heavy-duty carabiners on the ends.

'You'll be attached at all times,' their guide told them. 'You'll only unclip and move one line at a time. We'll go and do a bit of training on a low set of rungs and cables. You're both good with heights, yeah?'

'No problem for me,' Fizz assured him. 'And my

friend, Cooper, here dangles out of helicopters often enough so I'm sure it'll be a walk in the park for him.'

She smiled up at Cooper but he was finding it difficult to smile back.

He was only her 'friend'?

An echo of that beat of fear returned. How hard would it be to spend time with this woman if this stopped being fun for Fizz and it was over? Would she have any regrets?

Probably not. There was another echo in the back of his mind now. Fizz's voice saying something about living for the moment and enjoying something while it lasted. Moving on with no regrets when it stopped being fun.

Cooper saw the flash of concern in Fizz's dark eyes. She stood on tiptoe to plant a swift kiss on his lips.

'Don't worry,' she murmured. 'It'll be as safe as houses. Just like climbing a ladder.'

Finally, Cooper could find his smile. Fizz thought he was simply concerned about how safe this was going to be. Maybe it *was* going to be possible to hide how he felt about her and keep things going a whole lot longer.

With the faint tingle of the touch of her lips still on his own, Cooper set off, lengthening his stride enough to catch up with Fizz and walk by her side.

This adventurous afternoon had been an inspired choice for something exciting to do in a very beautiful place.

Fizz was having the time of her life. This might be a very safe thing to do but it didn't actually feel like that when you were halfway up a completely sheer cliff or crossing a bridge that was no more than a single cable to put your feet on, with extra cables for both hands and an overhead one that your carabiner clipped onto. With a drop of hundreds of feet below and the rush of water almost close enough to touch, the sense of doing something intrepid and brave was…well, it was just perfect.

It wasn't the sort of thing that she would have expected safety-conscious Cooper Sinclair to be enjoying. It wasn't that he didn't do dangerous things in his job but he did them to help others, not purely for the personal enjoyment of an adrenaline rush.

He was doing this for her, wasn't he? Because he knew how much of a thrill she got from successfully challenging herself like this. Because he wanted to impress her, perhaps?

Not that he needed to. He was impressive enough just the way he was, even with that annoying overprotective edge that he had. Cooper was a clever, very skilled, warm and caring person. He was mischievous enough to be great fun to be with and he was certainly the best lover Fizz had ever had.

Right now, he had taken his first step onto the cable bridge and, with his extra height and weight, he was swaying a lot more than Fizz had. She saw him try to control the sway by going still and she saw the deep breath he took when he turned from looking sideways, at the panoramic view of green flat land with a lake and snow-capped mountains in the distance, to the drop beneath that slim cable he was trying to stand on.

'You're doing great,' their guide encouraged him. 'Just take it slowly. One step at a time.'

Cooper nodded and then looked directly ahead, to where Fizz had reached the other side of the ravine and was waiting for him before tackling the next upward ladder of rungs.

Steadier now, Cooper took a careful step forward. And then another. He was holding Fizz's gaze and she could feel her smile widen into a grin. She was proud of him, she realised. He was really stepping out of his comfort zone here and he was doing it with style. That he was probably doing it only because she was with him made her feel curiously protective. She wanted him to enjoy this. To want to push his boundaries. To believe that he could do anything and be anything he wanted to be in life.

That he could have everything he deserved.

Like a family who would adore him.

Not that there was any hurry for him to go and find the person he could create that family with. Fizz didn't want this adventure to end any time soon. Being with Cooper was more than fun. It was kind of like that space you got when you'd done something incredibly exciting and then arrived at safety. The time when adrenaline levels had lowered enough to make you feel tired but happy.

When you got the heightened feeling of how great it was to be alive but you only appreciated it that much because there'd been a chance that you might not be alive now. It was about being totally in the moment and taking a deep breath to revel in it but also knowing that it would be possible to experience that thrill again sometime soon. A feeling of being safe but with no limits on what could happen next. Safety laced with pure excitement.

How much more fun was it going to be sharing her spare time with Cooper if they could both go out and pursue adventure together? She could take him on four-wheel-drive outings that were a lot less tame than Ocean Beach had been. Or maybe they could both get involved with a mountain rescue team after the course this weekend and get deployed on missions that would take them into countryside like this. Challenges that might not have a guide and so many points of safety to clip onto.

Fizz would still feel safe. Who wouldn't with someone like Cooper watching out for you? She could feel the solid shape of his body as it came closer to her end of this bridge. Solid and warm and totally trustworthy.

Oh, yeah…she didn't want times like this to end anytime soon.

They rode the gondola—advertised as being the steepest cable car lift in the southern hemisphere—up to the restaurant perched high above Queenstown. It was the perfect place to watch daylight fade over the stunning view of the lakeside town with its backdrop of the dramatic skyline of the Remarkables mountain range. The twinkle of lights coming on bit by bit sprinkled a note of celebration to their evening. They were drinking a local, Central Otago wine that was delicious and the food they were sharing was equally good.

'I think this has been one of the best days of my life,' Fizz sighed happily. 'How amazing was that climb?'

'It was extraordinary,' Cooper agreed. 'I knew it was safe enough but I have to admit it had its moments.'

'I know… Like when we were halfway up that longest set of rungs on that totally smooth rock face. I got a bit of vertigo when I looked down.'

'And I thought of what might happen if one of the rungs came loose from the rock.'

'It would have been okay. We were clipped onto the cable as well.'

'And those bridges. The plank was hard enough but tightrope walking on that single cable felt impossible.'

'But you did it.' The slow way that the corners of Fizz's mouth were curling was the most gorgeous smile Cooper had ever seen. 'I'm so proud of you, Coop.'

'You know what?' Cooper smiled back at her. 'I think I'm quite proud of me, too. I learned something about myself today—thanks to you. And I would never have thought of doing something like that by myself.'

Fizz's eyes darkened with empathy as her smile faded. 'Because of Connor?'

Cooper's breath caught in his chest. Or maybe it was something else catching his heart. The feeling that Fizz saw parts of him that nobody else ever would? That she cared about the things in his life that had shaped who he was today and who he would be in the future? That she understood, so well, what it was like to lose someone so important in your life?

He found himself nodding slowly. 'I was thinking about him a lot. He would have loved to do that climb *so* much. He was an adrenaline junkie, I guess. Like you.' But Cooper was smiling, to let Fizz know that wasn't a criticism. 'That look on your face when you let go in the middle of that bridge and you were just sitting in space with your weight in your harness and your arms out wide and you had that…glow… It's what I remember about Connor whenever he was doing something that excited him. It always made me happy to see *him* so happy. So…alive… If only I'd…'

Fizz reached out to touch Cooper's hand. 'Don't do that,' she said softly. 'No more "if onlys". It wasn't your fault. Maybe he wouldn't have even listened to you if you'd tried stopping him because he was chasing that feeling of being so alive that nothing else mattered in that moment.'

'I kind of get that now. But I still feel that I should have stopped him. I knew it wasn't safe enough. It had been raining. The rocks were slippery.'

'It was an accident,' Fizz said. 'They happen. And sometimes you can be too careful and you'll miss out on a lot of good stuff that way. The only way you could ever make yourself totally safe would be to shut yourself inside an empty room and never do anything, and what kind of life would that be?' Her smile was wry. 'You could still get sick, too. Or fall over and break your neck. Things happen, Coop. You lose people. You lose people that you love very much, but if you let that hold you back, you may as well be shut in that room, don't you think?'

Was she talking about herself as well as him? Was this, in fact, an invitation to a different kind of future? The vision of a future Cooper wanted more than anything he'd ever dreamed of was filling his head. And his heart. A future with this woman he was loving more with every day that passed. A future that didn't have a 'use-by' date for when the 'fun' stopped. A real relationship? After those passionate words Fizz had just uttered, the hope surrounding that dream was so real he was convinced that they were on the same page. Thinking the same thing. That they were both prepared to take the risk of truly loving someone and committing to spending their lives together.

'I love *you* very much, Felicity Wilson,' he said quietly. He turned his hand that she was still touching so that he could catch hold of hers. 'And I never, ever want to lose you. To be honest, I'm starting to have trouble imagining my future without you.'

Time seemed to stop in that instant. He could almost see the moment his words reached her brain and she understood what he was saying. Precisely the same moment that the colour began to leach from her face.

'*No...*' The sound was no more than a whisper.

He could feel her hand dragging itself free of his.

'Excuse me.' Fizz pushed her chair back and got to her feet. 'I need to...um...go to the loo.'

Really? Cooper wondered. Or was it that she needed time to find the words she needed to let him know that she didn't feel the same way?

He could see the way her chin tilted before she shook her head sadly. 'Oh, Coop,' she said quietly. 'Why did you have to go and say something like that?'

'Because it's true.' Cooper wasn't going to apologise. He felt sick at having clearly misjudged the moment so badly but he couldn't feel sorry for being honest. He didn't want to have to hide how he felt. It was far too big to be able to hide, anyway. 'And it's not something that's going to change.'

For a long, long moment, Fizz stood there staring at him. So long that Cooper actually felt a beat of that hope again. That she might tell him that she felt the same way. That, maybe, there was hope that she could get past the trauma of losing the man she had planned to spend the rest of her life with and that she was ready to try again.

It was hard to tell in the candlelight around their

table but there was a glint in her eyes that could be due to unshed tears. Or possibly anger.

'You've ruined everything,' Fizz murmured.

Cooper still couldn't be certain whether she was angry or sad and he didn't get any more time to wonder because Fizz had turned on her heel and was leaving the restaurant so quickly she was virtually running away from him.

Running out of his life…

CHAPTER TEN

THERE WAS NOWHERE actually to run to but Fizz couldn't go and shut herself away in a bathroom.

They were on the top of a small mountain and, as far as Fizz knew, the only way down was in the gondola or via the tracks in the mountain bike park, which was undoubtedly closed after dark. She kept going, anyway. Past the bathrooms and the entrance to the restaurant. Past the area where you waited for a gondola cabin to arrive.

'Oi!' The crew member in charge of getting people safely in and out of the gondolas called after her. 'Where are you going, love? The next stargazing tour doesn't start for thirty minutes.'

'Just need a bit of fresh air,' she called back. And freedom, she thought. She was feeling trapped. By walls. By words. By the thought that she might risk everything by trusting a future that couldn't be trusted.

'Well, don't go far,' the man warned. 'It's dark out there. Easy to get lost.'

Fizz nodded but kept going. She simply had to get away.

Cooper loved her?

He couldn't see a future without her? It had probably

only been a matter of minutes before he'd want to start talking about a wedding. A honeymoon. Having a family and planning how they could fit their careers around shared parenting. Making promises about 'for ever'.

How had she not seen that coming?

Fizz had always sensed when one of her male friendships was getting out of control and someone wanted far more than she was prepared to offer them. It hadn't always been easy but each time she'd managed to escape without hurting anyone too much in the process.

But she hadn't seen it coming with Cooper. Why not? Because she'd believed that he was held back by the same barriers she was. The kind of barriers that were built, brick by painful brick, from the pain of losing someone so special that life could never be the same. Losing hope that the future would be the way you assumed it would be. The way you wanted it to be.

Fizz knew the answer to that question, of course. It had been so blindingly obvious in that moment when she'd turned her back on Cooper and tried to get as far away from him as she possibly could. She'd been drawn to him from the moment she'd met him. She admired every quality he had. She believed that he deserved the best that life could offer and she'd believed that she could help him achieve that by being his friend. By pushing him to overcome any barriers that might be holding him back.

Well, that had just backfired in a fairly spectacular fashion, hadn't it?

Cooper *had* overcome his barriers. And by doing so, he'd given Fizz a clear glimpse into what had been sneaking up on her. She'd come *so* close to falling into that moment when he'd been holding her gaze and telling her that he loved her. So close to telling him that she felt the same way. To making promises and those plans for a shared future.

She had recognised what Cooper Sinclair was searching for because…because it was what she was searching for herself. She'd just been too blind to see it.

She wanted all the good things life could offer to Cooper because…because she loved him. She loved everything about him. She had wanted to keep this friendship with benefits going as long as possible, not just because she enjoyed his company so much but because she felt the same way Cooper did. She was having trouble imagining her own future without him as a part of it.

This was the worst thing that could have happened. She was in love with Cooper and she wanted that future, too—possibly more than he thought he did. She wanted to see him every day for the rest of her life. To hear his voice. To feel the touch of his hands or his lips.

She wanted his babies…

Fizz was in the position she'd sworn never to be in ever again. With dreams and hopes for a future. And it felt like a huge, emotional, wrecking ball was swinging through the air directly at her. Waiting to show her how destructive it could be when those hopes and dreams were wiped out in an instant.

She couldn't go there again.

She wouldn't survive a second time.

Fizz had gone past a helipad now, and signs showing her the direction to take if she was here for a luge ride or a tandem paraglide. Good grief…that was kind of ironic, wasn't it? As if she needed reminding that clearly of how easily dreams could be snuffed out.

She turned away from the signs, away from the defined pathway, heading for the edge of the pine forest. Maybe being amongst trees with no sign of human habitation for a few minutes would ground her again and this feeling of panic would subside. That wrecking ball would not be able to get close enough to do any damage at all. Trees were huge and solid and safe.

Like Cooper was?

Oh…help. Half-blinded by tears, Fizz set off into the forest. There was a warning bell sounding somewhere in the back of her head with tones of getting lost, of tripping over a tree root and breaking her ankle, but there was no way she could stop just yet.

She'd tried to persuade Cooper to stop feeling guilty over his brother's death by telling him that he might not have been able to stop Connor from having that accident because his brother had been living so much in the moment he wouldn't have listened. That's what Fizz felt like right now. Even if Cooper was somewhere behind her and yelling at her to stop, she wouldn't be able to. It wasn't the thrill of an adrenaline rush that was pushing her forward, though. It was fear.

Fear of putting her arms out to hold tight to what had become so incredibly important to her only to have it snatched away again.

Cooper…

A sob escaped her lips at the same moment that Fizz felt the ground beneath her feet begin to slide away. She reached out to catch a tree branch but it snapped and slipped through her hands as her speed increased. And then she lost her balance and hit the ground hard. She could feel herself rolling now and protruding rocks were hammering at her body, which was scary but not nearly as terrifying as when that pain suddenly stopped and Fizz knew she was falling over the edge of a cliff.

She was going to die, she realised in that moment, but the sound that came from her lips wasn't a scream of terror.

It was simply a name.

'Cooper...'

He sat there for several minutes.

Well, he couldn't have chased Fizz into the ladies' toilets, could he, however much he might have wanted to. And he trusted that was where she'd needed to go because Fizz wasn't someone who would simply run away from something. She was the bravest person he'd ever met.

It was clear that he'd said too much, too soon. That he'd ruined everything. So, for a few minutes, Cooper sat there and felt a bit sorry for himself. Sad that a future he'd truly believed would be all he could ever hope for in his life was not going to be possible. Sorry for Fizz, as well, because she needed more in her life than a brilliant career and the excitement of chasing adrenaline rushes.

Everybody needed to be loved and he could do that. He could love her with all his heart and soul for every day they were lucky enough to have together.

The way she'd been looking at him, on more than one occasion today, caught in his mind. Sharing the excitement of flying into Queenstown this morning and looking as if he was the only person she wanted to be here with. When he'd been walking towards her on that single cable tightrope, swinging over a scarily high drop to the rocks below, and she'd looked...well, *proud* of him—as if his achievements were just as important to her as her own.

And, just minutes ago, when her empathy for the loss of his brother had been written all over her face and the touch of her hand on his had given them a link that had seemed so much more than merely physical. It had felt as if their hearts were connected. Their souls, even. It had been enough to make Cooper believe that she was thinking that they could both escape from a space where a real relationship was not going to happen. That they could both get out of that safe but confined space—that empty room she'd been talking about that was no kind of living—because surely being too careful applied to emotional safety as much as anything physical.

The more Cooper thought about it, the more he could remember what he'd seen in Fizz's eyes and he could add that into so many moments when they'd been together in these last weeks and wrap those moments inside the cloak of the extraordinary physical connection they'd found in their lovemaking.

He got to his feet.

He wasn't going to push Fizz into doing anything she didn't feel comfortable doing but he wasn't going to let this die by letting her run away without at least talking about it. At some level, he really didn't believe that she wanted that, either.

And…she'd been in the toilets for rather a long time, hadn't she? Cooper went to take care of the bill. They would have to both return to the motel room where they'd left their bags, so that would provide an opportunity to talk if nothing else.

A woman with a small child was coming out of the ladies' toilets when Cooper left the restaurant.

'Is there anyone else in there?' he asked.

'Don't think so,' the woman replied. 'No, I'm sure there wasn't.'

Cooper went further. He got to the gondola station. 'Did a woman take the gondola back down?' he asked. 'About ten to fifteen minutes ago?'

The man shook his head. 'I saw her, though,' he said. 'She said she needed a bit of fresh air. I thought she might be waiting for the next stargazing tour.'

'Which way did she go?'

The man shrugged. 'She won't have gone far, mate. It's too dark on the tracks now. You'll find her.' His sympathetic glance suggested that he thought they were an arguing couple that needed to make up. 'Good luck,' he added, before shaking his head. 'Women, huh? Can't live with them, can't live without them...'

Taking the gondola down these steep slopes would be the only safe way to descend at night but Cooper knew all too well that Fizz wouldn't hesitate to take a less safe option. She would probably prefer it, in fact.

He wandered the areas that were well lit, ignored barriers that carried warnings of being out of bounds and used a flashlight app on his phone when he followed a smaller track and found himself in the darkness of a fairly dense pine forest. It would have been useful to have already done the course they were intending to do tomorrow, he thought. He could do with some extra knowledge of how to tell if someone had walked along these tracks recently. How long ago had that branch been broken, for example, and had it been done by a human or an animal? Was that a fresh footprint or a scuff from a mountain bike tyre? He tried sending a text message and calling Fizz but received no reply.

He should go back, he realised a short time later. He could ask for help in searching for Fizz. But what if she'd simply walked down one of the main tracks and was now safely in their motel room? Sending out a search party that could actually involve some of the personnel they might meet in their course this weekend could end up being a source of acute embarrassment. It would also increase the distance appearing between himself and Fizz by shining a spotlight on how differently they approached life, and that was the exact opposite of what he'd hoped to achieve by joining her in some adrenaline-producing activities today.

Nobody would launch a search and rescue mission at this time of night, anyway. They would wait for first light so that they could see what they were doing and keep everybody in the search team as safe as possible. And perhaps Fizz hadn't headed back to the motel. She could have circled back to the restaurant after giving herself a bit of breathing space and be in there now, wondering where on earth *he'd* got to.

Cooper turned back, looking for the gleam of light through the trees to show him the direction he needed to take.

And that was when he saw it. The pale gleam of a small branch where it had been snapped.

It had to be fresh. Part of the branch was hanging on by a thread of bark that would snap at any moment due to the weight that was gradually tearing it from the rest of the branch. Cooper approached cautiously, using his torch to scour the surrounding ground. He could see that the ground was starting to slope steeply even before he got near the broken branch. And he could see the marks where someone had slipped and where those marks suddenly vanished.

All Cooper's training was telling him exactly what he should be doing right now. Marking his trail as he went to call for professional help. People who had the kind of gear that would make navigating this landscape so much safer. Headlamps, for example. And ropes. Abseiling gear. A stretcher in case it was needed for someone that was badly injured…

That did it. Cooper couldn't turn around. Not when that injured person could be the woman he loved.

Very carefully and slowly, he edged down the steep slope towards the drop, using tree branches and rocks for support. He lay down then, to peer over the edge, but he couldn't see anything but more rocks and vegetation.

'Fizz?' His call was tentative. 'Are you there?'

He listened carefully but could hear nothing apart from the sound of the gondola mechanism as its cars moved along the cable not far away. The hum and clicks slowed and then got quieter and it was in that moment that Cooper heard something that sounded very much like a groan.

'Fizz?' He scrambled a bit further down the slope, hoping that the branch he was using for support was not going to snap under his weight when he felt his feet slipping at one point.

'Cooper?' The call was faint. 'Is that *you*?'

'Yes… Where the hell are you?' Stupid question, he realised as soon as the words left his lips. How on earth would she know? 'Keep talking,' he called. 'I'll find you.'

'I'm sorry...' The words floated through the darkness. 'It was a stupid thing to do...'

'That doesn't matter right now...' Cooper pushed sideways towards the sound of her voice but found a barrier—a deep fissure between two rocks. 'Are you hurt?'

'I'm not sure. I slid over a few rocks on the way so I'm sure I'll have some bruises. There were some bushes that broke the fall quite a bit and I might have bumped my head when I landed. Scratched it, anyway.'

He was much closer now. The place where Fizz had landed was right behind the rock on the other side of this fissure, where there appeared to be a ledge. As Cooper shone his torch on the rocks to try and assess whether it was possible to get across the gap, the light caught movement on the other side. A hand appeared on the top of the rock and then he could see Fizz's face as she hauled herself upright. He hair was a wild mess around a face that looked far too pale and she had a streak of blood on her forehead and cheek.

'Don't move,' he told her. 'I'm coming over.'

'No...' Fizz looked dazed but she was staring at the gap in the rocks between them. 'You can't do that. It's far too dangerous.'

'You're hurt.'

'I'm okay. I can wait for help. Coop...don't *do* that...'

It was too late. Cooper had chosen a foothold on this side. All he had to do was make sure he could catch what looked like a suitable handhold on the other side and he would be able to scramble onto the ledge.

If he missed—or slipped, of course—it could be disastrous but Cooper felt completely confident. Plus, he didn't give himself time to tap into any familiar safety checklists.

There was a split second as he hung over the gap when Cooper thought his confidence might have been misplaced but he found a boost of strength so that he could push with his feet on one side as he hauled himself up on the other and then there he was, right beside Fizz. Close enough to gather her into his arms.

Except that she pushed him away.

'How could you have done that?' Fizz sounded furious. 'Have you *any* idea how scary that just was for me?' She burst into tears. 'I could have *lost* you…'

Cooper's heart stopped. He'd never seen Fizz cry. Her head injury must be worse than he feared. But then her words sank in. She'd been afraid of losing him? She would only feel like that if she felt the same way about him as he did about her. If she *loved* him?

'It's okay,' he said softly. 'I'm here, babe. I'm not going anywhere if you don't want me to.'

But she was still crying as she shook her head. 'You have no idea how that felt,' she said again. 'I thought you were going to fall. You could have been injured. Or *killed*…'

'I know exactly how it feels.' Cooper found himself smiling wryly as he gathered her into his arms. 'How do you think *I* feel every time *you* do something risky?'

'Really?' The word came out as a hiccup.

'Really.' Cooper was holding Fizz gently. Part of his brain was trying to assess whether she was in any pain or having trouble breathing from an injury rather than being upset. 'I wouldn't stop you doing those things,

though. It's who you are and I love your courage but…
you might have to get used to me trying to protect you
sometimes or making sure you don't do something
stupid—like running off the edge of a small cliff like
this one. Now, let me check you out and then I'm going
to call for some help to get us out of here.'

'Not yet… I don't think I'm hurt much. A few
bumps and bruises maybe. Don't move, Coop… Just
hold me, please?'

Cooper shifted enough to give him a more secure
position on the ledge and he pressed a kiss to Fizz's
head as she snuggled against him.

'I always thought you were a human rock,' she told
him. 'I just didn't realise that you were *my* rock.'

Cooper liked that. 'Always,' he murmured against
her hair. 'I'll always be your rock.'

'I was running away because I thought it was all
ruined.' Fizz lifted her head and Cooper could see her
face clearly as moonlight appeared between clouds.
'Because after you said what you did, I realised that
I felt the same way…that I couldn't imagine a future
without *you* in it. That I…that I…'

Say it, Cooper pleaded silently. *Say that word*…

'That I…*love* you,' Fizz whispered. And then she
burst into tears again.

Cooper held her tighter. 'It's actually a good thing,'
he told her. 'You'll see.'

But Fizz was shaking her head. 'It means we'll be
in a real relationship.'

'I hope so.'

'And that implies a future.'

'It certainly does.'

'Things like getting married and having babies.'

'Well…not straight away but…we can talk about that sort of thing later, babe. We don't have to plan our entire future the moment we find out that we're in love with each other. One step at a time, hey? And the first step is getting us off the side of this mountain and getting you properly checked out. Are you sure nothing is really hurting?'

'My ankle's aching a bit.'

Cooper sighed. 'Knowing you, that probably means you have a compound fracture. Let me see.' He eased her out of his arms. 'No…don't move there. It's too close to the edge of this ledge.'

Fizz froze.

'It's safe here,' Cooper told her. 'You're safe now.'

'You can't always keep me safe, Coop. No one can know what's going to happen in the future.'

'I know.' Cooper was carefully taking her shoe off. 'But it's like watching someone you love do risky things because that's who they are. You have to do what you can to make it as safe as possible and then all you can do is hope that everything *will* be all right. And it usually is.' He cupped her foot in his hand as he examined her ankle, shining his torch on the skin and then starting to palpate the muscles and joint. 'Does that hurt?'

'A bit. Ow, yes…that hurts.'

'There's no bones poking out. I think you might be lucky and it's only a sprain but it'll need an X-ray.'

'Okay…'

Fizz had never been this subdued before. Cooper looked up, searching her face. 'I'm still worried about that bump you had on your head. Do you know what day it is today?'

Her eyes looked huge in the moonlight. A corner of her mouth twitched. 'It's the first day of the rest of our lives. Together.'

A huff of laughter escaped Cooper. 'Now I'm *really* worried you've got a serious head injury. That's the cheesiest thing I've ever heard you say.' But he straightened up and cupped her chin instead of her foot and then he leaned closer and kissed her lips with a tenderness he could feel coming from his entire body. 'It's also the most beautiful thing I've heard you say,' he told her when he stopped kissing her. 'Particularly that last word.'

'I don't have a head injury,' Fizz said. 'My thinking is crystal clear. That's why I'm still a bit scared.'

'I get that. It *is* scary.' Cooper kissed her again. 'But you know what?'

'What?'

'Somebody said something to me once that sounded quite wise. Something about being too careful and missing out on a lot of good stuff. About how the only way you could make yourself totally safe was shutting yourself in an empty room, and what kind of life would that be?'

Fizz wrinkled her nose as she nodded. 'That person does sound quite wise. It's a good thing you remembered it after all this time.'

But Cooper was being serious. 'I reckon the same goes for taking the risk of losing somebody you love. If you don't take that risk, you're just going to sit around with an empty room in your heart, aren't you? You're going to be hiding in case you get faced with the pain of loss, but if you hide from that, you're also hiding from the flip side of that coin. The joy it can bring to be with someone that you love.'

'I guess…'

'You'd be choosing to be lonely when…when you could be…' Cooper had to swallow a big lump in his throat. 'Happy,' he finally managed. 'Together. I want you to be happy so much, Fizz. I want to be part of that happiness. To help create it.'

'You already are. I love working with you. I love being with you. I love… I just love *you*.'

'Only you had to take a running jump off a cliff to find out?'

Fizz sounded like she was trying to laugh but it turned into a groan.

'Don't do that again, okay?'

'I'll do my best.'

'If you ever get scared again—of anything…' Cooper wrapped his arms around Fizz again. 'Don't try and hide. Run *towards* me, not away from me, okay?'

He could feel Fizz nodding against his chest. Over the top of her head he could see a flicker of movement well above them.

'*Oi!* Is someone down there?'

Fizz jerked her head up. 'It's the man from the gondola station.'

'Yes,' Cooper shouted back. 'We're down here. Stuck on a ledge.'

'Turn your phone on again. Someone saw the light from the gondola when they were on their way up. We can get some help on the way when we know exactly where you are.'

Cooper turned on the torch app again and held his

phone up with one hand. He kept his other arm firmly around Fizz.

'Let's get out of here.' He smiled. 'So we can get on with the rest of our lives. Together...'

EPILOGUE

Six months later...

'DON'T MOVE...'

'What?' Fizz turned to where Cooper was standing in the doorway. She paused in her action of winding her hair into a knot on the top of her head because something in his expression was giving her a melting sensation deep inside. 'Why not?'

'Because, right now, you look exactly like you did the first time I ever saw you. You were wearing those same jeans and that T-shirt with the knot, and you were putting your hair up to get it out of your way.'

Cooper walked towards her, that look on his face becoming even more tender. His hands were large enough that they went right around her body as he took hold of her waist. Fizz loved that. She would never get tired of the size of this bear of a man she loved so much. Of his combination of both strength and gentleness. When he lifted her off her feet, a bubble of joyous laughter escaped and she released her hair to let it cascade down her back as she wrapped her arms around his neck.

'You looked like a warrior woman standing on that rock.'

'I *am* a warrior woman.' Fizz had to bend her head to kiss Cooper because he was still holding her well off the ground. 'That's why I need to get on with sorting these boxes.'

'We only moved in yesterday. We made the bed. What more do we need?'

'Things to cook with. And eat off.' Fizz kissed him again as she slid down to escape his hold. 'We're supposed to be having a house-warming party with Maggie and Laura and Jack later, remember?'

'Maybe they could bring stuff. Like tacos and beer. That way, we could go back to bed for a bit.'

'Hmm...' Fizz grinned. 'Tempting, but no. This is our house, Coop. Our first house...'

She took a moment to let her gaze roam the main room of this small, old villa, with its honey-coloured wooden floors, pretty tiled fireplace and high ceiling. A glance through the sash windows showed the greenery of a garden that was overgrown enough to give them complete privacy. It was a bit run down but full of character, and both Fizz and Cooper had fallen totally in love with the property the first time they had seen it. High in Wellington's hillside suburbs, they had a view from their veranda of the harbour in all its glory. They could even see helicopters taking off and landing from the Aratika Rescue Base when they weren't on duty there themselves.

'I want this place looking its best when our friends come to see it,' Fizz added. 'Oh, that reminds me... I must call Tom and invite him as well. He wasn't at work in the ED yesterday.'

'Did I tell you I asked Shirley? She's bringing cake for dessert.'

'That's fantastic. Except now we really do need to get things properly tidy or Shirley will start sorting things herself. Is Joe coming?'

'Yes. And Don and Andy. Pretty much everybody from Aratika, apart from the people on shift.'

'What about that new guy—what's his name?'

'You mean Adam—the new HEMS doctor? You're right. It would be a great way to welcome him to the team. I'll try and find his number.' Cooper turned towards the dining table that was covered with boxes and picked up the closest one. 'Where does this one need to go?'

Fizz gave him a look. 'What's in it?'

'Feels heavy enough to be books.' But Cooper laughed as he put the box down again and pulled the flaps open. 'Okay... I guess I'm a bit excited. We've bought a *house*, babe. Together. How good is that?'

'Very good.' Fizz stepped closer to peer into the box. 'That's your training manual from the mountain search and rescue course, isn't it?'

'Yep. You said you wanted to read it, remember? When you couldn't get time off to go back to Queenstown on the next course they offered us.'

'I was too embarrassed to go back to Queenstown. Have you forgotten all those jokes those guys made about being a bit too keen to see how mountain rescue worked?'

'I shouldn't have told them we were due to do the course ourselves the next day. Guess I was just happy you weren't badly hurt.' Cooper was reaching into the box. 'What's this?' He had a much smaller box in his hand and was starting to remove the lid.

'It's nothing,' Fizz said quickly. She tried to take it from Cooper's hands but she was too slow. He was unfolding the small square of newsprint.

'It's the photo that was in the newspaper!' he exclaimed. 'From the rescue on the day we met.'

'Yeah…' Fizz smiled. 'I ripped it out of a paper a few days after that incident so I could keep it and look at you again. I did it so often I got a bit of a crush on you and I was so embarrassed when I did meet you again on base, I pretended I couldn't remember your name very well.'

'I remember.' Cooper nodded. 'I was devastated.'

'Don't think so. It was the same day when you almost kissed me. When you insisted on looking after my thumb.'

'And there I was thinking it was you who'd almost kissed me.'

Fizz grinned as she folded up the newspaper cutting again. 'I'm admitting nothing.'

Cooper had pulled the other object out of the box. 'A shell?'

'Mmm.'

Fizz was a little embarrassed by this. She'd never been particularly sentimental in her life and had nothing more than a few photos to remind her of her time with Hamish, but she hadn't wanted to throw that shell away when she'd found it in a pocket of her flight overalls a while back now. So far back, in fact, it was part of another life. The life before she and Cooper Sinclair had become so much more than a professional team. Or friends who could have fun without being in a 'real' relationship. They were a personal team, now—as close as two people could ever be and equally committed to their future together. A relationship that was as real and meaningful as it was possible to be.

'You were holding it,' she told Cooper. 'That day you told me about Connor. When we were sitting outside Sarah's house and I asked you how you knew so well what to do to help in a situation like that when someone so young was dying.'

Cooper turned the shell over in his hands but he was looking puzzled.

'I think I kept it because it was the day I realised how kind you are. How caring. What a truly special person you are. When I thought how lucky the person who got you for a partner would be, but I didn't ever think it was going to be me.'

'Ah…' Cooper held her gaze. 'Were you right? Does the person who got me for a partner feel lucky? Do you feel lucky now that we're in a real relationship that everyone knows about? That we've not only moved in together but we've bought our very own house?'

Fizz forgot about the huge list of tasks she had in her head to get their home ready for its first party this evening. Nothing mattered other than this man standing in front of her and that look in his eyes that told her he didn't need an answer to that question at all because he trusted her. He trusted that they were perfect partners and he trusted that they would always be together to cope with whatever the future had in store for them.

Best of all, he'd taught her that it was worth having that trust herself. That, without it, she would have been missing out on a joy that had made her world so much bigger and so much brighter that she had never felt so alive. So incredibly happy.

'I *was* right,' she whispered, reaching up to put her arms around Cooper's neck again. To invite him to bend his head and accept the kiss on offer. 'I feel like the luckiest person ever.'

'Me, too,' Cooper murmured as his lips touched hers.

This conversation could well be leading to one they'd had not so long ago when they'd tentatively explored the idea of getting married, but Fizz hadn't quite been ready to take that step into planning their future and instead they'd turned their energy into finding a home for themselves.

Now that they were in their own home, the fear of tackling something that could tap into old fears was receding. Fizz was here, with her human rock. She had never felt so safe or so happy. If Cooper asked her again, she was going to say yes. If he didn't ask her, maybe she'd just ask him. Would he say yes? Could they turn their housewarming party into an engagement party as well?

It was Fizz who broke the kiss. She kept her arms around Cooper's neck, though, and only pulled back far enough to be able to see his eyes clearly. Then she took in a slow, deep breath. Cooper held her gaze. He clearly knew that she wanted to say something and he was waiting for her to say it.

But their eyes were having their own conversation and, in the end, they both spoke at the same time. With the same words.

'Marry me…?'

Their laughter was no more than a soft huff of mingling breath as they closed the gap between them for another kiss. There was just time to say one more word.

'Yes...'

* * * * *

MILLS & BOON

Coming next month

MENDING THE SINGLE DAD'S HEART
Susanne Hampton

Harrison's head was telling him to pull back but his heart was saying something very different.

They were two professional people who had spent time getting to know each other outside of work and he had allowed it to go too far. Now he needed to take her cue and set boundaries. Jessica had been upfront about her intentions. Stay six weeks and leave town. There had been no deceit, no false promises. He had to try and colleague zone Jessica immediately and put some distance between them. He had no choice, for his own sake. But he doubted how successful it would be after the kiss they'd shared.

'I can assist with that...'

'You've done enough.' Enough to unsettle him. Enough to even at that moment make him want to pull her close again. Enough to make him kiss her again. He was so confused, and she had made him think clearly when he'd felt her pull away. Now he had to do it too. 'I'll email hospital admin when I get home and let them know to roster cover for you until eleven. It's not the entire day off, but it's a few extra hours' sleep. I arranged the same for the other staff before I left. And the neuro-surgeon is flying in from Sydney mid-morning, to consult on the two suspected spinal cord injury patients.'

'You certainly have everything under control.'

'It's best for everyone that way.' Though Harrison knew he was losing control with Jessica. And that was not the best option for a man who had finally gained control of his life.

His tone had changed and he could see it hadn't gone unnoticed by Jessica. Torn best described how he felt. He didn't understand what he had seen in her eyes only moments before. It confused him. Her gorgeously messy blonde hair fell around her beautiful face and she looked less like an accomplished temporary Paediatric Consultant from a large city hospital and more like a fresh-faced country girl. She was so close he could reach out and cup her beautiful face in his hands and kiss her again.

He had to leave before he went mad with the gamut of emotions he was feeling.

Opening the door, he walked into the icy night air without stopping to put on his jacket.

Or say goodnight.

Continue reading
MENDING THE SINGLE DAD'S HEART
Susanne Hampton

Available next month
www.millsandboon.co.uk

COMING SOON!

We really hope you enjoyed reading this book. If you're looking for more romance, be sure to head to the shops when new books are available on

Thursday 2nd May

To see which titles are coming soon, please visit

millsandboon.co.uk/nextmonth

LET'S TALK
Romance

For exclusive extracts, competitions
and special offers, find us online: